# PITCHING UP IN AMERICA!

Deborah Aubrey

ISBN-13: 9798397496353
ISBN-10: 1477123456

Cover design by: Art Painter
Library of Congress Control Number: 2018675309
Printed in the United States of America

*To Dave, the used-t'be cowboy we met in Las Vegas, and to Youtubers, TheLongLife, who helped me more than they'll ever know xx*

# CHAPTER ONE

**DAY 1**

The flight was incredibly long, the plane full to capacity. Four hours in, people started getting restless and began walking up and down the aisles. Brian was so wide he had to shuffle sideways, careful not to concuss anyone with his elbows on his way past, and was forced to enter the space at the back of the plane in order to have enough manoeuvring room to turn round without causing injury to anyone.

"Captain's going to make an announcement about the heavy load tilting the airplane to the left at any minute," Mark sniggered. "Oh, no, he's gone 'to the other side' and the plane's tilting to the right."

Olivia gave a little giggle, despite herself. Even Faye smirked.

After three laps of economy, Brian squeezed himself into the end seat of the middle section. He left his legs out in the aisle, hoping no one would notice and he could keep his blood supply going for a little longer, but then the flight attendant came down and asked him to put them in as he was blocking the gangway and it was against safety regulations. After he'd contorted himself fully into his seat, nudging Faye into near insanity and making the man in the seat in front turn round and tut several times, he managed to drag his legs in. His knees were up near his chest and he had to cross his arms over them to stop them hanging limply at his sides like an Orangutan.

"Should have booked one o' seats at front with more leg room," he said to Faye. "I feel very foetal."

Faye sympathized with him, but she wasn't having a fun

ride of it either, having to sit at an uncomfortably acute angle in her seat to allow for the width of Brian's shoulders, which in turn made Olivia, sitting next to her, lean sideways into the aisle. Behind them sat Sophie, Tel and Mark, who reached forward periodically to stroke Olivia's arm and hold her hand.

The instant the flight attendant had disappeared up the plane Brian tried turning again. The man in front hissed, "Can you stop moving, *please!*" and Brian had to stop, one leg out, one leg bent double in front of him.

"Very squashed," he squeaked.

"Try watching a film," Olivia suggested.

"Can't see the screen, there's a bloody great leg in the way."

"Read a book," said Mark.

"How?"

He fidgeted for a bit more, then prised himself out of his seat, saying, "I'm sorry, Faye, I have to do this."

"Do what, Bri? Bri?"

Brian wriggled free with some effort and shuffled sideways up the aisle until he came to the front seats in economy.

"What's he doing?" Olivia asked.

"Where's he going?" said Tel.

"He's not going to throw himself out of the plane, is he?" Mark gasped.

"Excuse me," Brian boomed at the people sitting in the front middle seats. They stared up at him, startled to have the giant who'd been wandering like a crab around the plane address them directly. They all, Brian noticed with envy, had their legs stretched out luxuriously in front of them. "I will give any of you one 'undred pounds *in cash* if y'let me have your seat f'rest of flight."

"Pounds aren't much good to us Americans," the man in the middle laughed. "Besides," he added, languidly crossing his legs, "I'm perfectly happy where I am."

Brian looked at the man's uncramped position and said,

"One hundred pounds for *one hour* then?"

The man laughed and shook his head, as did the passengers either side of him.

"I'll do it," said a man in the right section.

Brian turned awkwardly and looked at the space in front of the right-side man, noticed it wasn't as much as those in the middle aisle, and said, "Let me try it first."

The man got up and negotiated his way around the giant. Brian sat down, nudging the woman in the next seat with his shoulder. He stretched out his legs, not as far as the middle aisle but at least his knees weren't under his chin. "Fifty pounds for two hours," he said.

The man shook his head, "Nah, you said 'undred for an hour."

"The middle aisle has more leg room."

"'Undred or nuffink, makes no odds to me, mate."

"Brian!" Faye cried.

"Shush, woman, I'm negotiating my own survival. Hundred for two hours?"

"Yer on."

The woman next to him whined, "I don't want a complete stranger sitting next to me, Martin!"

"They don't come any stranger than Brian," Mark laughed, as the man said, "'Undred extra spending money, innit, love."

Brian pulled out his wallet and handed over a wad of cash. Then he leaned back into his seat and the whole plane heard his heavy sigh of contentment. The man came and sat next to Faye. He nodded once, plugged in his headphones, stared at the TV screen in front of him, and didn't utter a single word for two whole hours.

Brian, however, regaled the woman sitting next to him and those within earshot with tales of Yorkshire, about their escapades on a Cotswold campsite, and why they were headed for the bright lights of Las Vegas. Faye kept raising her eyes from the film in front of her when Brian's laughter or the women's high-pitched tittering cut through her headphones. To distract herself, she turned and pushed her head between the headrests to look at the others in the seats behind. Tel immediately cried, "Here's Johnny!"

"What are you doing?" Faye asked, lowering her eyes to the laptop on the table in front of him.

"Watching *Flight of the Phoenix*," he said, "You know, just in case."

"Oh." She turned her eyes to Sophie, who also had her laptop open in front of her. "What are you doing?"

"Just catching up on my emails."

"You work too hard."

"Just last-minute stuff."

Brian's laughter filled the plane. Faye tried not to hear it and craned her eyes over to Mark, who was holding a book. "What you reading?"

"*Alive*," he said, "It's the story about the Andes plane crash when they had to eat the dead passengers."

"Eugh" Faye said, as the woman's high-pitched hilarity echoed down the aisle.

"Yes, I'm picking up tips in case – "

"Don't say it," Olivia said from the seat in front of him.

Faye pulled her head out from between the headrests, resisting the urge to glance at her husband, who appeared to be having a whale of a time in front, and turned to Olivia, who tipped the cover of her book and said, "*438 Days*. Two men lost at sea. It's very good."

"In case we find ourselves in the same situation?" Mark laughed. Several people around him tutted.

After two hours, the man sitting next to Faye got up and went to reclaim his seat. Brian grumbled as he reluctantly got to his feet. The woman sitting behind him handed him a business card and said, "Call me."

Faye's head went up like ET. "He won't," she shouted.

The woman turned and said, "He'll be great at dinner parties, very funny."

"Very *married*."

"Welcome back to squish-town," Tel said, as Brian prepared to enter the seat of infinite compactness.

It felt even smaller now. The man in front of him tutted like a metronome as he shifted and squirmed, pulling a muscle in his back and losing all sense of feeling in both feet.

"Have a drink to relax," Faye suggested, so he did.

One hour later, standing in the aisle with his third plastic glass of brandy, Brian asked the passing flight attendant in the other aisle, "How much longer before we land?"

"Oh, we're halfway there," she said.

"Oh, we're halfway there?"

Brian then led the economy class section in a resounding rendition of Bon Jovi's *Livin' on a Prayer*. After which, he lay down on the floor in the aisle and fell fast asleep, snoring loudly and refusing to wake up, even when the flight attendant threw a glass of water in his face. In the end, when even the captain was unable to rouse him, they left him there, the attendants dispensing food and drinks from the right aisle, which everyone quite happily passed along to the left.

\* \* \*

"Brian!"

"What?"

"Brian!"

"WHAT?"

"There's no need to shout!"

"Then stop saying *Brian*!"

"Brian!" She was shaking him now. He opened his eyes and saw her looming over him. He wondered where he was for a moment, wondered if Faye was feeling a bit frisky, then turned his head and saw a long aisle of empty seats.

"We're here, Brian. We've landed."

\* \* \*

There were police officers standing where the crowds were gathering in a queue to show their passports.

DEBORAH AUBREY

"Oh look," Olivia said to Mark, "I forgot American policemen wear guns."

Mark looked. Mark saw. Mark's eyes widened as he was suddenly overwhelmed with the urge to panic. Guns! He'd never actually seen a real gun before, certainly never in public. His brain exploded with potential doom. What if one of the officers was unstable, had some sort of mental breakdown as they passed and pulled out his gun? If one pulled out their gun would the others automatically follow?

Mark gasped for air. Sweat dribbled down his face as he tried and failed to tear his eyes off the weapons all around him. Now he really did look suspicious, staring and sweating and swiveling his head round as they walked towards the checkpoint.

"Are you okay?" Olivia asked him.

Ahead, Brian turned round at the sound of concern in her voice. "Mark?"

"G-g-guns," Mark gasped. "They have g-g-guns."

Brian recognised the signs of impending panic and stepped back to take a firm grip of Mark's arm. "Just act natural," he whispered, "And keep walking."

Mark's eyeballs detached from the weapons and The Scream impersonation on his face whipped forward. He was still breathing heavily and sweat poured out of him.

"There's no cause for alarm," Brian said, pulling him along. "They're not going to shoot you for no reason."

"They ... might," Mark panted, "I look very ... suspicious."

"Stop looking suspicious then."

"We Brits just aren't used to seeing guns, are we," Faye said.

"We see guns in London a lot," said Tel.

"Oh, do you?"

"Yes, machine gun type things, especially around the Palace and Downing Street, always police holding guns there."

"Can we *p-please* stop talking about g-guns," Mark spluttered.

"Think of something else, darling. Think about Las Vegas and the film they're making about us."

"We're going to be famous," Tel said, "In an anonymous type of way."

"It's all good," Brian said, stoically dragging Mark along, "Deep breaths, calm thoughts."

They stood in the queue, passports at the ready. A police officer walked past, casually scanning faces, and Mark flinched and made a tiny whimpering sound.

"You're not drawing attention to yourself at all," Sophie drawled. "Pull your head out of your shoulders and relax."

"If he starts shouting 'We're all going to die' I'm leaving him behind," said Tel.

"Nobody gets left behind," Brian said.

"Don't leave me," Mark whimpered.

"We're not going to leave you, darling."

"I might," said Tel.

"Tel!" hissed Sophie.

"Deep breaths, lad, we're nearly there."

They stepped forward in the queue.

"I can't do it," Mark suddenly hissed, his eyes once again rivetted on another officer's weapon, "I'm not going to make it."

Brian hitched up his arm, supporting Mark's sagging weight, as Olivia whispered soothing words to him.

They made it to the front.

A good-looking security guard took Sophie's passport, looked at the photo, looked at her, grinned and said, "Very nice, ma'am."

"Yes, she is," Tel said, slapping his passport on the counter. "My *wife* is lovely."

"I love the Briddish accent," the guard said.

Sophie winked at him and he winked back.

Tel sighed. The guard checked his passport, handing it back and saying, "I'd keep a good eye on your wife while you're here, sir."

"I intend to. Sophie, wait for me!"

Mark was speechless and sweaty when the security guard checked his passport photo, glancing up at him several times. His heart was pounding so hard in his chest he could feel his ribs moving, and his legs were wobbling sticks of jelly.

Brian was still holding him up. "Jet lag," he said to the guard, nodding at Mark's almost white face.

They let him through, along with the others, and Brian helped an unsteady Mark to the baggage carousel to collect their luggage.

"Is this ours?" Brian kept asking, as identical black sports bags sailed by; Sophie, in charge of the itinerary, had insisted they all 'travel light'.

"No, ours has a pink ribbon around the handle," Faye said.

"Like this?"

"No, a lighter shade of pink, more baby pink than fuchsia pink."

"It might have fallen off."

"I double knotted and dabbed superglue on it, it won't fall off."

"This one?"

"No, I'd say that was more a shade of – "

"What about this one?"

"No, Brian, that's not – ! Oh, actually, yes, that's yours."

Brian let go of Mark, who wavered unsteadily on his feet, and quickly chased it down. As he hauled it off the conveyor belt, he saw Sophie struggling with her bag and helped, as Tel chased after another further round the carousel. Olivia was vainly tugging at hers, whilst Mark fought with another passenger over his, victoriously pulling it to him after they'd checked the label.

Faye saw her bag sailing by and yelled, "BRIAN! BRIAN! THIS ONE!"

He ran over to retrieve it, already exhausted and sweaty. "Bloody hell, woman," he cried, almost dislocating a shoulder as he pulled it off, "What have you got in here?"

"Just some clothes and a few books."

"How many books?"

"A few."

"How many is a few?"

"I don't want to say."

"I thought you'd brought your Kindle?"

"I did, the books are for … backup."

Brian gave a low growl at the back of his throat.

Reunited with their luggage, they turned as one, slipped on sunglasses, and walked like characters from *Reservoir Dogs* towards customs, dragging their bags behind them.

Brian glanced at Mark, who looked like a very hot, wobble-eyed animal caught in the headlights of an oncoming truck. "You okay?"

Mark nodded.

"Nearly there."

"You're doing brilliantly, darling."

"They're …" Mark gulped. "They're all looking at me."

"They're not," Brian scoffed, noticing that the police officers did, in fact, all seem to be looking in their direction. "Just act normal."

"I d-don't know what n-normal is."

"Perhaps try walking on your own." Brian let go of Mark's arm, and Mark slumped sideways and staggered like Bambi across the ice for a few steps. Sweat dripped from his face and his eyes were abnormally large.

"Nothing to declare?" Faye asked.

"Nothing," Sophie said.

"Unless you're carrying- *umph*."

"You don't make jokes at customs," Sophie hissed at Tel. "Whatever you were about to say, zip it."

"You're suddenly very bossy," Tel said, rubbing his side where she'd elbowed him, quite fiercely. "Don't let the title of 'wife' go to your head, it's early days and I could revoke it at any time."

"Feel free. Meanwhile, I'm aiming for us to get out of here

without drawing any more attention to ourselves."

Mark started whimpering. "They're c-closing in on m-me," he squeaked.

"They're not, darling, they're moving away."

"They're r-regrouping, ready to s-surround and detain me."

"Watch many cop shows, do you?" Brian asked. Mark didn't answer, he was too busy whimpering, so Brian said, "Have you never flown to another country before?"

"Europe," Mark spluttered, "I've f-flown to Europe. They don't have guns in Europe."

"Get a grip," Tel hissed.

As they started passing through the 'Nothing to Declare' corridor, Mark's whimpering became louder, making officials behind the desks look up.

"He's an anxious flyer," Brian said, raising a placatory hand. "He'll be alright once he gets some fresh air." To Tel he whispered, "Take his bag and walk fast."

Tel did, and they all hurried out of customs.

They had made it.

When Mark saw the crowds and yet more police officers in the arrivals lounge, he started hyperventilating.

"Slap him," Tel said, "He's clearly hysterical. Slap him before the CCTV cameras pick us out."

"C-cameras!" Mark cried.

"Little aggressive, Tel."

"I'm tired, Soph."

"We're all tired, but no one else is suggesting violence on our travelling companions."

"I just want to get out of here."

"Don't we all."

"You did it, darling," Olivia breathed, planting a kiss on Mark's sweaty cheek, "You can calm down now."

"Calm down?"

"Yes, we've arrived. We're in America, darling."

Mark straightened up and took a quivering breath. "It's

over?"

"Yes, darling, you can relax and enjoy yourself."

Mark inhaled deeply and ran his hands down his wet face. "Right," he said, striding ahead as if he hadn't just acted like a complete drama queen through security and customs, "Let's get on with it then."

Sophie looked around the crowds and said, "They said they'd send someone to collect us."

"Over there," Brian pointed.

A young, slightly scruffy man was standing outside the barriers with a rough cardboard sign that read, 'Cotswold Campers'. They hurried over to him. He seemed quite alarmed to have a crowd, led by a hairy giant, suddenly bearing down on him. Tel removed his sunglasses in a sideways manner and said, "We are they."

"Pardon me?"

"We are they, the Cotswold Campers."

"Oh hi." The man enthusiastically shook their hands one after the other. "I'm Michael, the Chairman of MGN Movie Production Company and Director of the camping project." They were mesmerized by his mouth, which seemed to deliberately shape itself into a pinched expression, as if he had something distasteful stuck in his teeth, whilst simultaneously jutting his chin out in an awkward manner.

"So glad you made it," Michael continued, after they'd introduced themselves. "I can't tell you how happy we are to have you *Brits* on board."

"We're very pleased to be here," Tel said.

"Please, follow me."

Still smiling and still making an effort to jut his chin out for some inexplicable reason, Michael turned and urged them all out into the dusk of Las Vegas. The heat hit them immediately.

"Oh my god it's hot!" Faye cried, coming to a standstill inches from the air-conditioned airport and fanning herself, first with her hand, then with her passport. Already red in the face, she snatched up a free newspaper from the stand by the exit doors and furiously fanned herself with that.

"Good God, woman, we've only been outside for forty-five seconds and you already look like a boiled lobster."

Faye could feel sweat prickling her skin, seeping into her hair and dribbling down her face. "It's hot!" she snapped.

"Temperatures are starting to drop this time of year," Michael said, leading them to a battered blue people carrier parked at the kerbside that had one yellow front side panel and one grey one. There was no rear bumper, and spots of rust ran amok over the battered metal. "Only eighty-five degrees today."

"Only?" Faye gasped.

"Reached one-hundred and ten last week."

Faye fanned herself faster.

"It'll cool off now the sun's setting."

"This is cool?"

Michael slid open the back door, revealing sagging brown seats inside, and indicated for them to get in. He was still twisting his lips and jutting his chin in a very strange way.

"Not quite the stretched limousine I was hoping for," Tel muttered.

"Lower your expectations," Sophie whispered to him, as Faye hurried past and positively leapt into the shaded interior of the car. "This is Las Vegas, not Hollywood."

Mark tilted a middle seat and he and Tel clambered into the back. Olivia got next to Faye, followed by Sophie. Michael jumped in behind the steering wheel and took three attempts to slam the door shut, sprinkling rust onto the ground with each bang.

Brian stood on the kerbside and looked down at the mountain of baggage round him. He pointed to them as he peered through the window at Michael. Michael said, "Oh yeah," and popped open the boot.

Brian grumbled as he dragged the bags and lifted them one by one into the car, before concertinaing himself into the front passenger seat.

"Can you turn the air-conditioning on?" Faye gasped.

"Can't," said Michael, "It's broken."

"I'm going to die," she gasped.

\* \* \*

They pulled out of the airport with Faye hanging her head out of the open window. Despite the setting sun, the air that rushed past her face was still hot from the day. The seat was hot, the inside of the car was hot, the air she breathed was hot. She could barely stand it.

"I'll go this way to give you a look at the Las Vegas Strip." Michael turned right onto the freeway. "How was your flight?"

"Long," Brian said. "We left London – "

"Wow, *London*."

" – at midday-ish. Ten hours flying across the Atlantic, and it's now – " He looked at his watch, then said, "Anyone have their watch set to Las Vegas time?"

"It's 8.35pm," Sophie said.

"So what's the real time?" Olivia asked.

"8.35," she repeated.

"What time is that at home?"

Sophie shrugged and said, "Early hours of the morning?"

"No wonder I feel exhausted!"

"That'll be the jet lag. Brian won't have jet lag because he slept for most of the way."

"Did not!" he boomed from the front, "I had a quick nap."

"A quick *three-hour* nap. You're fully rested and spritely, while we all feel like death warmed up."

"Fried!" came Faye's voice outside the window, "I feel fried! There's no air here, I can't breathe."

From the back seats, Mark's head was lolling on one shoulder and Tel was gently snoring into his chest.

"You slept!" Brian said. "It was like an episode from *T'Twilight Zone* when I came out toilet and found everyone unconscious and dribbling in their seats."

"I love the way you guys talk," Michael enthused. "I just love the Briddish accent."

"We like yours," Olivia said. "Where are you from?"

"What's that now?"

"Where are you from?"

Michael glanced across at Brian. "What's she say?"

"She said, where are you from?"

"Ah. I live in Vegas, but I'm originally from California."

"Lovely."

Michael glanced at Brian again. "She said, lovely."

"Oh."

"Can he not understand me?" Olivia asked Sophie.

"No class system in America," Sophie said, "They've never heard posh accents before, except on *The Crown*."

"And that film where Colin Firth walks wetly out of the lake," Faye yelled from outside.

"Oh. I'll 'ave t'talk more lower-claass then."

"It's working-class and that's our domain," Brian bellowed back, "Leave well alone, lass."

"Oh look!" Faye suddenly screeched, "It's the Strip!"

They all peered through the windows like children outside a toy shop as famous hotels flashed by on either side, glowing in the fading light. The pyramid-shaped Luxor, The Tropicana, Excalibur, New York New York, the Waldorf Astoria, Planet Hollywood.

"There's our hotel," Olivia shrieked, pointing ahead, "Caesar's Palace."

"Place," Michael said casually.

"Pardon?"

"*Pardon*," he laughed, "Just love that accent."

"Place?" Sophie asked.

"Yeah, Caesar's Place."

All necks craned back as they drove past Caesar's Palace.

"Did y'all not read the email?"

There was some shifting and some rustling as everyone looked in their hand luggage for the two-page email they'd been sent.

"I thought it was a typo," Sophie said, finding hers in a neat plastic folder.

"No, Caesar's *Place*," Michael said again. "It's where the film studio is, and the film set. It's also where we live."

"Oh," said Sophie.

"Oh," said Olivia.

"We're just finishing off the first scenes of the movie before moving out into the desert for the rest of the filming, but it all takes money. We have a very tight budget."

"Isn't the film studio paying for it?" Brian asked.

Michael laughed. "We are the film studio."

"MGM?" Sophie asked.

"MG*N*, Michael, Graham and Norman Movie Production Company, although Meryl, our Executive Producer, seems to think the first M relates to her and we've had some arguments about using MGNM, but this is our baby, so … MGN."

"N?" Sophie repeated, "MG*N*?"

"Yeah. We're a small independent set-up, just starting out, in fact."

"Oh," said Sophie.

"Oh!" said Olivia.

"Are we going round to the back entrance of the hotel?" Faye laughed, pulling her head in again. "Are we too common to go in the front?"

"We're not staying at the Caesar's Palace Hotel," Sophie told her, "We're staying at somewhere called Caesar's *Place*."

"It's not far," Michael said, "About thirty minutes out."

'Thirty minutes?' Sophie mouthed.

"Is it a hotel?" Olivia dared ask.

"What?"

"Is it an 'otel?"

"No, not a hotel. You're seasoned campers, you'll like it."

"Is it a … " Sophie gulped nervously, " … campsite?"

"No, no, not a campsite," Michael laughed. "Well, it depends how you define campsite, but you'll see."

"Scared now," Olivia whispered to Sophie.

"Me too."

* * *

After twenty minutes, Sophie leaned forward in her seat and said, "Are we still in Vegas?"

"Yeah," Michael laughed, "The outskirts."

"Are we staying in the desert?"

"Not actually *in* the desert, but you can see it from where we are, just over the fence."

After another ten minutes driving through increasingly desolate areas, Michael slowed down and turned right. They all peered through the windows and saw a sign with *Caesar's Place* roughly painted on a piece of wood, nailed to another piece of wood that sat crooked in the ground. Behind the sign were what looked like static caravans in various stages of decay, and a very large car park to the side that had some motorhomes grouped at the far end with two tall spotlights towering over them. Michael parked in front of them and leapt out, opening the doors for them whilst painstakingly arranging his lips and chin into an arrogantly constipated expression.

"TEL!" Sophie yelled as she got out, "WAKE UP! WE'RE HERE! I think."

A muttering noise came from the back, but Sophie was too tired and too hot to follow up.

"Mark, darling?" Olivia said, as she shuffled across the seats, "We've arrived."

Mark remained silent and motionless. Tel shifted his position until his head was resting on Mark's shoulder. Mark slowly raised a hand and patted his head.

"OI, YA DOZY LIGHTWEIGHTS!" Brian boomed into the car, shocking the living daylights out of them both. "GET YOUR POSTERIORS OUT HERE AND HELP WITH THE BAGS!"

Mark sucked in air like he'd just been saved from drowning. Tel's eyes flew open and he looked around, lost and bewildered.

"Vegas," Brian told him. "We're in Vegas, remember?"

They both struggled to extricate themselves from the back seats. Brian immediately started throwing bags at them from the boot of the car. Catching one in the chest and losing all air from his lungs, Tel spun with the momentum and faced the parked-up motorhomes, six of them grouped together, three facing three. There were a few people standing around, pretend fighting, reading from sheets of paper or adjusting electrical equipment.

"Where are we?" Tel gasped, spotting a tiny, blonde-haired woman wearing what appeared to be the tiniest dress in the history of the world, with frills. "This isn't Caesar's Palace."

"We've already had that conversation," Brian grumbled, "I'm too hot and tired to have it again."

"Caesar's *Place*," Sophie said, by way of explanation.

"Not Caesar's Palace?"

"No."

"Here?"

"It appears so."

"Oh."

Olivia tapped Michael's arm and said, "Oo are all these pee-pul?"

He stared at her, confused. Brian boomed, "She said, who are all these people?"

"Oh, let me introduce everyone. Most have gone home for the day, but we needed a dusk shoot for the main characters so they're still here."

The group followed him, dragging their bags across the cracked, weed-filled concrete towards the dilapidated motorhomes.

"Brits," he announced loudly, "This is our lead actor, Shane. He's playing the Brian character in the film."

They all looked at Shane, who was going through the motions of a choreographed fight with a big stick and only had time to glance in their direction and nod once. He was tall, with floppy blond hair and a square, clean-shaven jaw. Mid-twenties, tops, and wearing torn jeans and what looked like a series of intertwined leather belts across his chest.

Mark was the first to laugh. *"He's* playing *Brian?"*

Brian grinned behind his beard. Faye's mouth popped open and she had to force herself *not* to say 'I wish!'

"Shane, come and say hello to our honoured guests."

Shane threw the big stick down and sauntered over, his shoulders leading each step. "Pleased to meet you," he squeaked, giving each of their hands a hefty shake.

He pumped Faye's hand and she started fanning herself faster with the newspaper. "You know who he looks like, don't you, Livs," she whispered.

"Who?"

"A young Brad Pitt."

"He does," Brian said, nodding, "I think he captures the essence of me very well."

Faye fanned faster as she watched his shoulders lead him back to the stick.

Michael waved an arm at the tiny woman with intricately styled blonde hair and an enormous, shelf-like chest. "Hey, Tammy, come and meet the Brits."

Tammy tottered over on high heels and, in a helium-pitched voice, said, "Howdy, folks, right nice to meet y'all. I'm sorry I can't stay, ma boyfriend's coming to pick me up, he don't like me stayin' out late."

"Who are you playing?" Tel asked.

Tammy looked down at the papers in her hand and said, "I'm playing … Sophie."

Sophie looked startled. "Me?"

Tel looked from Tammy – tiny, delicate, massive chest, a huge pile of coiffured hair – to Sophie – tall, with a mass of black curly hair. "I can definitely see it," he laughed.

Michael, once again twisting his lips into a sneer, said, "We had to make a few changes to the characters – "

"You can say that again," said Sophie.

" – due to actor availability and financial constraints."

"I gotta go," Tammy said, "But I put brand new sleeping bags and pillows on your beds – you still owe me for those, Mike – and a little welcome treat like they do in all the best hotels. Nice meeting y'all."

"See you tomorrow, Tam."

They waved her off.

"This is Christofer," Michael said. "He's playing Tel."

Sophie snorted as a man with a very short, blond haircut came marching over to them. "Guten Tag. I am very pleased to meet you." His voice was abrupt and sharp. He didn't smile. "Michael, I've been going over the script for tomorrow and I am not happy with my scene."

"We'll talk about it later, Christofer, I just want to get our guests settled in first."

Christofer wandered off, tutting.

"Can we get out of the heat?" Faye said, swaying slightly on her feet.

"We're all pretty tired," Olivia said.

Michael looked at Brian for translation and he said, "Knackered, lad, we're totally knackered."

"Yes, yes, of course. Let me take you to your quarters, you must be worn out after your travels. You'll meet Graham and Norman in a bit, they've just nipped out for food for the barbecue we're having in celebration of your arrival later."

"Later?" Sophie whispered to Olivia, glancing at her watch, "It's gone nine already!"

"What's that in real time?"

"You don't want to know."

Olivia slumped on her feet.

"Follow me, Brits."

"There's no air!" Faye wailed, hurrying after Michael with her sports bag and hand luggage, hoping there was air-conditioning wherever he was taking them and vaguely wondering why he was walking towards the back of the car park.

Michael had only taken a few paces before he suddenly raised an arm and went, "Ta da!"

The others trundled their way up to Faye, whose face was a drenched red sponge.

"Ta da?" Sophie dared to say, when everyone else remained nervously silent.

"*Tar dar*," Michael laughed. "Your accommodation."

"You appear to be pointing, with both hands," Sophie laughed, a little hysterically, "At some battered old motorhomes?"

"RVs," Michael grinned, whilst also trying to maintain his strange sneer. "Recreational Vehicles, one each! Take your pick! Except for the one at the front, which is set up for interior scenes, and that one over there where we store all the costumes and the cast use it to change in, and that one has all the on-location equipment inside."

"So, these three then?" Brian boomed, looking at the motorhomes at the back that seemed the shabbiest of them all. "The one with a broken windscreen, the one listing to the left due to *two* flat tyres, or the one being held together by rust and copious amounts of gaffer tape?"

Michael gave an awkward laugh. "They're all we could afford, but you're welcome to share with me or the boys if you'd prefer?" He pointed over towards the static caravans. "Except, I've got props in my trailer, Graham's an introvert and doesn't like company, he's our script editor, and you'll probably die of electric shock if you stay in Norman's trailer; he's the cameraman and Video Editor and his place is just a death ... You're all looking at me kinda strange."

"Trailers?" Tel muttered. "This is a *trailer* park?"

"We're staying in a trailer park?" Sophie gasped.

"Bit of a comedown from Caesar's Palace," said Brian.

"We couldn't run to a proper hotel due to financial constraints, and since you all like camping so much – "

"Caravanning," Brian said, "We like caravanning, with *on-site facilities*."

"Well, these are caravans, trailers, RVs, what's the difference?" He gave another nervous laugh. "Not much in the way of facilities, but we've hooked up electricity to each one and there's plenty of bottled water in the fridges. There's also a shower area at the back."

"The back?" Olivia asked.

"Of the parking lot."

Brian grunted. The others looked disappointed, and tired, very, very tired.

"We thought it would be good for you to stay on site, give you a flavour of our operation," Michael continued. "This is where we live and work, and we're able to use this vacant lot for free, so it's a win-win situation and very … You don't look happy."

"We're all a little … surprised," said Brian.

"We thought it was a two-night stay at Caesar's Palace," Sophie said.

"Place," said Michael. "Caesar's Place."

"Yes, we get that … now."

"I don't care!" Faye said, dragging her sports bag to the door of the nearest motorhome, the one made almost entirely from rust. "I just need to cool down and go to sleep. Jesus wept!" she cried, opening the door, "You could cook a chicken in here! No air-conditioning?"

Michael slowly shook his head.

"I'm definitely going to die out here." She disappeared inside, lifting blinds and opening the windows. One side window fell out completely and crashed to the ground. She ignored the gaping hole and screamed, "So bloody hot! I can't breathe!"

Brian hauled the bags up the steps, which bent under his weight. "What's that smell?"

"They might be a little musty," Michael said, "They've been here a while."

"Musty? Smells like something died in here."

"We did have a little rat problem a while back."

Tel widened his eyes and took a step towards Michael, shaking his head and breathing, "No, no, no."

Sophie gasped, "*Rats?*"

Tel kept shaking his head, staring deep into Michael's eyes, willing him to take it back. Sophie hated rats, if she thought there were rats here she would leave. He didn't want to leave, he just wanted to go to sleep, so he kept on shaking and staring and practicing his telepathic abilities.

Brian prodded Michael in the back and he spun round, wondering what was going on.

"They don't have rats in Nevada, do they?" Brian urged. He glanced over at Mark and said, "This is Nevada, isn't it?"

Mark shrugged.

"I think," Brian said, "You meant chipmunks, those cute, little furry things. You had a problem with *chipmunks*, that's what you told me earlier, isn't it, Michael."

"Did I?"

"Yeah, cute little chipmunks."

"Chipmunks?" Sophie said. "You're not just saying that because of my rat phobia, are you, Bri?"

Brian was torn between lying, which he hated, or keeping Sophie calm. In the end he decided on a single nod of his head and hoped that would do.

"Ah, chipmunks are lovely," Olivia grinned broadly. "They're the ones with the stripes down their backs."

"What happened to them?" Mark asked.

Michael, completely lost now, raised his palms and said, "They just ... went."

Olivia grabbed Mark's hand and said, "We'll take the one with the broken window, unless you wanted that one, Soph?"

"No, no, you're fine, Livs. It's Hobson's Choice really, isn't it; bad, bad or bad."

"Madam," Tel said, sweeping an arm in front of her, "Your hot, crooked motorhome awaits."

"RV," Michael muttered as they all stomped passed. "You settle yourselves in and I'll call you when we have the barbecue going."

They vanished into the motorhomes and collapsed, fully clothed, onto the lumpy, musty beds.

Outside, Michael clapped and yelled, "That's a wrap, folks!"

"I don't suppose … ?" Tel said, cuddling up to Sophie, but Sophie was already asleep and Tel fell unconscious before he could finish his sentence.

* * *

Despite their semi-squalid accommodation, they had a good sleep, broken only when Sophie screamed, "SOMETHING TOUCHED ME!" in the middle of the night, and Tel's voice cried, "It was me, it was me!"

Even Brian's thunderous snoring, booming out of the gap in the RV where a window used to be, didn't disturb them.

# CHAPTER TWO

**DAY 2**

"Coffee," Brian croaked, stirring on the lumpy bed. "Need coffee."

"Water," Faye cried, "About 150 gallons. I'm so dehydrated I'm practically a crisp. Look at my skin!"

"Can't, it's too dark."

"What time is it?"

"Dunno, dun't care."

Faye scrambled off the bed straight into the kitchen area, where she pulled open the lower cupboards until she found the fridge. She gulped down a whole bottle of water. "Seems a bit cooler today," she burped.

"That's because it's still dark and the day hasn't started yet."

"I hope it's not as hot as yesterday."

"We're in the desert, Faye, it's not going to get chilly, is it."

"It felt like I was in an oven yesterday."

"You'll adapt."

"Or just burn to a – *AAAARGH!*"

The inside of the motorhome was suddenly filled with a bright, white light. Everything was illuminated in high definition; the tatty cupboards, the stained walls and ceiling, the shabby surfaces.

"My eyes!" Faye cried, "*My eyes!*"

Brian leapt to his feet, making the motorhome shift under his weight. Faye spun around, shielding her eyes from the light streaming through the windows and screamed again. Brian lumbered to the door and threw it open, fully expecting to see an alien spacecraft lowering for an abduction. It was so bright he couldn't see anything for a moment, and then, slowly, moving figures came into view, just like the end scene of *Close Encounters of the Third Kind*.

"AND CUT!" a voice yelled through a megaphone.

Shane, standing outside the motorhome and still wearing a tangle of leather belts, halted his pole in mid-air. Beneath the pole, Christofer hauled himself to his feet and brushed the dust off what looked suspiciously like a safari suit.

"Kinda ruined the shot for us there, Bri," came Michael's magnified voice.

Brian held his hand up to his eyes to stop his retinas from burning. "What's going on?"

"We were filming a night scene before the sun comes up."

"What time is it?" Tel asked, staggering out of his motorhome.

"You've got to be kidding me!" Faye said, following Brian down the steps. "Four o'clock in the morning?"

"It's midday at home," Brian said, "So kind of a lie-in."

"Doesn't feel like a lie-in," Mark yawned, joining them. "What the hell's going on?"

"They're filming."

"At this hour of the morning?"

"Appears so."

"We have a very tight schedule." Michael's voice boomed across the parking lot and beyond. He was sitting in a director's chair with two men standing beside him, one with a camera on a tripod and one holding a cat on a stick. "Okay, folks, take five."

Faye was furiously sucking on her second bottle of water. She'd never been so thirsty in her life. She must have sweated buckets since they'd landed. She must stink. Her scorched hair hung limp and slightly crisp around her face and, because she had no sense of smell, she automatically raised an arm in Brian's direction to test his reaction. He gagged.

"You've got something on your face," Brian said.

Faye frantically slapped herself. "What? What is it? A spider? Is it an insect? A cockroach?"

Brian poked a finger into her cheek, then brought it to his lips and licked it.

"Ew!" she cried, "That's disgusting."

"Chocolate," he grinned, "Courtesy of Tammy, left on our pillows, just like in all the best hotels."

"Yours is on your forehead."

Brian peeled it off, looked at Mark and laughed.

"What?"

"You sleep on your left side."

"I do, but how do you know that?"

"It's where your pillow chocolate was."

"Didn't see the chocolate, but did notice our motorhome is rammed with mugs and giant tins of coffee, and the fridge is full of milk cartons. There's also plastic chairs and a table outside."

"Ooh, get you with your fancy table and chairs," Tel crowed. "I'll have a coffee when you're ready."

"Tel doesn't appear to have encountered a chocolate on his pillow," Brian said. "Did Tammy forget you?"

"We never made it to our pillows, we woke up half on, half off the bed on account of the 45-degree angle of the van."

Michael leapt out of his chair and came charging towards them. In the glare of the overhead lights they watched his face change from slightly annoyed to a chin-jutting sneer.

"Why does he twist his face like that?" Mark asked.

"Constipation?"

"Morning, folks," he sneered. "Sorry if we woke you but we're on a very – "

"Tight schedule," Tel said.

"Don't come too close," Brian told him, holding up a hand, "The wife is ripe, she could blow at any minute."

"Brian!"

Sophie came running over. "Shower, shower, shower!" she cried. "They don't work in the motorhome and I *need* one as a matter of urgency. Where are they?"

Michael pointed behind them and said, "Green are the showers, black are the toilets."

Sophie glanced over her shoulder, expecting to see a shower block, or at least something solid and substantial. "Tents?" she gasped.

"There's a clip on the hosepipe to keep the nozzle open."

"Hosepipe?"

"Yeah, they're connected directly to the water tap."

"The *hot* water tap?" Sophie quizzed, tilting her head and squinting an eye.

"No, the … cold."

"We're abluting in tents?" Olivia said, coming over.

"I'm not sure what that means," Michael said, letting his sneer be taken over by a frown.

"Tents," Sophie snapped, "We're washing and abluting in *tents*?"

"Still unclear about the A-word."

"Weeing," Brian boomed, "And pooing."

"Oh! Yeah, we brought them onto set for the cast and crew, but you're welcome to use them. They're almost brand new."

"I shall be sure to admire the newness of the tents as I wash under *cold water*," Sophie snapped, stomping off. She came to an abrupt stop halfway towards the shower tents and asked, "Are there towels in there?"

"Er, no."

Everyone looked at Faye, who could always be counted on in these situations to have a stash of essentials hidden in her caravan, from spare sheets and pillows to giant, bendable umbrellas. "It's … it's not my caravan," she shrugged.

Everyone turned to Michael.

"It's a bring-your-own kind of situation regarding towels."

"But I haven't brought any towels," Sophie snapped, "I *assumed* Caesar's Palace would provide them."

"You could borrow mine," Michael said, "They're a bit crispy but – "

"Hard pass on that," Sophie said.

"I'm not sure when I last washed mine," Norman said, coming over.

"That's fine," Olivia said, holding up her hand.

"Say again?"

Olivia vigorously shook her head.

"Shake," Tel suggested. "It's humid enough, jump up and down for a couple of minutes and you'll dry."

"And during those damp, drippy minutes when I'm jumping up and down and shaking myself like a wet dog, should I parade around naked?"

"Yes, please," he laughed, before catching Sophie's expression and quickly adding, "No, no, of course not."

"There's torches in your trailers," Michael said.

Tutting, Sophie turned and stomped back to her motorhome for toiletries and clothes. Faye and Olivia did the same, and minutes later the three of them were hurrying towards the green shower tents at the very back of the car park. Shortly after came the sound of three women furiously screaming under a stream of ice-cold water.

"Any food on offer?" Brian asked. "I'm starving."

"Sure."

"Oh, thank god."

To the sound of women still screaming, Michael led them to a wooden picnic table next to a shabby trailer. "We tried to wake you last night but you were out for the count. Boys couldn't find any meat, couldn't find the barbecue in the weeds either, but they brought back burgers. You like MacDonalds, right?"

They nodded nervously, and Michael shouted, "MERYL! THROW THOSE HAMBURGERS IN THE MICROWAVE, WILL YA? THEN COME AND MEET OUR BRITISH GUESTS."

"Reheated MacDonalds for breakfast," Tel sighed. "Not quite what I was expecting."

"Stop complaining," Mark said, lifting his head up from the table, "We're all suffering."

"This jet lag is a killer," Brian croaked, rubbing his red, puffy eyes. "It's gone midday at home, and the sun hasn't even come up here yet."

"Probably best to think in local time," Tel said, "You'll acclimatise quicker."

"Time check?"

They all lifted their wrists and looked at Michael, who looked at his and said, "Four twenty-five in the AM."

They synchronized their watches like robbers before a heist.

A woman with jet-black hair cut into an immaculate bob around her jawline strode towards them with a tray of still-wrapped burger buns and several cans of Coke. She was wearing a grey suit and an irate expression. She slammed the tray down on the table and stared at them one-by-one.

"This is Meryl," Michael said.

They all muttered some sort of greeting, which Meryl didn't reciprocate as she continued to glare at them.

"Meryl is my sister, and our Executive Producer here at MGN Movie Production Company."

"I organise everything," she said fiercely. "Both on and off set."

"Meryl has very kindly invested into this project."

"And I will not be losing a single cent of that investment." She turned to Michael and said, "Are they investing? It's their film, after all."

"No, no," Brian said, laughing and holding up his hands, "We're not investing."

"Why not? Why else are you here?"

"We were invited," Tel said.

"You'll have to excuse my sister, she's very abrupt and undiplomatic."

"Yorkshire ancestry?" Mark snorted.

"I get things done," she snapped. "If it was left up to you

lot you'd be broke in weeks and working at ... " She looked down at the tray. " ... MacDonalds. Enough chit-chat, we need to finish the night scene before the sun comes up. Do not make any noise while the camera is rolling and do not wander like lost children onto the set."

"Wouldn't dare," Tel breathed.

Meryl marched off, shouting, "Is Shane ready?"

Michael's strangely contorted mouth relaxed as he said, "She's rude, but she gets the job done."

The women came running back to the table with drenched hair and damply clinging clothes. They snatched up the wrapped burgers.

"Bloody starving," Faye said.

Sophie hesitated. "Are these fresh?"

"What do you think?" Tel laughed.

"Oh." She shrugged, stared at the steaming, reheated burger in her hands, then ravenously bit into it, as did Faye and Olivia. The men, who hadn't yet picked up theirs, watched intently.

"No signs of salmonella thus far," Mark said, staring across the table at Olivia.

"Mine seems unaffected," said Brian. "Looks like she's just walked through a waterfall – "

"I have, and it was bloody cold!"

" – but other than that, she looks pretty good."

"Ah, thanks, Bri."

Brian and Mark's palms met in mid-air above the table. "One for the Little Book of Men's Answers," Mark laughed.

"Mine eats like a dainty little bird," Tel said dreamily. "No signs of discomfort or tummy rumbling ... except for yours, Bri."

Brian snatched a burger off the tray, ripped off the paper, and pushed it into his mouth. "Bugger it," he chomped, "Do as the locals do."

"You having one, Michael?" Tel asked.

"No, no," he replied, fervently shaking his head and

notching up his sneer, "I've, er, already eaten." When they'd finished and cracked open their cans of Coke to wash it down, he said, "So, what do you think of our set-up?"

They all stared back at the half empty car park with the dilapidated motorhomes and overhead spotlights.

"Well," Brian said, "Nothing says middle of the English countryside like a vast expanse of cracked concrete."

"Surrounded by a chain-link fence," said Tel.

"And palm trees," said Sophie.

"And sand everywhere," said Olivia.

"And clear blue skies," Faye said, already starting to sweat.

"So yeah," Brian said, "Looks good."

"We had to change the script to suit an American market," Michael explained. "We'll be adding trees and thunderous skies in post-production, you know, with special effects and everything, which is Norman's job. NORMAN, COME OVER AND SAY HI."

A tall, pale man with long, pale hair wandered towards them holding a video camera. He was followed by a small, bald man wearing thick-rimmed glasses who was fussing over a sheaf of papers in his hands.

"If we can just get this last scene in the can," the short man said, "We can move onto the desert scenes and film the extra trailers in the morning."

"We're showing the first rushes tonight," Michael told them excitedly. "Just the first ten minutes of the movie to give you a taste. This is Graham, he's our screenwriter."

The small, bald man raised a hand but didn't lift his eyes off his papers.

"Have you revised the scenes for tomorrow yet, Graham?"

"As best I can with Christofer texting me every five minutes suggesting rewrites."

"Norman's our cameraman and Video Editor extraordinaire," Michael said, nodding towards the tall, pale man. "He puts the whole thing together using his laptop and some pretty neat software."

"NERDS!" Meryl called across, "GET OVER HERE AND START FILMING, WE'VE WASTED ENOUGH TIME AND *TIME IS MONEY*!"

Michael immediately jumped up, rearranging his face into a sneer and chin jut again.

"Can I just ask?" Mark said.

"Sure, bro, ask away."

"Why do you keep … What would you call that?" he asked, turning to Brian, "A smirk? A sneer?"

"Oh," Michael laughed, "You mean the Tarantino look?"

"The Tarantino look?"

Michael closed his eyes and took a deep breath, turning his hands in front of him as if directing the winds of good fortune towards himself. "I'm channeling Quentin Tarantino for this movie," he said, hitching his upper lip. "The greatest director of our generation. I'm encouraging the universe to gift us with the Tarantino Effect, which is what they call, in his honour, the transition of a low budget film into a Hollywood hit, like *Reservoir Dogs*, a masterpiece which was voted one of the best independent films of all time. We may be small," he continued, opening his eyes and raising his palms to the heavens, "But we have the ambition, we have the spirit, and we have the greatness inside us to become – "

"Rich," Norman interjected, "Hopefully before we end up sleeping on the streets and begging for change."

Michael hauled himself from his reverie and glared at Norman. "We're not going to get anywhere with an attitude like that. Have a little faith, why don't you?"

"I have faith. What I don't have – what *we* don't have – is the money to pull it off, or indeed enough cash to survive. Has he asked you yet?" he directed at the group around the table.

"Asked us what?" said Brian.

"For the money to finish the film?"

There was a moment of pure silence, before Tel said,

"We're not here to invest in your project."

"No, no, of course not," Michael laughed. "That isn't why we invited you here at all."

"Why did you invite them then?" Graham asked, still not raising his eyes from his shuffling pages.

Michael's laughter became a little harsher, a little more hysterical. "To show off our little venture, I guess. To let fresh eyes see how we operate, and how we can, if we absorb as much of Tarantino's style and characterisation as we can, become – "

"NERDS!" Meryl hollered through the megaphone, "THE SUN'S COMING UP AND WE'RE WASTING TIME, AND *TIME IS MONEY*! GET A MOVE ON!"

The film crew scampered off.

"Bloody cheek!" said Mark. "Invites us for a two-night stayover in Las Vegas, all expenses paid, sticks us in old motorhomes, feeds us botulism burgers, and then asks us for money!"

"They did pay for the flight over," Faye said.

"Ian Flemmingway paid for those," Sophie explained. "He mentioned it in the emails and when he rang to say he wouldn't be able to meet us here when we arrived because he had a meeting in New York with a major film studio about his new book."

"Read it," Mark said.

"It's excellent," said Olivia.

"So," said Brian, "We find ourselves in a bit of a sticky situation."

"I'll say," Faye said, pulling the shiny, damp shirt away from her body.

"We could make a run for it," Tel suggested, "Just pack up and go."

"Go where?"

"There's a Hotel 8 down the road," Mark said, tapping on his phone. "Forty-six dollars a night, which is about … twenty-eight quid."

"It would only be for one night," Tel said to Brian.

Brian looked up, sensing something in their tone but not quite sure what it was.

"Wouldn't it seem a bit *rude* to suddenly up and leave?" Faye said. "We've only just got here, and they've been so welcoming, putting chocolates on our pillows and everything."

"I'd quite like to see what the film looks like," Olivia said, squeezing out her hair, which immediately sprung into perfect damp curls around her face.

"When did you have time to put makeup on, Livs?" Sophie asked.

"I don't wear makeup," she giggled, "Foundation makes me go all itchy, and I'm always rubbing my eyes, so I'd end up looking like a – "

"You don't wear makeup?" Faye gasped, leaning forward to peer at Olivia's face.

"No."

"You mean," Sophie said, gently running a finger down Olivia's flawless cheek, "Those long, dark eyelashes are *natural*?"

"Yes."

"Those eyebrows arch like that on their own?"

"Well … yes."

"What do you use to make your lips go all rose-buddy like that?"

"Nothing."

"*You lucky cow!*" Faye hissed.

"Lucky man," said Mark, winking at her.

Faye huffed. "I'm going to have to go au naturelle while I'm here too on account of the heat."

"Brace yourselves," Brian laughed, "It's not for the faint-hearted."

"Shut up. My makeup totally slid off my face yesterday."

"I wondered what that stuff was on your neck," Brian howled.

"CAN YOU KEEP THE NOISE DOWN!" Meryl shouted

through the megaphone, "WE'RE TRYING TO FILM HERE."

\* \* \*

They watched from the wooden picnic table, too terrified to move, as Shane, wearing torn jeans and leather belts around his torso, went into the first motorhome. Graham ran over, turned off one of the spotlights and turned on something which shrouded the vehicle in smoke. Michael sent a drone flying into the air. With Norman behind the camera on the tripod and Graham once again holding a cat on a stick, Michael positioned his drone and shouted, "ACTION!" A few seconds later Shane burst out of the motorhome holding a rifle, which he proceeded to 'fire' silently in all directions. The drone flew in and over his head.

The group around the picnic table dropped their mouths. Tel said, "What the … ?" before he was distracted by Christofer, running into shot holding a knife in the air and screaming wildly. Shane went to kick the knife out of his hand and belted him in the side of his head with a sturdy boot instead.

"CUT!"

"You *idiot*!" Christofer hissed, holding his head.

"SHANE, WE'VE PRACTISED THIS!"

"I'm sorry, it was an accident."

Christofer pushed him and he fell against the side of the motorhome. A window popped out and crashed onto the concrete.

"Nobody sneeze or cough loudly round here," Brian whispered to the others, "Whole place will collapse like a deck of cards."

"I think he is kicking me on purpose!" Christofer shouted. "He is jealous of my talent."

"What talent?" they heard Shane say, and Christofer pushed him again.

Meryl hurried over and whacked them both across the back of the head. "Stop fighting!" she screamed, "You're wasting time and – "

"Time is money!" everyone said in unison.

"You will lift your leg higher and kick the knife out of his *hand*," Meryl screeched, whacking Shane again. "You will not concuss the cast. Now, do it again and do it *properly* this time!"

Shane clambered back into the motorhome. Meryl stomped back and stood behind Michael's director's chair with her arms crossed and her face pinched. Christofer moved off to the side, still rubbing his head.

"AND ... ACTION!"

Shane leapt out of the motorhome, swinging his rifle. The drone buzzed around. Christofer rushed over with his knife and Shane froze. Christofer pretended to plunge the prop knife into his chest, cackling like a maniac. Shane stared plaintively at Michael. "I'm worried I'll kick him again," he said, as Christofer continued to stab him. "Also," he added, pulling at the leather belts around him, "I'm chafing."

"HOW HARD CAN IT BE TO KICK A KNIFE OUT OF HIS HAND?" Michael bellowed through the megaphone, "HE'S ONLY FIVE FOOT SEVEN!"

Christofer stopped stabbing and spun round to face Michael. "I am five feet and ten inches!" he screeched. He shuddered in indignation and stormed off, stomping past the picnic table muttering obscenities.

"Meryl, go calm him down."

Meryl tutted and chased after him. The first thing she did when she caught up with him was whack him across the back of the head and yell, "You're such a drama queen! Get back over there and do your job!"

"No, I will not. I am offended. I am *five feet ten inches!*"

Back at the table, Faye asked, "Why does Shane, playing Brian, have a gun?"

"Beats the hell out of me," Mark shrugged.

"Michael said they'd made some changes to suit the American market."

"Campers in the middle of the English countryside to Battle of the Somme is quite a significant change," Brian said.

Sophie leaned forward and whispered, "Do you think this film is any good?"

Before anyone could answer Michael, dragging his director's chair behind him, threw himself down on it next to them. "It's going to be the next *Reservoir Dogs*," he said. "The Tarantino Effect is all over this. You wait and see, I'll be picking up my golden trophy at the next Oscar Awards."

Michael looked from one face to another. Nobody said anything. Instead, they smiled. Mark briefly nodded.

"Christofer says he needs a break," Meryl said, stomping back.

"He's only been working for three minutes!" Michael glanced at his watch. "And the bloody sun is coming up soon, we need this night shot!"

"He says he feels under-appreciated, physically abused, and traumatized."

"By?"

"Everything and everyone."

"Maybe he should consider a different career if he has such a delicate demeanor." Michael sighed heavily. "Never work with actors," he told them, waiting for a laugh that didn't come.

"Am I coming today?" Faye suddenly asked.

Brian's head swiveled towards her, his eyes wide, his mouth gaping behind his beard. "What?" he boomed.

They all stared at her. Olivia giggled.

"The character playing me," she said, surprised by all the attention, "Is she coming today?"

Brian pressed a hand to his chest and sighed, "Oh thank God for that, I don't think I have the stamina after all that travelling."

"Colette?" Michael said. "Yeah, I think she's in later."

"Ooh, *Colette*, nice name."

"You'll like her, she's scatty and insecure and very, very pretty."

"Got you down to a T," Brian breathed in her ear.

"Ah, thanks, Bri."

Still looking at her, he and Mark slapped palms across the table again.

Graham wandered over. "Is Christofer still working on this project or has he gone full meltdown."

"Full meltdown," Meryl snapped.

Graham sighed heavily.

"What time is Colette in today?" Michael asked him.

Graham consulted his pile of papers and said, "Love scene this afternoon, but … " He peered at them through his thick glasses, " … it'll be a closed set, Colette hates getting her clothes off."

"Was that the sound of your jaw hitting the table, lass?" Brian asked, and Faye nodded.

"Do we have any large Band-Aids to cover her frontal area?" Meryl said, waving her hands over her flat chest.

"We can always crisscross small ones and listen to Shane repeatedly saying 'X marks the spot' for the *entire* scene." Graham sighed again, then wandered off towards one of the static caravans.

"Are we getting *anything* in the can today?" Norman asked, impatiently stomping over. "We're gaining light, I can't do anything in post-production if there's shadows all over the place."

"Yes, yes." Michael pulled himself out of the director's chair and dragged it back to the camera tripod. Norman followed. Meryl went in the opposite direction. She knocked on the door of a static caravan and they heard Christofer shouting, "I'm not getting paid enough to be kicked in the head!"

"You won't be paid at all if you don't get back to work."

The door flew open and Christofer hissed, "That is not in my contract! I get paid regardless of whether the film gets finished or not! Do you know how many films don't even get –?"

Meryl grabbed one of Christofer's arms and hauled him

down the steps, pushing him back to the film set and barking, "Get back out there *now* and be more *professional*, you tiny twerp."

"I will remember this when I am writing my biography," Christofer wailed, "You will not come out well, Meryl, you mark my words."

"Interesting, isn't it," Brian said, as Christofer was shoved passed them. "I didn't know film making was like this."

"It probably isn't," Mark laughed. "It all seems a bit– "

"Amateur?" Tel suggested.

"I was going to say sloppy," said Sophie.

"Unfeasible," Olivia said.

"I think it's very exciting," said Faye.

They watched Shane bursting out of the motorhome over and over until, finally, he managed to kick the knife out of Christofer's hand without giving him a serious head injury, and Michael called it a wrap. The sun was now rising, along with the temperature.

"I haven't brought enough deodorant," Faye said, fanning her sweaty face as the crew ambled over to the table. "I need some toiletries."

"Me too," Sophie and Olivia said in unison.

"What time do the shops open?"

The Americans all laughed.

"Have you heard of the city that never sleeps?" Michael asked.

"That's New York, isn't it?"

"Las Vegas told New York to hold its beer."

"That's not strictly true," Graham muttered, scribbling on his pages, "Walmart doesn't open until six. Maybe Vegas told New York to hold its *lemonade*."

Norman rushed past with his digital camera and disappeared into a static caravan.

"Is there a supermarket close by?" Tel asked.

"There's a Walmart Supercenter about ten minutes down the road."

"Great. Can you take us?"

"Meryl will drive you."

"I will not!" Meryl snapped, "I have a lot of Executive Producer things to do, I don't have time to waste running *errands*."

"As Executive Producer of MGN Movie Production Company you take care of everything," Michael said, "Including visitors to the set. It's in your contract."

She huffed.

"I need something to stop me bursting into flames," Faye said, now fanning herself with the tray Meryl had carried the burgers on. There were already sweat stains forming on her shiny shirt.

"Your clothes don't help," Sophie said softly.

"What do you mean?" Faye glanced down at herself, feeling slightly offended. These were new, bought in a sale at Asda just before they left.

"You're wearing jeans, that won't help with the heat."

"They're cotton, cotton's good for hot weather, isn't it?"

"Denim's too heavy, it's not breathable," Olivia said. "You'll chafe, and it'll give you a very hot crotch."

"Interested!" boomed Brian.

"You weren't a minute ago," she huffed.

"You need natural fibres," Olivia added, feeling the hem of Faye's shiny shirt. "Nothing man-made."

Faye shrugged. Sophie glanced at Olivia, who nodded and got up. She casually wandered behind Faye. "Oh," she said, reaching out for the back of Faye's neck, making her shiver, "Your label's showing, I'll just put it back in for you." She nodded again at Sophie.

"Be at the car in five minutes," Meryl said, striding off.

"Was hoping to have a quick shower first," Tel said.

"No time for showers!"

"Bugger." Mark sniffed under an arm. Olivia fanned her face with her hand and coughed. "Bit ripe, darling."

"Wet wipes," Brian said, standing up, "Just grab a wad and

do the main bits."

"Pits, tits and bits," Faye laughed.

"Hurry!" Meryl snapped. "I don't have time to waste."

They all jumped up and headed for their motorhomes. On the way Sophie fell into step with Faye and looked down at her trainers. "Oh, look how small your feet are compared to mine! What size are you?"

"The one above four."

Tel, slightly ahead of them, started laughing. "What size is that, Faye?"

"The one below six."

"Which is what?" Tel insisted.

Faye tutted. "Foive," she said, in her Midlands accent.

They all laughed, except Brian, who knew better.

* * *

Meryl huffily drove them, windows down, to a Walmart Supercenter, and they all gasped at the enormity of the building.

"Be quick," Meryl snapped, "If you take too long I'll leave and you can make your own way back."

"Sweet little thing, isn't she," Olivia said, as they raced towards the store.

"Sweet like that cartoon character in *The Incredibles*."

"Just grab a trolley and lob in what you need," Mark said. "Don't pither, just run."

They hurried inside.

"Food in small packages," Sophie cried, reading off a piece of paper Etta, her PA, had prepared for her, "Tins and dry goods only, nothing fresh will survive in this heat."

"I know just how it feels," Faye mumbled.

"Don't overbuy, there isn't the storage space, but get a crate of bottled water each."

Faye immediately ran to the toiletries section, with Brian in hot pursuit.

"Don't go mad," he said. "Remember, we've set ourselves

a budget for this trip."

"I need this, and this, and," she said, eyeing a can of cooling mist, "several of these. Oh, and some cooling wipes."

Brian peered over her shoulder. "Those are haemorrhoid wipes, Faye."

She tossed them back onto the shelf. Brian grabbed six cooling mist cans out of the trolley and replaced them with several sticks of deodorant, dropping them in with a flourish. Faye pouted and raced off.

Olivia and Sophie, following closely behind, put several cooling mist cans into their trolleys. Mark and Tel trailed along, smugly saying they'd brought everything they needed and casually admiring the enormity of everything.

Until they rounded the corner into another aisle.

"Guns?" Tel laughed, "At a supermarket?"

Mark instantly clutched at his chest, struggling to breathe. He couldn't take his eyes off the sign reading 'Rifles and Ammunition'. Even as he stared, a man standing at the gun counter turned and seemingly aimed a rifle straight at him. Mark cried out in alarm, his cry ending abruptly as he fell backwards in a dead faint. It was only Tel's quick reaction that stopped him toppling like a tree to the floor, grabbing him and lowering him down like a toppling tree in slow motion.

"BRIAN!" he yelled, and Brian immediately came thundering over. "They sell guns at Walmart! Who knew?"

Brian leaned down and tapped at Mark's face. "Mark! Mark! Can you hear me, Mark?"

"Uh."

"He's okay."

"Uh?" Mark lifted his head. "Where am I?"

"On the floor in Walmart," Tel said.

"Why am I – ?" His eyes settled on the gun counter again. The man was no longer aiming a rifle at him. He struggled to his feet, his head swimming. "I was taken by surprise. I didn't expect to see firearms in a supermarket."

"That's some phobia you've got there," Tel said, then he

looked at Brian and said, "How about you, Bri, are you scared of anything?"

"Faye," he said, "I'm afraid of Faye left unsupervised in a shop.  You okay now, Mark, only I fear for the contents of my wallet?"

"I'm fine," Mark said, waving him away, "Go save your wallet."

"Come on, chap," said Tel, "Let's go get you a bottle of water.  You sure you're okay?  I've never seen anyone faint so abruptly before."

"It's a skill I've only recently acquired."

"It needs work if you don't want to faint your way across the American West."

Brian found Faye furiously throwing items into her trolley: a pack of neck cooling tubes, a cooling headband, and a cooling ice vest.

"You don't need that," he said, putting the vest back.

"I need *everything*!" she snapped sweatily, "So I don't spontaneously combust from the intense heat!"

Her hand hovered over a pair of ice pack slippers and Brian growled, "Don't do it, Faye."  She put them back with a huff and hurried on.

Behind them, Sophie and Olivia picked up a few things.

Mark, staring over at another customer, said, "Is that a man in a dress, or a woman with a beard?"

Tel looked.  "I don't think it matters these days."

Brian poked his head between them and whispered, "Why is that man wearing a dress?"

"I guess he identifies as a woman," Tel said.

"He has a beard."

"He's comfortable as a woman with a beard."

"Can't he make his mind up?"

"It's called gender fluidity."

"Now you're just throwing random words at me."

Brian pulled his head away and continued chasing after Faye, who was frantically lobbing things into the trolley in his absence. He passed a tall, skinny woman slinking passed wearing a full-body catsuit, complete with whiskers and a swishing tail. A man coming into the aisle was wearing a bin bag, thigh high boots, and a leather hat. Brian briefly spun around and raised his palms at Tel and Mark. They laughed.

In the clothes section Faye threw a six-pack of 'anti-chafe, anti-sweat boxer briefs for women' into the trolley, and a t-shirt on special offer that felt thin and cottony. Olivia and Sophie furiously scoured the racks, giggling and choosing several items. Faye felt a tiny bit jealous.

They moved into the food section.

"Small packets," Sophie reminded them, "Essentials only. I'll get the condiments."

"Oh!" a woman near to them cried, "You're English!"

"Yorkshire," Brian boomed.

The woman turned to the woman she was with and laughed, mimicking, "York-sha."

"God's own country."

"We love your accent," the other woman said to them.

"We love yours," Olivia gushed.

"Say what now?"

"We love your accent."

With a slight shake of their heads, the women stared at them for a while as if they were animals in a zoo. Then one suddenly screamed, "OH!" and they all took a careful step back. She hurried off, returning with a small brown bottle in her hand, which she thrust up into Brian's face. "What do you call this?" she shrieked, hyper-excited.

Brian read the label and smiled behind his beard. "What do you call it?"

The woman slowly and painfully read the name. "Wor-ces-ter-shy-er. How do you pronounce it?"

"Woo-ster-sher."

"Woo-ster-sher," they repeated, giggling into each other. "That's much easier to say."

Tel said it in his deep, husky voice and the women

stopped giggling and simply ogled at him.

"Stop flirting," Sophie whispered.

"I said Woo-ster-shire!"

"That'll do it."

"Wor-ster-shire," Olivia said.

"Say what now?"

Olivia shrugged and the women wandered off, still giggling, with their bottle of sauce.

"Maybe lower the tone of your voice a little," Sophie suggested, "And speak slowly, like Margaret Thatcher."

Olivia coughed.  In a low, slow voice she said, "This woman … is not … for turning."

"Turning into what?" Mark laughed, sidling up with some clothes on hangers.

"Margaret Thatcher."

"Oh."  Mark retracted his head like a tortoise going back into its shell.  "Not sure I could put up with that for long."

They picked up tins and dry food, and then Faye started racing towards the checkout.

"No!" Brian bellowed in horror, "Not yet!  We're not finished!"

For a moment they watched him lumber in great haste down the aisle, and then Mark and Tel gasped out loud and inexplicably gave chase.

"But we've got everything we need," Sophie said, checking her list and their trolleys.

"Not quite everything," Faye said. "BRIAN!"

His distant voice bellowed, "WHAT?"

"PROSECCO!"

The men returned as the women stood in the checkout queue, carrying a box of beer and a bottle of prosecco each. Faye tutted and said, "One bottle?"

"Couldn't carry any more."

"Go back and get a box."

"Storage," said Sophie.  "We won't be able to fit it all in."

The men hesitated.  Faye grimaced.  Sophie said, "We can

pick them up along the way."

Faye and Brian stood first in line at the checkout. In front, with her back to them, lumbered a large woman who was wearing a pair of denim shorts so tiny they barely covered her posterior; it looked like a fabric belt with a dangerously straining gusset. Her buttocks exploded out of them like dimpled bread rolls. Brian could barely tear his eyes off the mounds of exposed flesh … until the woman suddenly spun round and caught him.

"What are you looking at?" she spat, her face a multicoloured mass of twisted features.

"I'm sorry, I couldn't – "

"Are you staring at my *ass*?"

"I thought maybe you'd forgotten to put on a skirt or … something."

"*Excuse me?*"

Brian instinctively took a step back. Faye sucked in air. From the red clown mouth drawn across the woman's face came a barrage of abuse as colourful as her makeup, the volume of it echoing across the massive floor, making everyone turn their heads. A hole appeared in Brian's beard. He felt every follicle on his head cringing from the force of the onslaught.

Behind them in the queue Tel yelled, "RETREAT, BRI! RETREAT!"

Faye quickly turned the trolley around and scurried off to a distant checkout. Brian didn't move, he was stunned into paralysis by the force of the woman's verbal assault. There were words he didn't even recognise, but the woman's jabbing fingers, jerky body movements and furious expression suggested they weren't good ones.

Tel stepped forward and grabbed Brian's giant arm, pulling him back as best he could. "Come on, Bri."

Brian finally moved, turning and saying, "She was obviously a sailor with an anger management issue in a previous life."

With the woman still screaming obscenities, now aimed at several quickly departing customers, Brian sidled up to Faye and helped empty their trolley onto the conveyor belt with wide, startled eyes.

"You okay, Bri?"

He shrugged, looking back at the woman, who was now spitting obscenities over her shoulder at the security guard, who was valiantly attempting to push her towards the exit doors. "And I thought the lads at work were foul mouthed!"

When Sophie started emptying her trolley, Faye glanced back and said, "Oh, nice dress."

"Yes, it's cotton."

"And shirts too."

"Yes."

"Those shorts look nice?"

"Natural fibres, very cooling."

Faye forced a smile.

"And these are cute," Sophie said, holding up some baseball caps. "Big brims, keep the sun out of our eyes. I got us one each."

"Oh that's nice, Sophs."

"And folding fans." She shook one open with a flourish and fluttered it in front of her face. "Very Marie Antoinette. Should help with heatstroke."

"You're so kind."

"Teamwork," Sophie winked. "I've researched everything we might need. Well, my PA has."

They packed quickly and raced back out to the car park with a bag each, except for Mark and Olivia, who had one in each hand.

"We were only supposed to get minimal supplies," Sophie said.

"I need *everything* in these bags," Olivia insisted.

As they were walking across the car park Meryl drove passed them on her way to the exit. Tel had to step sideways in front of her to get her to stop. They scrambled in. Meryl tutted and huffily drove them back to the trailer park.

* * *

Back at camp, the men raced for the shower tents waving their new towels.  There followed a lot of shouting and hollering.  When they came back to the RVs, towels around their waists, the women laughed and said, "We told you it was cold."

"Refreshing," Brian said.

"My external bits are now internal bits," Mark said.

The men dressed while the women forced their new purchases into the sports bags.

"Damn it!" Sophie yelled from her motorhome. "I bought the wrong size! They're *all* the wrong size! Faye, what size are you?"

"I'm not shouting it out for all the world to hear!"

"I'll come over."

"Me too," Olivia said.

Faye opened the RV door to be met by them both holding a pile of clothes over one arm, a pair of shoes in one hand, and baseball caps on their heads.  Sophie also had a plastic Wal*Mart carrier bag.

"What's all this then?" Faye asked.

"We only went and bought the wrong sizes," Sophie tutted, dramatically rolling her eyes.

"Both of you?"

"What are the odds, eh?" Olivia giggled. "Silly us."

"You both bought the wrong sizes in shoes as well?"

"Linen flats," Sophie said, holding out a pair of espadrilles, "Very cool for your feet.  I was really looking forward to wearing them but," she tutted and rolled her eyes again, "they won't fit me. They'll fit you though."

"Same here," Olivia sighed, holding out a pair of soft, slingback sandals.

"How do you know they'll fit me?"

"I asked about your trainers, earlier, remember?  I must

have got confused between my size and your size when I picked them up."

"You forgot what shoe size you are?" Faye asked, raising an eyebrow.

"Yes, must be the heat, or the jet lag."

"And the clothes?"

"American sizes confused me," Olivia said, bowing her head.

"Me too," said Sophie.

"How do you know they're my size?"

"I checked your shirt label earlier," Olivia confessed.

Faye glared down at them.

"What's going on?" Brian asked, coming to stand behind her in the doorway.

"That's what I want to know."

Sophie rolled her eyes. "We bought *all* the wrong sizes, Bri."

"We got mixed up with the American sizes," Olivia said.

"Excellent acting," Brian grinned. "You should ask to be in the film."

"You'd better come in," Faye said.

Brian wandered off as the two women excitedly showed an unsmiling Faye their purchases: wide linen trousers in two cool colours, two pairs of lightweight shorts, the cotton dress Faye had admired earlier, and a couple of cotton shirts. "All natural, breathable materials," Sophie said.

Faye crossed her arms and pursed her lips. "So, what's really going on?"

"Genuine mistake," Sophie said.

When Faye's arms and lips remained tight, Olivia added, "They're a gift, from us, to help keep you cool."

Faye eyed them both.

"You don't look happy," Sophie said. "We thought you'd be happy. You're not offended, are you? That wasn't our intention."

"We were only trying to help, you were so hot and sweaty

and uncomfortable."

Faye picked up a shirt from the small pile of clothes on the lumpy bed. It felt lovely. The colours were lovely. The gesture was lovely. And her hot feet were crying out for the shoes and sandals. There were several cans of cooling mist and a couple of packs of deodorant wipes in Sophie's plastic bag, along with a pretty folding fan.

"Oh, and this," Olivia said, taking the baseball cap off her head and putting it on Faye's. "There's one for Brian, too."

Faye was still frowning. She took the cap off her head and rearranged her sweaty hair.

"We didn't want you gasping and swooning all over America," Sophie said. "It would ruin our trip, and shipping your crispy husk back to England would be *so* expensive. This is cheaper."

Faye idly fingered the clothes. She shrugged. She sighed. The frown evaporated and a small smile tugged at the corner of her mouth.

"You'll feel so much better wearing these," Sophie urged.

"So much cooler," said Olivia.

"Thank you, it's … it's really thoughtful of you."

"You're not offended?"

Faye shrugged.

Olivia looked at Sophie and said, "I think we might have gone a bit overboard."

Sophie snatched the baseball cap off Faye and held it to her chest. "How about now, are you less offended without the cap?"

Faye laughed.

Olivia picked up two cans of cooling mist and held them tight. "Better now?"

Sophie was just reaching to take back a shirt when Faye snatched it back and said, "I'm not *that* offended." She hugged them. "Thank you, you're both so kind."

"Selfish," Sophie said, "We did it purely for selfish reasons."

"And because you've always helped us out when we needed it. Call this payback."

Faye smiled, and took back the cans of cooling mist.

* * *

Brian wandered over to where Mark was sitting at the back of his motorhome, in the shade, on the ground, leaning against the wheel and sucking on a large water bottle.

"Girls okay?" he asked.

"Yeah, they're fine." Brian slowly lowered himself to the ground and looked up at the clear blue sky. "They're just doing their bit for charity."

"Charity?"

"Yeah, Sophie and Liv bought Faye a whole load of clothes and some other stuff."

"Ah." Mark looked down at the ground. "They're only trying to help."

"I know." Brian picked at a weed growing between them. "Thing is, Mark, while I understand their motives and acknowledge their kindness, my pride is a little bit … stung."

"I get that."

"I can take care of my own wife. Faye wants for nothing. Except natural fibres, apparently."

"We just thought, because of the new caravan, and the other thing that cannot be mentioned, you might be a bit … skint."

Brian remained silent.

"It's not charity, Bri, it's friends helping friends. You'd do the same for us."

"We're not destitute, we're just a little … *financially constrained* at the moment."

"Where have I heard that before?" Mark gave an awkward laugh. "Does that mean you won't be interested in the chambray shirts I got you at Walmart, then?"

Brian lifted his hairy chin. "Chambray, you say?"

"Yeah."

"Triple-X?"

"Of course."

"Expensive?"

"At Walmart?"

"Quite happy to buy them off you."

"Cheers, Bri, you'll be doing me a favour."

Brian gave him a sideways glance.

"Well, would you look at that!" came Tel's irate voice through the window of his RV, "I only went and bought the wrong size in these really comfortable cargo shorts in cool but manly colours!"

Brian's beard puckered around his mouth as Tel came bounding out of his motorhome carrying several clothes hangers. He held them out towards Brian. Brian didn't take them. Tel said, "Consider it payback for encouraging Sophie to marry me."

"And for helping to deal with Richard all those times," Mark added.

"And for being an all-round good bloke."

"Decent."

"Friendly."

"The calm voice of reason."

"Our mentor."

"Stop!" Brian cried.

"Just take the shorts and shirts, Bri!"

He did. Reluctantly.

# CHAPTER THREE

While Faye took another freezing-cold shower before putting on her new, cool clothes, the others gathered around the picnic table between the two static caravans. There was no one about. The other statics looked empty and dilapidated. It was eerily quiet.

"Where is everyone?" Olivia whispered.

"They've abandoned us because we won't invest," Tel said.

"No, surely not."

Faye tottered over and sat down next to Brian. He stared at her for a moment, then said, "Hello, can I help you?"

"Don't embarrass me, Bri."

"Who are you?"

"Bri!"

"What are you wearing?"

Faye broke into a huge smile. "My new cool clothes."

"And?" Brian persisted.

"And what?"

"What else are you wearing?"

"Oh, you mean my cooling head and neck bands?"

"Is that what they are?"

"Yes, Bri, I haven't suddenly turned into a hippie."

"Suits you," Sophie said.

Olivia smiled and nodded.

"That's a very funky necklace you got there, Faye," said Tel.

"It's a neck cooling tube. Hasn't been in the freezer long enough really, it's more of a slushie tube, but the other two are in there, and this fan," she said, fanning herself, "Is amazing."

"We're forgiven for spoiling you then?" Sophie asked.

Faye reached across the table and put her hand on Sophie's. "Yes. Thank you. I feel like I might actually survive this climate now. This all benefits you, too, Bri."

"Oh yeah? How so?"

Faye lifted her arm in the air next to him and he instinctively recoiled and gagged. Then he tentatively sniffed the air between his nose and her armpit, and said, "Great improvement, lass. I thought I was sleeping next to a compost heap last night." He was already laughing as Faye slapped his enormous, chambray covered arm.

"You're looking very dapper yourself, Bri," Mark said.

"Skip it, lad."

"Fair enough."

"Where do you think they all are?" Olivia said, looking around.

"They could have gone off to film somewhere, I suppose."

"Without us? I thought they wanted to show off a bit."

"And incite the Tarantino Effect."

"And encourage us to part with some pie and mash."

"Pie and mash?" Olivia asked.

"Cash," he told her.

"Who do you think you are?" Mark laughed. "You're not an East End gangster, you live in Kensington."

A bump came from inside the static caravan next to them.

"I think they're in there," Sophie whispered.

"All of them?"

"I don't know, but I'm getting human occupation vibes."

"Vibes would be more your area of expertise, wouldn't they?" Brian chuckled, staring at Faye's headband. "Tell my fortune later, lass?"

She slapped his arm again, then left her hand there, stroking the material.

"Chambray," Brian said, "A gift from the lads."

"Ooh," Faye said, "We're both getting spoiled."

"We are indeed."

"There, I heard it again, something moving in that caravan."

"Could be wolves," Mark said, already tapping on his phone for a list of local wildlife.

"Do they have wolves in Nevada?" Olivia asked.

"Wolves, bears – "

"Bears?"

" – coyotes, mountain lions."

"Lions and coyotes and bears, oh my," Brian sang. "I doubt the local predators come into populated areas much."

They all looked around. The place was deserted.

"Is that tumbleweed rolling across the cracked concrete car park?" Tel asked.

"Don't suppose you bought a cattle-prod at Walmart, did you?" Brian asked Faye. "Or a gun?"

"*A gun!*" Mark gasped.

"Funnily enough, that wasn't on my shopping list, Bri."

"Pity."

"HELLO?" Sophie suddenly yelled, making them all jump.

"Bloody 'ell, woman, you could warn us first!"

"Sorry, I just wanted to give the impression that this was a populated area, you know, in case there's any nearby lions or tigers or bears."

"You'll have scared them off with that sudden screaming, or else they, like us, are clutching at their pounding, terrified chests, stunned into shocked paralysis."

"Nice one, Bri."

"Thank you. I read a lot."

"Shows."

The door to the static caravan next to them suddenly flew open and they gasped out loud. Olivia gave a little scream of surprise.

"Sorry, folks," Michael said, stepping down. "We're just putting the finishing touches to the scenes we have in the can. It's looking really good, I think you're going to like it."

"Once we get Christofer to actually do some acting," Graham yelled from inside. "A mannequin could have done a better job."

"I heard that!" a voice from a nearby static cried.

"Good! You're not even phoning in your performance, it's more like texting. A corpse would have more expression."

"I can't work under these conditions!" Christofer yelled.

"You won't work ever again if your acting in this movie is anything to go by."

"Shut up!"

"I'm not sure there's enough explosions in the background," they heard Norman say.

"Any more digital pyrotechnics and it would look like the world exploded," Graham said.

"You sure?"

"Yep, and I don't think the air force jet flying overhead adds anything either."

"What can I put in the background then?"

"Godzilla?"

"Really?"

"No, Norm."

"We're looking forward to seeing it," Faye said to Michael, who was busy rearranging his face into a Tarantino smirk.

"Hmm," said Sophie.

The others nodded vaguely.

"We've got a couple more scenes to shoot today, it should be ready to view by … " He glanced at his watch. " … around four this afternoon."

"Can't wait to see an English campsite *Americanised*," Mark said.

"Camping … in the Nevada desert," boomed Brian.

"With guns," Tel laughed.

"*Guns!*" Mark gasped.

"And explosions," Faye said.

"Possibly Godzilla?" Olivia shrugged.

"It's going to be the next *Reservoir Dogs*," Michael said

proudly.  He glanced at his watch again, adding, "Colette should be here soon."

"Oh good," said Faye.

"We've got one quick scene with her and Shane inside the mobile trailer, then we're off to film in the desert.  You're welcome to join us."

"Pass," Faye said, frantically fanning the fan.  "Too hot for me."

The others said nothing.

Graham lumbered down the trailer steps holding a wad of paper.  "Is the interior ready?"

"MERYL!" Michael yelled, "IS THE TRAILER READY FOR SHOOTING?"

"YES!" she screeched from a trailer further down.

"So we just gotta wait for Colette to show up."

"*If* she shows up," Graham muttered.

"She said she would."

"She said that yesterday."

"And the day before," Norman called out.

"She'll show."

Graham lifted a hand and crossed his fingers.

"It'll be a closed set," Michael told them.  "We're doing a nude scene and Colette's a bit shy."

"No problem," said Brian.

"MERYL, DID YOU FIND THE BAND-AIDS?"

"THERE'S ONLY THREE LEFT!"

"Oh.  Graham, check the first aid kits in the mobile trailers."

"Check them yourself!"

"I'm the director."

"And I'm an as-yet unpaid scriptwriter."

Michael gave them a quick smile, which turned into a Tarantino sneer, before he marched off across the car park.

Meryl appeared, as if from nowhere.  "Is Colette here yet?"

"No."

"Where is she?"

Graham pulled out his phone, looked at it, tapped it, and said, "She's a mile away."

"You track her?" Mark asked, surprised at the violation of privacy.

"Have to. She's from New York and gets lost a lot. Oh, she's driving in the wrong direction."

"Call her," Meryl snapped.

Graham brought the phone up to his ear. "Colette, it's Graham. You're going the wrong way. No, I can see you on my map." He looked at his screen and turned on the speaker. "You're definitely going the wrong – "

"I don't know what to do!" came a woman's high-pitched, panicky voice. "I'm following the sat-nav."

"Have you got it upside down again?"

"No." There was a long pause. "Yes. Okay, I'm turning round." A clatter and a cry of, "Dammit!"

"Turn right, then right again."

"Okay, okay. Am I going in the right direction now?"

"Yes."

"How about now?"

Graham sighed. "Any particular reason you decided to take a random left turn?"

"It looked like the right way. Oh wait, there's a delivery truck blocking the street."

"Turn right, Colette."

"I can't, there's a del-. No, no, it's a furniture van, someone's moving in to one of the apartments."

"You'll have to back up."

"I can't, there's cars behind me now."

"How long do you think the van will be?"

"I don't know, but there's a lot of stuff in the back and they're not moving very fast."

"Ask them," Graham snapped, "Ask them how long they'll be."

"Excuse me! Excuse me, van man! How long do you think you'll … ? Oh, rude. Hello? You there in the overalls, how long do you think – ?"

"We'll be as long as it takes, ma'am," came a distant voice.

"Hey, I'm not old enough to be called ma'am, and I'm single!"

"We'll be as quick as we can, ma'am."

"Graham! Graham! I'm going to have to wait."

"Get here as soon as you can, we're all set up."

"I'm so nervous, I've never been filmed naked before."

"You'll be fine. It's something an actor has to overcome in this business."

"Is it?"

"Yes. It's in the script, you signed the contract, they both say some nudity is required."

"Does it?"

"Yes, Colette. There's no avoiding this. Get here and get it over with.

"Okay, if you're sure."

"I'm sure."

She hung up.

"She sounds lovely," Faye said, smiling broadly.

Graham circled the side of his head with a finger. "Crazy as a sprayed cockroach."

"Ugh," said Sophie, brushing at her arms.

"No idea how she's made it to adulthood," Graham said. "Nice boobs, though."

"The original character is much the same," Brian said.

"Shut up, Bri." But she smiled as she said it.

* * *

As they waited for Colette to show up, Olivia got up to make drinks in her trailer. She'd taken one step away from the bench before Michael said, "Tea, two sugars, splash of milk."

"Ditto," Norman called from inside the static.

Meryl said, "I'll take a coffee, strong, black, no sugar. Bring it to my trailer." She promptly marched off.

"I'll have tea with four sweeteners and the tiniest drop of

milk," said Graham. "And cookies, do you have any chocolate chip cookies?"

"I don't have the ingredients to make cookies," Olivia said.

"He means biscuits," said Tel.

"Oh. I didn't buy any biscuits."

"No biscuits?" Mark cried in mock horror, "How will we survive?"

Olivia wandered off, chanting the order under her breath and frowning.

Michael sat in her place at the table. "Wait until you see it," he said, "It's a masterpiece. Tarantino will tremble in his boots. You'll be *begging* to put money into it."

"We won't," Brian said, deadpan.

"You should grab this exciting opportunity while you can, before it's too late. You'll kick yourself later for missing out on something so *epic*."

"We won't."

"Think of the prestige, the fame, the glory. Your names will be up on the big screen, on the closing credits, obviously. I'll give you titles, I'll list you as producers, how about that? Or the opening credits, whatever it takes. Think of the – "

"If I could just interject," Tel said, leaning forward. "None of us are investors. Why don't we wait until we've seen the film – "

"Rushes."

" – before we make any financial decisions."

"I wouldn't hold your breath though, lad."

"Just out of interest," Mark said, "How much investment are you looking for?"

Michael told them. They sat in stunned silence for a moment, before Brian started laughing.

"I don't expect you to come up with the *entire* sum," Michael said.

Brian laughed louder.

"A substantial contribution would suffice."

And louder.

"You've no chance, mate," said Mark.

"Has the writer invested in it?" Tel asked, "This Flemmingway guy?"

Michael grimaced. "We did ask, but he said he writes to *make* money, not to give it away, and that it was our project now and we should just get on with it. He'll take twenty-five percent of the profits though."

"Interesting," said Tel, glancing at the others.

"Wait until you've seen the rushes," Michael gushed, "Meryl has a PowerPoint presentation for you afterwards, she'll inspire you much better than I can."

"I doubt that."

"Just wait, you'll see."

Olivia, standing in the doorway of their RV, shouted, "There's not enough mugs!" She was hoping she wouldn't have to make as many drinks if there weren't enough mugs, it was too hot to be standing in a compact space with a steaming kettle.

"They're all in Graham's trailer," Michael shouted.

"No, they're not!" Graham yelled.

"Norman, bring out the mugs!"

There was stomping as Norman moved about inside the trailer, making it creak, followed by the clattering sound of mugs being gathered. He came down the steps with several in each hand and shouted, "MUGS!"

"I'll say," Brian drawled.

Olivia rushed over to get them, glancing frantically at Mark, who said, "You'll need paying if you're going to act as the tea lady."

"Tea lady?" Olivia gasped.

"Paying?" gasped Michael.

* * *

A car pulled onto the car park just as Olivia was struggling out of the RV with two full mugs in each hand. A young, very pretty woman got out looking flustered. She spotted them at the picnic table, started to walk towards them, then turned and ran back to her car for her bag. Brushing the long, streaked-blonde hair from her face, she passed Olivia carrying the drinks and said, "Oh, good, you've hired a caterer. Black for me, please, strong enough to stand a spoon in."

Olivia pounded the mugs down on the table and went back into the RV. Mark chased after her. Brian stood up and offered Colette his seat. She looked up at him in amazement.

"Are you one of the cast members?" she asked. "I don't remember a giant being in the film, is this a new development?"

Tel burst out laughing.

"Anyway, sorry I'm late," she said, talking in a fast and breathless New York accent, "Damn van took ages, I had to drive onto the sidewalk in the end and nearly hit a kid coming out of a building."

Michael closed his eyes tightly.

"And then I scraped passed this car that was *incorrectly parked* and knocked both our wing mirrors off."

Michael groaned.

"It's okay," she said, waving her hands around, "I'll glue it back on and put some nail varnish on the scratched bits, the hire company won't notice."

Michael leaned forward and whispered, "Don't tell Meryl, she'll throw a fit."

"I won't, I won't." She looked around the table. "Hello."

"Hi," they all said.

"Are you the British people? Pleased to meet you." She shook each of their outstretched hands with her delicate fingers. "Apologies for my lateness and for looking like I got ran over on the way, and first impressions are so important too, aren't they."

"You're very pretty," Faye couldn't help saying. "You look a bit like Jennifer Aniston."

"Yes," she giggled, waving a hand, "I get that a lot. Mike, I'm so nervous about this scene, I hardly slept a wink last night."

"You'll be fine. It's a closed set. We'll keep everything very tasteful."

"Yes," Graham said, "We're not making a porn movie."

"No." Colette giggled nervously, scrunching up her face. "Is it absolutely essential, this scene?"

"It's part of the storyline."

"Are you sure?"

"Yes, Col, we've been over this several times."

"I know, I know, I'm just nervous."

Mark and Olivia came staggering over with more hot mugs and put them on the table.

"So," Michael said, standing up, "Shall we get it over and done with?"

Colette sipped her coffee. "Just give me five minutes to ingest my caffeine and I'm all yours, figuratively speaking, of course, I don't *literally* mean I'm yours, you understand that, right?"

"You're mine for the duration of the shoot," he winked, and she gave a dry laugh. He sat down again.

Meryl strode over. "I thought you were bringing my coffee to my trailer," she barked at Olivia.

"I said I was making a drink," Olivia said firmly, "I didn't say I provided a delivery service."

A heavy silence fell around the table as Meryl glared at Olivia and Olivia glared back. Meryl pulled her eyes away first. "Is Shane ready?"

"Isn't that your job?" Michael said, "To organise the cast and the set."

Meryl glared at him. Michael looked away first.

"Graham," she snapped, turning to him, "You're standing there doing nothing, go and drag Shane from his trailer. He's probably playing Quest games again."

"Why me?"

Meryl stood up straight, all five feet of her, and took a deep breath. "Do I detect a sense of mutiny in the group?" she asked. "If you're not happy with me as Executive Producer I'd be happy to resign and take my investment with me."

"No, no," Michael said, jumping up and helping her to sit in his place, "We're very happy with you as Executive Producer, Meryl, you do an excellent job, *excellent*."

Norman and Graham swapped glances, before Graham wandered off with his mug to Shane's trailer.

"Where shall I get … undressed?" Colette asked, chewing on her nails.

"First trailer, the one with all the windows open and the lighting and camera inside."

"How much lighting?"

"Can't fit the stadium lights in there so we're using … flashlights."

"Small flashlights?" Colette asked.

"Super bright LEDs," Norman said, and Michael threw him a glowering look.

"Oh," she said, "Okay, but not directly on me, right?  I mean, it's a trailer, it's supposed to be dark inside, isn't it?"

"You'll barely be seen," Michael soothed.

"Barely," she laughed. "Funny.  Where are the, er, Band-Aids."

"They're in there," Graham said, coming over with Shane lumbering half-naked behind him.

"Shane," Colette said, lowering her eyes.

"Col," he said, before quipping, "You get your clothes off, girl."

"Right, let's get this show on the road," Meryl thundered, "We're wasting time, and time is money."

Colette scuttled off.

\* \* \*

The campers watched from the table.  The door and blinds were closed as Colette got undressed.  Everyone stood waiting outside with their backs turned, Meryl standing guard by the door with her arms firmly crossed.

"Okay," Colette eventually called out, "I'm … I'm ready. Well, as ready as I'll ever be."   The blinds were opened and they could just make out Colette, wrapped tightly in a blanket, before she disappeared into the dark again.

"Mike, can I just question the *absolute necessity* of having a love scene in this movie?" she called out.

"We're doing this, Col, it's in your – "

"Contract, yes, yes, I know.   Remind me to phone my agent after this."

"Brace yourself, baby," said Shane, climbing the steps, "I'm coming in."

"Oh God."

Norman followed him inside with the camera, shooting from the doorway.  Graham stood next to him holding the flashlight and the cat on a stick.  Michael was outside, pointing another camera through the window.  The mood was tense.

"You okay there, Col?  Pull the blanket down a little.  A bit more."

"Way-hay!" Shane cried, "X marks the spot!"

"Okay, Shane, do your thing."

"Hey!  Be careful!"

"My bad?"

"Don't injure her," Michael said, "Our insurance might not cover it.  Okay, comfy?"

"Not really."

"And … ACTION."

There was some puffing, a little huffing, a slight wobble of the motorhome, and then Michael yelled, "OKAY, CUT! Colette, sweetheart, could you not cover your entire face with the blanket?"

"His breath *stinks*!"

"Shane, have you been chomping on garlic cloves again?"

"It's good for the blood and stuff."

"Not so good for your co-star though, is it."

"I'd do it," Faye said under her breath.

"What are you muttering, wife?"

"How did you hear that?"

"I get heightened hearing when my wife expresses an interest in galivanting naked with other men."

"I meant because I can't smell, Shane's garlic breath wouldn't bother me."

"Sure you did."

Michael shouted, "Okay, let's go again."

Puffing, huffing and wobbling ensued, followed by Colette suddenly shouting, "I just don't get what my motivation is for this scene, Mike."

"Your motivation is to be paid," Meryl snapped.

"Eventually," Michael muttered. "We've been over this, Col. He's your husband, he's just saved your life, and you're grateful."

"This grateful, though?"

"Yes! Okay, let's give it one more try, and please, get it right this time."

Puffing, huffing wobbling. Then Colette start laughing.

"AND ... CUT! Colette, this is supposed to be a serious love scene."

"I'm know, I know. Sorry, Mike, he just looks so funny hanging over me like that."

"View's not that good from up top, either," Shane said.

"Excuse me?"

"I'm pulling ya chain, you look gorgeous, you know you do."

"Ew, you're not coming on to me again, are you?"

"Always."

"Just stop it. Mike, I can't work if he's going to keep leering at me like that."

"It's my sexy look."

"It's not, really it's not."

"People, can we just get this scene in the can? And ... ACTION!"

Huffing, puffing, wobbling, and then Colette started laughing again.

"CUT!"

"Mike, I'm so sorry. I guess I'm just nervous and overcome with garlic fumes."

Brian glanced at Faye. She kept her face expressionless and said nothing.

"And Shane's belts keep catching in my hair. Ow!"

"You're supposed to be professionals!" Meryl barked, "Act like proper actors and not like children!"

"Yes, Meryl."

Michael, peering through the window, said, "Shane, could you shift over a bit, we can't see Colette's face."

"Can't you bring in a body double, Mike? I mean, if you can't see my face anyway I don't see why I should have to – "

"And ... ACTION!"

Colette burst out laughing. "It's nerves!" she cried, "I'm so sorry." But she didn't stop, and then Shane started laughing too, yelling, "X marks the spot!"

"Get off me, you perv."

Outside, Michael huffed and stepped away from the camera, staring up at the sky with his sneer and his jutting chin.

"Sorry, Mike."

Meryl stormed inside the motorhome, pushing Norman and Graham aside. "Shane, shuffle down. Put your leg here and your arm here. Colette, turn your head this way."

"OW! You nearly pulled my head off!"

"I'll do just that if you don't get this scene finished. You think we *like* standing around watching you two get hysterical?"

"Quite enjoying it myself," said Mark.

"Me too," said Brian.

Meryl stomped out again and began walking away, then stopped and turned round.

"CHRISTOFER!" she screamed. "I SEE YOU HIDING AT THE BACK OF THE TRAILER! THIS IS A CLOSED SET. LEAVE *IMMEDIATELY*!"

At first there was silence. Nothing and nobody stirred. And then, very slowly, with his head hanging, Christofer stepped out from behind the set trailer and sloped off.

"Has he gone?" Colette asked.

"Yes."

"Is there something wrong with him? He keeps sneaking up on me in the shower tent. Have you sorted out the hot water yet, by the way?"

"QUIET ON SET!" Michael yelled. "Gather yourselves, people. Become the characters. You can do this. And ... ACTION!"

* * *

It took another five takes before Michael was satisfied, by which time the campers at the table were starting to feel the effects of jet-lag creeping over them again.

"What time is it?" Mark asked, his head on the table.

"It's half-ten, darling."

"What time is that at home?"

"Early," Tel yawned, "Really, really early."

"I suggest," Brian said, rubbing his face, "That we all get some kip, then head into town later."

"Oh yes!" Faye cried.

"I concur," said Sophie.

They all stood up.

Michael, noticing their movement, raced over. "What are you doing? Where are you going?"

"Quick nap in the RVs."

"You can't do that."

"Er, I think you'll find we can," Mark said. "We're not on your payroll, we can come and go as we please."

"Well, yes, but I was kinda hoping you'd be available before lunch."

"For?"

"It was going to be a surprise." Michael swapped his sneer for a smile and started rubbing his hands together. "We want you to be in the movie."

"Oh, how thrilling!" Olivia squealed, as Faye's mouth fell open.

"In what capacity?" Tel asked.

"As extras. We need you for a crowd scene."

Brian and Tel sighed heavily.

Mark said, "I don't think I have the energy for a crowd scene."

The women, however, seemed overtly excited. "We're going to be in a movie!" Faye screeched. "This could be the start of something *big*."

"Don't get carried away, lass."

"Allow me to dream a little, Bri."

"This could be the start of something big," he grinned behind his beard.

"I'll get noticed, people will clamour after me, I'd work on a film with *Chris Hemsworth!*"

"And all this from a crowd scene," Brian laughed, as they all sat back down again.

"So, you'll do it?" Michael asked.

"Looks like it," said Mark, watching Olivia clapping her hands together.

"Great. We've got Singent and Maria coming in at midday, they're playing Mark and Olivia."

"Singent?" said Mark.

"Exciting!" said Olivia.

"*Singent?*" Mark said again. "I'm being played by someone called *Singent?*"

"Yes," Michael said. "You won't like him, he's tetchy, acerbic and massively pretentious."

"Exactly the words I used to describe you the other day," Brian snorted.

"Did you, Hagrid?"

"He's impossible to work with but an excellent actor," Michael added. "So, drinks all round?"

"It's a bit early," Sophie said, glancing at her watch.

"It's never too early," said Brian.

"I meant coffee." He looked straight at Olivia. "If you wouldn't mind?"

"When did I get delegated as tea lady?"

"I'll help," Mark said.

Colette came over, fully dressed. "I could do with a shot of vodka after that little fiasco. Man looks like a Greek God, acts like a three-year-old. Anyone making a coffee to get rid of the rancid taste of garlic?"

Graham came over and said, "Can I have a word, Mike? I've made some changes to the crowd scene, Singent's not going to like it."

"He doesn't like anything."

"He particularly won't like this."

Michael and Graham stood reading through sheets of paper. Tel yawned loudly.

"We could go for a walk to keep us awake," Sophie suggested.

"No!" Michael suddenly cried, looking up with wide eyes, "Don't go beyond the chain-link fence!"

"Why not?"

"It's … not safe. Neighbourhood's a bit … rough."

"Oh, we have rough neighbourhoods in England," Brian said.

"Carry guns in England, do they?"

"*Guns!*" Mark gasped.

"They carry guns here, and knives. It's dangerous for you out there."

"And you do look like tourists," Colette said, "You wouldn't last five minutes."

"Well, that's reassuring," Tel said. "Trapped in a trailer park in uptown Las Vegas."

They glanced nervously at each other, then Tel dropped his head on the table and cried, "I'm so tired!"

Michael shouted, "WHERE'S THAT COFFEE?"

# CHAPTER FOUR

A man stepped out of a battered, rusty car that spluttered onto the car park. He was wearing a shabby Panama hat, a white goatee beard, and a creased grey suit that flapped around his huge frame, under which was a stained t-shirt with a faded logo.

"He's as wide as you, Bri," Tel gasped.

"And half the stature," said Sophie.

"It's Orson Welles!" Faye cried.

"The one who died thirty years ago?" Tel laughed.

"Which is roughly the age difference between him and me," complained Mark. "How can *he* be playing *me*?"

The huge man lumbered towards them with the use of a gold-topped cane and glared down at the faces around the wooden picnic table.

"Investors?" he bellowed gruffly at Michael.

"Possibly."

"Not," said Brian.

"Then who are you?"

"We're the Brits," said Mark. "You're playing me." He stood up and offered a hand. The man didn't take it. "I'm Mark."

"Good for you." He took a hip flask out of his baggy jacket pocket and swigged at it, before concentrating his glare on Colette. "You still here?"

"I work here. This is *literally* my job. I don't know why you hate me so much, Singent, I've never done anything to you."

"You annoy me."

"Why, because I'm pretty and talented?"

"Both are *highly* debatable. Get up."

Huffing, Colette stood up and leaned against Graham's trailer. Singent sat down on the edge of the bench. The opposite end lifted up off the ground. Brian shifted further along to counterbalance.

"I have one hour," Singent thundered.

"But we're shooting scenes in *two* different locations!" Michael cried. "It'll take all afternoon!"

"One hour. Where's my coffee?"

Olivia and Mark came over carrying multiple mugs.

"Is there bourbon in this?" Singent growled, looking down at the mug she'd placed in front of him.

"No," Olivia said.

"No?"

"I don't have any bourbon."

"Then I'm not drinking it!"

"Suit yourself," said Brian, nodding for Olivia to sit down.

"Do you know who I am?" Singent said, piercing Brian with his yellow-tinged eyes.

Brian shrugged.

"I am *Singent Carruthers*."

The campers faces remained blank.

"Ac-tor extraordinaire, *star* of both stage and screen. I have trodden the boards of Broadway and been nominated for a Tony."

"He wasn't," Colette whispered to Mark, as they leaned against the trailer sipping at their coffees, "He started that rumour himself.

"I have graced the small screen and was longlisted for an Academy, an Emmy *and* a Golden Globe," Singent continued.

"Never happened," Collette whispered.

"*And* I was nominally nominated for an *Oscar* for my powerful portrayal of Big Daddy in *Cat on a Hot Tin Roof*."

"That's true," Colette breathed, "But he didn't make the final list."

"Directors fete me and women *fall* at my feet."

"A few decades ago maybe," Colette muttered.

"Have you been in anything we might have seen?" Sophie asked, and Singent's head spun round to glare at her. "I very much doubt it."

"I think that says more about you than it does about me," she said.

"Are you an imbecile?"

Tel quickly leaned across the table towards the big man and quietly said, "Do *not* speak to my wife like that."

Singent gave him a withering glare from his beady little eyes.

"We're lawyers," Tel explained, sitting back again.

"The very definition of an imbecile." Singent started laughing, loudly and with apparent effort. His whole body wobbled like jelly. Up against the trailer Colette crinkled up her nose. He finished with a hearty cough.

Michael hurried over. "Don't upset the Brits," he said quickly, "You never know when we might need them."

"God forbid we should ever need the British!"

"Singent, you're being very – "

"Singent-like," Colette said. "Would it kill you to be nice every now and again?"

"Yes, it would. Now where's my bourbon?"

Graham slipped into his trailer and came out with a bottle. He poured some into the steaming mug of coffee.

"More than that! Don't scrimp on the star of the show!"

"I ... I thought I was the star," Colette whined.

Michael nodded and mouthed, 'You are.'

Faye preened.

"Look," Michael said, "If you're only here for an hour we'd better get started."

Singent slowly raised the mug to his lips.

"There's one scene here at the lot and another in the desert."

"I'm not going into the desert."

"It's in your contract."

"I don't care, it's too hot. I won't jeopardise my health by subjecting myself to heatstroke."

"But you're willing to jeopardise it with bourbon, cigarettes and a massive addiction to Taco Bell," Colette huffed.

Singent turned to glare at her. She sipped her coffee.

Michael said, "Norman, have you set up the crowd scene?"

"Just got to get the plastic rifles out of the props trailer and then we're good to go."

"Who are they actually fighting in this film?" Tel asked.

"I bet it's zombies," Mark laughed.

"The Democrats!" Brian howled.

"Aliens," Michael said.

"Aliens?"

"We did consider zombies," Graham said, "But the makeup would have cost way over our budget with all the foam-latex prosthetics – "

"Although there were those Halloween masks in Walmart."

" – and having to look for people with missing limbs would have been time consuming."

"And time," Meryl declared, "is money."

"So we went for aliens. Invisible ones, like the one in *Predator*. Norman can add the special effects afterwards."

The Brits silently digested this piece of new information.

"Funny," Tel said, "When you say 'Quentin Tarantino' you don't automatically think of aliens, do you."

"It'll have a very Tarantino vibe to it," Michael explained, "Hence all the violence."

"Violence?"

"So," Brian squinted at Michael, "The story is about British folk – "

"Americans."

" –fighting off invaders – "

"Aliens."

" – from a campsite – "

"Trailer park."

" – in the middle of the English countryside?"

"Middle of Western American."

"And this is based on Ian Flemmingway's book?" Olivia asked.

"Loosely based," Graham said. "I obviously jazzed the script up a bit."

"A bit?" Tel laughed. "Sounds like a whole new story!"

"Same basic plot though," Michael said. "And we wanted to keep the characters, we were very careful about matching the right actors to the characters."

Mark looked at Singent, surreptitiously tipping something from a hip flash into his mug. Brian glanced across to where Shane was fighting off invisible forces with a big stick. Faye smiled broadly and waved her fingers at Colette, who waved back.

"Right, let's get a move on," Michael declared. "If you could just mess yourselves up a little."

"Pardon?" Sophie said.

"You need to look like a desperate gang of people fleeing the alien invasion."

"We're British," Faye said, smoothing her shirt and glancing down at her lovely new sandals. "We look smart whatever the situation."

"You're playing Americans, so you need to look particularly scruffy. Can you muss up your hair and put a few wrinkles in your clothes?"

"No!"

"They'll be fine as long as you shoot it from high enough," Norman said, and Faye exhaled in relief.

"Here's one for the grandkids," Brian whispered to Faye. "Nanny and grandad were once in a film! That's them, in the crowd, shot from fifty feet in the air."

"There go my dreams of working with Chris Hemsworth."

"CHRISTOFER!" Meryl screeched.

"I AM COMING!"

"Singent, are you ready for your running scene?"

"I don't run."

"It's in your – "

Colette's phone started ringing. She cried out in alarm and frantically searched in her bag before pulling out her mobile phone. "Hello?" She stopped leaning against the trailer and started shaking a nervous hand. "Yes, yes, I'd love to! Now? This minute? No, no, it's fine, I'll be there." She thrust the phone back in her bag and glanced at her watch. "Audition!" she cried, "Big part in a big film and I have to be there within the hour, so can we hurry this up? CHRISTOFER!"

*"I AM COMING!"*

The crew ran off in all directions. The gang nervously stood up and Meryl quickly herded them towards the RVs. Michael ran to the middle of the car park with his drone, standing next to Norman behind the camera tripod. Graham handed out plastic guns.

Singent, still sat at the table, filled his empty mug with the remains of the hip flask.

"SINGENT!"

Singent emptied his mug in three gulps and staggered towards the set with his walking cane. Graham handed him a gun and picked up the furry microphone on a stick.

Christofer sauntered casually towards them.

"Hurry up!" Colette hissed, "I have an audition to get to!"

Christofer deliberately slowed his pace.

"All gather at the far end of the car park," Michael yelled through the megaphone, jutting out his chin and twisting his mouth. "Then run like you've got aliens chasing after you. Look really scared, picture panic in your mind. You could die here, people! Ready?"

They were all gathered outside the shower tents like relay racers waiting for the baton. Graham stood next to them with his cat on a stick. Michael put down the megaphone and picked up the controls for the camera drone, lifting it into the air, higher and higher.

"Grandkids will never recognise us from that high up," Faye muttered.

A car suddenly skidded into the car park and two women jumped out; Tammy, and an equally tiny woman with a wild mass of black hair. "Sorry we're late, y'all," Tammy cried as they raced across the car park, "One of Maria's kids was sick."

"Just get with the others."

"That's you," Mark said to Olivia, nodding at the woman with wild hair. "She's playing you in the film."

"Oh, I can see the resemblance."

Tel leaned in, laughing. "Singent and Maria, don't they just scream 'couple'?"

"OKAY, AND ... ACTION!"

The drone swooped towards them. They ran as fast as they could, except for Singent, who casually wandered after them leaning heavily on his cane, and Tammy, who tottered on her heels and gripped onto her boobs. Graham sprinted alongside them with his boom mic in the air.

They'd barely passed the rows of RVs before Michael yelled, "CUT!"

They all stopped, breathless. The drone returned to the middle of the car park.

"BRITS, YOU CAN'T SMILE WHEN YOU'RE BEING CHASED BY INVISIBLE ALIENS."

"WE'RE JUST ... SO EXCITED ... TO BE IN A ... FILM," Faye gasped.

"I WANT YOU CRYING AND SCREAMING! I WANT YOU TO BE *TERRIFIED!*"

"Just think of our last fuel bill," Brian said.

They walked back to the shower tents. When Michael yelled 'ACTION!' they ran, screaming and howling, except for Singent, who sauntered, and Brian, who was quite puffed out.

"CUT! AND AGAIN!"

The crowd turned and groaned. The woman with the wild hair shouted to Michael in strangled English.

"Yes, Maria," he responded, "We'll get it done as soon as we can."

Maria started shouting in Spanish, gesticulating with her hands, then joined the crowd in front of the tents.

"She really captures the essence of you," Mark said to Olivia.

"I can speak Spanish," she said.

"Say something dirty to me in Spanish, my little señorita."

"Not now," she giggled, "Maybe later."

"HURRY UP!" Mark yelled.

"DESPERATE! TERRIFIED! AND … ACTION!"

The drone swooped. The crowd ran and screamed. Singent sauntered. Brian threw his head on an arm against the last RV, gasping for breath. "I'm more … " he puffed, " … a lifter than a … sprinter."

Shane bumped into Colette and sent her sprawling across the cracked concrete.

Michael yelled, "CUT! YOU'RE STILL SMILING, BUT I LIKE THE FALL, COLETTE, DO THAT NEXT TIME."

"Bloody brute," she hissed at Shane, checking herself. "I can't go to an audition with blood all over my hands. Oh, now it's on my shirt!"

"Take the shirt off," he leered. "You'll definitely get the part, and I speak from experience."

"Ew! Creep!"

"AND AGAIN!"

They ran. They screamed and yelled. Shane bounced into Colette, who fell in front of Tammy and Maria, tripping them both up.

"CUT! AGAIN!"

"You okay, Bri?"

"May … die … soon."

"The heat!" Faye gasped, red faced and sweating.

"MY AUDITION, MIKE!"

Maria yelled something in Spanish that made Olivia gasp.

"DID WE HAVE TO DO THIS AT MIDDAY?" Christofer shouted.

"Mad dogs and Englishmen," Tel laughed.

"What?"

"Never mind."

"AND … ACTION!"

The drone swooped. They ran. They shrieked. They raced across the car park towards the camera on the tripod. They stopped before they knocked it over, Tammy clinging on to her boobs, the rest gasping. The drone landed. They all stared expectantly at Michael.

"Got it!" he said, grinning, and they all cheered in a hoarse, sweaty kind of way. "Now for scene two."

They groaned.

* * *

On a close-up, the camera mere inches away from him, Singent gently lowered himself, first onto his hands and knees, then into a comfortable seated position on the ground.

"That's what you call throwing yourself down on the ground in a wild panic to escape the aliens?" Michael asked.

"That's as close to throwing myself down as it gets."

"Do it again."

Singent grunted. "Help me up."

It took three of them.

Second shot, Singent threw himself, protruding stomach first, face second, onto the ground, and was immediately engulfed in a shocked cloud of sand. Air exploded from both his mouth and his rear end, shifting the cloud around.

Third shot, Singent stood and stretched out his left leg, gripping tightly onto Graham's steadying and out-of-shot hand. He half slid to the ground, let go of Graham's hand, and landed like a felled tree.

"Ow!"

"I guess that'll have to do," Michael said.

"Where should I send the medical bills for my broken

coccyx?"

"You're fine."

"I'm in pain."

"We're all in pain," Colette snapped.

"Did *you* just crash to the ground?" Singent snarled at her.

"As a matter of fact, I did," she replied, glaring at Shane, "Quite a few times, in fact! And look at my hair, it's full of sand and dirt! I'm supposed to be auditioning in – " She glanced at her watch and shrieked, "Fifteen minutes! Michael, I *have* to go, I have to go *now*."

"Let's finish the scene."

"I can come back later."

Maria said something in Spanish, furiously shaking her head.

"Ma boyfriend kinda wants me home for lunch," Tammy said, "He gets real hungry this time of day."

"Come on, people! Let's make this happen! Singent, sit with your back against the wheel. The rest of you, gather round him. Graham, hit him with the fake blood."

"We're out of fake blood, but I've got this." He aimed a plastic red bottle at Singent and squirted tomato sauce on his jacket and t-shirt.

Singent looked down at it and snarled, "That had better not leave a stain."

"It will," Olivia breathed.

"Concentrate, people. You're losing Mark – "

"Oh Mark!" Olivia said to the real one, clutching his arm, "We're losing you."

" – a beloved member of your army – "

Colette huffed.

" – your brave comrade, your magnificent leader."

"Oh Mark, you're the leader!" Olivia gasped.

"The leader!" Mark grinned.

"Don't let it go to your head," said Tel.

"The leader," Mark said again. "Go me!"

"I wanna see *emotion*," Michael yelled, "I wanna hear

*devastation* in your voices."

"We are actors," Christofer snapped, "We know how to fake it."

"Some of us do," Shane whispered to Tammy, who giggled.

"Let us get on with it."

"*Please*!" Colette urged, tapping on her watch.

They got to their knees around Singent, who was sweating profusely and stank of alcohol.

"SAD!" Michael directed through the megaphone. "DEVASTATED. YOU'RE HOLDING BACK THE TEARS."

"Holding back the urge to barf," Colette said, covering her nose with a hand. "He stinks of stale bourbon."

"It's not stale, I just imbibed it."

"It must be yesterday's bourbon oozing out of your pores then!"

"Stop arguing and concentrate!" Michael snapped. "Maria, your husband is dying, you are inconsolable, start crying. The rest of you, sad, sad, sad, and ... rolling."

"Mark!" Maria screamed like a banshee, throwing herself across Singent, making him *humph*. She then wailed something nobody could understand, and screamed again.

"We can dub that bit in," said Norman.

"Our fearless leader," Shane said, wiping a tear from his eye and getting sand in it.

"Keep going."

"How will we carry on without you?" Shane said, winking and squinting. "You're an inspiration to us all."

"We love you," Colette said, deadpan.

"Don't roll your eyes," Michael breathed, "Resist the urge to roll your eyes."

Maria wailed unintelligibly.

"Why do you think they hired an actor who can't speak English?" Brian mused.

"She is speaking English," Olivia whispered, "Just not in a way that anyone can understand. She told me she's the wife of one of the investors who would only invest if she was in the movie."

"It has been an honour to fight alongside you," Christofer said stiffly. "We will never forget what you have done for humanity."

Norman moved the camera closer, until it was solely focused on Singent. The others, out of shot now, moved back and relaxed. Colette checked her watch and pulled a face. Christofer walked off. Shane furiously rubbed at his eye, making it worse.

"We must fight the battles facing our country and the world," Singent said in a slow, deep voice, tinged with pain and regret. "Humanity must endure, as it has always endured against those who threaten it. We must fight, we must banish the invaders from our planet. We cannot cower in fear, we cannot be weak and hide. We must stand tall and face the enemy, even if we cannot see it. We are fighting a common adversary and we must put our differences aside as we claim humanity's right to exist in the universe. We *will* survive and we *will* recover."

"And cut," Michael said softly.

"That was quite good," Colette said.

"It will be the best scene in the movie."

"Modesty becomes you, Singe."

"It genuinely brought a tear to ma eye," Tammy sniffed.

"Mine too," Shane said, rubbing it.

"You get all that, Norman?"

Norman nodded, smiling.

"Help me up."

Again, it took three men to raise Singent to his feet. He immediately headed for his car.

"Singent, the desert scene?"

"It's been over an hour. I'm hot, I'm tired, I'm off to the nearest bar."

He got in, slammed the door, and turned the car around.

"Damn," said Graham, clutching the script as he watched

Singent skid with some urgency onto the street. "He's integral to the next scene."

Michael was silent for a moment, then said, "Do we have a Panama hat in props?"

"I'm off!" Colette cried, leaping into her car.

"Are you coming – ?"

She shot off before Michael could finish.

"That's two down," Graham said. "Rats and sinking ship come to mind."

Michael glared at him. "It's going to be a masterpiece of filmmaking!"

"Of course it is, Mike. Absolutely."

Tammy and Maria were just walking to Tammy's car, and Michael was just about to ask if *they* were coming back, when another car skidded onto the parking lot.

"Oh no," Tammy said. "It's ma boyfriend. I'm getting real tired of him following me around."

A chubby, scruffy man jumped out of the car, slammed the door, and stormed straight towards Tammy.

"I told ya, honey," she said, not looking the least bit alarmed, "I said I'd be home to make you your lunch."

"It's gone lunchtime!" he yelled, jabbing at his watch. "You said you'd only be an hour."

"Well, it overran a bit on account of … well, a lotta things. Don't you get yourself all riled up now, y'hear, I ain't but an iddy-bit late. Hey, y'all, this is ma boyfriend, Snoop."

"Snoop?" Brian asked, "Like the dog in the *Peanuts* cartoon?"

"What you talking about, bro?" Snoop snapped, "Snoop like Snoop Dogg, bro."

"Snoop Dogg?" Tel laughed. "Tall, thin, black rapper?"

The campers looked at Snoop; short, chubby, white as a pint of milk.

Mark shook his head and said, "I don't see it."

"And, just like the real Snoop Dogg, his name is Calvin," Tammy said gaily.

"What you talkin' 'bout, woman? I told you not to tell people that."

"Well, it's your name, darlin'."

Fists clenched and mouth pinched, he hissed, "Get in the goddamn car!"

Mark subconsciously took a step forward. Olivia gently held his arm.

Christofer came striding over. "Are me and Tammy doing the kissing scene today or is that tomorrow?" he asked Michael.

"Kissing scene?" Snoop snarled. "My girlfriend ain't doing no kissing scene with *anyone*!"

"Hang loose there, darlin'," Tammy soothed. "No need to be pitching yourself a hissy fit now."

"You get in the car *right now*."

He shoved her shoulder.

"Hey!" Mark snapped.

"Not terribly chivalrous," Tel said, instantly regretting how English it sounded.

"What you say? Chivailerous?"

"It's not really the done thing to push a woman around."

"The done thing? What you talkin' about, bro? Have you 'done' ma girlfriend?"

"Done? Done what?"

"You been sleepin' with Tammy, bro?"

"Sleeping? Mate, I *just* got married!"

"I ain't your mate, bro."

"I'm not your bro, Calvin."

"Gentlemen," Tammy said, standing between them, "I am quite capable of taking care of myself, been doin' it since I was fifteen years old."

Snoop/Calvin glared down at her. In a deep, gruff voice he said, "You get yourself in that car, and don't even think about coming back here to be filmed *kissing other men*."

Tammy's sweet smile dropped from her face like a rock. She turned, wriggled her way across the parking lot, grabbed the back of Michael's Director chair and dragged it back. Placing it in front of Snoop/Calvin, she clambered up onto the canvas seat, threw back her arm, and punched him full in the face.

While he clutched his now bloody nose, whining, she said, "Ain't no man tellin' me what I can and can't do. We're done here, Snoop, y'hear? I ain't standin' for it no more. Bye now, you have yourself a nice life."

Tammy stepped down from the chair and brushed her hands together. "It's time for you to move on, ain't nothing for you here no more."

Snoop/Calvin hurried back to his car, still whining. He got in and, clutching his nose, he roared off with one hand on the steering wheel and the other trying to stem the flow of blood.

"Wow," said Mark. "That's some punch you've got there."

"You think with these," she said, indicating her mighty chest, "I ain't learned how to take care of m'self? My daddy taught me good, he's the only man that tells me what to do, and he's dead now."

"You killed him?" Faye gasped.

Tammy laughed. "No, course not. Heart attack took him." Turning to Michael, she said, "I'm just going to drop Maria off and come right back."

"Meet us at the desert location."

"Will do, honey."

"Three down," said Graham. "It's not going to be much of a crowd scene with three people."

Michael glanced at the group in the middle of the parking lot. "She's got the same hair colour as Colette," he said, nodding at Faye, who grinned for a brief moment, until he added, "Dyed, is it?"

"None of your business!"

Turning to Norman he said, "Just don't get her face in focus."

Faye turned open-mouthed to Brian, who shrugged.

"And she's a shoe-in for Maria," Michael said, indicating Olivia. "And ... we have the Panama hat." He looked straight at Brian. "I think," he said, smirking and sneering at the same time, "we have ourselves a crowd scene."

\* \* \*

After the running and the run-in with Tammy and her now ex-boyfriend, Mark had peeled away from the group, yawning, and taken himself off to their RV, where he swiftly fell into a coma. Tel and Sophie sneaked off and did the same.

It took 10 minutes to spark the first three equipment-laden RVs into life. The engines coughed and spluttered, billowing smoke from the exhaust pipes, and something cracked in one of them as they started to move forwards.

"Let's get this show on the road!" Michael shouted through the car window, leading the way.

Next to him in the passenger seat, Olivia giggled nervously. Behind sat Brian and Faye; Faye, wearing the cooling headband and a frozen neck collar, fluttered the fan in front of her face, occasionally spritzing with cooling mist. Christofer, Graham and Shane, and Norman followed in the RVs.

Despite the noise of them all leaving, Mark, Tel and Sophie didn't stir in their exhausted slumber.

They stopped off at a Burger King on the way to the location.

"Is this what was meant by all expenses paid?" Brian asked, when they pulled into the drive-through, "Just fast food? Burgers for breakfast, burgers for lunch. What are we having for tea? Oh, let me guess, burgers!"

"Tight budget," Michael said. "Also, we don't have the facilities to cook at the trailer park. Plus, none of us can cook."

"Remind me to have my cholesterol tested when we get back," Brian said to Faye, who sucked furiously on a large cup of iced water.

They drove along the highway for twenty blistering

minutes, before Michael pulled off the road.  Brian's head banged repeatedly against the car roof as they bounced across the rugged terrain.

They were literally in the middle of nowhere, pulling up at the base of a steep, scrubby incline.

* * *

"JUST PUSH IT UP THE HILL!"

"*Just*, he says," Brian gasped, as he heaved a shoulder against the back of an RV, the Panama hat slipping to the back of his head. "Does he know how much these things weigh?"

"I'm still not sure how we got talked into doing this," Faye said, pushing next to him, her face redder and sweatier than ever.  "Why are we pushing an RV up a hill again?"

"Yes, what is my motivation for doing this?" Christofer grumbled beside them.

"Sure is hot out here," Shane said, "As an Australian I'm used to hot, but not this hot, this hot is *hot*."

"JUST GET INTO CHARACTER," Michael yelled from his Director's chair at the bottom of the hill.  "THE ALIENS ARE COMING, YOU HAVE TO MAKE GOOD YOUR ESCAPE FOR THE FUTURE EXISTENCE OF HUMANITY."

"There's a perfectly good road down there we could use," Olivia puffed.

"There's aliens on that there road," Tammy said, "Remember?"

"PUSH!" Michael screamed.  "REALLY PUT YOUR BACKS INTO IT."

"I'm sure I've seen this scenario somewhere before," said Brian. "Pushing a van up a hill. I bet the van slips the brake and rolls back down."

"*Ice Cold in Alex*," Faye said.

"That's it! I can taste that cold beer now."

"I have seen this film," Christofer said.  "I do not think a man would gently put a hand on the woman's shoulder to comfort her after she had let the ambulance roll down the hill,

I think they would be more likely to slap her."

"I don't think slapping a woman is allowed anymore," Olivia gasped.

"What is this you say?"

"I don't think slapping a woman – "

"I do not understand what you are saying.  Do you have something in your mouth?"

"She *said*," Tammy explained, "Slapping women ain't allowed no more, honey."

"Oh?  Since when?"

"Since forever really, darlin'."

"Maybe a hefty push, then, and a few pertinent expletives."

"OKAY, MEN REST UP, WOMEN HOLD THE VAN IN PLACE.  FAYE, CAN YOU PUT MORE EFFORT INTO IT?"

"Not in this bloody heat," she rasped.

"STAY IN CHARACTER, PEOPLE!"

Faye, Olivia and Tammy braced themselves against the back of the van as the men fell to the ground, wiping sweat from their faces.

"HOLD IT!  THAT'S IT, HOLD IT!"

"I ain't nothing but an iddy-biddy thang," Tammy said, her feet slipping in the sand. "My weight ain't nothin' against this vehicle."

"I can't hold it either," Olivia gasped.

"My lovely new clothes are ruined," Faye sniffed, looking down at herself. "Oh, it moved."

"It's moving!"

"Bri!"

"*It's going!*"

Brian leapt to his feet like a giant cat and pulled both Faye and Olivia away from the back of the RV. Tammy managed to jump out of the way just in time as it started rolling backwards down the hill, slowly at first, then gathering speed.  Brian clutched the women to his enormous chest, panting in shock.

"AND … JUST LET IT GO!" Michael directed.  "WE'RE

STILL ROLLING.  STAY IN CHARACTER.  MARIA, JUST KNEEL ON THE GROUND, AND SHANE, PUT A SOOTHING HAND ON HER SHOULDER."

"WHICH ONE'S MARIA?"

"MARIA'S THE POSH ONE WE CAN'T UNDERSTAND WHO'S STANDING IN FOR MARIA, SO LITERALLY PLAYING HERSELF IN THE MOVIE."

Frowning, Shane glanced from Faye to Olivia, both still pressed into Brian's chest.

"CHRISTOFER, RUFFLE COLETTE'S HAIR."

"NOBODY'S TOUCHING THE HAIR!" Faye snarled.

"Bri," Olivia muffled into his chest, "Can't breathe, Bri."

With his heart nearing normal rhythm again, Brian released his tight hold on the women.  Flooded by a furious burst of adrenaline, he yelled, "YOU PLANNED FOR THIS TO HAPPEN?  WITHOUT TELLING US?  WHAT KIND OF LUNATIC PUTS WOMEN AT THE BACK OF A HEAVY VEHICLE ON A HILL?  DON'T YOU HAVE HEALTH AND SAFETY REGULATIONS IN THIS COUNTRY?  *I NEARLY LOST MY WIFE!*"

"It's okay, Bri. I'm okay. Calm down."

At the bottom of the hill, next to the now stationary RV, Michael consulted with Norman.  He looked up at them and shouted, "YEAH, WE'RE GOING TO NEED YOU TO DO THAT AGAIN, FOLKS."

Brian pulled the Panama hat off his head and tossed it into the air like a frisbee.  He stomped, sand bursting from beneath his feet, down the hill, his huge arms pumping like pistons at his side.  Michael slowly stood up from his chair as the big man approached.

"OKAY!" Michael cried, holding up a hand as he turned towards another RV, "TAKE A BREAK."

"Come here!" Brian bawled after him, "I'd like a bloody word with you!"

"Just got to revise the script," Michael cried, hurling himself into the RV, "*Graham!*"

Graham leapt into the RV and the door was slammed

shut. Brian pounded on it furiously. "GET OUT HERE! I WANT TO SPEAK TO YOU ABOUT NEARLY FLATTENING MY WIFE!"

"Brian!" Faye cried, scrambling and falling down the hill, "Don't kill him, Bri!"

"YOU'VE GOT THREE SECONDS TO OPEN THIS DOOR BEFORE I RIP IT OFF AND COME GET YOU!"

Shane laughed. "I'll huff and I'll puff and I'll blow the bloody doors off."

The RV door opened. Michael held up both hands as he tentatively came down the steps. "Completely unintentional," he grovelled, "It won't happen again."

"I know it won't!"

"I want to go back to camp," Faye said, swooning into the Director chair. "It's too hot out here."

"Take us back!" Brian insisted.

"Okay, okay, we're almost finished."

"We're finished now. Take us back!"

"Little irate," Christofer said.

"Brian's very protective of Faye," Olivia told him.

"I cannot understand a word you are – ?"

"Who's Brian?" Shane asked, "And Faye?"

* * *

On their way back to the trailer park they stopped at Taco Bell.

"Kill me now," Brian breathed. "No, wait, the massive amount of fast food will do the job."

They watched Michael, along with Norman, Graham and Shane, return with their orders in paper bags. Michael got into the car and handed back the food.

"Is this the cheapest item on the menu?" Brian asked, opening his small parcel. "It looks like a large, salad filled crisp, and I use the word 'large' loosely."

"No, it's not the *cheapest*," Michael said.

"One up from the cheapest?"

Michael deliberately took a big bite out of his taco so he

couldn't answer.

"Do they sell drinks here?" Faye asked, parched beyond belief.

"Yes, but they're – "

"Expensive," Brian huffed.

"I could ask them for some water, if you like?"

"Biggest cup they have, with ice," Faye gasped, "*Lots* of ice."

Michael huffed and got out of the car, thinking these Brits were a bit demanding.

"And get another of those crisp things," Brian shouted after him, "One just isn't going to cut through the raging hunger."

\* \* \*

The others were asleep in their RVs when they got back. Faye immediately ran off for a shower, sucking from a water bottle as she went.

Brian knocked on the wall of Tel and Sophie's RV. "You in there?"

"No," Tel grunted, "We're off in the land of nod."

Olivia went into their RV and some giggling ensued. Brian envied them their energy. He was knackered.

He was fast asleep across the lumpy bed by the time Faye came back. She lay down next to him and instantly slipped into unconsciousness.

# CHAPTER FIVE

There was a hammering on the wall of the RV. Brian woke with a start, cried out, turned to look at Faye and pulled her close.

"Nightmare," he croaked.

"You've been shouting 'You almost killed my wife!' over and over."

"Sorry, love."

"No, it's nice that you care," she said, kissing his hairy cheek.

"Of course I care."

She snuggled up to him. "Good to hear after twenty-five years of marriage."

"HEY, WAKE UP!" a voice yelled from outside.

They shimmied off the bed. "Are there rocks under this mattress?" Faye asked.

"WAKEY-WAKEY, BRITS!"

Brian, bleary-eyed and yawning, opened the door.

"RUSHES!" Michael cried excitedly.

"What rushes where?"

"The film rushes, they're ready! And there's food."

Brian was suddenly wide awake and leaping down the steps.

* * *

They dragged the plastic chairs from outside Mark's RV over to 'the viewing area' by the picnic table. The cast sat around the wooden bench, which was heaving with a huge delivery of pizzas and sides and drinks, including beer, and even paper plates and napkins. Brian headed straight for it, pulled out a steaming slice and pushed it into his mouth. The baby being bounced on Maria's knee looked up at him with wide eyes.

"Oh!" Sophie cried, picking at the basil leaves on top of one pizza, "Green stuff, thank God! Oh!" she cried again, spotting the plastic boxes of salad, "I'm in heaven!"

"I know how much you women worry about your weight," Michael said, just as Faye threw a couple of slices, some dough balls and a few chunky chips onto a plate. She hesitated for a moment, then picked up a salad box. "No expense spared our prospective investors."

Brian threw a few slices onto a plate, hoping to get as much in as possible before money was mentioned, picked up a couple of cans and ambled over to a plastic chair.

"It looks lovely," Olivia said.

"How did the audition go?" Sophie asked Colette, who was nibbling vaguely on a lettuce leaf.

"Oh, you know, they said they'd let me know."

"What was the part?"

"Extra," she nodded heartily, "But I'm counting on my star potential shining through. It could be my big break."

"I'm sure it is. Fingers crossed."

Maria bounced the grisly baby on her knee, talking to it in Spanish. When she offered it a dough ball it threw up. Tammy moved down the bench away from it, taking her nail polish with her. Mark dry-wretched and firmly turned his head away, concentrating on the TV screen in front of them all.

On the back bench Shane and Christofer were slapping each other's hands as they reached for the last slice of margarita, while Meryl furiously chewed on her nails.

Michael sat fidgeting in his Director chair, wearing his most extreme Tarantino look.

"Upset tummy?" Brian asked him. "It'll be those crisps from Taco Bell."

"Just nervous, man, just nervous."

Graham stood to the side, furiously shuffling through

papers. Norman had put a large TV screen outside his trailer, beneath the window, shielded from the sun by a strategically placed cardboard box.

"Ready?" he cried from inside.

"We're ready."

They settled down, munching and slurping. A picture appeared on the screen, followed by several animations of varying standards depicting company names. The background music sounded suspiciously similar to Jeff Wayne's *War of the Worlds*. The company names continued to come and go.

"Production logos," Michael explained, "All our financiers, software companies we've used, several restaurants and cafes who've invested for product placement, and mom and dad's craft shop in California. Your names could be up there too if you decide to contribute."

Brian pushed more pizza into his mouth. On the TV screen, to the sound of familiar music and a backdrop of space, a voice that sounded like Richard Burton started speaking, outlining the arrival of the aliens and the decimation of humankind. The film suddenly stopped.

"Sorry," Norman shouted from inside his trailer, "Technical issue, won't take a sec."

"Hasn't this been done before?" Tel said to no one in particular. "The film, I mean."

"No, no," Michael insisted, "It's a brand-new concept."

"Is it?" Brian said. "How old are you?"

Offence took some of the intensity from his Tarantino face. "Twenty-eight."

"And this is new to you?"

"Is it not new to you?"

"I think there's been at least three other versions," Tel said.

"Of?" Michael snapped.

"This film."

"Perhaps you ought to watch it first!" A pout overtook his

sneer. "There's frequent references to popular culture, some dark humour, non-linear storylines, intense violence, lengthy dialogue, and a *lot* of profanity, just like Tarantino's work."

The actors looked at each other across the wooden table.

'Intense violence?' Colette mouthed at Tammy, who shrugged.

"What's your budget?" Sophie asked.

"*Reservoir Dogs*, before Keitel invested his own money, initially had a budget of thirty thousand dollars."

"And yours is?"

"You don't have to tell them," Meryl snapped. "They don't need to know."

"Slightly less than that."

"How much less?"

Michael shifted uncomfortably in his chair. "A third."

"You're making this film for ten thousand dollars?"

"That's why we're working on it for free," Norman shouted from inside, "We believe in this project, so we're taking a cut of the profits instead."

"But *we're* getting paid, aren't we?" Colette quickly asked. Turning to the others, she added, "Have you been paid yet?"

The cast shook their heads.

"But we *will* be paid, won't we?"

"Of course," Michael said, "Absolutely."

"When?"

"We will discuss the matter after we have watched the rushes," Meryl said.

"You're gonna love it," said Michael. "Come on, Norman, let's show them what we've done."

There was a brief sparking sound from inside the trailer, and then, on the TV screen, they saw the parking lot from above. CGI spacecraft broke through the CGI clouds. People ran out of the RVs and stared up at the sky, some pointing and screaming, others running off into the surrounding forest. The audience turned to look over at the parking lot, at the chain-link fence and the Nevada desert beyond.

"Good special effects," Tel whistled.

"Thanks," Norman yelled.

The spacecraft started firing shards of light at the people on the ground. Shane, playing Brian, jumped out of an RV shooting a rifle. Explosions detonated all around him. A military plane flew overhead.

Mark leaned towards Brian and, with a smile, whispered, "I don't remember any of this happening at the campsite?"

"Don't you? Happened every time you popped back to your garden centre, aliens everywhere."

"And you never thought to mention it when I got back?"

"Didn't want you to feel as if you'd missed out on anything, we thought you'd notice the explosion holes and the dead bodies lying about."

"Nah, didn't," Mark chuckled.

"Pity. It was quite exciting."

"Excellent, isn't it," Michael said, rubbing his hands together. "There'll be a short piece before this which depicts the aliens invading and – "

"Shhhhh!" Christofer hissed, "My bit's coming up."

Christofer, playing Mark, attacked the gun firing Shane with a knife. More explosions. A skirmish. Christofer running away holding an arm bloodied by tomato sauce. A victorious Shane going back into the RV, where Colette, playing Faye, was waiting for him on the bed. The audience cringed their way through the love scene. At one point Shane was whispering to her but his lips didn't match the dialogue.

"We made some script changes here," Michael said, glancing at Graham, who was grimacing, "You can hardly notice, can you."

On screen, Shane was saying, "I have to leave you. I have to go fight the aliens. Stay here where you're safe."

"No, Brian, I want to come with you. I can help."

"Let me do this, Faye."

"I can't let you go."

"You have to. It's our only chance of survival."

"But Brian – "

On screen, Shane bent to kiss Colette into silence. In real life, Brian nodded as Faye reached out and held his hand.

At the table, Colette covered her face with both hands. "Too much," she whined, "I'm showing too much *boob*. I hope this doesn't come back to haunt me when I'm famous."

"Stay here, my love," said Shane/Brian. "I'll be back as soon as I can."

Shane headed for the door.

"Be safe," Colette called after him. "Come back to me, my love."

"My love?" Brian laughed. "She normally calls me poo-breath. Don't know why, she can't smell!"

"*Shush!*" hissed Christofer.

Cut to an outside scene; Shane racing across the cracked parking lot that was dotted with burning bushes and scorched RVs. The camera rose up, showing Shane running towards the CGI forest. Behind him, shimmering shapes followed. Shane spun round with his gun and shot at them. The aliens crackled and disappeared. The camera lowered and closed in on his face.

"Good angle," Shane grinned, rubbing his square jaw. "Really brought out the colour of my – "

"*Will you be quiet!*" Christofer hissed.

There was some running through a field of wheat, some shooting at the spaceships in the sky, some shooting at the shimmering aliens behind him. Explosions, more running, meeting up with the group that had run off the parking lot earlier, a lot of talk about 'plans of action' interspersed with expletives, which was a bit boring.

"Big fan of the *Alien* franchise?" Mark asked Michael.

"That's set in space, isn't it?" said Sophie.

"We couldn't afford space," Michael said. "The software required to create space was too expensive, so we kept it terrestrial."

On the screen, Tammy, playing Sophie, was wielding a

gun that was almost as big as she was. Maria wrapped bullet belts around her and shoved large knives into sheaths around her waist. Shane argued with Christofer about who should save the world and win the love of Colette, ending in a fight scene with a crescendo of music and everyone shouting.

Brian got up for another beer, bringing cans back for Mark and Tel. The hissing of tabs made Christofer tut theatrically.

Running. Shooting. Shards of light hitting unknown characters, who grossly overacted their sizzling deaths. Close-ups on Shane, staring masterfully into the distance. Close-up of Tammy, who tried to look tough but just looked pretty. Close-up of Christofer, looking shady and bitter, pretty much as in real life.

And then it ended.

"Is that it?" Tel asked.

"We've only been shooting for two weeks. What do you think?" Michael's face was a plethora of expectation, terror and desperation.

"It's ... good."

"You like it?"

Everybody nodded, some more enthusiastically than others.

Michael stood up and turned to them all with a huge smile. "So, what do you think?"

There was some murmuring from the table, some nodding of heads, a double thumbs up from Shane. Michael seemed satisfied and intensified his Tarantino scowl. "You can see where we're going with this now, can't you. Epic. Apocalyptic. Boundary breaking."

"Unconscious plagiarism," Sophie whispered to Tel.

Brian said, "I'm just not sure where we come into this."

"How do you mean?"

"Us, British campers on a British campsite, as written by Iain Flemmingway."

"Like I said, we had to change it slightly for an American

market."

"Slightly?" Mark laughed. "It's a completely different story."

"Did Iain Flemmingway not tell you about the script?"

"We've not seen any scripts," Sophie said.

"Oh." Michael looked flummoxed for a moment. "Well, a major film studio picked up the option for the British story, then dropped it. Another big studio looked at it and eventually decided it wasn't for them. It was touted to smaller studios, and then we heard about it and managed to secure a deal."

"Does it bear any resemblance to Flemmingway's original script at all?" Sophie asked.

"It has the same characters."

"And the storyline, campers on a Cotswolds campsite?"

"Adapted for an American market."

Mark looked at Brian, who shrugged and emptied his can.

Meryl suddenly stood up and walked to the front.

"Here it comes," Brian said in a low voice, "Brace yourselves for the big pitch, and keep a tight hold of your wallets."

The cast at the table stood up and wandered off, talking animatedly about their scenes. The campers glanced nervously at each other.

"It's like that feeling you get when they try to sell you timeshare in Tenerife," Faye whispered.

"Worse," Sophie said, "There's no place to run."

On the TV screen came the first slide of a PowerPoint presentation:

*WHY YOU SHOULD INVEST IN MGN MOVIE*
*PRODUCTION COMPANY*
*PROJECT 1: WAR ON THE PLANET*

"I'd like to start ..." Meryl began, and they all sighed.

\* \* \*

"So, in conclusion," Meryl said, some twenty-five minutes

later, "I'm not going to pressure you in any way, all I'm going to do is put this box – " She held up an intricately carved wooden box and carried it like an unexploded bomb to the picnic table. " – over here, and I'd like you to consider investing in our brand-new start-up." She opened up the lid. There was a small sheet of paper tucked inside. "All our bank details are there when you're ready. Get in early, while you can." She tried to smile and failed, resorting to a burst of harsh laughter instead.

"We're going to take the world by storm!" Michael cried.

"You don't have to do it now," Meryl continued. "Think about it, consider what you're willing to invest in the project, how much you want to see yourselves and your story up on the big screen."

"Our story?" Tel sniggered.

Mark pressed his lips together so as not to question 'their story' in the extract of film they'd just watched. The others glanced furtively at each other.

"Take your time." Meryl left the open box on the table and stepped back with her hands clasped in front of her grey suit. "It doesn't have to be bank transfers or cash, it can be pledges written on a piece of paper."

"Are you accepting Amber Heard pledges?" Brian couldn't resist asking, and Meryl tilted her head slightly. "Amber Heard, when in court against Johnny Depp – "

"Gorgeous man!" Faye sighed.

" – said that she used the words 'pledge' and 'donate' synonymous with one another."

"You'll pledge to donate to MGN Movie Production Company." Meryl shook her head, a little confused. Brian wondered if his sense of humour was suffering from jet lag, then decided it was probably an American thing.

The others looked awkwardly at Meryl for a moment, who was expectantly standing by the box on the table.

"We'll … think about it," Tel said, to break the heavy silence.

"Don't think too long," Meryl said with a strained

smile, "You don't want to miss out on this once-in-a-lifetime opportunity."

Brian stood up. "Right, if we're done here, I thought we might go and explore Las Vegas."

"Yay!" Faye cried, and shot off towards the RV, closely followed by Sophie and Olivia.

"Anyone want to tag along?" Mark asked the others.

"We've seen it already."

"Fair enough. Michael?"

"No, Meryl's keeping a close eye on my gambling addiction, but I can drop you off."

"Very kind of you," said Brian, popping the last of the dough balls into his mouth and picking up a couple of extra cans before heading off towards the RV.

"Vegas, baby!" Mark cried.

* * *

The women took an age to have yet another shower and get ready. The men stood around drinking their own supply of beer.

Meryl had brought the open 'pledge' box over to the plastic table outside Mark's RV and hovered in the periphery, watching them like hawks . Michael, Graham and Norman were buried away in the trailer next to the now empty picnic table. The cast had gone home.

"What do you think?" Tel asked.

"About the film or the free weekend of fast food?"

"Both."

"Film's crap," Brian said.

"Say it like it is, Bri."

"I always do."

"It's not the worst bit of film I've ever seen," Tel said.

"Isn't it?"

"Not *the* worst."

"I'd say it's on a par with *Alien vs Predator*," Mark said, "The *Requiem* one."

"*Snakes on a Plane*," Brian laughed.

"We've only seen fifteen minutes of it," Tel said. "It could actually be the next *Reservoir Dogs*."

Brian nodded. Mark raised his eyebrows.

"So," Brian said to Tel, "Are you thinking of investing in it then?"

"I'm giving it serious consideration."

There came the distinct sound of someone hissing 'yes!' from the end of their RV.

"You okay there, Meryl?" Mark asked.

A pause, and then a tiny voice said, "Yes, I'm fine, thank you."

Michael came over jangling car keys. Brian boomed, "Come on, women, or we'll leave you behind!"

The women hurried out, converging in a giggling crowd in front of them. They wore pretty dresses with pastel cardigans hung over their handbags. Faye also sported a frozen neck tube, a can of cooling mist in one hand and the fan in the other. They all had their hair up, their faces painted, and were positively fizzing with excitement.

The men wolf-whistled.

"Viva Las Vegas!" Mark cried.

Michael unlocked his car and pulled back the side door. The women stopped smiling.

"Have you got anything to cover the seats?" Sophie asked, looking down at her white, flowered dress.

Michael peered inside. "They look dirty but they're not."

"They do, and they are."

"Towels," said Faye, and they all ran back to their RVs. By the time they returned, Tel and Mark had crawled into the back seats, Brian in the front. They took an age to arrange the towels over the seats before gingerly getting in, resuming their fizzing excitement in high-pitched voices.

"Can we go now?" Brian drawled.

"Yes, yes, of course."

"Oh, isn't this exciting!"

"I might have a bet," Olivia giggled. "I might go mad and have two."

It took thirty minutes to reach the bright, shiny bit of Las Vegas. Michael used the time to rave about the movie, how much they'd appreciate any financial support, and how hard they'd all worked because they *believed* in it.

They made the right noises at the right time, and stared in awe as the lights got brighter and bigger.

"I'll drop you off outside the Bellagio," Michael said.

"Where else would you recommend?" asked Mark.

"Anywhere. Everywhere. As much as you can cover before exhaustion sets in. The Venetian's pretty neat, it's got this sky effect on the ceiling."

"I've read about that," said Olivia.

"Definitely want to see that," said Sophie.

"Oooh," Faye cried, as Michael turned right off the Strip and drove under the enormous covered entrance to the Bellagio. "I feel so important, like a film star."

"Wow!"

They got out and Michael drove off. The women huddled in a tight ball of energy.

"I'm channelling Audrey Hepburn," Olivia said, draping her cardigan over her shoulders and lifting her chin.

"We're terribly important people," Sophie laughed, doing the same.

Faye, fumbling with her cardigan, said, "No photographs please, innit."

As one, they put their bags into the crook of their arms, shoulder straps dangling, and daintily held out their hands. They wriggled past the giant Chinese lions and through the enormous revolving doors, the men chuckling and following at a discrete distance.

Their eyes lit up at the sight of the impressive, multi-coloured ceiling, the vast acres of marble and rising columns; the lights, the sumptuousness of everything, and the people milling around, so many people. Multiple voices echoed all around them.

When Olivia managed to catch her breath she said, quite loudly for Olivia, "Yes, I think this place might be sufficient for our needs, darlings."

"Oh yah," Sophie cried, trying not to giggle, "More than adequate."

Faye opened her mouth to say something, when two elderly women rushed over to them. "Are you Briddish?" one squawked.

Olivia, keeping firmly in character, raised her eyebrows and said, in an accent the Queen would have been proud of, "Why, yes, we are indeed British."

"We thought so," the other woman squealed. "We love the Briddish accent."

"I think I know her," cried the first, thrusting a finger towards Faye. "Are you … Helen Mirren?"

As Faye sucked in horrified air she was instantly overcome by two clashing emotions; on the one hand she was flattered that anyone would liken her to Helen Mirren, and, on the other, Helen Mirren was at least twenty years older than her, if not more.

"No, no," hollered the second woman, "You're thinking of Dame Maggie Smith."

A noise accompanied Faye's inhalation of horror. Sophie wrapped a comforting arm around her shoulder and pulled her close. "I'm sorry, ladies," she said haughtily, "If you'll excuse us, we have terribly urgent business to attend to."

They sashayed off, chins high, their arms extended bag holders.

Brian, standing behind watching, like the others, laughed and said, "I think I know why we all get along so well."

"Why's that, Bri?"

"Our ladies are all as mad as a box of frogs."

"I think they'd say the same about us," Mark grinned.

"Mine was pretty normal before she met yours," said Tel.

"Everyone's normal until they meet Faye."

"Are you sure it's Faye and not you, Bri?"

"Cheek. Ey up, they're off."

The men diligently followed as the women sauntered passed statues and crowds of people, their dainty hands posturing through the air. At one point they passed a man who was shouting over to his mate, "Hey, Pete, I've just been propositioned by a prostitute!"

"Bit early for a prostitute," Mark laughed, glancing at his watch.

"It's never too early for a prostitute," Tel said, and they both looked at him. "You see it all the time on certain London streets, day or night."

"Night?" Brian grinned.

"So I'm told."

"Told by who?"

"It's common knowledge."

"Is it?"

"Yes, it is."

"Does Sophie know you know about this common knowledge?"

"I don't know, it's not something we've ever discussed."

"Isn't it?" Brian laughed at the look on Tel's face. "Shall I throw a rope down the hole you've just dug for yourself?"

Tel laughed. "You know I'd never *entertain* a lady of the night, right?"

Mark nodded towards Sophie who, from the back, looked just like an exotic princess sashaying down the corridor with swathes of people parting before her gorgeousness. "Oh, we know," he said, "We know."

They watched at their excited partners wriggling in rhythm down a sumptuous marble corridor; Olivia in a wraparound dress, Faye in a flared flowered dress, and Sophie in a figure-hugging linen dress with a plunging neckline and a hem that finished just above the knee.

Mark said, "You don't think they'd be mistaken for – ?"

"SOPHIE!" Tel suddenly yelled, "LET'S GO SEE THE

FOUNTAINS!"

* * *

They merged into the crowds standing around the Bellagio fountains. The girls marvelled at the display, pouting and taking dozens of selfies. The men were bored within minutes.

"Women are weird," Mark laughed.

"New discovery, is this?" Brian asked.

"No, but it's just … splashing water and a few lights."

"To us. To them it's magic and glitter and sparkles."

Sophie turned her head and said, "There's nothing wrong with magic and glitter and sparkles, Bri."

"This is how you are at Big Boys Toys in Dudley," said Faye.

"No it isn't!"

"Tis. Eyes wide, mouth open, dribbling into your beard."

An endless wave of cars drove up and down the tree-lined boulevard behind them. The Eiffel Tower reared into the sky, one foot on the pavement. People pushed passed, talking and laughing, eating and drinking. It was lively and loud and bright. Music came from everywhere. The buildings were enormous, like giants peering down at them.

They ambled up the road, taking photos of each other and themselves. Sophie led the way into Starbucks. "In here," she said, reading from a piece of paper she'd pulled from her handbag, "It'll take us across the bridge to the other side."

"The other side," Faye breathed spookily.

They followed the crowd up the escalators and over the bridge. Everything seemed so big and opulent. They walked past a Gucci shop, the women's eyes rivetted on the window display, minimalist amongst all the giant splendour.

Outside, Olivia suddenly cried, "Hell's Kitchen!" and pressed her face against the windows, hoping for sight of the great man himself. Mark had to peel her away.

"Your favourite chef?" Sophie asked, quite surprised that

gentle, quiet Olivia would like someone so loud and sweary.

"No, I prefer Jeffrey Epstein."

They all stopped and stared at her.

"Stein," Mark said, "She means Rick Stein."

"Yes, that's the one."

"Phew," Tel sighed, "You had me worried for a second there, Livs."

Through a marble-balustraded garden with lines of fountains and a decorated shrine, towards Caesar's Palace.

"We were going to stay with you!" Sophie howled, holding her arms out towards it.

"The strip *is* pretty impressive," Tel said.

"Better than Broad Street," said Faye.

"Better than the West End," said Sophie.

A group of young men ran across the roads at the foot of a giant Roman statue, making traffic screech to a halt. Several people yelled, "Clowns!" or "Jaywalkers!" Brian tutted and said, "Tourists!" as they waited with the crowds to cross.

A fountain at the foot of a building looked like the hugger creature from *Alien*. Archways. White columns, black columns. Giant screen billboards, so big you could walk under them.

"Fancy one of those for your next camping trip?" Brian laughed, nudging Tel. "Will it be big enough for you?"

Harrah's on the right, the Mirage on the left, places they'd only ever seen in American films. The women kept huddling together to take photos.

"I can't believe we're here," Faye breathed, her eyeballs trying to take it all in at once.

"Me neither," gasped Olivia.

Still following the crowds, they turned to cross the road. They waited. The lights changed, the traffic stopped, and a flashing countdown started from twenty.

Tel suddenly panicked. "Come on!" he cried, urging them on with a windmilling arm, "Hurry up or we'll never make it to the other side in time!"

"There's safety in numbers, lad."

"Calm down," Sophie told him.

"I will, when we get to the other side. *Hurry!*"

Once safely on the path again, Tel exhaled with relief. They ambled passed so many shops, so many flashing lights, so many bright billboards, so many accents and faces from across the world. The roar of traffic and the pounding of music. Fast food restaurants and foot-long sausages. It was almost overwhelming.

"It's like a big playground for grown-ups," Tel said.

"Disneyland on steroids."

A crowd of women all dressed in white with feathered wings on their backs came towards them, screeching and giggling and waving their wands around.

"A fluster of fairies," Mark laughed, as they were engulfed in the feathers.

One of them wrapped herself around Tel and ran her wand down his face. "You're very handsome," she said. "Do you fancy joining us for my last fling? I'm getting married next week."

"Do you not see the woman standing right next to him?" Sophie drawled, as Tel grinned and the other fairies reached out to him with their sparkly, star-shaped wands. "The one with a gold band on her finger?" She held up the recently acquired ring in front of the fairy's face. The fairy laughed, undraped herself, and carried on down the strip with her fellow fairies.

"You didn't tell them to stop," Sophie said to Tel.

"I was enjoying it."

"Could you enjoy it less the next time a bunch of drunken fairies fawn over you?"

"No, not really."

Canopied escalators rose up to The Grand Canal Shoppes and The Venetian. At the top, Madam Tussaud's. They stood on a moving walkway, up and down, like an undulating magic carpet carrying them inside. A balustraded walkway. Outside, gondoliers punted across a vast body of water using red and white striped poles.

And then they were in the casino. Noisy, bright, crowded, electrifying.

Brian spotted a bar and made a beeline for it. The men followed. The women wandered around the tables, laughing and looking at everything and everyone.

Tel quickly jumped in front of Brian at the bar and ordered a round of beers, with mojitos for the girls.

"This place is amazing!" Olivia cried, joining them.

"My mind is blown!" Sophie shook her head.

Faye quickly tipped her drink back. "Thirsty work, all this walking," she said, indicating at the bartender, a pretty young woman, for another.

"Steady on, Faye," said Brian. "Pace yourself."

"What happens in Vegas," she began.

"Yeah, but you tend to take the hangovers home with you."

"Good point," she said, flopping onto a bar stool. "Just one more."

"Australian?" asked a man next to them.

"British."

"Oh." He didn't seem to have anything more to say and went back to nursing his beer.

Further down the bar a middle-aged couple stared at them. "British, did you say?" asked the woman.

Mark nodded.

"I have a cousin living in the UK."

"Oh, do you?"

"Yes. Maybe you know her?"

"Possibly," Brian boomed, "There's only several million people in the UK, we're bound to have crossed paths at some point."

"She lives near that chapel that was featured in a Dan Brown book." They all looked blank. "Just outside a big city. Oh, what's it called?"

"London?" Tel suggested.

The woman shook her head, deep in concentration.

"Manchester?" said Sophie, "Leeds? Newcastle?"

"Birmingham, in the Midlands?" Faye said.

"Mid!" cried the woman, "That sounds familiar.  Mid ... Mid ..."

"The Midlands?" Faye said again.

"No, Mid-something."  Her eyes suddenly widened. "Midlothian!"

"Scotland."

"Yes, where the Loch Ness monster lives!"

"We're all from England," Olivia said.

"England, Scotland, it's all the same, isn't it?"

"No, Scotland's a completely different country."

"Country," the woman laughed, "A different *country* on such a tiny island."

"Scotland's hundreds of miles away from where we live."

"People travel further than that for a coffee round here," she scoffed.  "Jean Granner, do you know her?"

"Oh!" Brian boomed excitedly, "No."

"Long blonde hair, five feet four inches, talks with a New York accent?"

Brian contemplated for a moment, running his fingers through this beard, then said, "No."

"Oh, never mind."

The group eyeballed each other over their drinks, stifling giggles.  And then Sophie suddenly cried, "Well, would you look at that!"

They all turned and saw, strutting and nodding their way through the casino, four Elvis Presley impersonators, complete with rhinestone suits and shiny black wigs.

"What's the collective noun for a group of Elvises?" Tel asked.

"Elvi?" Sophie suggested.

"An encore of Elvi?" said Brian.

"An ensemble?"

Mark laughed and said, "A *king*-dom of Elvi," which earned him a hearty pat on the back from Brian.

The kingdom of Elvi strutted by. Faye waved. One of them waved back and she cried, "Ooh, I've pulled."

"You're very hyper, lass."

"I'm in Vegas, Bri."

"It's almost a prerequisite to be hyper in Vegas," Olivia said.

"On account of being slapped round the senses by *everything*," said Mark.

Tel slurped down his beer, eyeing the gambling tables. "I promised myself I'd try out some roulette while I'm here," he said, and promptly marched off.

"I promised to watch him win big," Sophie said, chasing after him, "Or stop him from losing our life savings."

"I promised myself I'd kiss a real cowboy," Faye said dreamily.

"Drunk, woman."

"No, he doesn't have to be drunk."

"I meant you," he howled. "Put the drink down and step away from the bar."

Faye raised her now empty glass to attract the bartender's attention.

"I hope I won't be carrying you home over my shoulder, lass."

Faye ignored him. She was excited by all the people, the lights and the noise. She was adrenalined up to the eyeballs.

The bartender came over.

"What do you fancy, Livs?" Faye asked. "Anything you like, Brian's paying."

"Am I?"

"Is that the howl of a Yorkshireman opening his wallet I hear?" Mark laughed.

Olivia ran her finger down the list of cocktails on the menu card. "I think I'll have … a Long Island Iced Tea."

"Are you sure about that?" asked the bartender with a

warning look.

"No, not now."

"You don't strike me as a woman who drinks a lot."

"And you call me a lush," she giggled at Mark.

"You own a pub!"

"Can I recommend something that *isn't* likely to have you splayed out on the floor in an alcoholic coma?" asked the bartender.

"Oh, yes please."

"Vodka tonic?"

"Lovely."

"And another beer," said Brian. "Mark?"

"Same."

"Faye? Faye? FAYE?"

Even though half the people in the bar had turned at the sound of his baritone voice, Faye remained sitting with her back to him, staring at the entrance.

"Faye?"

"Cowboy," she breathed, slowly lifting her hand and pointing.

They turned. A man stood just inside the doorway. He was middle-aged and very distinguished looking, tall and broad shouldered. He had a handsome face, the kind of face you'd run to if you were in trouble or if you just wanted to talk, he seemed like a man who would listen. He was wearing a chambray shirt, jeans with a silver bull's head belt buckle, and a white Stetson.

"A Stetson doesn't make him a cowboy," Brian breathed in her ear.

"Oh, he's a cowboy," she said, "I can tell, I can *feel* it."

"You want me to ask him if you can kiss him?" Brian was joking and was surprised when Faye gasped, "Yes."

Feeling that he couldn't back down now, Brian moved away from the bar towards the man in the hat.

"Excuse me," he said, and the man, equal in height and width, turned to look at him. "My wife and I are from England

and she promised herself she'd kiss a cowboy in Las Vegas. Are you, by any chance, a cowboy?"

"Used t'be," said the man.

"Oh, okay. Sorry to have bothered you."

"No bother at all."

Faye was suddenly at Brian's side before he could turn and walk away, grinning like a Cheshire cat at the man in the hat. "Hello," she beamed.

"He's not a cowboy," Brian said.

"Used t'be," said the man, in a deep, husky voice. "Then I was in the military for a time, served in the police force for a while, and now I drive an 18-wheeler truck. Name's Dave."

Dave tipped the brim of his hat and, despite the noise surrounding them – the talking, the laughter, the pinging of slot machines and, strangely, the sound of someone screaming blue murder in the background – Brian actually heard his wife gulp.

"Would you mind *terribly*," she gasped, channelling Joanna Lumley for all she was worth, "if I kissed you on the cheek?"

Faye stared up at him. Brian stared first at his wife, astonished, then at the man in the hat, who looked totally unphased, as if he had women running up to him asking for kisses all the time – and maybe he did.

"Well, ma'am," he said, and Faye made a noise Brian had never heard her make before, "I'd have to ask ma wife first."

"Of course, of course."

The man tipped his hat again, which made Faye make that strange noise once more, and strode off into the throng of gamblers.

"Wife," said Brian.

"Don't ruin it, Bri," she squeaked, "Let me dream, just a little."

They wandered back to the bar. Mark and Olivia were canoodling and giggling.

"Do you sell balls and chains here?" Brian asked the

bartender. "I might need one to keep the lusting wife in check."

"Brian!"

The bartender laughed.

"You do look a bit flushed," Olivia giggled.

Faye brushed the hair from her face. "Yes, well I've just met a cowboy, a real one."

"Really?"

"Yeah." Faye grinned and fanned her face with her hand.

"Did you kiss him?" Mark asked.

"No. Sadly. He said he had to ask his wife first."

"You're aware I'm standing right here, aren't you?" Brian boomed, pointing up and down at himself with both hands. "I haven't just disappeared and you're now single to chase after cattle ranchers."

"Cattle ranchers," Faye sighed.

"They just ride horses!"

"In chaps and hats," Faye laughed, amused at the expression on Brian's face.

"They just chase after cows, Faye, *cows*."

"I know, I've seen them on those cowboy films you watch."

"That you've never shown any interest in, until now, apparently."

"I like *Tombstone*."

"Because they wear long coats, you said."

"And the hats."

"Are you deliberately winding me up?"

"Calm down, Bri, you don't want to upset your rising cholesterol levels. Anyway, cut me some slack, it's not every day a girl meets a cowboy, is it."

"Thankfully."

"Howdy, ma'am."

Faye nearly fell off her chair when she turned and saw Dave standing right next to her. A tall, very striking woman stood at his side, her long brown hair hanging over one shoulder and onto a stunning blue cocktail dress. Her eyes were ice blue and mesmerising, her smile wide and bright.

"I'm Angela," she said, nodding at each of them, "But you can call me Angel."

"Call her Ange and she'll shoot you dead where you stand," Dave laughed, which made Mark sit bolt upright on his stool with his wide eyes zigzagging over Angel's body.

"You'd better not be checking out ma wife there, buddy," said Dave.

"I'm checking to see if she's carrying a gun."

"In this dress?" she laughed. "No, I ain't carrying no gun."

Faye was still staring up at Dave with her mouth open. Brian fervently hoped she wouldn't start dribbling.

"My wife and I were just heading on over to Gilley's for some food," Dave said, "We were wonderin' if you'd care to join us?"

"I could eat," Brian said, nodding.

Wide-eyed, Faye slipped off the chair and threw her handbag over her shoulder. Brian thought she would have gone with them without so much as a backwards glance, which worried him a bit. Well, a lot.

"Where are we going?" Mark asked, untangling himself from Olivia.

"Gilley's," Faye breathed, still staring up at the man.

"You British too?"

"We are," Olivia giggled.

"Is it far, this Gilley's?"

"Just across the street."

"Well, that's very kind of you."

They followed the used-t'be-cowboy and his wife to the exit doors, where Brian held up a hand and said, "Hang on a minute, I promised myself I'd have a bet in Vegas."

"Careful, Bri."

Brian took out his wallet, took out a single dollar bill, and tried to put it in a slot machine. He eventually had to be helped by the man in the hat.

The reels spun. Brian looked bored, Faye looked

expectant.

The wheels stopped. He didn't win.

"Right, I can cross that off my bucket list now. TEL!" he yelled over to the roulette table, and a shocked hush fell over the whole room, "TEL, WE'RE GOING TO A PLACE CALLED GILLEY'S ACROSS ROAD, COME FIND US WHEN YOU'VE FINISHED."

Tel raised a hand but not his glazed eyes, which were rivetted to the rolling ball in the middle of the table.

"WE'LL SEE YOU THERE IN A BIT," Sophie shouted, and everyone turned as one to look at her.

"British?" one of them asked.

* * *

They walked into 'Gilley's Saloon, Dance Hall and Bar' and were instantly transported into a cowboy country barn. It was full and busy and bursting with excitement, with people drinking and eating and line-dancing to a live country band.

"Oh wow," Olivia breathed.

"Look at all the cowboy hats!" Faye cried. "I'm in heaven!"

Brian and Mark nodded their approval.

What also met with their approval were the skinny Gilley Girls wearing bikinis and leather who served their huge wooden table. Brian and Mark's eyes were out on stalks the entire time.

"Stick your tongue back in," Olivia drawled at Mark.

"Watch your eyeballs don't fall out, Bri."

"Like yours did earlier?" he grinned, "And still are."

"They don't even look old enough to be out this late," Faye snorted.

"Late?" Brian managed to tear his eyes away long enough to glance at his watch. "It's not late."

"On a school night too!"

They talked and laughed, ate and drank.

"I'll get the next round," Brian insisted, taking out his wallet.

Dave held up a huge hand and said, "You're guests in our fine country and we're honoured to have you here."

Faye swooned.

They line-danced with the crowd and sang along to country music. Mark even climbed up onto a mechanical bull, and promptly fell off again.

"Rubbish!" someone cried from the audience, "Don't you have bulls where you come from?"

"We don't tend to ride our bulls in the Cotswolds," Mark said, cricking his neck.

Quite a few people started mimicking the way he said 'Cots-wolds'. Olivia hugged him and said, "My Cotswolds cowboy."

"You having a go, Bri?"

Brian howled with laughter. "I don't think my travel insurance would cover it, and," he added, firmly turning away, "I'd rather stick rusty nails in my eyes."

"But we're in *Vegas*, baby! What happens in Vegas stays in Vegas."

"Returning home sporting plaster casts and a neck brace would indicate otherwise."

Faye randomly screamed like a teenage fan at a pop concert, "I'm with a *cowboy* in a *cowboy bar!*"

"And your husband," Brian reminded her.

"Yes, yes, the husband." She stopped lifting a cocktail to her mouth and said, "If you could tear your eyes away from the Gilley Girls, that would be great, Bri."

He did, for a brief moment.

At some point, Tel and Sophie burst through the door and into the throng; Sophie looked furious, Tel looked uncomfortable. Brian waved them over.

"Had to physically drag him away from the roulette table," Sophie shouted above the noise. "He was completely mesmerised by the ball."

"I was close to winning."

"How do you know?"

"Because I lost so much."

"That's not how it works, Tel." She snapped her head away and locked eyes with a tall, wide man wearing a Stetson who had risen up from the table.

"Howdy, ma'am," he said, holding out a giant hand as he tipped his hat.

"Oh, hello."

"Could I buy you a drink?"

"Well, I'm married, actually."

"No," Faye hissed at her, "This is Dave, he's a *real-life cowboy!*"

"And I'm Angela, but you can call me Angel," she said, leaning forward to shake her hand. "Don't mind me, I'm only here to make sure he doesn't get kidnapped by British women." She laughed. They all laughed. Except Faye, who was drunkenly wondering if she could get a suitcased cowboy through UK customs. Brian, who knew exactly what she was thinking, they'd been married a long time, said, "We don't have the space for him at home, lass."

* * *

At gone ten, overdosed on brisket and nachos, beer and cocktails, line-dancing and bull riding, they began to slump.

"I can barely keep my eyes open," Olivia yawned.

"Unlike my wife," said Brian, "Who can barely keep her wide eyes off our friend, Dave."

They all looked towards the dance floor, where Dave, Angel and Faye were kicking up their heels and screaming, "Yee-ha!" a lot. Faye looked so happy, her eyes bright, her smile wide, her hair in glorious disarray as she stepped along with everyone else.

Brian watched her and felt something inside him he'd rarely experienced before; a smidgen of jealousy. Dave was tall, like him, and wide, like him, and he had a strong accent, also like him. Faye definitely had a 'type', and she appeared to have lost her head over an American cowboy.

What Dave had that Brian didn't was a Stetson. Brian briefly wondered how hard it would be to procure a cowboy hat in Nevada.

When Brian turned back to the table, Mark and Olivia were leaning against each other with their eyes closed. Sophie's head was nodding on Tel's shoulder, and Tel's head kept jerking backwards and forwards.

"TIME FOR BED!" Brian boomed, standing up. "FAYE!"

"WHAT?"

"TIME TO GO?"

Faye's face fell and she glanced at her watch. "IT'S ONLY JUST GONE TEN!"

"WE HAVE AN EARLY START IN THE MORNING."

She tottered over unsteadily. Dave and Angel followed.

"You folks off now?"

"I'm afraid so," Brian said. "Thank you for giving us such a good time, we've really enjoyed ourselves."

"It's been our pleasure. It's been real nice meeting you."

"Likewise."

Brian shook his hand. Nice bloke, funny, down to earth. In another place, somewhere more local perhaps, they might have been friends.

"It's been fantastic," Faye breathed up at him, vigorously shaking his hand. "Really, *really* fantastic."

They stirred the others, and Dave led them to the pick-up point round the corner for taxis; they had to use two. After effusive hugs and handshakes and multiple farewells, Sophie and Tel got in the first one, Mark and Olivia in the second.

"It's been brilliant," Faye said, hanging off the open taxi door.

"We've had a great time," said Brian, "Thank you for your generous hospitality."

"No problem. You take care now, and stay in touch, we're both on Facebook."

"Will do."

Brian turned to get into the front passenger seat, then

realised Faye wasn't moving into the back, next to Mark and Olivia. She stood on the pavement, hanging off the open door, smiling up at Dave.

"It's been lovely meeting you," she said.

"Yes, ma'am, we had a real good time. It's been nice meeting y'all."

And still she stood, smiling.

Angel leaned into Dave's ear and whispered something to him. "Oh!" he said, "Of course."

Brian was just getting back out again to retrieve his errant wife, when Dave bent down and gently kissed her cheek. She turned her head and kissed his.

"Bye, Dave," she breathed.

"Bye, Faye."

Brian held onto the back door, encouraging his wife inside. She eventually managed to tear her eyes away and got in, staring through the window and keeping her eyes on him as the taxis pulled away.

The drive back to the trailer park was silent. Mark and Olivia slept. Brian stared straight ahead, going over the events of the night in his head.

Faye sighed dreamily the entire time.

# CHAPTER SIX

It was still dark when Brian woke up the next morning. He checked his watch. It was almost six o'clock.

Enough sleep. They had a big day ahead of them and he was itching to get going.

He shimmied down the lumpy bed, glad it would be the last time.

"What time is it, Bri?"

"Time for pastures new."

Faye quickly lifted her head up off the pillow. "Is it today?" she said, cracking a smile.

"It is."

She quickly dragged herself down the bed until she sat on the end next to Brian. "Exciting, isn't it."

"It is."

From the corner of his eye he saw his wife raise a hand to her face and touch her cheek. A tiny spasm of jealousy washed over him, but he pushed it away. It was a silly thing and he shouldn't ponder on it, but he pondered on it anyway.

As Faye started pushing things into their sports bags, Brian ambled outside, stretched, and looked around. It had been … interesting. Not many people could say they'd stayed on a film set and starred in an American film, however bad it might be.

Tel and Sophie's door opened and Tel came down the steps.

"Bri," he said.

"Tel."

They both looked at the plastic table outside Mark and Olivia's RV. The ornate wooden box sat on top with its lid open. Next to it was a lamp, shining down like a spotlight, the cable curling across the ground and into one of the trailers.

"Subtle," said Tel. "Do you think they'll let us go without putting anything into it, or will they hold us hostage until we've emptied out our pockets?"

"We could make a run for it?"

Tel laughed quietly. "What time does the place open?"

"We have a couple of hours yet."

"Maybe we should hide until then."

"We could feign our own deaths," Sophie gently laughed from inside their RV.

Mark and Olivia's door opened and they stepped down with several steaming mugs on a tray.

"Coffee," Olivia announced quietly, putting them on the table next to the wooden box, "Good and strong."

"Hangover levels?" Mark asked everyone. "Mine may have merged with the chronic jetlag to produce a general sense of *bleurgh*, marbled with excitement and a healthy dollop of terror."

"I didn't have that much to drink," Brian said.

"Weird!" Tel said.

"I know. I was too busy keeping an eye on my philandering wife."

"I don't need keeping an eye on!" Faye said, stepping down and joining them around the plastic table.

Brian glared at her. "You were like a teenage groupie at a rock concert in front of Dave!"

"I was not!"

"I've never seen such fawning adulation!"

"That's not true!"

"I had visions of you running away to round up cattle on horseback."

Faye smiled. "Did you? How did I look?"

"Pretty good, actually."

"I could have gone home with them."

"That's what I was afraid of."

"I doubt Angel would have liked that," Mark laughed.

"I can dream," Faye sighed, picking up a mug and giving Olivia a wink. "It was nice while it lasted."

"Have you got it out of your system now?"

She nodded. "Unless we see another cowboy, then I won't be held responsible for my actions."

Brian rolled his eyes.

"Watch out," Mark hissed, "Incoming."

Meryl came striding over from the statics, a large lipstick smile wedged onto her face. She glanced at the open box, still empty, and her smile dimmed a couple of notches.

"Good morning, I hope you all slept well. I was just wondering what time you'd be leaving us this morning, and if you'd come to any decisions about investing in our small but ambitious company?"

"Just entered consciousness," Brian said, raising his mug, "Caffeine hasn't hit the brain cells yet."

"Ah, right. Well, I'll leave the box there until you've made your minds up."

Michael came over, looking like he'd just forced himself, his hair and his crinkled pyjamas out of bed. He hadn't yet arranged his face into the Tarantino grimace; without it he was a good looking bloke.

"Hi," he said, yawning and scratching his head, "How you all feeling today?"

They muttered their responses, and then he peered inside the box. "Have they ...?" he whispered to Meryl, and she briefly shook her head.

"We're still thinking it over," Tel said, feeling, like the others, a bit uncomfortable.

Graham hurried over. He went straight to the box, then glanced at Michael, who shrugged. Meryl had given up on the smile.

"I'm just nipping out for breakfast," he said, hurrying

towards the car. "Does anyone have any preferences."

"For?" Brian asked.

"McDonald's. Or there's a Chick-fil-A if you're into that sort of thing?"

"Anything," Faye said, "I'm easy."

"So I've witnessed," said Brian.

Meryl stood with her hands clasped in front of her, looking from each of them to the empty box. Michael nodded his head as they sipped at their coffees. Tel broke under the pressure and, sighing, took out his mobile phone, took a picture of the bank details, and said, "We'll come to a decision shortly."

Meryl huffed and walked off.

"I don't want to push you or anything," Michael said, "But we are financially constrained and a bit of fresh investment could make all the difference to the end product."

"Sure."

"What time are you off?"

"This morning."

"Early," Mark added.

"Good, good. Well, not good, we'll be sad to see you go. You've been an inspiration to us all."

"Have we?" Sophie asked, surprised.

"Yes, your Britishness. Brits always do well at the awards and we're hoping some of that will rub off on our little masterpiece."

"I'm sure it will," Brian said.

"When do you think you'll finish it?" Olivia asked.

"We're aiming to have it ready for the Cannes Film Festival in May."

"Tight schedule," Tel whistled.

"Tight schedule, tight budget, but we'll get it done, somehow."

"I'm sure you will."

"Right, I'll leave you to it." He turned to leave, then turned back again. "I don't suppose I could borrow you for one more crowd scene before you go?  Maybe two?"

"I think we're quite keen to be off," Sophie said.  "Not that we haven't enjoyed our stay here and seeing all the workings of a real film set, we're just … "

"A bit pushed for time," Tel finished.

"Yes, yes, of course."  Michael scratched his head again, smiled, and then abruptly walked off.

"I feel a bit bad now," Faye said, watching him go.

"Bad enough to put something in the box?" asked Brian.

"No, not really."

"Harsh, Faye."

"Oh don't, you'll make me feel worse."

"I've got the bank details," said Tel, "I'll take care of it."

"Take care of it *frugally*," Brian said, "And we'll all chip in."

Mark and Olivia nodded.

"Do you have anything left after that roulette rampage last night?" Sophie asked Tel.  "I mean, we don't have to sell the apartment and all our worldly possessions when we get home, do we?"

"No, of course not, Sophs."  He paused for a moment, then added, "Probably just the car."

Faye gasped out loud and grabbed Brian's huge hand.

Sophie broke into a sardonic grin.  "I hope you're joking. You'd better be joking or this is going to be a very short marriage."

Tel mirrored her grin.  "Of course I'm joking."

"Are you?"

"I'm just winding you up, Sophs.  Did your sense of humour disappear when I put that ring on your finger?"

There was a sharp intake of breath from everyone as the newly married couple glared at each other across the plastic table.

"Are we witnessing their first spat?" Mark asked Brian.

"Shh, you'll scare them.  Don't make any sudden moves."

Annoyed, Sophie said to them, "Did he tell you what he said to the dealer when he got to the roulette table last night?"

"Oh don't, Sophs!"

"The dealer asked him if he wanted any chips and he said he wasn't hungry."

Brian burst out laughing.

"Are we finished now?" Tel asked, dead-pan.

"I think so. Arguing is a bit boring, isn't it. Even more so when you're married, it takes all the frisson out of it."

"Oh," Brian boomed, "You've only just started! Give it another twenty-three years and you'll have it down to a fine art, with object throwing and death threats and everything."

"Brian!"

"What, my love?"

"I don't throw things!"

"Clock off the living room wall," he said. "You flung it across the room like an Olympic discus thrower. I felt all the hair on the top of my head move as it skimmed millimetres from a concussion."

"That was *fifteen years ago*!"

"Feels like yesterday," he squeaked, wiping an imaginary tear from his hairy cheek.

"And why did I throw the clock, Bri?"

"Something I'd done, presumably. Could have been anything. Whatever it was, it was undoubtedly my fault." He doubled over with laughter as Faye gently punched him on the arm and snapped, "It's *twenty-five* years, Bri. We've been married for *twenty-five years*, not twenty-three!"

"Time seems to stand still after twenty," he sighed.

"I'm not sure I like all this marital discord," Olivia said, turning to Mark. "Do you think you'd prefer *not* to marry me?"

"No, definitely not."

"You'll get used to it soon enough," Brian told her. "It's like psychological warfare to see whose mental stability crumbles first. He who survives, wins."

"He?" Faye punched him again. "*She* who survives, by the skin of her teeth!"

Brian draped an arm across her shoulders and pulled her

close to him, kissing the top of her head. "You know I love you, wife of mine."

Tel looked at Sophie. "Love you too, wife."

Sophie looked at Tel. "I quite like you, too."

"Ah, newly married love," Brian sighed, "I remember it well."

"*Brian*!"

* * *

After yet another burger breakfast, this time fresh-ish, Graham drove Brian, Tel and Mark away from the trailer park. The women took a screamingly cold shower and finished packing; it didn't take long. They sat on the plastic chairs around the plastic table with fresh coffees.

"Is Meryl still staring at us through the static window?" Olivia asked.

Faye glanced over. "She's got binoculars trained on us now."

"It suddenly feels very awkward, doesn't it."

"We'll be going soon."

They sat. They waited. Michael wandered passed, going nowhere, and smiled at them. Norman did the same. As did Graham. The wooden box was like a beacon, drawing everyone's eyes and tormenting them with its emptiness.

* * *

Colette arrived. She didn't park the car, it sort of came to a juddering stop in the middle of the concrete car park, coughed once, and belched out a cloud of grey smoke. She got out, already flustered as she gathered a collection of bags together, muttering furiously under her breath.

As she hurried towards them, Sophie asked, "Heard anything about the – ?"

"Don't ask me about the audition," she said, dropping her bags next to the table and kicking them underneath. "They say they'll get back to you and then they never get back to you."

"Meanies!" hissed Olivia.

"Well, it's only been – "

"I don't want to talk about it, I don't want to think – " Her phone went off and she struggled to snatch it out of her jacket pocket, almost dropping it. "Hello? Oh hi, mum. No, I've not heard anything yet."

"I'll make you a coffee," Olivia said, jumping up into her RV.

Tammy arrived. "I'm so glad I caught y'all," she cried, tottering over to them. "I'd hate for you to have left and me not wishing you well or saying g'bye."

She gave each of them a warm hug. "You'll never believe it, but that Snoop had the cheek to come round last night, with flowers! I sure told him where to go. Damn fool cried."

"Oh no," Olivia said.

"I don't pay me no heed to no fake tears. Nobody cries faster an' harder than a man that ain't got no place to stay. I told him if he didn't go away I was gonna break out my Indiana Jones whip, and he raced on off down the road like there were wolves snapping at his heels." She gave a high pitched giggle. "If he comes back again I'm gonna take out my rifle, that'll show him I mean business."

"Blimey!" Olivia gasped.

"She's joking," Sophie told her.

"I sure ain't," said Tammy.

Maria arrived, complete with a grizzling baby balanced on her hip. Singent roared into the car park shortly after, driving towards them so fast and so close they thought he was going to plough straight down the middle of the RVs and mow them down, but he slammed on his brakes at the very last minute, making the bonnet bow down and the car rock. He opened his door and half fell out; only strategic use of the cane prevented him from tipping head-first onto the cracked concrete.

"If you good ladies could kindly give me a hand," he said, struggling to raise himself.

The women approached, stopped halfway and began

taking steps back.

"Stinks!" Sophie whispered, waving her hand in front of her face.

"Hello?" Faye called back, "I can't straighten up a huge man on my own even after years of training at the care home!"

"You're gonna have to, darlin'," Tammy said. "He smells like a cigar dipped in stale beer, an' I ain't going nowhere near it."

"I don't drink *beer*," Singent snapped, still leaning heavily on his cane, "I drink *spirits*."

"It's all alcohol, honey, and none of it smells nice the morning after."

"Great," Faye sighed, "Just me then!"

"You can't smell." Olivia was holding her nose. "You should consider yourself very lucky."

"Oh yeah, I feel lucky, about to get my vertebrae crushed."

Faye took a tight grip on the top of the cane to steady it. It wobbled as Singent used it to lever himself upright. Once standing, he wavered slightly on his feet. When he staggered forwards the others stepped back.

"I'll make him a strong coffee," Olivia said, rushing off.

"Don't bother," Singent called after her, "I've brought my own refreshments." He pulled a flask out of his baggy jacket pocket and brought it up to his mouth.

"How can you come to work like this?" Colette asked. "It's highly unprofessional. Meryl's going to throw a fit."

"I'm not afraid of Meryl." He staggered over and lowered himself carefully onto a plastic chair. The arms splayed to accommodate his bulk and the legs bent like a donkey with a heavy load. "Uh-oh, talk of the devil."

"Are you all here?" Meryl snapped, striding towards them in her grey suit and neat black bob. "We need a full cast for the scenes today. Maria, why have you brought a baby onto set with you? There are no babies in any of the scenes, and we'd much rather not have them on set at all."

Maria said something in Spanish, which Meryl clearly

couldn't understand and decided to ignore.

"Where's Shane and Christofer? MICHAEL!"

"I'M ATTENDING TO A PERSONAL MATTER," Michael yelled irately from his static.

"WHAT PERSONAL MATTER?"

There was a beat of heavy silence before he yelled, "I'M IN THE JOHN!"

"Does John mind?" Olivia giggled.

"I'M THE DIRECTOR!" he hollered, "I'LL TURN UP ON SET WHEN I'M GOOD AND READY!"

"Clearly not a morning person," Faye sniggered.

"SHANE!" Meryl shrieked.

"I'M *COMING!*"

Christofer marched towards them with a sheaf of papers in one hand. "It is precisely eight o'clock and I am here, ready to work."

"Which is more than can be said for some of us," Colette said, eyeballing Singent, who stuck his tongue out at her. "Have you even been home and showered?"

"I'm a method actor," Singent said, "I have to stay in character."

"I'm pretty sure the leader of a rebel gang of alien fighters wouldn't look, or smell, like you."

"It's just a horror movie," he snapped.

"IT'S NOT A HORROR MOVIE!" Michael yelled from the static, "IT'S SCIENCE FICTION!"

"I have come dressed accordingly," Singent finished. "It's in my contract that I can wear my own clothes."

"I didn't know your character was a heavy drinker with an aversion to personal hygiene," Colette sniffed.

"Where is Graham?" Christofer asked. "I have been reading through the script and I have some suggestions for the scenes we are filming today."

Meryl rolled her eyes. "I'm sure he'll be thrilled."

"He's taken the men into Vegas," Olivia said.

"How long will he be?"

Olivia shrugged and said, "As long as it takes, I suppose."

"You specifically said eight o'clock," Christofer snapped at Meryl. "I got up early to do my yoga and my vocal exercises – "

"Oh, was that the howling we heard earlier?" Faye asked.

" – and I have memorised my lines, including the new ones I wrote this morning."

"WE'RE NOT MAKING ANY MORE CHANGES!" Michael yelled. "WE'RE ALREADY BEHIND SCHEDULE!"

"They are small changes that will make a *big* difference."

"WILL YOU BE JOINING US ANYTIME SOON?" Meryl called over.

"NOT IF YOU INSIST ON TALKING TO ME WHILE I'M … IN DISPOSE!"

Shane arrived, his freshly washed and blow-dried hair hanging as straight as curtains on either side of his handsome face. "I'm trying a new look," he said.

"Part way through filming?" Meryl screeched, "Are you insane?"

"Does it make me look more Brad Pitt or Leonardo?"

"Neither. Put it back the way it was when we started filming or Norman is going to have an aneurysm doing continuity."

Shane pushed his fingers into his hair and flopped it over to the left, where it fell perfectly into place. Faye was so impressed she tried it with her own hair and looked at Sophie, who shook her head. Faye struggled to put it back again.

Christofer huffed and fell cross-legged onto the floor. He looked up at Olivia and said, "I take my coffee strong and black."

"Oh, do you? How fascinating." She lifted a straight arm and pointed back at the RV, where all the mugs and tins of coffee were kept. "All the necessary components for a strong, black coffee are in there," she said. "Knock yourself out."

"Oooh!" Faye laughed.

"Go, Liv!" Sophie breathed.

"I am on the ground," Christofer said, pointing with both

hands at the ground he was sat upon. "You just watched me sit down!"

"And I'm more than happy to watch you get up again." She pushed her empty coffee mug across the table towards him, maintaining strong eye contact. "I take mine with milk, no sugar."

Christofer huffed and clambered to his feet.

"Milk and four sugars for me, mate," Shane said, leaning against a tree with his bulging arms crossed over his leather belts.

Norman sauntered over. He heard the tinkling of a teaspoon in a mug coming from the RV and said, "Someone making coffee? MILK, NO SUGAR!"

"Is there any tea?" Tammy asked.

Maria, bouncing the still whinging child on her knee, said something in strangled English. "She needs milk for the baby," Olivia translated.

"GET IT YOURSELVES!" Christofer yelled, "I AM NOT THE TEA LADY!"

"Me neither," Olivia grinned.

Michael stormed out of the static caravan, slamming the door behind him, and marched over, mumbling about not being able to take a moment to himself. Meryl looked down and said, "Don't let your puppy fly out the open door there, Mike."

"What?"

"Don't let the horse out of the stable."

"Have you completely lost your mind, Meryl?"

"Not yet," she sighed, "But I can feel it slowly slipping away day by day. Your *zipper*, Mike, you're hanging loose." She nodded down at his jeans and Michael hastily closed the stable door.

"Right," he said, "Let's get the RVs loaded up with all the equipment we'll need for today, and get this show on the road. Oh, are you making coffee?"

Christofer came down the steps and leaned against the

RV, making a big show of sipping from his mug. "For myself," he said.

"Get one for me, will you?"

"Get it yourself."

"I'm the Director."

"I'm the star."

"Er?" said Shane.

"I thought I was the star?" Colette said, looking at each of them.

Michael grinned and said, "I have the final say on any close-up shots, and even who we should and should not film."

Christofer pursed his lips and stomped back into the RV.

"Milk and four sugars!" Shane said again.

"Tea!" cried Tammy.

"Milk, for the baby," Olivia shouted.

"Oh!" Faye suddenly cried, standing up and looking towards the entrance of the car park, "The men! They're back!"

# CHAPTER SEVEN

They filed onto the car park; Graham in the first car, followed by three identical motorhomes, each with a giant mural of the Grand Canyon on both sides and 'RVS 4 U' printed on the front and back.

"That's not going to stand out much, is it," Faye said. "We won't look the least bit like tourists. Might as well have 'Tourists, rob me' signs on it."

"Well, aren't you the little cynic," Sophie said.

"I think I'm nervous. Are you nervous? I'm nervous, foreign country and all that, unknown journeys, unknown people."

"This is America, Faye, not deepest, darkest Africa."

"We're going on an adventure," Olivia squeaked excitedly.

"Hopefully one we'll survive."

They went to greet the men, now parked up and sitting in the vans, turning on indicators and windscreen wipers and bibbing the horns.

"What do you think?" Brian beamed through the open window at Faye. "It's got a pull-out canopy on one side."

"Nice. Bit overkill on the advertising though."

"Doesn't matter, it hasn't cost us anything. Hey, Sophie," he called over, "I can't believe you got such a good deal on these motorhomes."

She gave him the thumbs up and said, "I know, right!"

"Hire two, get one free!"

"Yes," she said.

The other four swapped nervous glances.

"I'll get our things," Olivia said, hurrying off.

"You're keen," Mark shouted after her.

She turned and pumped her fists up and down, shrieking, "I'm *so* excited!"

"Me too!" Sophie laughed, chasing after her. "Come on, Faye!"

The men started playing with the walkie talkies.

"Breaker one-nine," Brian said into his.

"Ten-four," came Mark's crackly voice.

"What's your twenny?" Tel laughed.

"About six feet to your left."

"How many times did you watch *Smokey and the Bandit* before we left?" Mark asked. "I did both of them twice."

"Same here," said Brian.

"Sophie said if I didn't stop watching them every night and take her out to dinner there would be repercussions."

"So what did you do?"

"Took her out to dinner, of course, then came home and finished watching them."

"Wise lad."

"We need handles," said Mark.

"There's plenty of handles in the RVs," crackled Tel. "Is there a specific handle you have in mind?"

"No, nicknames for the walkie talkies. Brian can be Big Buddy."

"That's a ten-four," said Brian, quite pleased.

"Mark can be Gollum," Tel laughed, "I always thought you bore a striking resemblance."

"Funny ... not! Just call me Burt, as in Reynolds, as in the young, handsome version, and you, Tel, can be ... Teletubby!" Mark's laughter crackled over the airways.

"I know what names the womenfolk would give us," said Brian, watching them struggling across the car park with the luggage, handbags and hangers of clothes flung over their shoulders.

"What's that then, Bri?"

"Mud, our names will be Mud."

The men jumped out to help the women load up the RVs.

The women took a good look around – it didn't take long.

"It's very compact, isn't it," Faye said, opening cupboards.

"That's what this model is called, Compact."

"Very apt."

"It comes with kitchen equipment, towels, a sleeping bag, two camping chairs, a folding table and GPS, although Mark's isn't working properly. Mark and Tel hired a couple of barbecues, too." He opened a tall, slim door next to them. "Shower and lav, and up here," he said, sweeping a huge arm to the cabin above the front seats, "Is our bed! It's a good set-up, we've everything we need."

Faye, opening another cupboard, said, "Why is there a small, folding spade in here?"

"To bury any bodies along the way."

"What bodies?" Faye gasped.

"Anyone you mow down on the highway, the fatal conclusion of any long festering resentments in the party, nagging wives."

"I don't nag," she snapped, "I remind."

"Repeatedly."

"Which I wouldn't do *repeatedly* if you just did what I asked you to do first time."

"You're absolutely right, lass, you always are."

"So why are there *really* folding spades?"

"In case we do any wild camping."

She looked blank.

"If we don't park on a campsite and have to go off into the wilderness to do … you know, poopy stuff."

"On a spade?"

Brian laughed. "Not *on* it, lass. You use the spade to dig a hole and then bury it."

"Ugh, I won't be doing any of that."

"Then you'll get very uncomfortable."

She looked around again and said, "There's not many cushions in here."

"Just a couple of pillows."

"Maybe we can pick some up along the way?"

"I've heard America is a cushion-free zone."

Faye's mouth dropped. "Really?"

"Americans don't go for that kind of fancy European stuff."

"Oh. What do they have instead?"

"Space," Brian told her, "They have lots and lots of space."

In the second RV, Olivia was carefully putting food items into cupboards. "I can't wait to cook something," she said.

"Me neither," said Mark, imagining future culinary delights.

"We'll have to stop off at a supermarket somewhere and stock up on fresh provisions now that we have a fridge."

In the third RV, Tel said, "Where have you stored my electric razor, Sophs?"

"I haven't seen your razor."

"It was in the sports bag."

"Probably still is, then."

"You've not unpacked my stuff?"

"No, just mine."

"That's not very wifely of you."

Sophie, pushing her clothes into the tiny wardrobe and said, "I'm not your mother, Tel, you're perfectly capable of unpacking your own stuff." When Tel said nothing, she turned to him and added, "Can we be clear on this, just so there's no future misunderstanding; you're not going to come home from work and find me in the kitchen wearing a frilly pinny, ready to wait on your every whim."

"No, Sophs."

"I will not be some subservient woman picking up after you and ironing your clothes."

"No, Sophs." He paused. "I'm sorry, it's just that I've never been married before."

"Me neither," she laughed.

"I don't really know how to behave as a husband, or how to treat you as a wife, or what you expect of me."

She put her arms over his shoulders. "You behave and treat me as you always have, and I don't expect anything from you except love and respect. Nothing's changed, Tel, we just have a piece of paper and a ring, it doesn't affect how we are together or how we feel about each other."

"You're right."

"I'm always right."

He laughed, but knew enough to say nothing.

Michael came over. "We've loaded up everything we need for the shoot and we'll be heading out in about ten minutes."

"Well," said Brian, getting out to shake his hand, "It's been fun. Nice to have met you all, and thank you for your hospitality."

"You can follow us there, it's only a couple of miles away."

"Follow you where?" Mark asked, joining them.

"To the desert scene we have scheduled for today."

"We're about ready to leave," Mark said. "Nobody said anything about being involved in a desert scene."

"Oh, did Meryl not mention it?"

"No," said Brian.

"We've planned to use the extra RVs, your RVs."

"Planned, but failed to mention?" said Mark.

Michael's eyes glazed over. His face morphed into the Tarantino sneer. "My vision is of a convoy of survivors driving out across the desert just as the sun's setting. Filmed from above using the drone, the RVs casting long shadows on the ground, like that famous picture of camels in the desert. It'll be very atmospheric, humankind running from the alien invaders. The music will be bold and spectacular and signify mankind's – "

"Sounds good," Brian said, "Pity we don't have time."

Michael looked surprised. "It'll only take an hour, two at most."

"I think the women really want to be off," Mark said.

"But … we need your RVs!"

Mark looked at Brian, who shrugged and said, "Faye and

the desert don't really go together."

"You just have to drive while we film."

Brian looked at Mark, who looked at his watch and said, "We'd love to help, we really would, but it's not worth the stick we'll get from the women."

"Stick?" Michael repeated, aghast, "They beat you?"

"The nagging," Brian explained, "The sulking, the pouty bottom lip, the general sense of doom a woman can incite when she doesn't get what she wants, that kind of thing."

"MERYL!"

Meryl hurried over.

"They're leaving!"

"Now?"

"Yes!"

"But … you can't leave," she told them, just as Tel and Sophie came over. "We've scheduled scenes with the extra RVs."

"I think you'll find we *can* leave," Tel laughed. "That was the plan, a two-night stay, followed by us leaving to explore the American West."

"But," said Michael, staring wide-eyed at them, "We can't do it without you. We need six RVs to signify mankind's escape from the – "

"No."

"What about the fight scene?" Meryl asked.

"What fight scene?" said Mark.

"There's a big crowd scene where the aliens find them and – "

"Brian?" Faye came out of the motorhome. Olivia, sensing something going on, came hurrying over. "Are we leaving soon?"

"We're just discussing the terms of our release," Tel said.

"What?"

"It's in the contract," Meryl suddenly said.

"What contract?" Sophie asked. "We haven't seen or signed any contract."

"It was one of the stipulations when we purchased the rights from Iain Flemmingway, that you'd make crowd appearances in the film to save on hiring extras, and RVs. We thought you'd enjoy being part of the process."

"Don't enjoy being made to stay," said Brian.

"It's not legally binding," Sophie said. "We haven't agreed to anything."

"We're lawyers," Tel added, giving his most sinister look, "We know about these things."

"Oh," said Michael, turning to Meryl, who pursed her lips.

"I guess we can't keep them here against their will," she said.

"No," said Brian, "You can't."

"Anyone know the number for the British Embassy?" Mark asked, taking out his mobile phone. "I imagine they're the experts at hostage negotiations."

Meryl huffed loudly, spun round and stormed off. Michael, after pleading with them with his eyes and seeing only stoic determination in theirs, strode back to the statics scratching furiously at his head.

It took longer than they'd expected to leave the 'film set'. There were lots of hugs from Tammy and Collette, even Maria said something sweet-sounding in Spanish, which they couldn't hear anyway on account of the screaming baby in her arms.

"Let me know about your audition," Sophie said to Colette, kissing her cheek. "You've got my number, haven't you?"

"Yes, yes, of course."

"It's been real nice meeting you folks," Tammy said, wiping a tear from her eye. "I hope one day to come visit your cute little island."

"You'll be more than welcome," Olivia laughed. "You can stay with us."

"Can I?"

"Of course!"

"Why, that's real nice of you."

"What about me?" Shane asked.

Mark patted his huge shoulder. "No offence, mate, but I don't want somebody who looks like you staying in the same building as my fiancée."

"We'll take him!" Faye laughed.

"We won't!" said Brian.

"I have a pub, plenty of room for everyone."

"Olivia!"

"What? It's *literally* what a pub is for, to put people up."

"Yes, but … "

"But what?"

"Look at him! He looks like a Roman god!"

Shane preened proudly.

"Oh, you silly sausage," she said, giggling, "I only have eyes for you."

"I'm going to hurl," Tel laughed.

"And someone like Shane wouldn't be interested in little old me anyway."

"I would," he winked, making Olivia giggle again.

"There is no room at the inn," Mark said firmly.

"It has been nice to meet you," Christofer stated abruptly. "Enjoy the rest of your vacation."

"Thank you, Chris."

"Tofer, the name is Chris*tofer*."

"Photos!" Colette cried, and everyone took out their phones and started posing in small groups. Brian seemed to be the one they all wanted to capture, followed by Tel and Sophie.

Faye, Mark and Olivia stood in the background, redundant and unwanted.

"It's just like games at school," Faye muttered, "I never got picked for the team there either."

"I hated games," Olivia said.

"It's hard being ugly," Mark sniffed.

"You're not ugly, darling."

"Nobody loves me!"

"You'd make a terrible actor," said Faye, "Very hammy."

"Well," Brian said, breaking away from the cameras and walking up for a final farewell with Michael, Graham and Norman, who were huddled miserably around the wooden picnic bench, "Good luck with your venture and I hope it all works out for you."

"Won't be my complete vision without the RVs driving across the desert scene," Michael sulked, "But thanks."

They nudged knuckles.

Brian turned and boomed, "RIGHT, HERD 'EM UP AND MOVE 'EM OUT!"

As they ambled towards their motorhomes, Michael cried, "Norman, quick, get the camera! Film them leaving, we can use the footage."

There were a few last-minute hugs before they clambered up into the RVs.

"One last look at Vegas?" Brian shouted over to the others.

They nodded, waving at the crowd gathered on the cracked concrete car park.

"Don't wave!" Michael yelled, "Norman, try not to get their faces in. No, it's okay, we can do a digital face replacement in post-production."

"There's a lot going on in post-production," Norman drawled.

"Drive slower! Stop waving! Although they would wave at their fellow survivors, wouldn't they. Okay, wave, but look miserable about it."

They started up their engines, waving out of the windows and blowing kisses. Norman ran along beside them with the camera while Michael shouting instructions. Through the trailer park fencing and out onto the road; Brian leading, Tel following, Mark bringing up the rear.

And then they were off.

"WAGONS ROLL!" Brian hollered.

\* \* \*

"Darling," Olivia said.

"Not now, Livs, I'm concentrating."

"Yes, you look very pensive."

"I'm driving on the wrong side of the road, I need to focus."

Mark gripped the steering wheel so tight his knuckles were white. He was leaning forward in his seat, peering intensely through the windscreen. Outside, the shabby area got less shabby and turned into high towers as they approached The Strip; the towering STRAT, Circus Circus, Resorts World, Trump Tower ("I wonder if he's looking down on us right now?" Olivia said, and Mark shivered and said, "Creepy!"), the Palazzo and the Venetian with Treasure Island on the opposite side, Harrah's, Caesars Palace ("Bye, hotel we never stayed in!" Sophie cried, waving), and the Bellagio, all glistening like giant, colourful shards in the sun.

"We didn't get to see all the hotels," Olivia sighed, "Or a show. We'll have to come again to take it all in." She turned her gaze to Tel's RV ahead of them. "Aren't you a little close, darling?"

"GPS isn't working and I don't want to lose them, can't lose them, mustn't lose them."

She looked over at him. "Darling, you need to calm down. Take some deep breaths."

"I am breathing!" he cried.

"No, you're hyperventilating. *Deep* breaths, darling."

In the middle RV, Tel gasped, "Oh my god, Sophs, this is the first time we've been alone in *days*."

"I know."

"Fancy stopping off for a quick snog once we get out of Vegas?"

"I do."

In the front RV, Brian was humming along to country music on the radio as he pressed buttons on the GPS. "You okay, Faye?"

"I'm fine," she grinned. "I still can't believe we're

in America. I never thought I'd actually see Las Vegas. Everything here is just so *big*!"

Brian smiled. Happy wife, happy life.

"Where are we headed?" she asked.

"I can see you didn't do your homework, lass. Sophie prepared a detailed itinerary of our journey, day by day, did you not read it?"

"No, couldn't seem to find the time. So where are we headed first?"

"Somewhere really exciting, and it's not far."

"Ooh, where?"

Brian turned right. The others followed.

Into a supermarket car park.

"Fresh stuff to see us through the next couple of days," Sophie cried, jumping out and handing Faye and Olivia a piece of paper from a plastic folder. "I'll get the meat and barbecue charcoal. Livs, you get any fancy ingredients you think we might need. Faye, you're on salad and sauce duty. Right, let's go!"

"It's like a military operation," Brian chuckled, watching the women run off into the supermarket clutching their lists.

"Organised woman, my wife," said Tel.

Brian felt a tiny flame of hope light up inside him. "I'm sensing that our presence might not be required on this particular shopping – "

"BRIAN! WE'LL NEED HELP CARRYING THE BAGS!"

The flame died.

Brian bought a couple of country music CDs, and they each bought an electric cool box, which made Brian very happy as he stacked cans of beer on top.

After fiddling with the CD player, and with Alan Jackson filling the RV, they were off … again.

"Where to next?" Faye asked, fidgeting excitedly in the passenger seat.

"You'll see, just enjoy the views."

Further down the road the GPS directed them to turn left,

across three lanes of oncoming traffic. Brian came to a stop at the lights and checked his mirrors to see if they were all behind him. They were.

"Oh god," said Tel.

"What?"

"Left turn."

"You've done left turns before."

"Not from the wrong side of the road, I haven't."

"You can do it, Tel, I have every faith in you. Just follow Brian."

He took a deep breath and stared at the traffic lights.

Behind them, Mark was muttering, "Left turn, left turn," over and over again.

"Darling, you're shallow gasping."

"I'm just breathing, Liv."

"Rather fast."

"If I slow down I'll pass out."

"Do you want me to drive? I drove mummy from New York to Florida when we came over."

"No, I can do it, I'm sure I can do it."

"Okay. We can swap places anytime if you're not comfortable or if you want a rest."

"No, I'm fine. I'm sure it'll be fine. Left turn, left turn."

The traffic lights changed to green.

Brian turned smoothly, glancing in his mirrors, where he saw Tel not turning at all but carrying straight on down the main road. Mark, suddenly unsure about anything now that Tel had broken away, wavered in the middle of the road, before finally deciding to stick with Brian and stomped on the accelerator. The RV kangarooed across the three lanes.

Sophie said, "Tel, you didn't turn."

"I tried, I couldn't ... I just couldn't do it."

"We're going the wrong way now."

"I know!"

Brian picked up the walkie talkie. "Tel, do you copy?"

Sophie picked up the walkie talkie, pressed the button

down and held it out towards Tel, who was sweating profusely.

"Copy, Bri."

"You didn't *copy* what I did at the traffic lights."

"No."

"Was there a problem?"

"I just couldn't do it, Bri."

"Are you planning on turning any time soon?"

"I'm building up the courage to take the next left, alone and unsupervised."

"Turn next left," Brian said, glancing at the GPS, "Then left again and – "

"Two lefts?" Tel gasped.

"Well, if you're not planning on taking any left turns on our trip you'll end up in…" Brian ran through a map in his head and said, " Mexico. I hear it's quite nice at this time of year. Send us a postcard."

"Okay, I'm doing it. Lights are red. I'm ready to turn left. Lights are green and there's cars hooting behind me."

"Probably best to get a move on, then."

"I can't, I can't do it."

"Tel!" Sophie shouted, "Hit the accelerator and turn the wheel! Do it now!"

Tel, normally very calm and composed in all situations, gave a continuous high scream as the RV lurched forward, hauling left, left, left on the steering wheel and then frantically right, right, right to straighten up again.

There was radio silence.

"Tel?" said Brian.

Nothing.

"Tel?"

A burst of static and Tel shouting, "I did it! I did it!"

"Well done, lad. Sophs?"

"Yes, Bri?"

"Could you update the itinerary so the route doesn't involve any left turns?"

"No, Bri, I couldn't."

"Then have a word with your husband, would you?"

"Already planning a severe tongue lashing at the first available opportunity." Leaving the button down, they all heard Tel shouting, "Okay, I think I have it, I'm turning left, left, left."

Another scream of terror, and then, "I've done it! I've bloody done it! Oh, this is easy, I don't know what I was worried about."

"Practice makes perfect," said Brian. "Now take an easy right turn and you should be on the same road as us. Can you see us?"

"YES!"

"Good. Follow us and do exactly what we do. Above all else, don't panic."

\* \* \*

They were on the freeway, or it could have been an interstate, they weren't sure. Brian followed the GPS directions, constantly checking the other RVs were behind him, while Faye wondered where they were heading. The GPS just showed a lot of straight roads and some blank stuff, with no destination in sight.

"This could be anywhere," she muttered, watching the passing buildings. "It could be Birmingham."

"Yeah," Brian laughed, "Hot, sandy Birmingham."

"You know what I mean."

"I don't. I never do."

"It's just so hot!" She swished the fan in front of her red, sweaty face, then reached down to take a can of cooling spray mist out of her bag, liberally coating herself with it.

"I thought you'd have acclimatised by now, love."

"I feel like I should be having hourly showers. Do I stink?"

Having no sense of smell herself, Brian knew Faye was sensitive about bad odours; was the cheese off in the fridge, did the hallway cupboard smell damp, were her armpits whiffy. Brian delicately said, "A bit."

"That means a *lot*."

"No, no." He quickly ran through the database in his mind for an answer that wouldn't have Faye howling with malodorous misery. "You expect to sweat in this heat."

"You're not."

Another quick glance through his database. "I'm a man, it's different for men, we have … thicker skin."

"Oh," said Faye, and Brian felt a mini-drama had been deftly avoided.

He drove on down the road. The others followed.

\* \* \*

Slowly, the buildings and the bustle of traffic fell away, and the landscape metamorphosed into flat, scrubby desert on either side of the road.

"It's so big!" Olivia cried. "You can almost see to the edge of the world."

"If the mountains weren't in the way," Mark laughed, slightly calmer now that he was away from traffic, it was just them and the almost empty road running as straight as a die into Olivia's edge of the world. He liked this bit.

"I had a quick look at Sophie's itinerary before we lost it," Olivia said. "Faye's going to really like the next stop."

"Why, where is it?"

She told him and he grinned. "Does she know?"

"No, sneaky Sophie didn't put it on their itinerary."

"Excellent. Can't wait to see her face when we pull up."

\* \* \*

"Tel."

"Yes, my love."

"My love? Yuk, you can knock that on the head for a start."

"What should I call you then?"

"Sophie."

"Yes, Sophie?"

"I've been thinking about tonight."

"Have you indeed."

She couldn't stop herself from smiling. "I can sense an early bedtime coming on."

"Oh yes?"

"Only … "

"Only?"

"It might be a bit awkward, you know, with the others parked right next to us."

"We'll find a completely different campsite in a different state."

She laughed. "If we could put a bit of space between us and them when we pull up?"

"Several RV spaces away, you mean?"

"Or at least one, unless we can find a quiet corner somewhere."

"Your wish is my desire, my … Sophie."

Sophie pondered for a moment. "Should we have adoring nicknames for each other now that we're married?"

"I don't know, should we?"

"I could call you … sweetheart?"

"Ugh, kill me now."

"Darling?"

"Olivia calls Mark 'darling'. What does Brian call Faye?"

"Lass, or 'wife'. Don't even think about either."

"Maybe we shouldn't force it, the names will come organically."

"Just don't call me 'missus', or worse, 'old lady'."

"I wouldn't dare."

She stared out of the window, still smiling, watching the vast desert landscape flying by. "Isn't the scenery beautiful, all that open space."

"It is if you're just passing by and not in it. In the event of a breakdown you should never leave your vehicle, apparently, people get lost out there."

"Really? Hard to imagine, coming from a crowded, boggy Britain."

"Iddy-biddy island," Tel laughed, "That's what Tammy called it."

"She was lovely."

"They all were."

"Except for Meryl."

"Yes, except for her."

"To be fair, though, she did have her work cut out for her, having to deal with everything, especially those three."

"I guess so."

"I did enjoy it, but I'm glad to be away, on our own, just the six of us, not being pestered for money all the time."

"Yeah, me too. HELLO, AMERICA!" he yelled out loud, making Sophie jump in her seat. "BRACE YOURSELVES, THE BRITS ARE COMING!"

\* \* \*

"Breaker ten-four," Brian said into the walkie talkie.

"What does that mean?" Mark crackled back.

"I don't know, but it sounds good. Turn off towards Boulder up ahead. You good for a turn, Tel?"

"Left or right?"

"It tells you on your GPS."

"I think mine's having an existential breakdown."

"That'll be the heat," Faye said, fanning herself. "I know just how it feels."

"It keeps turning itself on and off."

"Mine's done that since we picked up the RV," Mark came in.

"It's a left, Tel, a freeway-guided left. Piece of cake. Follow the signs to Boulder."

"Is that where we're going?" Faye asked.

"It is."

"What's in Boulder?"

"I'm not at liberty to say."

"Why not?"

"I've been sworn to secrecy."

"By who, whom, whatever?"

"Interpol."

"Interpol?" She stared at him with faux astonishment. "Are you a spy, Bri?"

"If I was I wouldn't be able to tell you, would I."

"I'm your wife, I have a right to know."

"Faye, do I look like a spy?"

"I don't know, what does a spy look like?"

"Well, can you see *me* jumping across rooves and clinging on to the sides of airplanes on take-off?"

Faye was quiet.

"Your eyes have gone glassy," he said, to bring her attention back. "Are you daydreaming about Tom Cruise in *Mission: Impossible*?"

"No, actually I was thinking of Colin Firth in *Kingsman*."

"Is he a spy in that?"

"I don't know," she sighed, "Doesn't really matter. I liked him in *Pride and Prejudice* as well."

"I remember." He glanced over at her, daydreaming and smiling. "Faye, are you getting bored of me?"

"How could I?" she laughed.

"It's just that you seem to be lusting after other men a lot lately."

"I suppose I'm caught up in all the excitement. There's not many handsome men at the care home and there seem to be lots here."

"I mean, we *have* been married for twenty-three years."

"It's almost twenty-five, Bri."

"Maybe the magic wears off after a couple of decades. It's a long time for a couple to be together."

"We don't do too bad," she grinned. "I've enjoyed it."

He grinned back. "Me too. Now, stop lusting after other men."

"I'll try, Bri, I'll try."

They drove into Boulder City, a town of low buildings, which emphasised the enormity of the clear blue sky. Fat palm trees lined the road.

"Oh look!" Faye cried, "An American *motel*! Oh look, *shops*!"

"Oh look!" Brian said, "So much to do and so little time."

"Not even – ?"

"If it's not on the schedule it's not happening. Sophie spent a lot of time putting them together, she's not going to like any deviation."

"Oh, Indian Jewelry! Spelt wrong."

"That's how they spell it here."

"Do they just get bored of writing long words and skip letters."

Brian laughed and started slowing down.

"Oh," Faye cried, "Are we stopping for a pizza?"

"No," said Brian, turning off the road and into a car park, "We're stopping for you."

"For me? Have you had enough of me, Bri? Are you going to leave me at the side of the road?"

"Hadn't thought of that, but no." He pulled into a parking space, Tel parked two spaces away and Mark two spaces after that. He turned to Faye's expectant face. "Look," he said.

Faye widened her eyes at him. "Looking. What am I supposed to be seeing?"

"Not at me, woman, outside, at the building.

Faye turned her head. She looked. She saw. Her mouth fell open. "For me?" she gasped.

"Sophie found it. She knows how much you like horror films."

"Oh wow!" She quickly scrambled out and stood in front of a nondescript building that had a very descriptive sign reading TOM DEVLIN'S MONSTER MUSEUM. Outside stood a Ghostbuster car and, as they walked round to the front, there was a life-size model of Frankenstein and a purple hearse with a coffin on top. "What is this place?" she asked.

The others came over, Sophie opening up her plastic folder and reading, "It's an amazing collection of screen-used

PITCHING UP IN AMERICA!

memorabilia, as well as meticulously recreated props and make-up from the greatest horror films of all time."

"No!" Faye squealed, racing for the door, "Really?"

"Really," Sophie laughed, quickly adding, "We might give this a miss, it's not really our thing. We're going to take an afternoon nap instead, give you plenty of time to wander round."

"Us too," said Mark, already stepping back towards his RV, stretching his arms up and yawning as Olivia hurried to open the side door. "Very tired. Siesta required."

"Oh," said Brian. "Faye, do you fancy a quick – ?"

"I want to see the monsters, Bri."

"Of course you do, love."

# CHAPTER EIGHT

Brian knocked on the side of Tel's RV. "Er," he said loudly, "Sorry to disturb, but according to the itinerary – "

"Yes, yes, we're up!" Tel shouted groggily.

Brian wandered over to Mark's RV and tapped on the door. "Ahoy!" he bellowed.

"A who?" came Mark's muffled voice.

"Ahoy. Nautical term."

"And how far are we from the sea?"

"A few 'undred miles."

"Wouldn't recommend the fish then. How was the House of Horror?"

"Horrific, but Faye seemed to like it. You ready for the off?"

"Give us two minutes."

Brian wandered back to their RV. Faye was in the passenger seat rifling through her Monster Museum tote bag of memorabilia from the gift shop. He'd stopped her from buying a Pennywise mask and a Freddy Krueger glove, knowing she wouldn't be able to resist playing tricks with them and potentially giving him a heart attack, now thankfully averted. She looked very happy; hot, but happy.

Brian got behind the steering wheel and waited for the others to appear in their windscreens.

"That was so interesting," Faye gushed, frantically fanning herself. "The waxwork models were amazing, so realistic, and that Gremlin spider! That would look good in our back garden, Bri."

"I doubt the neighbours would agree."

"We could build our own and make it a feature."

"I won't be building a spider, Faye."

"You have no imagination."

"I can imagine the kids next door screaming in terror. We might have to pay for their therapy and, as you know, we can't afford it."

Mark appeared behind the steering wheel first, with Olivia slipping into the passenger seat tidying up her hair. Tel and Sophie really did look as if they'd been asleep. Tel picked up the walkie talkie.

"How long does this jet lag last?" he groaned. "It's ruining my sex life."

In the background Sophie hissed, "Tel!"

"You're asking me about jet lag because I'm a well-travelled man of the world?" said Brian. "I don't know, probably until the day before we fly home."

"Can I just have a word with Sophie?" Faye asked, reaching out for the microphone, "Tell her how much I appreciated the – "

Brian snatched the microphone away and snapped, "No."

"No?"

"We've agreed that the walkie talkies are for serious travel business only, not for idle gossip."

"Who agreed this?"

"The men." Brian pumped his free fist into his chest and boomed, "Men take full custody of the walkie talkies."

"I can't see if you're smirking behind your beard or not."

"Entire reason for its existence, to keep you on your toes."

"Breaker, breaker," came Mark's voice. "Did Faye enjoy the museum?"

"She took so many photos we can join them all up and run a film tour with them later."

"We're ready to follow the lead."

"Copy," Tel said.

"Thank you for driving American RVS 4 U," Brian said into the walkie talkie as he reversed out of the parking space. "We hope you have a pleasant journey."

And they were off … again.

\* \* \*

After they'd navigated a successful left-turn, they drove down the road awhile, watching the scrubby desert and a spattering of white houses sail passed their windows. A slither of blue water came into view in the distance and grew bigger as they approached.

Faye pressed her sweaty face against the window. "Any house round here will do, Bri."

"We can barely afford the house we've got."

"Let me – "

"Dream, I know. Dream away, lass."

Sophie said, "I can't get over how big everything is here. Even the sky looks bigger."

"It's probably because you can see it from horizon-to-horizon, we only get to see pieces of it in London. You've been to America before, though, haven't you?"

"I've been to New York a few times on business," she laughed. "There's no horizon-to-horizon view of the sky there, and I was back home before jet lag had even noticed I'd left the country. I think Olivia's been before, I remember her telling us that she and her mother drove from New York to Florida. Oh, I forgot, I have an announcement to make."

She picked up the walkie talkie, pressed the button and, opening up her travel folder, said in her best BBC newsreader voice, "Ahead you can see Lake Mead, formed by the building of the Hoover Dam, which spans the border between Nevada and Arizona. Brace yourself as we cross the bridge because we will lose an hour of our lives."

"Lose an hour of our lives?" Faye gasped.

"Time zone," Brian said. "America's so big it's split into different time zones."

"A whole hour, though. I could have done great things with that hour."

"Such as?"

"I don't know, read an hour of my book, or caught up on my sleep, or started learning a new language."

"You barely have a grasp of English," Brian howled.

Faye gently punched his arm and said, "The, the, the. Go on, Bri, say it."

"'T, 't, 't.'"

"I rest my case."

Sophie's voice crackled over the walkie talkie. "I have historical facts and figures if anyone wants to hear them?" She paused. She waited. Nobody answered. "The Hoover Dam is considered to be one of the seven modern engineering wonders of the world." Still no response. She closed her folder and said, "There's a checkpoint before the dam where, you'll be pleased to hear, Mark, the security guards *don't* wear firearms."

"Copy, Soph."

The convoy pulled up at the at the RV checkpoint.

"Hey, guys," the guard said, approaching Brian's open window. "Any firearms in the vehicle?"

"No, sir."

The guard looked across at Faye, who instantly froze under his uniformed scrutiny.

"Any particular reason you're sweating so much, ma'am?"

"It's hot."

"We're from the UK," Brian said. "We only get temperatures like this once or twice a year, when the whole country fries and comes to a complete standstill."

The guard laughed. "Just going to have a quick check of your outside compartments."

The drivers clambered down from the RVs, stretched, and accompanied the guards on their inspection, both inside and out. It didn't take long, and then they were off … again.

"It's a bit bigger than Bartley Green Resa," Faye said, as they drove across Hoover Dam. "And look at all those people!"

"As agreed," Sophie said over the walkie talkie, "We won't be stopping here, so enjoy the view as we cross."

"Where do we lose our hour, Bri?"

"Just about ... *now!*"

"Oh," she cried, "I felt it. My life span shortened, just like that. I feel faint."

Brian shook his head. "You know you're a full sandwich short of a picnic, don't you."

"It's what drew you to me in the first place," she said proudly, "That, and my low-cut top."

"It was your eyes," he breathed, glancing over at her, "Your enormous brown eyes."

Faye fluttered her eyelashes at him, and the convoy crossed the dam and entered the great swathe of desert and mountains of Arizona.

* * *

"Anyone hungry?" Brian asked over the walkie talkie, spotting a place they could stop up ahead. He could do with moving his bones. Also, he was hungry.

"Wee," said Mark.

"Is that the royal 'we' or a statement about your manhood?" Tel laughed.

"Pull over and I'll explain it to you fully."

They parked next to a Mini Mart at Grasshopper Junction, in the middle of absolutely nowhere, and sat for a moment listening to the sound of silence. They got out stiffly and strolled under the covered wooden porch, with Tel and Mark jabbing at each other. A sign on the door read, 'Chloride, the town that refuses to die."

"Town?" Sophie said, looking around at the desert. "I don't see a town."

Tel shielded his sunglasses, looking far. "There's something over in the distance, at the base of those mountains. Could be a town."

They all looked, lost interest, and entered the small shop.

"Salad!" Sophie cried, rushing over to the display of plastic boxes in a fridge. "Do you want one, Tel?"

"I'm quite full from all the snack bags I've ploughed my

way through," said Tel.

"Which accounts for the orange dust all over your face," Brian said. "You look like an Oompa Loompa."

Tel slapped his chops.

"Olivia made us some lovely pastrami sandwiches on the way," Mark said, rubbing his tummy, "Followed by a chilled slice of cheesecake."

Brian's eyes jumped accusingly to Faye. He'd been hungry for ages.

"I was on salad and sauce duty," she said, looking over at Nigella Lawson and her well-stuffed fiancé. "I want to travel in their RV from now on."

"And miss all the scintillating conversation from your husband?" Brian asked.

"And the rumbling tummy," Tel laughed.

"If he plays *Big Country* one more time I'm throwing myself out the door."

"Australian?" queried the woman behind the counter.

"British," Tel said.

"Oh, you sound Australian."

"Yeah, we get that a lot."

"Long way to come," the woman continued, ringing up their purchases, "All the way from Australia."

"We're from the UK," Tel said again.

"Is that one of the islands off Australia?"

He sighed. "Yes."

"Tel, you're paying for our stuff there," said Brian.

Tel looked at the goods on the counter and said, "It's only a sandwich and some pasta. And some chocolate bars, some crisps, and a few cans of pop."

"Pop!" laughed the woman behind the counter. "I just love the way you Australians talk."

They rolled their eyes en masse and wandered outside onto the veranda to sit at a wooden table. As they were chomping down on their lunch a large and very loud motorbike pulled up next to their RVs, and a stubbled, leather-clad biker wearing a cowboy hat and a patched-covered waistcoat sauntered over and sat at the next table.

"I just stopped on by for a cee-gar," he said, lighting up and looking for all the world like Clint Eastwood in his spaghetti western days.

They all turned to look at Faye.

"What?"

"Nothing."

Sophie and Olivia giggled. Faye struggled to concentrate on her plastic box of chicken pasta and not glance over at the man, who was quietly puffing away on his cee-gar. She briefly wondered if the new vitamin tablets she'd been taken lately were playing havoc with her hormones, her hormones were certainly playing havoc with her. She reluctantly tore her eyes away when Brian gave a low growl.

"So, where are we stopping off for the night?" Mark asked.

Sophie tutted. "Did *nobody* read their itineraries?"

"Read it, lost it," said Mark.

She sighed and said, "I'm not telling you."

"Meanie," Olivia giggled.

"It's somewhere nice," Sophie relented, "Where we can do a bit of shopping – "

"Argh!" cried Brian.

" – and have a steak dinner."

"Ooh."

\* \* \*

They were on the road again, still heading south along arrow-straight roads that seemed to disappear into the distant mountains. Mile upon mile of desert rolled by.

"Kingman coming up," Brian said into the walkie talkie. "Easy left, Tel."

"I think I've got the hang of it now."

"Good lad. We're aiming for Route 66."

Everyone cheered.

It was more built up here, with more traffic. Tel and

Mark kept as close to each other and Brian as they dared; they couldn't begin to imagine getting lost, they might never find each other again.

"The road signs are good, aren't they," Sophie said, watching them fly by as they left the main road. "They tell you what hotels and restaurants are off the next exit. They should do that at home."

"What, in Australia?" Tel laughed, then carried on biting his lip as he meticulously followed Brian down the slip road and navigated another left. He quickly snatched up the walkie talkie. "Are you sure this is the right way, Bri?"

"Feel free to take the lead, lad."

"I don't know the way."

"Me neither, I'm just following the Route 66 signs and hoping for the best. GPS says to stay on the 93 to Exit 53."

So they did.

"There it is," Tel eventually cried, spotting a sign.

Down another ramp, under bridges, fighting for space with 18-wheel trucks.

"Route 66 straight ahead," said Brian.

"Oh, it's so exciting," Olivia giggled.

"I think," Brian eventually said into the walkie talkie, "I think we're on it. GPS says we're travelling down the AZ-66."

"Are we?" said Faye, looking around and feeling decidedly unimpressed by all the commercial companies on either side of the road, including a train track.

"Did you expect cowboys and Indians?" Brian grinned. "Covered wagons and women wearing bonnets?"

"No." But she'd expected something other than this.

The buildings gradually faded away and the desert encompassed them.

"Let's pull over," Mark suggested.

They parked.

"It's so desolate," Olivia said, getting out and standing at the roadside, taking in the vast view.

"So empty," said Tel.

"So big."

"So hot." Faye fanned herself, then sprayed her face.

"Sophs, aren't you coming out to have a look?"

"I can see from here," she yelled from the passenger seat.

"Come and soak up the atmosphere. It's splendidly quiet."

"I can't."

"Why not?"

"Because you said we should never leave the vans, and also," she said, sticking her head out of the window and looking down at the ground, "Are there snakes out there?"

"Possibly."

"Then I'm not getting out."

Olivia, feeling the sun boiling her brain, wandered back to the van and got in. Faye decided it was too hot to stand and stare, and did the same.

"Well, that was a momentous moment in our journey," Mark laughed.

"What should we do?" Tel asked. "We ought to mark the occasion somehow."

Brian thought for a moment, then held out a giant hand and shook theirs. "Welcome to Route 66," he said.

"Thanks very much."

"Lovely to be here."

"Let's go."

* * *

It took an hour and a half to drive the loop that was Historic Route 66. The few towns were sparse and far between. They waved at the longest freight train they'd ever seen and it blew its whistle at them. They spotted tiny houses way off in the distance, tucked in at the base of mountains.

"Who'd live way out here in the middle of nowhere?" Olivia wondered.

"Introverts," said Mark.

Tel crackled over the walkie talkie. "Sophie said we're

passing Grand Canyon Caverns, if anyone's interested?"

"Watched it on YouTube," Brian said.

"You're all a bunch of heathens!" Sophie laughed.

"Happy heathens who don't want to get concussion in remote caves," said Brian.

"Hot heathens," Faye gasped, fanning her face.

"Heathens sucking on ice-cold bubble tea," said Mark.

Brian glared at Faye. "Why didn't you buy me bubble tea?"

"Because you didn't ask and I'm not a mind-reading servant."

"I would have liked some bubble tea. Not entirely sure what it is, but it sounds nice."

"Should have got yourself some, then."

"I might trade you in for a newer model."

"Just say the word and I'll find myself an American sugar daddy."

Brian burst out laughing. "Dave, I suppose."

"Or Shane was quite nice, or that biker outside the death-defying town. Wish I'd got his number now."

"Shut up, woman."

"You started it!"

"Wish I hadn't."

"Don't give it if you can't take it."

"I accept defeat!"

"I accept your apology."

"Not sure it was an – "

"It was."

They drove into Seligman, passed the Roadkill Café and OK Saloon. Without even looking at him Faye said, "It's too early for a beer," and Brian grunted.

"Do you think they cook dead animals at the Roadkill Café?" Sophie asked Tel.

"That's usually the way it's done. It's more difficult to cook them if they're fighting back."

The convoy drove though the low-level, wide laned town.

Route 66 signs were everywhere. They approached an aqua-coloured building on the right with the back end of a plane sticking out of it, emblazoned with the American flag, which were also everywhere. A coach releasing its travellers was parked up outside Historic Seligman Sundries, surrounded by old cars and several Harley Davidsons.

"Aaaaah!" Faye cried, pointing at it.

"Which roughly translates as?"

"Shop! Stop!"

"You're not looking for the cee-gar biker, are you?"

"Don't be daft, I want souvenirs of our trip down Route 66."

"A likely story."

Brian turned the wheel. The others followed. Faye was out of the cab before he'd even turned the engine off, closely followed by the other women, all of them vastly over-excited.

"What's up with them?" Tel asked, coming over to Brian's RV.

"Women have an inherent need to shop."

Tel laughed. "Going in?"

"Only to stop the wife from buying everything."

"Yeah, me too."

"I'll stay out here and look at the cars and bikes," said Mark.

By the time Brian entered the shop, Faye already had several items in her basket. Sophie and Olivia were picking things up and ooh'ing a lot.

Faye came rushing over to him. "Postcards, stickers, a Route 66 sign you can put in your shed, a mug, a keyring, shot glasses for when we buy some real bourbon, and a t-shirt each." Brian sighed. "Do you think I should get an American flag, Bri?"

"No, I don't."

"You could build a wooden porch on the back of our house to hang it from."

Brian just looked at her, and she hurried off to the counter to pay, picking up another couple of items on the way. He caught Tel's look of boredom and they both went outside.

"Cars are good," Mark said. "They have the characters from the *Cars* movie."

They wandered around, admiring the old cars and the new motorbikes, every one of them a Harley Davidson.

The women eventually burst out of the shop, spotted the metal man standing on the porch outside, squealed a bit, and started taking selfies.

"This could take a while," Tel said, as the women moved en masse towards the cars and the motorbikes, huddling to photograph everything – they even got the bikers to pose for them.

Brian watched Faye. Was it his imagination or was she having a lot of fun with the crowd of leather-clad bikers mulling around the tables and chairs? He deliberately dragged his eyes away; he wasn't that man, and Faye had every right to have fun.

Tel looked over at Sophie and thought again how beautiful and elegant she was, and how lucky he was to have her as his wife. She was glorious. He felt a huge wave of pride.

Mark observed Olivia, posing and giggling, and smiled. He thought he'd never been happier.

"Come on!" Brian eventually bellowed, and everyone swivelled their heads towards him, which surprised him a bit. "Let's get back on the road."

The women waved at the bikers and clambered into their seats with their bags of goodies, waving some more as they drove passed.

"Was he there?" Brian couldn't help asking, instantly regretting it.

"Was who there?"

"The cee-gar smoking biker?"

He sensed her turning towards him, but kept his eyes firmly on the road.

"What's got into you, Bri?"

"I …" He shook his head. "I don't know. The heat, maybe? Jet lag, midlife crisis? Just ignore me."

"I will." There was a long moment of silence, broken only when she said, "You know, those leather-clad bikers with skinny white arms poking out of their Metallica t-shirts were all Germans, living the dream on Route 66. Not a real biker among them."

Brian laughed.

* * *

They travelled across mile upon mile of empty desert, until finally they pulled up in the town of Williams.

"Take water with you everywhere," Sophie told them. "Dehydration is a real thing in this heat. And wear sunglasses, unless you want crispy retinas and blindness."

"Yes, mum," Faye said.

"What would we do without you, Sophs?" Mark asked.

"You'd go blind before dying of thirst."

They walked in a group down the high street, where the cars parked at an angle to the kerb, peering into shop windows.

Brian suddenly stopped, his arms outstretched, and cried, "Whoa! This is it! This is *my place*."

They all looked up at the shop name – Western Outfitters.

"Go for it, Bri!"

"Step away, woman," he said, gently pushing Faye aside, "Let the man shop."

Sophie peered through the glass. "It's all very leathery."

"No shiny stuff," Faye said, peering next to her.

"We'll carry on down the road," said Olivia.

Mark grabbed hold of her hand in both of his. "I'll miss you," he cried. "Parting is such sweet sorrow."

"Stop it," she giggled.

"Farewell, my love," Tel called after Sophie. "Miss you already."

"Yeah, whatever."

Brian didn't say anything, he was already inside the shop.

* * *

"Oh, this is the one," Brian said, trying it on for size and finding it small. "Or," he said, putting that one down and picking another from the shelf, "Maybe this one is more me?"

Mark and Tel nodded.

"Really suits you."

"Your head was made for it."

Brian moved over to the mirror and checked himself out. The black leather cowboy hat was the hat he'd wanted since he was twelve years old and playing cowboys and Indians on the streets of Bradford. Bit tight though. He asked the shop assistant for a bigger one and she disappeared into the back.

Mark tried on hats and moved on to view the impressive cowboy boots. Tel was browsing through belt buckles. The assistant came back with Brian's hat and he tried it on. Like Cinderella's slipper, it fit perfectly.

He was just about to say, "I'll take it," when he caught sight of the tiny price tag dangling from the embroidered band. "Thank you," he said instead, handing it back, "I think I might leave it after all."

"What's that?" Tel asked, taking the hat from the assistant. "I thought you were getting this."

"Nah, I'd look daft wearing that in Birmingham."

Tel put the hat on. "I think I might have it then."

"It's way too big for you!"

Tel looked in the mirror. The hat wobbled on his head like a plate on a stick. "I don't like them tight," he said, "My head will be able to breathe in this."

"And invite several other heads to join it."

"No," Tel said, admiring his profile, "I like it."

"It looks like a UFO balancing precariously on your head!"

Tel pulled the chord tight under his chin. "See? Fits perfectly."

Brian felt his bottom lip give a little quiver, then forced a smile and nonchalantly walked off towards the boots, where

Mark engaged him in a discussion about heels or no heels for a man.

"I'll take this," Tel whispered, handing it back to the assistant. He picked another one off the shelf, tried it on in front of the mirror, and handed that to her too.

The assistant smiled and walked towards the counter.

Mark bought an embossed wallet, and Brian got himself a leather money clip for the money he didn't have, hoping it might have an attracting effect on his feeble funds.

* * *

Meanwhile, further down the road, the women had found a shop called Cruise'n on Route 66 that was full of shiny things and were having a whale of a time.

The first thing that caught Faye's eye was a colourfully decorated handbag with a long leather strap. She snatched it up, admiring it, *loving* it.

"That's nice," Sophie said.

"Isn't it. I love the colours, and the little tassels."

"You should get it."

Faye was just breaking out into a huge smile when she noticed the price tag.

She put it down and sulkily went over to where they were looking at colourful not-real cowboy hats. Sophie picked one and said, "You fancy one, Faye?"

"No, no," she said, forcing a smile, "It'll give me flat hair."

Olivia went wild over some embroidered cowgirl tops and picked three really pretty ones.

Faye chose a small dreamcatcher and took it to the counter, where Sophie was paying for three different cowboy hats and the handbag she'd admired earlier. She sighed and tried to think of the lovely caravan they had on their driveway at home, but she hated being broke, especially amongst friends who weren't.

"Here," said Olivia, paying for the tops and pushing one at each of them, "Do you want to be in my gang?"

"Oh Livs, you shouldn't have!"

"Well, I did.  Let's put them on and surprise the men."

As the shop was empty, Sophie immediately pulled off her t-shirt and slipped on the top, tucking it into her trendy shorts and instantly looking like a supermodel.

"Since I don't look like that," Olivia said, stepping behind a curtain at the back of the shop, "I'll take the more modest approach."

"Me, too," said Faye.  "Thanks, Liv."

"No problem, Faye."

\* \* \*

The door to Western Outfitters swung open and three men strode out.  One pulled apart two black cowboy hats. He slipped one onto his own head, the other he thrust into the chest of a tall, wide, bearded man, who looked down and expressed surprise – a hole appeared behind his beard.

"Take it," Tel said, "It was made for you."

Brian, genuinely touched, pulled it on and tilted it forward until the brim shielded his eyes from the sun.  He instantly felt like John Wayne.

Mark wore his Walmart cap.

They put on their sunglasses.

People sitting outside a restaurant on the other side of the road watched as the men turned as one and walked, as if in slow motion, down the pathway.

The door to Cruise'n on Route 66 swung open and three women strode out.  One handed colourful, not-real cowboy hats to the other two.  One woman positioned it on top of her curls, giggling and showing off her cute overbite.  The other looked like she was about to burst into tears as she slowly took the hat and put it on, instantly feeling like Calamity Jane.  They slipped on sunglasses.

"We look like country singers," Olivia giggled.

"Stand by y'man!" Faye wailed.

Olivia started singing *Jolene*.

"Those are absolutely the men Jolene was singing about," Sophie laughed, spotting them and their hats further up the road.

"I'd scratch Jolene's eyes out if she ever came near ma man." Olivia said, staring at Mark in his baseball cap

"I quite like mine," Faye sighed, "I'd fight for him."

"I'd take out a restraining order," Sophie said.

People outside the restaurant turned their eyes from the cowboy-hatted men and stared at the cowboy-hatted and trendily-topped women walking towards them. Long strides, solemn faces; until they met in the middle and started shrieking at one another.

"You look fab!" screeched Sophie.

"You look *incredible!*" said Tel.

Faye gasped, "Oh, Brian."

Brian tipped his hat, and Faye squealed and fanned herself with her hand.

"Hiya, cowgirl," Mark drawled, wrapping his arms around Olivia.

"Hiya, cap-boy."

Brian lifted his nose in the air. "I smell meat," he cried, glancing across the road at a bar and grill opposite that had a red car on its roof. "I could eat."

Still feeling like John Wayne, he held up a giant hand to stop traffic, and they all strode across the road.

There was a uniformed woman with a clipboard standing outside the doors. Brian approached her and, in his best John Wayne accent, honed to near perfection after 30 plus years of watching cowboy films, he said, "We'd sure like a table for six please, ma'am."

The woman looked up – and up – at the giant standing before her, and said, "Of course, sir. Right this way."

"That accent," Mark whispered to Tel, as the woman led them to an outside table, "It's like Yorkshire meets American, has a fight over vowels, with Yorkshire winning hands-down for sheer volume."

They both laughed as they settled around the table.

"What's the etiquette for wearing cowboy hats at the table?" Brian asked, not sure whether to take his off or not; he quite liked wearing it.

Mark quickly thumbed his mobile phone and read, "It is generally considered polite to take it off at a dinner table."

"Gosh darn it," he said, balancing it on the back of his chair, already feeling bereft.

Tel did the same, as did the women, except for Sophie.

"I'm keeping mine on," she said defiantly, "Ain't nobody telling me otherwise."

"Me too," Faye said, quickly putting hers back on to cover her already flattened hair.

Olivia flustered for a moment, then jammed hers back on her head. "Power in unity," she said, giving a little fist pump.

The waitress came with menus. She didn't say anything to the hat-wearers and simply asked what they wanted to drink. They ordered beer, in keeping with their new head apparel.

Brian made grunting noises as he roamed his eyes over the menu. "Starters, no point. Soups and Salads, no thank you very much. Burgers, never again. Ah, the meat!"

"Steak!" four of them declared.

"Steak, Bri?"

Brian glanced at the prices and said, "I'm not as hungry as I thought I was. I think I'll have the fully-loaded baked potato with brisket and pulled pork, that sounds nice."

"What?" said Mark and Tel together.

Brian turned his head to Faye. "You can have steak if you want, love."

"While you sit and eat a spud? I don't think so, Bri."

"No, really, I'm only a little peckish."

Mark laughed. "When have you ever been 'a little peckish'? You're like a human waste disposal unit!"

"It's the heat, kind of takes your appetite away, doesn't it."

"No," said Tel.

The waitress brought over their tray of drinks, set the glasses on the table, and took a notebook and pen out of her pocket. "Are you guys ready to order yet, or do you need a few more minutes."

"Large steaks for the men," Olivia said, thrusting her credit card at the waitress whilst staring unblinkingly across the table at Brian, "Smaller ones for the women, with *all* the extras."

Brian opened his mouth to say something, but Olivia held up a delicate hand. "My treat," she said firmly, "And I don't want to hear another word about it."

"Very firm and stern," Mark said, putting an arm across her shoulders. "I like it."

"Later," she giggled, and the tension evaporated.

The meal was delicious.

* * *

A couple of hours later, almost bursting at the seams with food, they drove onto a small, quiet campsite on the outskirts of town that Etta, Sophie's PA, had booked. Without discussing it, they each pulled up a pitch away from each other, unloading the table and chairs onto the empty space between Brian and Tel's RVs.

Brian dragged out his cool box, opened it, and handed out cans. The women busied themselves with glasses and bottles of Prosecco.

Brian stood up, pulled back his tab and, raising it aloft, said, "Here's to our first proper night alone in America."

They all cheered and lifted their hats.

"So," he said, sitting down, "How much did you two put in the wooden box?"

There was a slight hesitation before Tel said, "A hundred dollars," at the exact same time as Mark said, "Hundred bucks."

"Just to cover our food really," Sophie said.

"Two hundred then?" Brian reached into his jeans pocket for his wallet.

"No," Mark said, shaking his head, "It was for all of us."

"And our share would be … ?" Brian lifted his eyes, trying to calculate. "We'll call it seventy dollars."

"Honestly, Bri," Sophie urged, "Keep your money, it … it came out of the kitty."

"But we only put two hundred pounds each into the kitty."

"Yes, but … that's what it's for, miscellaneous items. Everything else is paid for."

"Everything?"

"Yes."

"Are you sure?"

"Yes."

"Okay, if you say so." He slowly put his wallet back in his pocket, frowning. "Did you invest in their film?"

"Might have," Tel said.

"How much?"

"Bit rude to ask, Bri. I tend not to talk about personal investments, but a five percent return on profits is a pretty good deal."

"Fair enough." Brian turned to Mark, who said, "I'm still thinking about it."

Olivia, sensing discomfort in the group, gave a little splutter and said, "How's your new caravan, Faye?"

"Oh, it's lovely," she gushed. "Everything's so new; the wood wallpaper on the doors – "

"Laminate," said Brian.

" – is all smooth and uncracked, the blinds don't fall off the windows, the cooker works, the bathroom *with* shower is *a-mazing*, and there's so much cupboard space."

"For Faye to stock all her emergency supplies," Brian laughed. "Was that an inflatable dingy I saw you pushing into one of the top cupboards the other day?"

"No, of course not. It was a blow-up paddling pool."

"For?"

"People to paddle in when it gets hot."

"Essential camping equipment," Brian mocked.

"Wish we had it here, I'd throw myself in."

"Haven't had a chance to use it yet," Brian said, "But I think we got a bargain, it looks like new, there's no wear or tear anywhere, and it's got *motor movers*!"

"Brilliant," Tel said.

"Neighbour chap came over for a look when I brought it home," Brian added, already starting to laugh. "We don't get on, he's a bit of a moaner, but he couldn't resist comparing our caravan to his. He says to me, 'Why is your hook-up cable blue?' It came with the caravan, just a normal cable, but I said – "

"Oh this is funny!" Faye cut in.

" – 'It supplies everything; electrics, t'internet, mobile phone network, Satellite TV, Netflix.' He looked a bit put out and rushed back to his house, and I knew, *I knew*, he was on Amazon looking for a blue hook-up cable." He roared with laughter. "Still tickles me now."

"You'll have to bring it to the Woodsman to show it off," Olivia said.

"We will, first chance we get."

Olivia turned to Sophie and said, "I've been dying to ask, did that gorgeous man and beautiful woman at your wedding get together in the end?"

"Oh, Lucas and Annie?"

"Did they ever!" Tel gasped.

"It was like a nuclear explosion," said Sophie. "Lucas, lovely man, but he only previously dated … what would you call them, Tel?"

"Airheads? Bimbos?"

"Cruel, but accurate. He was a serial monogamist – "

"We're monogamous, aren't we, Bri?"

"I certainly hope so, lass."

"Are we serial monogamists?"

He turned his head towards her. "Only if you're talking about cornflakes."

"A serial monogamist is where somebody has brief

relationships one after another," Sophie explained.

"Oh, that's not us," Faye declared, furiously swishing her fan.

"Thank God for that!" said Brian. "You had me worried for a minute there."

"Don't be daft, Bri, where would I find the time, or the energy?" Despite it being cooler, Faye frantically fanned her face and spritzed with cooling mist, pulling on her cotton blouse. "I'm never going to get used to this heat!"

Sophie glanced at Olivia, then leaned forward in her chair and said, very softly, "Faye, do you think it might not be the heat?"

"I'm sweating buckets, Sophs, of course it's the heat."

"Yes, but …" She glanced at Olivia again. "Do you think it might be … something else?"

"Is she ill?" Brian quickly asked.

"No, it's just … "

"Spit it out, Sophs."

Another look at Olivia, then she braced herself and said, "Me and Livs had a quick chat, not behind your back or anything, we just felt sorry for you and wondered why you were suffering from the heat so much when we're … not. We were just concerned."

"About?"

"Your hot flushes."

"They're not *flushes*," Faye said, lifting her chin to fan at her neck, "It's one constant explosion of hotness."

Sophie leaned back in her chair and looked pleadingly at Olivia, who leaned forward in hers and said, "We love you very much, Faye."

"Sounds ominous."

"And this is said out of love."

Everyone was leaning forward in their chair now. Olivia knew she should just spit it out. It was like holding an unexploded bomb in her mouth.

She took a deep breath and said, "Do you think you might

be going through the menopause, Faye?"

Brian gasped out loud in both surprise and horror and slowly stood up, ostensibly to get another can from the cool box but mainly because his fight-or-flight response had kicked in. The men shifted awkwardly in their seats. Olivia fidgeted, and Sophie looked down at her glass, shielding her face with the brim of her colourful hat.

There was a long moment of silence. Faye's expression didn't change. She stared poker-faced, first at Olivia, and then at Sophie. She said, "Don't be daft, I'm not old enough for that!"

She looked up at Brian, who looked back at her in restrained dread. "Brian?"

"Yes, my love?"

"Do you think I'm going through the menopause?"

They all heard him gulp. "Well, there have been one or two incidents."

"You're not going to mention the flying clock again, are you?"

"No, no, too scared now." He attempted a laugh, but it was dry and it ended in a cough. "You have been a bit … tetchy of late, love."

"You're very tetch-inducing, Bri."

"True, but I can't remember the last time you filled the dishwasher without using extreme violence. It's almost a Ninja attack. We always seem to be buying crockery and glasses at the supermarket, and I fear for the solidity of our doorframes at home, you're constantly slamming doors, quite impressively for a woman of your stature."

Faye glared at him. Even though he didn't want to, *really* didn't want to, his mouth carried on without his permission. "And sometimes, Faye, you have brief bouts of … senseless ranting."

Faye stood up, mouth tight, eyes furious. Brian took a step back, Tel and Mark shuffled uncomfortably in their seats. Olivia and Sophie chewed on their nails, wondering if they should have said anything at all.

"I am *not* old enough!" she snapped.

"Of course not, love."

She spun round to Sophie, who recoiled in her chair. "I'm not old enough!"

"No, no, we weren't saying that, Faye, we were just worried about your constant sweating."

Olivia quickly nodded.

"It couldn't possibly be the menopause," Faye said, "I've got *years* left yet."

She collapsed back down in her seat and dropped her head into her hands. Sophie and Olivia were at her feet in seconds, holding her as she sobbed. "I can't be that old already. It's gone so quickly. It's all *his* fault," she snapped, looking up at Brian, who pressed himself against the side of the RV, crushing the can in his hand. "Time goes so fast when you're enjoying yourself."

Brian relaxed, stepped forward and put a hand on her shoulder. "We'll get through this, lass, don't you worry."

"Together?" she sniffed.

"Of course together. I'm not going anywhere, hormone hell or not."

"It might not be hell. Some women sail through it without any symptoms." She frantically fanned herself.

"Of course, love. We'll just take it as it comes."

"I don't want to be old!" she wailed, and Olivia and Sophie hugged her tightly. "There's loads of things I haven't done yet!"

"You're not dying, woman, you could just be going through a short interlude of … "

"Recalibration?" Tel suggested.

"Changing direction," Mark shrugged.

"But I don't want to change direction, I like the direction I'm in!"

"Faye!" Brian boomed.

"What? Are you leaving me? Have you been building up the courage to tell me?"

"Get a grip, woman."

"I can't! I'm *hormonal!*"

"You might not be, in which case this is a terrible display of … " He couldn't think of a word that wouldn't have her screaming or crying, so left it hanging in the air. Tel and Mark said nothing, this wasn't their scene at all. "It'll be fine, Faye," he said, sitting down again and putting an arm across her shoulders. Sophie and Olivia shuffled back to their seats. "Absolutely fine."

There was an awkward moment of silence as Faye composed herself and started swishing the fan again. To break it, Brian looked at Olivia and said, "How's the Cotswold campsite going?"

"It's going well."

"Good, good." He pleaded at her with his eyes.

"It rained for most of the school summer holiday, the kids went feral, running around and breaking things. It was like *Lord of the Flies.*" She gave a tinkly laugh. "The parents just hunkered down in their tents and caravans, trying very hard to kill the pain of parenting with copious amounts of alcohol."

"Sounds pretty standard," Brian laughed, "Doesn't it, Faye?"

"What?"

"Kids going wild at campsites."

"Yeah."

"Talking to the parents did no good," Olivia continued, "They were either drunk or hungover, so I left it with Chelsea, the manager, to sort out, and she did. She was brilliant. Every night at nine o'clock she'd open the upstairs window in the pub and yell at the wildlings through a megaphone: 'OI, BRATS, BE IN YOUR BEDS IN TEN MINUTES OR I'M RELEASING THE DOGS, AND THEY *EAT* CHILDREN.' She was so good, she should be on the stage, even I was scared. She'd shout, 'YOU HAVE FIVE MINUTES TO FIND SAFETY WHILE YOU STILL CAN!' and then she'd pause for a few seconds and scream, 'THEY'RE FREE! THE DOGS ARE FREE! SAVE YOURSELVES! THEY'RE COMING!'"

They laughed at Olivia's dramatic recreation.

"Some of the parents came into the pub as they were leaving and shook Chelsea's hand, asked if she'd ever consider becoming a nanny. She told them she'd rather train wild tigers. They thought she was joking. She wasn't, she's not fond of children."

"There's never a dull moment, is there, Livs."

"Oh," she cried, on a roll now, talking about her favourite subject, the place where it had all started and where her new life had begun, "We had travellers invade the campsite a couple of weeks ago."

"Oh yeah," said Mark. "About twenty of them."

"No!" Sophie gasped, "What happened?"

"They came in the night and must have just lifted up the barrier. We woke up in the morning and there they were, spread out across the field. We waited a couple of days to see if they'd move on again, but they didn't, really seemed to settle in for the long haul. We tried talking to them but they weren't interested. All our campers left and we had to cancel the bookings for the rest of the week *and* the week after, just in case. The police couldn't do anything because they said it was private property and a civil matter. All the neighbours were sending me stern letters saying they were concerned about the state of their house prices."

"One of the travellers actually came into the pub and asked for ten grand to leave, can you believe it?" Mark said

"Did you pay them?"

"No," Olivia giggled, "I don't give away money anymore, not since I broke up with Richard. We were a bit naughty though."

"How naughty?" Brian grinned behind his beard.

"*Really* naughty."

"Do tell."

Olivia looked at Mark. He grinned and said, "We hired bikers from the local scrambling club, you know, the ones that came and terrorised us."

"No!" Faye cried, now out of her funk.

"You didn't!" Tel laughed.

"We did. There's more of them now and they did two shifts, 2am and 4am, every night for three nights."

"The travellers were properly cross," Olivia continued. "They even came into the pub to complain about it!"

"The cheek!" said Faye.

"When that didn't work someone, who shall remain nameless – "

Mark stared up at the sky and started whistling.

" – took pot shots at their caravans at night with a paintball gun."

"They set the dogs on me," Mark gasped, "Never run so fast in my life."

"They were furious and came up to the pub to complain again. I said to them, 'Why is this my problem? If you don't like it, leave!'"

"And did they?"

"No."

"We think," said Mark, "one of the neighbours got fed up with them and started plinking a pellet gun at their caravans. It didn't go through or anything, but it left a dint."

"They *really* didn't like that," Olivia said. "Told me it was criminal damage and they'd sue. I told them to go ahead. I also told them that the locals didn't take kindly to strangers, and there were a few 'unstables' amongst them who were capable of *anything*, and that one of them, a farmer with a trigger-happy finger, owned a shotgun and wasn't afraid to use it. They left the next morning, just drove passed the pub in their dented, multi-coloured caravans without so much as a wave or a thank you. I've put up a proper gate on the entrance of the camping field now with number plate recognition, and some cameras and an alarm, so hopefully that'll keep them out."

Mark crossed his fingers and they smiled and nodded at each other.

Sophie's phone rang. "Sorry," she said, glancing at the

screen and getting up, "I have to take this."

She walked off. They couldn't hear what she was saying but they caught the harsh tone of her voice when she snapped, "No!" and "Absolutely not!"

"Her work voice," Tel grinned.

"She win many cases with that voice?" Brian asked.

Tel nodded. "Almost all of them, including the odd one at home."

"Brave man."

"Lucky man."

Sophie came back, all smiles. "Work stuff," she said, rolling her eyes, "It's a hard life."

Eventually Tel stood up and stretched. "Much as I enjoy your company," he yawned, "I think we might have an early night."

"Big day tomorrow," Mark said, getting up. Everyone jerked their heads towards him and he quickly added, "The Grand Canyon."

But Faye had caught the looks, and a tiny smile played on her lips. They all knew.

Brian hadn't forgotten after all.

She suddenly felt a bit better.

* * *

Brian tentatively crawled into the sleeping bag on the platform above the cab, hoping it would hold him. The man at the hire place had asked him his weight and, of course, he'd lied, because when people asked him how heavy he was, being a big chap, and he told them, they generally sucked in air and looked him up and down in amazement or horror ("Do you have a cast iron skeleton?" someone had once asked). He'd nonchalantly asked what the maximum weight was for the platform and, when told, hoped a few extra pounds wouldn't make any difference; it was only the equivalent of six bags of sugar.

He lay down slowly, gently. Nothing gave way beneath

him and nothing cracked. He relaxed. The bed held.

He cuddled up to Faye and started whispering sweet nothings in her ear. She giggled.

"Oi!" Mark shouted.

"*What*?" yelled Brian, "I'm *busy*!"

"We know. You might want to shut your skylight there, mate."

"Jealous?" Brian mocked, quickly adding, "Not of my wife, of course."

"What's that supposed to mean?" Faye snapped.

"We can take them," Olivia whispered to Mark, and started moaning and stifling her giggles at the same time.

In the other RV, Sophie started groaning, interspersed with snorts of muffled laughter.

Brian, grinning, put a hand on the wall and started rocking the motorhome, shouting, "Oh! Oh! Oh!"

"Argh!" cried Sophie.

"Aaah," yelled Olivia.

Faye could barely breathe for laughing.

When the men started howling like wolves Brian bellowed, "Okay, that's enough now, I have a wife to take care of."

They stopped and heard, from the other parts of the campsite, people groaning and moaning and laughing. Eventually that stopped too, and all was silent again.

Except for the sound of multiple skylights slowly being closed.

# CHAPTER NINE

**Day 4**

The sun was barely up when Faye woke and found Brian and the others sitting outside at a collection of tables laden with coffee mugs, sauce bottles, and a huge plate of toast.

"Made you a coffee," Brian said, pointing at a mug next to him.

"Oh?" Faye grinned. "That's nice of you. Any particular reason? Any *special* reason?"

"I was up first. Whoever's up first always makes the coffee."

"Oh."

"Full English breakfast in five minutes," Olivia shouted from her RV.

"Smells delicious," Brian boomed.

"What's the occasion?" Faye asked, trying to sound casual.

"I haven't cooked in days," Olivia replied, "I was having withdrawal symptoms."

"Oh. Well, before we eat, Brian, I have something for you." She pulled up the bag she was carrying and took out a wrapped block of something.

"What's this?" he asked, taking it from her.

"Open it and see."

He pulled off the wrapping. It was the newest hardback book of his favourite author.

"There's something inside it," Faye said, and he opened it up to reveal a metallic bookmark with his name engraved in it. "It's not real silver," she said, "It's plated, I think, *silver* plated."

"Thanks very much," he said. "You don't normally wrap my books up, you generally just lob them at me as you come in from shopping."

Faye's smile faltered a little, but she carried on. "These," she said, taking envelopes from the bag, "Are from our kids, our friends, and our family."

"Oh?" said Brian. "Why are they sending us cards?"

"Brian!"

"What? It's a perfectly reasonable question."

The others sat at the table, pretending not to listen, except Olivia, who kept popping her head out the door as she cooked.

"You've forgotten, haven't you," said Faye.

"Forgotten what, lass?"

"It's our twenty-fifth wedding anniversary today, Bri. Twenty-five years!"

"Is it?"

"Oh Brian!"

"Before you burst into tears," he said, taking her hands in his, "I haven't forgotten."

"You have!"

Brian looked across at Mark. "Have I forgotten?"

"No, you didn't forget, Bri."

"Tel?"

"He's mentioned it a few dozen times."

"He has," Sophie agreed.

"Definitely hasn't forgotten," Olivia shouted from inside.

"Really?"

"Aye. I have a surprise for you later."

"Do you, Bri?"

"Yes, love."

"Did you get me a card, too?"

"No," said Brian, "I forgot the card, it's in a drawer at home."

"We got you one though," Sophie said, pushing an envelope across the table. "Happy anniversary to you both."

"A nicer couple there never was," Tel said.

Mark plonked his card down on the table and raised his coffee mug. Olivia stood beaming in the doorway, wiping her hands on a towel, and said, "Congratulations! What do you get for twenty-five years anyway?"

"A medal," said Brian, "And a letter from the King saying 'bloody well done'."

"Silver," Faye said, glaring at her husband. "What's the surprise?"

"I can't tell you."

"Is it nice?"

"I think you'll like it."

"It's not a silk scarf that I'll never wear, is it?"

"No, it's better than that, *much* better."

Faye turned to the others. "Do you know what it is?"

They all nodded, not daring to say anything else, just smiling.

Brian and Faye hugged. They all *ahhed*.

"Twenty-five years is quite an achievement," said Tel, "I hope Sophie and I make it that far."

"We will," Sophie said, and Tel thought he could detect a hint of teeth-gnashing determination in her voice. "I'm certainly never getting married again."

"Good to hear."

Olivia hurried down the steps of the RV with something in a fancy paper bag. "This is from me and Sophie. Forgot to buy wrapping paper," she giggled, "And sticky tape, *and* a gift tag."

Brian nodded at the paper bag. "Open it up then, lass. If we're lucky it might be pancakes."

"It's a bit bigger than a couple of pancakes, Bri."

"Could be enough for all of us, two each."

Faye excitedly opened the bag. "Oh!" she cried, taking out the beautiful handbag she'd admired in the shop yesterday, the one Sophie had bought. "You sneakies! You shouldn't have! I love it!" She clutched it tightly to her chest. Olivia and Sophie smiled at each other. *"Love it!"*

"I haven't bought anything," Mark said, "Have you, Tel?"

"No."

"It's from all of us," Sophie said.

Faye turned the bag this way and that, and gasped, "Thank you *so* much."

"With love," Olivia added, jumping up into her RV and shouting, "Lovely couple, lovely friends."

"Hear, hear," Mark and Tel said together.

"It's okay," Brian said, deadpan, as he sipped at his coffee mug and stared off across the campsite. "I wasn't expecting anything anyway. The man is always side-lined, forgotten, taken for – "

"Nice shirt and shorts you're wearing there, Bri," said Mark.

"Excellent cowboy hat," said Tel.

Brian plucked it from the back of his camping chair and slipped it onto his head, immediately feeling like a wild west cowboy. "Point taken," he said, "Ta very much."

"Phwoar," Faye laughed.

"Phwoar yourself, woman."

They kissed. Nobody *bleurghed.*

"Happy anniversary, lass."

"Happy anniversary, Bri."

"We're going to spoil you both all day," Olivia called out from the RV.

"And you're not to object to anything," said Sophie, smiling at Faye. The smile suddenly fell off her face. "Oh my God!" she gasped.

"What? Have I come out in a rash or something?"

"I have an extra present for you, Faye. You're really, *really* going to like it."

"But you've already bought me so – "

"I haven't bought this. This is free, and completely amazing."

Faye eyes widened. The others all stared at Sophie,

equally intrigued.

"Faye," Sophie whispered with a grin, "Faye, you're not fanning yourself or spraying yourself with cooling mist. You're not … *red in the face or sweating*!"

Faye stared at her empty hands, bereft of fan or can. Her palms were dry and so was her face. "OH MY GOD!" she screamed, checking her pits and the bits under her boobs, all dry, "I've acclimatised! I can't believe it! I've finally got used to the heat!"

"Well done, Faye!"

"Thanks, it was nothing."

"So, ignore everything we said last night," Olivia giggled, putting fry-up breakfast plates in front of them. "You're not menopausal after all."

"Not yet," Brian grunted, sawing into a sausage, "But I've had a taster and I'm not sure I'm going to like it."

"I might ignore it completely and take up drinking instead," said Faye.

"Hang on," Brian added, pausing with his fork of sausage, "If you're not menopausal, what's with all the rage with the dishwasher?"

"I like to see how fast I can load it."

"By lobbing everything in from the other side of the kitchen?"

"No, just quickly."

"And the door slamming?"

"That door sticks, I've been asking you to sand it down for ages."

"No, you … oh, I have a vague memory. First on my to-do list when we get home."

"Now open your cards and brace yourself for some really gooey stuff," Mark said. "Sick bags are available upon request."

\* \* \*

With everything cleared away, they drove to the on-site dump station, which was to become their daily ritual, and set off early to beat the rush.

"I'll drive," Olivia said.

"You sure?"

"Yes, since you already appear to be sitting in the passenger seat."

"Someone keeps moving the steering wheel."

"Should I drive?" Sophie asked Tel.

"I'd rather you didn't."

"I'm an excellent driver."

"You're not."

"You're not driving," Brian firmly told Faye before she could say anything. She pulled a face, but secretly she was pleased; everything was on the wrong side over here, she'd never cope.

"WAGONS ROLL!" Brian cried.

He pulled out of the campsite and onto the road. Tel and Sophie followed.

Olivia had just turned to follow when a black car suddenly appeared right behind them and sat irately on its horn.

"Oh!" Olivia cried, and pulled over, mostly out of shock.

There was a gentle bump as the car nudged into the back of their van. Two young men immediately leapt out and started yelling as they approached.

Mark and Olivia clambered out. "I'm terribly sorry," Olivia began, "I just didn't – "

The two men, one tall like a sapling, the other short and round like a ball, began swearing profusely, going red in the face and jabbing fingers in her direction.

"Hey!" Mark cried, "Don't talk to her like that, it wasn't her fault!"

"Whose fault was it then? She pulled out *right in front of us.*"

"I just didn't see you. I'm so – "

"You were driving too fast!" Mark said.

"Are you trying to blame us? You're not even American.

Don't they have roads where you come from? Do you even know how to drive?"

The skinny bloke, who seemed to have the loudest voice and the greatest rage, started wagging his finger in Olivia's distraught face, swearing and spitting and waving his free arm around in a menacing manner. Mark was about to lunge towards him when Brian and Tel came running down the road.

"Hey, hey!" Brian gasped, "Let's all calm down."

The two men were briefly silenced by the size of the big, hairy man bearing down on them. When he came to a puffed stop, they both glared up at him.

"Great, another foreigner on our roads."

"I'm not foreign," Brian said, "I'm *British*."

Tel ran to the back of the Olivia's RV to inspect the damage. "There's nothing broken," he called back, "Not even a scratch. I think it's more of a bump than a crash."

"It wasn't a full-on impact," Mark said.

"Yes it was!" the skinny man yelled.

"We could have died!" snarled the other. "It was only Burt's quick reflections on the brakes that saved our lives."

"There's no 'arm done," Brian said. "Nobody got 'urt, that's the main thing."

The men glared at him. "Where the hell are you from?"

"Yorkshire." The word boomed around them. "Born and bred."

"Can't even speak proper English," the round man snapped.

"We *are* English!"

"You drive on the wrong side of the road! You shouldn't be allowed to drive in this country, you ain't good at it, especially *her*!"

"Oi!" Mark snarled. "Keep your bloody fingers to yourself!"

"Let's not get carried away, lads, it was just a little bump."

"How do we know she ain't broken our ... manifold?" the skinny man snarled.

"The manifold?" Brian repeated, frowning. "Do you even know what a manifold is?"

"It's the thing at the front of the engine and it could be damaged."

"T'radiator is at front of engine, and since there was no actual impact I very much doubt there's any – "

"But you don't know that! There could be hidden damage, couldn't there, Lee."

The chubby man furiously nodded his head.

"We'll need some cash to cover any future repairs."

"You what?" Mark gasped.

"We want money, and we want it now!"

"Maybe we should inform the police?" Olivia said to Mark.

"No police," said the skinny man, "We ain't got time to wait around for the cops to turn up, we can deal with this ourselves. Call it two hundred bucks."

"We'll call it a slap round the back of the head for your cheek!" Brian boomed.

"Are you threatening me?"

"It's not a threat."

"He is, he's threatening you, Burt!"

Tel, who was still at the back of the RV checking out the vehicles, said, "Isn't this a rental car?"

"Is it?" said the round man.

"It's got barcode stickers in the windows, just like our rental vans."

"It's an *ex*-rental."

"Just give us some money so we can be on our way," said the skinny bloke, "We ain't got time to be talking about this all day, just hand over some cash."

Brian crossed his bulging arms across his chest and peered down at them both. "Are you trying to scam us?" he grunted.

"How dare you accuse us of that!"

"It was all *her* fault and we want compensating!"

"For?" Tel asked, joining them.

"Our distress and inconvenience," said the chubby guy. "I'm traumatised, we could have died. If it weren't for Burt's – "

"Yes, you've said," said Tel. "I'm a lawyer and I can tell you, from a legal perspective, that you don't have a leg to stand on. You hit the back of the van, you were entirely to blame."

"And a Grand Cherokee seems quite a nice car for a couple of young'uns like you." Brian glared down at them. "I don't know what you're up to but I have a pretty good idea. Best you clear off before we do call the police."

There followed some swearing, some fist shaking and some close eyeball contact, before the men finally gave up and stomped back to their car. They pulled away in a cloud of dust, extending fingers as they passed, and roared off down the road.

Olivia was gently crying. Mark pulled her into his arms, saying, "Don't upset yourself, Livs, it wasn't your fault."

Faye and Sophie came hurrying down the road; Sophie sprinting like a weightless gazelle, Faye holding onto her gloriously braless but now dangerously bouncing boobs.

Brian said, "Let's carry on," and started walking back to their RV.

"I just got here!" Faye puffed, patting Olivia's arm before turning and gripping onto her boobs again.

"You okay, Livs?" Sophie asked.

"Yes, I'm fine. Quite a shock. I can't drive now, Mark."

"You can and you will, straight back on the horse. You're an excellent driver, don't let a couple of rednecks put you off. Besides, it's only an hour up the road. I have every faith in you. Other drivers," he muttered, staring off up the road, "Not so much."

"We'd better get a move on," Sophie said, jogging backwards to catch up with Tel, "We have a full day of excitement ahead. Don't let this spoil anything, Livs."

Olivia got back behind the wheel, took a deep breath, and nervously drove on.

A short while later a police car with its lights flashing and its siren whooping sped passed them.

"Typical," Mark sighed, "Never around when you need them."

They could still hear the whoop-whooping as they turned left and headed north on the 64.

\* \* \*

The journey up to the Grand Canyon was uneventful and scenic; seemingly endless miles of scrubby, dry desert with a backdrop of gently rolling hills, a glorious blue sky, and the grey silhouettes of distant mountains. Up ahead, the single peak of a mountain sat dead centre of the arrow-straight road, like a beacon urging them towards it.

They saw dust devils running alongside and stopped to watch them, hoping they didn't turn into tornados. They saw rain falling from a solitary cloud far, far away, the odd cabin, the odd trailer, a tiny airport, motels and entrances to ranches that couldn't be seen. The shrubs slowly turned into trees.

"Must be tough living out here," Tel said.

"Doubt they do Ocado deliveries this far out," laughed Sophie.

And then a traffic island into Tusayan. Olivia navigated her way round on the right side, screaming a single note interspersed with nervous laughter the entire time, as Mark said, "Right, stay right."

"I am!"

In the front vehicle, Faye said, "So many American flags everywhere."

"They're very patriotic."

"I'm going to put the British flag on our back porch."

"What back porch?"

"The porch you're going to build on the back of our house when we get home."

"Am I indeed."

"Indeed you are," she laughed. "What's the surprise?"

"Not telling you."

They drove through the town without stopping, with Brian singing along to his Alan Jackson CD.

In the second RV, Sophie was singing along to a Shania Twain song. Tel was laughing because Sophie couldn't hold a note to save her life, but he enjoyed her enthusiasm, if not her wailing.

In the last RV, Mark sang along to the chorus of *Convoy* playing on the radio. He tensed a little as the two vans in front traversed another traffic island, but Olivia didn't scream this time.

"You look like a very sexy truck driver," he grinned.

She giggled.

As they passed the Grand Canyon National Park sign they all waved their fists in the air outside their windows, whooping.

"Never thought I'd see the day," Faye sighed. "This is so exciting. What's the surprise?"

"Wait and see."

They hit three lanes of traffic waiting to pay to go into the national park. Sophie's voice crackled over the walkie talkies. "I bought the digital entrance passes online, so we can go straight through."

They drove on, and on.

"Where is it?" Faye cried, sitting up straight in her seat. "I don't see it."

"Patience, wife, it's out there somewhere."

"Where? It's like that time we toured Scotland and couldn't find Hadrian's Wall."

Brian laughed. "Yeah, it's only seventy-odd miles long, you wouldn't think it was that difficult, would you."

"Never did find it."

"I think the Grand Canyon might be easier to spot."

"Hopefully by not driving head first into it, like *Thelma and Louise*."

Brian scoured the road signs, trying to figure out where to park. He followed the arrows to the RV parking and pulled up, the others pulling up beside him.

Faye was out of the cab in a flash, spinning around, looking everywhere. "Where is it? Where is it?"

"Follow the crowds," Sophie called over.

"They could all be going to the toilet en masse," Tel laughed, "You know what women are like."

"Oh funny!"

"I'm here all week."

They followed the throngs, all heading in the same direction. Faye was slightly ahead of the others, urging the people in front to go faster. She couldn't remember the last time she'd felt so excited. She never thought she would ever actually visit America and see, with her very own eyes, the Grand Canyon.

Brian watched his wife scurrying like an impatient mouse and smiled to himself. He hoped very much that she would like his surprise.

And then, finally, it was there. They all came to a sudden stop, as did several people around them, as the utter vastness of the canyon they had only peeked at through the trees suddenly came into full view. They could hardly take it in. It was *enormous*, the most impressive thing they'd ever seen.

Faye kept gasping, "Wow! *Wow!*"

Brian said, "Bit bigger than Cheddar Gorge."

"This makes Cheddar Gorge look like a crack in the pavement," said Tel, his eyes wide and unmoving from the scene in front of him.

They walked on, heads turned, hardly able to tear their eyes away.

"I can't believe I'm here," Faye kept saying.

Mark glanced back at Brian. Tel glanced back at Brian. Brian surveyed the people around him and thought, 'Too many. Not yet.' He briefly shook his head.

A crowd came down a pathway to the left, most of them blindfolded, being led by others who weren't. They were slowly taken to a railed viewing area and their blindfolds removed. They all gasped. People around them clapped.

"Oh, how lovely," Olivia said. "What a surprise for them!"

"What's my surprise, Bri?"

"Not telling you, Faye."

"Tiny clue?"

"No."

"At least tell me *when*, I'm on tenterhooks."

"Soon."

"How soon?"

"Sooner than tomorrow."

"Brian!"

"Patience, lass."

A short while later he saw it, the perfect spot. An empty viewing area jutting out over the canyon with a rail around it, so he wouldn't inadvertently topple off and Faye wouldn't fling herself over the edge when she realised what she was letting herself in for. He looked at Mark, who looked at Tel, and they both nodded. They stood in a line behind him and Faye, waiting and smiling.

Faye still had her eyes rivetted on the canyon. It was beautiful. Magnificent. A million times better than what she had ever imagined. The colours. The light. The sheer size of it.

"Faye."

She saw a bird swooping elegantly below. Its high-pitched whistle echoed off the rocks. Was that an eagle, an American eagle?

"Faye."

She peered at the river winding through the canyon so far below, the sun glinting off the water.

"*Faye!*"

"What?" Were those buildings at the bottom? Were those people walking down that long, long path? Were they completely insane in this heat?

"*FAYE!*" Brian bellowed, drowning out the sound of the eagle and making several people turn to look at them, which he'd been hoping to avoid.

Finally, Faye tore he eyes away and turned around, to find Brian down on one knee.

"Oh, Brian, what are you doing down there? Have you fallen? Is your back playing up again?"

"It wasn't," he said. "Is now." He held up a small, velvet box. "Faye," he said softly, "You've been my wife for twenty-five years and I've loved every minute of it. Well, not *every* minute, there was that brief phase when – "

"Brian!" Tel hissed.

"Yes, sorry, nervous."

Faye stood with her hands at her face, her mouth partially open.

"Anyway," Brian continued, looking strangely anxious, "Faye, I want to tell you, I love you very much, I've always loved you and I always will. You're a lovely wife and mother, a kind woman, generous to a fault, which is why we're probably broke all the time. We've had many adventures together and I look forward to sharing many more. Faye," he said, and Faye made a tiny squeaking sound, "Do you think that you would agree to be my wife for another twenty-five years? I promise to love you, honour you, and make you laugh at every opportunity."

Faye burst into tears. Brian, horrified, and with his knee really starting to hurt now, looked back at Tel. "Is that a yes, do y'think?"

"Oh Brian!" Faye cried, bending to hug his head.

"'Ave a look inside the box before you decide, you might change your mind."

"Way to build up expectation, Bri," Mark laughed.

Faye delicately took it from his fingers and opened it up. She expected to see a silver ring, or a silver brooch, even though people didn't tend to wear brooches any more, or maybe silver earrings, or ... what else was made of silver?

She looked. She saw. She gasped, "Brian, you can't afford this!"

"I can, love."

"No, it's too much." Still shocked, she pulled the gold

ring with a cluster of tiny diamonds from the box. It sparkled brilliantly in the sun.

"Don't drop it!" Sophie said under her breath.

"Are these … real diamonds?" Faye asked.

"They are, love. I couldn't buy you the engagement ring you deserved way back then, thought you deserved it more than ever now, having put up with me for so long. You're the best wife a man could have, and you make me really, really happy."

"How can you afford something like this, Bri?"

"I think the more important question is, do you want to spend the next twenty-five years with daft old me. We'll be into our seventies by then, like, but I promise not to fart too much or clack my false teeth while you're trying to watch *Coronation Street*."

Everyone looked at Faye, who was staring at the diamonds sparkling in her fingers.

"I know it might be a difficult decision to make," Brian said, "And I understand your hesitation, but a quick nod would put me out of my crushed knee misery. Unless, of course, the answer is no."

Quite a few people had gathered around them by now, watching and waiting and smiling.

"Oh Bri," Faye cried again, and Brian fervently hoped she wasn't about to make a run for it, or leap off the edge of the rock to escape another twenty-five years of purgatory. Then she said, "Of course I will, Brian. I couldn't imagine life without you, you're my rock and my best friend."

She went to put the ring on, when Olivia whispered, "Wrong hand, Faye."

"No," she said, "I'm not replacing my real engagement ring, it holds a lot of memories far more precious than diamonds."

"Did I waste my money then?" Brian asked, struggling to his feet.

"No, no, jewellery and holidays abroad are excellent

gifts." She jumped up to wrap her arms around his neck. "You're an excellent husband, Brian Bennett, and I'm glad I'm your wife."

"Excellent, eh? Does that mean I'll have to give up all the mistresses now?"

"Obvs."

"Fair enough."

The crowd around them clapped and cheered. Both Sophie and Olivia wiped away tears. Tel looked up at the sky to dry his up, and Mark bit his bottom lip, which hurt and brought even more tears to his eyes. Sophie briefly thought about rushing forward to hug them both, but they were dangerously close to the edge, poled barrier or no poled barrier, and she didn't want to risk killing them both in their big moment. She waited for them to step towards them, and they all indulged in a group hug, the women crying, the men remaining stoic, blinking a lot.

The women put their hands together, displaying their various engagement rings. It was like an explosion of bright light in the sunshine.

"Together we can dazzle the world," Sophie cried.

"Girl power!" Olivia squealed.

"Paid for by men," Mark laughed.

"We'll give you some time to yourselves," Sophie said, gripping Tel's hand and starting to walk away.

Olivia glanced at her watch and said, "We'll meet back here in ninety minutes, okay? I have a surprise for you all."

"Oooh," said Faye, "Another surprise? What is it?"

"I can't tell you."

"Why not?"

Olivia shrugged. "Because it's a surprise."

"I've already had one surprise today, I'm not sure if I can stand the anticipation of another. Just tell me." She stepped closer to Olivia with her ear turned.

"Don't tell her," Brian said, "She's terrible at keeping secrets."

"I am not!"

"I always know what I'm getting for Christmas and birthdays because Faye's told me at least three times beforehand."

"Did you know about the book I gave you this morning?" she retorted.

"No. Did you forget about it?"

She looked sheepish, then nodded.

"I rest my case."

"Probably best not to eat too much before this surprise," Olivia winked.

"Intrigued," said Brian.

"Excited," Faye beamed.

They wandered off for to marvel at their surroundings. Brian and Faye stood on the viewing platform, arm in arm, looking at each other and smiling. Faye looked down at her ring again. It felt strange and heavy on her finger.

"I had no idea," she said.

"You like it then?"

"You shouldn't have, Bri."

"Wanted to."

"It's far too expensive."

"You're worth it."

"How could you afford it?"

"Not telling."

"You didn't get a *loan*, did you?"

"You're speaking to a Yorkshireman here who believes if you can't afford it, you can't have it."

"So how – ?"

"Just enjoy it, love."

She looked at the ring again. "It's beautiful."

"Good, glad you like it."

"I still love my other ring, despite it being a can tab and shiny glass prised from the headlights of toy cars."

Brian stared at her. "What?"

"It has a lot of sentimental value, twenty-five years'

worth."

"A can tab?"

She nodded. "You said your mate did it for you at the steel factory."

"We cut great beams of steel for buildings, Faye, we don't sit around gently tapping out delicate pieces of jewellery."

"Oh."

"You think the original engagement ring is a can tab and toy car headlights?"

"That's what you told me when you proposed."

"And you've believed that for *twenty-five years*?"

"You never said otherwise."

A hole appeared in his beard. "It was a joke!" he gasped. "It's gold, with CZs, not car headlights!"

"Oh! You probably should have said."

"I wish I had now! Bloody 'ell, woman, I was laughing my head off when I said it, relieved you'd said yes, did you not cotton on?"

Faye was looking at her not-can-tab engagement ring, puzzled.

"A can tab is silver, Faye. Your ring is nine carat *gold*." Brian could barely comprehend the long-term conviction he had slotted into his wife's mind all those years ago. "It was quite expensive, a whole week's wages."

"Was it? I like it even more now."

She smiled. Brian pulled her to him and gently hugged her. "You thought it was a can tab and shiny glass, and you *still* agreed to marry me?"

"I'd have agreed if it had been copper wire, Bri."

"I'm a lucky man."

"We're lucky together, Bri."

"We are."

He lowered his head to kiss her. Mark, a long way down the path, yelled, "Put him down, Faye, you don't know where he's been!"

Faye looked up at her husband. "Everyone's looking at us

now, aren't they."

"They are, love."

"Come on, let's go wander."

\* \* \*

Tel and Sophie were sat on a wooden bench, watching people starting their walk down into the canyon or riding down on mules.

"In this heat though?" Tel said, fanning himself with his cowboy hat

"Fancy it?"

"I'd rather run around naked for the rest of the day."

"Go, Tel!"

"Wonder what it's like down there."

"There's pictures online," Sophie laughed, "Safer to look at pictures and much less exhausting.  There's a ranch at the bottom."

"Big trek to get your shopping home."

"I read it's ten miles down."

"Definitely get your shopping delivered then.  I wonder if you'd have to put the delivery driver up for the night?"

"Probably."

He hugged her close.  "Shame we're not staying longer, we could have sat on a rock and watched the sun go down."

"I wouldn't recommend it," said an elderly gentleman with a strong Welsh accent, who was standing and admiring the view next to their bench.  "A friend of ours came here a couple of months ago and did that, didn't he, Brynn?"

A little woman at his side nodded.  "Said it was the worst thing he ever did," she said, in an even stronger Welsh accent. "He thought it would be romantic, like you, but he said he'd never been so scared in his life.  Apparently, things come out from the rocks at night."

"Things?" Sophie asked.

"He said they only caught fleeting glimpses from the corners of their eyes, just dark shapes scurrying about and flying around their heads."

"They ran back to the car in the dark," the man said.

"Ran for their lives, he said."

"He's a horror film fan," said the man, "That probably didn't help, but he's a big bloke, y'know, proper rugby player type, but when they finally got back to the car and opened the doors he said he could actually hear the rusty squeak of a psychopath's scythe behind them." The man threw back his head and laughed. "Scared out of their wits, they were."

"Oh!" Sophie gasped.

"Good job we're not staying after dark then," Tel said.

"English, are you?" asked the man.

"Yes, from London."

"We're from Cardiff. Evan, and my wife, Brynn."

"Tel and Sophie." They briefly shook hands, compatriots in a foreign country. "Are you staying nearby or touring?"

"Going round the whole canyon, then back to Vegas."

"We're doing the same," said Sophie.

"Yes, we were hoping to arrive at the canyon earlier, but we had a little trouble with the car." Evan and Brynn looked at each other and winced. "Back on track now though. Anyway, we won't keep you. Take care, and enjoy yourselves."

"You too."

Smiling, the elderly couple wandered off hand in hand.

"Aren't they lovely" Sophie said. "Will we be like that at their age?"

"Absolutely. We'll grow old happily and disgracefully."

"I like the sound of that." She admired his profile. He was very handsome. She was glad she had married him, he was a good man. "You look very sexy in your cowboy hat."

"Thanks," he said, tipping it up. "Had to wear the jeans and chambray shirt to complete the look. Bit hot, actually."

"Suffering for vanity in double denim."

"Living a childhood dream."

"Maybe I should dress up as a fairy then."

He looked at her. "I can't see you as a fairy."

"No? How do you see me?"

"Amazonian woman. Legs that go right up to your cheekbones. My Queen of Sheba."

"Oh, I say! Flattery will get you everywhere."

"I certainly hope so."

He leaned in for a kiss, soft and lingering. When he sat up again he took off his hat and put it in his lap.

"You'll get sunstroke."

He stared off into the canyon.

"Do you fancy a short walk down the trail?"

He kept his eyes averted. "Just give me a minute."

"Why?" She looked at his hat. "Oh Tel!"

"Can't help it," he grinned. "You have that effect on me."

* * *

Mark and Olivia sat on a rock, far back from the edge, to soak up the view.

"Isn't it beautiful," she sighed.

"Not half as beautiful as my fiancée."

"You old charmer."

"Less of the 'old', if you don't mind." He turned towards her. "You're a bit of a dark horse, aren't you, arranging a surprise and not telling me."

"Wouldn't be a surprise if I had."

"Tell me now, I won't blab."

"Won't."

"Oh, go on."

She firmly shook her head and looked out over the canyon again. "It's nice, isn't it, doing this trip with friends."

"We'd have a lot more 'private time' if we were on our own." He planted a kiss on her neck and wailed, "I miss private time."

"I know, but this is fun too, and there's safety in numbers. I'd be quite nervous about doing this on our own."

"Yeah, have to agree with you there. Brian's always so calm and grounded, nothing seems to phase him."

"Love Brian."

"Yeah, someone to look up to."

"They seem so happy."

"They've had twenty-five years of practice."

"A lot of couples don't make it that far."

"We will," he said, putting an arm across her shoulders.
She smiled. "I know."

\* \* \*

"Christ!" Faye gasped.

"What? Are the diamonds blinding you?"

"No. Well, yes." She admired the ring again. How could
Brian have afforded it? She pushed the thought from her mind;
she would interrogate him later. "I was watching those people
perched on the edge of the rocks! They're just jumping from
one ledge down to another without a care in the world. They
could slip and die!"

"All for a good photo," Brian sighed, watching them.
"Madness."

"Do they not know how dangerous it is?"

"Young people think they're invincible."

Faye gasped again as two girls slid down onto a lower
ledge. She fervently hoped their laughter wouldn't suddenly
turn into screaming.

"Let's go get a drink," she said, unable to tolerate the
suspense any longer, "I've run out of water."

They wandered into the Grand Canyon village and found
a café surrounded by bicycles.

"We could hire one of those each," Brian said, "Get to the
bottom of the canyon in 8.3 seconds, none of this arduous
trekking or mule riding."

Faye laughed. "I can't remember when I was last on a
bike."

"Two years ago. Along the canal into Birmingham. You
hit a rock on the path and headed straight for the cut."

"Oh yes! And you saved me by hauling me back and

pulling me on top of you to give me a soft landing."

"Bruised ribs, hurt like hell for weeks."

"I think we'll give the bikes a miss, Bri."

"Probably best."

They sat at a table. "What surprise do you think Livs has planned?"

"I bet she's found the only place in America that serves cream tea."

\* \* \*

At the allotted time they met up with each other and made their way back to the RVs.

Halfway across the car park Mark said, "Isn't that the car from earlier?"

They looked at the black Cherokee.

"Same number plate," said Tel.

"Are you sure?"

"Positive, I gave it a good looking over."

They glanced around. No sign of the two men they'd encountered earlier.

"Do you think they're following us?" Olivia said nervously.

"It's probably a coincidence."

"Just a fluke," Tel added.

Sophie whispered, "Do you think it is?"

"Yes," he said, still looking around for the men.

They got to their RVs and clambered in, Mark on the passenger side. "Damn," he said, "Someone stole the bloody steering wheel again."

Olivia laughed. "I'll drive."

She picked up the walkie talkie and said, "Breaker, breaker, Liv speaking."

She heard the laughter from the other two RVs nearby and Tel shouting, "We know who you are, Livs."

She put the walkie talkie down and yelled, in her high-pitched voice, "Follow me, I'll lead the way."

"To where?" Faye cried.

"You'll see."

"*Meanie!*"

Mark looked down at the GPS on the dashboard. It had completely given up and wouldn't even turn on, so he had no idea where they were going either.

It was only a short drive.

When Tel saw the sign at the entrance to their destination, he groaned.

# CHAPTER TEN

"How you feeling?" Brian asked.

"Ugh."

"Better than the dry barfing you were doing earlier."

Tel nodded weakly as he sat, crunched up and holding his stomach, in the waiting area of the airfield. Olivia sat on a chair next to him saying, "Sorry, Tel, I'm so sorry," over and over again.

"It's not your fault, Livs."

"I forgot he didn't like heights," she said to everyone, her face a picture of misery. "I should have remembered his jump from the plane last year. A helicopter ride over the canyon is something I've always wanted to do, and I thought what better way than to do it with friends, but … I'm so sorry, Tel."

Tel took another shaky sip of water from his bottle. His eyes were still bulging from his face like pickled onions.

"I enjoyed it," Faye said.

"We could tell from all the hysterical laughter."

"Mixed in with Tel screaming that we were all going to die," Mark snorted.

"And Sophie trying to convince him that we weren't."

"And the poor pilot trying to quieten us all down," Brian laughed. "I'm sure that last sharp drop was just to get us all to shut the hell up. I bet his ears are still ringing."

"I'm sorry, Tel."

"It's fine, Livs. Honestly, I'll be fine."

"Are you okay to drive?" Sophie asked. "You look very pale, and your hands are still shaking."

"I'll be okay."

"You don't want me to – ?"

"No! I think one close encounter with death is enough for one day."

Sophie pulled a face, but was secretly relieved.

They helped him to his RV and manoeuvred him behind the steering wheel. He tried to smile, but it looked like a grimace.

"Just take your time," Brian told him, "And pull over if you need to."

It took a little over three hours to drive from the airfield near the Grand Canyon to Monument Valley, with a couple of stops to let Tel dry heave by the side of the road and one stop for burritos. During one of Tel's bent-double session, the black car that had almost run into them that morning sped past.

"Again?" Brian said, watching it disappear in a haze of dust.

"More than a little suspicious," said Mark. "Don't tell Livs, she's freaked out enough as it is."

They drove through Tuba City – "City?" Faye cried. "It's *tiny!*" – heading towards Kayenta down the endless I-160 that was lined either side with miles of flat desert. Hundreds of telephone poles followed them, electric pylons flashed by. Single tracks in the dirt disappeared into the distance. They stopped for fuel and water, a rest break at a petrol station, and at 'scenic points' to stretch their legs.

"Are you sure we're going the right way?" Faye asked Brian, after it seemed they'd been travelling forever.

"It's one road, lass, can't really go wrong when there's only one road."

"Unless you're going the wrong way."

"I'm not going the wrong way, Faye."

"Where's Monument Valley then? It all seems pretty flat."

"Patience, woman."

Behind them, Sophie asked Tel, for about the tenth time, how he was feeling.

"Better, actually. In fact, I feel a bit hungry."

"Good sign. Shall I get you that burrito?"

He dry heaved.

"I'll take that as a no, then. How about a biscuit and some water?"

"Yes, please."

On and on. Mile after mile. A tiny town. Left at an actual traffic island at Kayenta, onto I-163, and then, gradually, they saw the familiar red rocks start to rise up in the distance.

"Oh!" Faye cried, "This is *so* exciting!"

Finally, a sign reading 'Welcome to Utah'. Several cars were parked beneath it and a crowd of people stood taking photographs. The magnificent Monument Valley formed the backdrop.

"Pull over!" said Faye, bouncing up and down in her seat.

He did, and they took their turn in the crowd to take selfies.

"We've passed through some unseen barrier into a different time zone," Sophie told them as they headed back to the RVs. "We've lost an hour crossing the border, or gained an hour, I'm not sure any more."

"Doesn't matter," Tel said, "We're on 'vacation', time has no meaning."

Back on the road again, until they came to a sign reading, 'Lording's Resort. Movie location 1m'.

Brian whooped with joy, making Faye jump in her seat. "The Duke was here! I can feel the Ford vibes already."

Faye looked at him blankly. She didn't watch cowboy films and couldn't share in his excitement. She faked it instead with a weak cry of, "Yay!"

"You'll never win an Oscar, lass."

Another long road, and then they could see the lodges embedded into the side of a red cliff.

"Ooh," said Faye, "It looks just like that hotel in *The Shining*."

Brian glanced at her, then back at the lodges. "Apart from the lack of trees and the snow, you mean?"

"A hot version then."

*"The Sweating?"*

She laughed.

After booking in, they drove onto the RV site, which was busy but not packed, and were pleasantly surprised to find a pitch big enough to park all three RVs. They parked in a U-shape and opened up the canopies, providing a shaded area in the middle.

The women immediately ran to the showers. The men set up camp.

"Nice place," Brian said, admiring the monumental scenery. "Must have cost a pretty penny. Are you sure we've paid enough for all these sites?"

"Yeah, yeah," Tel said distractedly, arranging the chairs in a circle and wondering if it was too formal.

"Are you sure?"

Tel looked up. "It's all taken care of, Bri, we've all pitched in for the camping fees." He laughed. "Pitched in! Get it?" Mark gave a fake laugh. Brian could have smiled behind his beard but it was hard to tell. "You're going to love this place, Bri, it's called John Wayne Land, or something."

Brian inhaled deeply and looked up at the red cliffs towering above them, the red cliffs further out, and the general sense of John Wayne-ness it all elicited. He thought he already recognised some scenes from the western films he'd watched.

The women returned, all fresh and giggly.

"You having a shower, Bri?"

Brian punched his chest with a fist and said, "Men are tough, we don't require hourly bathing."

"I'm down to one a day now that the sweating has stopped," Faye said, scurrying passed him. "You could have terrible body odour and stink to high heaven for all I know, Bri."

Mark leaned into to Brian and inhaled, coughed, grabbed his throat and gasped, "He *reeks!*"

"Does he?" Faye frowned.

Mark shook his head. "Oddly not."

"I sweat and suck it back into my body."

"Too mean to sweat, eh?" Tel laughed.

"I practice recycling and excellent water management."

Tel settled himself into a chair.

"Don't get comfortable," Sophie told him, "We have lots to do."

"Such as?"

Sophie threw her arms up in despair. "Honestly, did *nobody* read the itinerary? Etta spent *ages* working out every detail. There's a museum here, which I think you're going to like, Bri."

"Food," said Brian.

"And a walking trail to an archway."

"Food."

"And there's a swimming pool on site."

"Ooh," said Faye.

"I hope you all remembered to bring your swimming costumes, as per my email?"

"It all sounds very exercise-y," said Brian. "Talk to me about the food side of things."

"You want to eat first?"

"Starving," said Brian.

"Okay. Well, it's a change to the itinerary, but I supposed we could eat at the *John Wayne Dining Room* first."

Brian's eyes lit up. "The *John Wayne Dining Room*?"

Sophie nodded, smiling.

"Lead the way!" he cried, jumping up and walking off.

"It's too far to walk," Sophie called after him, "We'll drive up."

"Which RV?"

"Ours," Tel said. "You can sit in the front."

"Oh, the washing!" Faye cried. "Can we stop off on the way? I saw they have a laundry room up by the grocery store, we could load up and pick them up on the way back."

Everyone dispersed to gather their clothes, except for Brian, who impatiently sat in Tel's passenger seat, tapping his fingers and waiting for them all to come back so he could see the John Wayne Dining Room and *eat*.

\* \* \*

It was big and pretty and busy, with panoramic windows overlooking Monument Valley and Native pottery water jugs on the tables. John Wayne paintings and photographs hung on the wall and Brian posed in front of each of them taking selfies, dragging Faye and the others in for a few.

Tel pushed two wooden tables together to accommodate them all.

A pretty waitress came over for their orders.

"Three pints of whatever lager you have, lass," Brian boomed, "And three large glasses of your finest Prosecco."

The whole dining room fell silent. Brian looked up from his menu. Some people had turned their heads to look at him. Maybe it was his British/Yorkshire accent.

It wasn't.

"We don't serve alcohol," said the waitress.

"Say again?"

"This is Navajo Nation."

Brian nodded, waiting for the punchline. A restaurant without alcohol? Tel and Mark were obviously playing a cruel joke on him.

"The sale of alcohol is prohibited on Navajo-owned tribal parks," the waitress said into the silent vacuum. "Nowhere around here serves or sells alcohol."

Brian stopped nodding. "No ... alcohol?"

"We do have a selection of non-alcoholic beer and wine."

"Non-alcoholic?"

The waitress nodded, pen poised over her notepad, smiling.

"No alcohol at all?"

The waitress shook her head.

"Anywhere?"

Another shake of the head. Brian looked aghast.

"We were going to get you a bottle of champagne to celebrate your anniversary," Tel said.

"Oh, that's nice," said Faye. "It's the thought that counts."

"I thought about getting you champagne."

"I'll sit and think about drinking it. Hmm, lovely."

"Have you lost your marbles, woman?" Brian asked.

"After twenty-five years with you, Bri, it's possible."

"We'll all have water," Mark said, filling their glasses from the colourful pottery jug.

As they placed their orders, Brian leaned into Faye and whispered, "Do we have any cans in the van?"

"Two, I think. We were going to stock up at the nearest shop once we got here but … we forgot."

"Two?" Brian inhaled and held it for a long time. "Do we have anything else to drink?"

"No. Oh, there's a miniature bottle of Absinthe I bought to try because it was a pretty colour, but it's horrible."

Brian was too shocked to even say 'Absinthe makes the heart grow fonder'.

Tel leaned forward and breathed, "We have half a bottle of medicinal brandy that Sophie bought for snake bites, scorpion stings and alligator attacks, if you're interested?"

"Alligator attacks?" Mark laughed. "In the middle of the desert. How would brandy help with an alligator attack anyway?"

"I'm assuming," Tel grinned, glancing at Sophie, who raised an eyebrow, "The plan was to get the alligator to drink the brandy until it was drunk enough to flip onto its back and drown."

Sophie tutted. "For the *wounds*, of course!"

Mark leaned towards Brian and whispered, "I might have a couple of cans left."

"Come on, Bri," Faye hissed, "You can go one night without beer."

Brian scrunched up his face. He could, and often did, but beer was part of his relaxing ritual, his holiday habit.

"Bugger," he said.

They helped themselves to the salad bar, with its tiny plates, and the soup bar, with its tiny bowls, followed by the authentic Navajo cuisine that was brought to their table – fried bread and chilli, except for Brian, who had a steak; red wine sauce wasn't even an option.

"I'll pay for this," he said, when they'd finished.

"No, no," said Mark, "It's your anniversary, our treat."

"I think we've been treated enough, our shout this time."

Tel wiped his mouth and got up. "Just nipping to the little boy's room."

Brian sat at the table, strumming his fingers.

"Stop that," Faye said.

He started biting his fingernails instead. He had to do something with his empty, beer-less hands.

"Brian!"

Sighing, he stood up and lumbered towards the 'restrooms'. He saw Tel at the cash counter and wandered over.

Tel didn't see Brian watching him hand over his credit card or listening when he said, "Send the remainder of the bill to our table."

He was putting his wallet back in his pocket when he turned and jumped at the sight of Brian standing right behind him.

"Brian!" he gasped.

Brian said nothing. He stared down at him with a strange look in his eye. His beard twitched.

"Everything okay, Bri?"

Brian humphed and carried on to the toilets. When he came back to the table he kept eyeballing Tel, making Tel feel more than a little uncomfortable. Tel hoped it might simply be beer withdrawal, but more likely Brian was onto them.

* * *

"Oh wow," Brian said.

"You've been wowing for a solid five minutes already,"

Faye said, climbing up a set of wooden stairs behind the restaurant. "You didn't wow this much for the Grand Canyon."

"Wow," said Brian, standing and staring at a stagecoach, a small sheriff's jail, a life size effigy of the Duke himself beneath a Saloon sign, and a building that had a 'John Wayne's Cabin' above it. The cabin was locked. He was bitterly disappointed. He immediately started taking selfies of everything, his expression the same in every one – extreme joy, verging on hyperventilating hysteria.

"*She Wore a Yellow Ribbon* was filmed here," he enthused, "And those rocks over there, I'm sure that's where the Duke got shot in *The Searchers*."

"I think Brian's in heaven," Tel laughed.

"Look at the view!" he cried, taking more selfies of the monuments, the huge sky and fluffy clouds in front of a gently setting sun. "Doesn't it just scream John Ford!"

"Certainly makes me want to scream," Faye sighed.

"Who's John Ford?" Olivia asked Mark.

"Film director, I think."

Brian stared down at the ground. "I can't believe I'm walking in the steps of – "

"John Wayne?" Faye sighed again.

"Don't you feel the magic of the place?"

"I feel full, and a bit tired, but no magic."

"Maybe later," Mark snorted.

"Two of the greatest men in western film history have stood here and admired *this* view. Did you know that John Ford paid the Navajo Nation to film on their land?"

Faye groaned. She wished she hadn't eaten so much. She wished there was a seat or a bench where bored wives could sit and wait for their husbands to calm down.

"They called him The Tall Leader."

The others mumbled and nodded. Faye made her way back down the stairs, eager to get settled into a camping chair. Brian, after a few more 'wows', a couple of gasps and some hysterical laughter, stomped down after her with a huge, satisfied grin on his face.

And then he spotted the gift shop and lumbered towards it.

"Bri?" Faye called after him, "Where you going, Bri?"

Brian carried on lumbering, almost breaking into a trot.

He bought a few items with the Duke's face on it; a mug, a set of coasters, a calendar, playing cards, postcards, and a tea towel for Faye ("Don't say I never buy you anything," he laughed, as she rolled her eyes). He whimpered over a bronze statue of the great man himself, and a signed photograph in a frame that had a lot of numbers on the price tag. He furtively took a photo of it on his phone.

"And you say I spend too much on junk?" Faye said, following him to the counter.

"This isn't *junk*, woman!"

"One man's junk is another man's treasure," Mark said.

"This is treasure," Brian breathed, hugging it to his chest. "This is John Wayne memorabilia from the place where he filmed. I will never get this opportunity again."

"Pretty sure you can get all that stuff on Amazon, Bri."

"It's not the same." He stroked the plastic wrapped calendar. "This has red Monument Valley sand on it." The man behind the counter glanced up at him. "A grain of this sand might have touched one of the Johns!"

"Therapy?" Mark asked Faye.

"Possibly."

"We could bury him up to his neck in sand outside the RVs until he comes to his senses?" Sophie suggested.

"In the middle," Tel added, "And use his head as a coffee table."

"It's certainly big enough," Mark howled.

"You'll have a long wait," said Faye, "He's *obsessed* with John Wayne and all things cowboy. There is no cure, believe me, I've tried."

"You take no notice," Olivia told him, "It's good that you have a passion."

"Yeah," Tel agreed, "Makes us feel better about ours."

"Oh yes?" Sophie breathed, "And what passions would those be?"

"Show you later," he winked.

Brian wore the huge, satisfied grin as he carried his precious stash back to the RV. They picked up the washed and dried clothes on the way, and Brian settled into a camping chair with them on his lap, looking at them one by one, running his fingers over the Duke's image and looking at the red dust on his hands.

Faye, watching him, was suddenly struck by a brilliant idea.

She slipped inside their RV and found the small bottle of Absinthe she'd bought, which looked pretty but tasted disgusting. She'd meant to throw it out, but she was glad she hadn't – she had a plan.

She went to pour the contents down the sink, then paused, shrugged, and necked it until it was empty, afterwards gagging and wincing at the rancid taste of liquorice.

She rinsed it out, soaked off the sticky label, and put it in a hidden corner to dry.

Brian was really, really going to like this. It would be the *ultimate* anniversary present.

* * *

"Excuse me," said the young man from a huge RV parked on a neighbouring pitch.

They all looked up and instinctively smiled.

"I couldn't help overhearing your conversation in the restaurant," he said.

"I apologise for the disturbance," Brian told him. "Shock is a terrible thing."

The man held out a plastic bag. "I come bearing gifts. *Cold* ones."

Brian took it from him and looked inside. It was a six-pack of beers with condensation dribbling down the sides.

He'd never seen anything more beautiful.

"That's ... that's very kind of you."

"No problem at all."

The young woman from the huge RV wandered over holding two bottles of wine in her hands. "Hope you like red," she said.

"We've been here before," the man explained. "We came prepared this time."

"Over-prepared," the woman laughed.

"Are you sure?" Faye asked, taking the bottles and throwing a silent scream over at Olivia and Sophie.

"Oh yeah."

"Couldn't have visitors to our great country going dry now, could we?"

"What's that?" a man prodding a smoky barbecue outside an Airstream yelled over, "Folks are dry?"

"They didn't know," yelled the first man. "They're Briddish."

The woman lounging outside the Airstream hurried into it and out again with two more bottles of wine. The man opened up a giant cool box next to the barbecue – which made Brian sigh in longing for his own giant cool box at home – and took out another six pack.

"We couldn't," Mark shouted.

"We could!" Brian countered.

As the man and the woman from the Airstream came over with their alcohol, they passed an elderly couple sitting outside their RV. "Dry Brits," he said as he passed, galvanising the couple into action.

The three camping tables outside their U-shaped RVs were suddenly filled with cans and bottles.

"There's way too much," Tel gasped, "You're too generous."

"Have a drink on us at your next campsite," one said, as they all started walking off.

"Won't you join us?" Sophie asked.

"Mighty kind, ma'am, but we have a barbecue planned."

"Love your accent," the Airstream woman gushed.

"We won't impose," said the first man.

"It's no imposition, really."

"Just don't keep us up late with your drunken revelry," said the elderly couple.

Sophie put her head on Tel's shoulder and said, "I love it."

"What, the freebies?"

"No, the kindness of campers."

"The world over, it seems."

With a huge smile, Brian cracked open a can as he stroked his John Wayne purchases. "Do you see this?" he said, raising his can to the sky, to the rocks, to the campsite around him and the people at the table, "This here is what's known as heaven on earth."

An while later, Mark rested his head back on his chair to stare up at the black, star-infested sky. "Amazing," he yawned.

"Isn't it."

"And so quiet."

Mark yawned again, which set off a chain reaction around the table.

"We should probably have an early night," Sophie said, "It's been a long day and we're up early in the morning."

"Are we?" Faye said.

"Yes." She glared at them all. "Can you *please* read your itineraries?"

"Couldn't find ours," said Mark. "We tried to remember where we'd put it for safekeeping, but do you know how difficult it is to search an entire pub?"

Brian looked at Faye, who said, "I think it's in the bottom of the sports bag."

Sophie sighed. "We have to be up by five o'clock."

"What o'clock?"

"We're doing the sunrise tour around Monument Valley." When they all continued to look surprised and a little shocked, she added, "You all agreed to this!"

Again, Brian looked at Faye. "Did we?"

"I think so."

"Five o'clock?"

She shrugged.

"I thought it was the sunset tour," Olivia said.

"And yet here we are, sitting in the dark, sans tour."

"Oh. Right. I see what you mean."

Mark still had his head back on his chair, now with his eyes closed.

Brian got up from his and said, "We'd best be hitting the sack then, catch what zeds we can before getting up in the middle of the night."

They wearily dispersed, leaving the cans and the bottles on the table.

* * *

Brian and Faye clambered up into bed, and Brian's breathing became heavy and rhythmic almost immediately.

"Brian."

There was no response, so she shook him. He woke with a start.

"Are you asleep?" she whispered.

"I was."

"Oh, sorry."

He started breathing heavily again.

"Brian."

He grunted. "Yes, my love?"

"How did you pay for the ring?"

"I sold a kidney. Nobody needs two kidneys."

"I'm serious, I want to know."

"I sold a couple of things."

"What things?"

"Just things."

"Like?"

"That silver photo frame my mother gave us as a wedding present, bloody 'orrible thing. I'm sure somebody gave it to her and she just wanted rid."

"You shouldn't have!"

"I should have, ages ago, we both hated it."

"I didn't *hate* it."

"No? I found it hidden behind the boxes of Christmas decorations in the garage."

"Oh, is that where it went?"

"Yes, Faye, you put it there."

"Did not!"

"I saw you on the security camera footage when I was checking for rats."

"Oh. And that paid for the ring?"

"Mostly."

"Did you borrow the rest?"

"I don't do debt, Faye."

"How else did you pay for it then?"

"Can't you just accept it without interrogation? You deserve it, and I didn't go into debt to buy it."

"Please, Bri, I can't sleep for worrying about it."

He sighed heavily and opened his eyes. "I sold a couple of guns out the loft that I haven't used for years."

"Your granddad's shotguns are in the loft."

"Should be in a museum."

"Did you give them to a museum?"

"No, I sold them to a gun shop."

"Oh Brian!"

"What? They were old, and I didn't dare fire them in case they blew my face off."

"They were family heirlooms."

"They were a liability, dangerous, and I was sick of renewing the shotgun certificate every five years. I was glad to see them go, to be honest, and I thought, 'What's the best use for this money?' and I decided to buy the ring I'd always wanted to give you for our anniversary."

"Oh Bri." She snuggled up to him. "You're a lovely husband."

"Tired husband."

Faye tilted her head to look through the skylight, at the stars twinkling in the black sky above them.  She felt very happy.

"Bri."

"Hmm?"

"I could live here."

"You've only had a glass and a half of wine and you're already planning to relocate. It would be a bit of a – " He yawned. " – commute to work and back."

"I could, I really like it here."

"You said that when we were leaving the Canaries, and again when we left Rhodes, France and Spain."

Faye snuggled up to him.  "Now that I'm used to the heat I like it, and the vastness of everything, and the people are lovely.  We could find a house, we've seen some really nice ones, or maybe one of those ranches we drove passed, a small one, and keep horses and go riding every day, and you could pretend to be ... Brian?"

She lifted her head to look at him.

He was fast asleep.

* * *

"What are you doing?" Mark asked, watching Olivia taking things out of cupboards and loading up the toaster, two by two.

"Oh, just prepping.  Won't be a minute."

Mark climbed up onto the bed.  He intended to stay awake until she lay down next to him, maybe have a bit of a cuddle, but he fell asleep within seconds.

* * *

Sophie snuggled up to Tel.

"About these obsessions," she said.

"Worcestershire," he breathed.

"Oooh."

# CHAPTER ELEVEN

**DAY 5**

At five o'clock on the dot, six mobile phones started beeping inside three RVs.

Brian thrust his under his pillow with a grunt, where it buzzed directly into his good ear. He turned onto his bad ear, but he could still hear it. He fumbled with it in the dark until it fell silent.

Faye reached over with the phone buzzing in her hand, prodding him with it, and mumbled something that sounded vaguely like 'Make it stop'.

"Tel."

"Shh."

"We have to get up."

"Shh!"

"It's five o'clock."

He pretended to cry as he rolled over in bed and nearly fell to the floor below.

"Need coffee," Sophie groaned, gently pushing him until he clambered down. "Strong, and lots of it."

"Why have I got to make it? This was your idea."

"It was a group decision." She yawned and stretched. "And I'm following Brian and Faye's routine for morning coffee; whoever's up first makes it."

"I wasn't up."

"You are now. Get to it, lad, and stop swinging your manhood about like that, we don't have time."

He wiggled his hips at her. She laughed and got up.

Mark took the phone from beneath his pillow and blindly

prodded it until it stopped making a noise. With his eyes still closed he patted the bed next to him. It was empty.

He opened one eye and saw the lights were on down below. Olivia was busy in the kitchen area. Delicious smells filled the RV.

"Have you been up all night?" he croaked.

"No, silly, about half an hour." She took something out of the oven. "These should be cool by the time we leave."

"What are you doing?"

"Prepping."

"Still?"

"Almost done, just the washing up to do."

* * *

Brian pounded as quietly as he could on Tel and Sophie's door. "If I'm up," he hissed, "You're up. Are you up?"

Tel opened the door a crack and nodded.

Brian walked over to pound quietly on Mark and Olivia's door, when it suddenly flew open.

"All ready," Olivia beamed, a heavy-looking sports bag hanging from her shoulder.

"I'll take that," said Mark.

"You're both bright and breezy, considering it's – " He went to look at his watch, then thought better of it. " – the middle of the night."

"We're excited," Olivia said.

"I'm too stunned by the hour to feel anything," said Mark.

Faye came down the steps with two large bottles of water and said, "What time's the coach coming?"

"It's a jeep," Sophie said, "And it'll be here at five-thirty." She took a sheet of paper from her jeans pocket and opened it out. "Provisions check, meticulously researched by my amazing assistant. Do you all have masks for the sand?"

"Check," they said, tapping their pockets. Faye felt the Absinthe bottle in hers, all clean and dry and ready to go.

Sophie glanced at them one by one, reading off, "Water?

Hats?  Sunglasses?  Suncream?  I see you're wearing zip-up hoodies."

"Because it's *bloody freezing*," Mark grumbled, rubbing his hands together in front of his mouth.

"What's in the sports bag, Livs?"

"Oh, just some things we might need."

Faye pulled a face.  "It's my job to have things we might need."

"We, and everybody else in the area," Brian drawled.  "Yet here you stand, holding only two giant bottles of water.  Your standards are slipping, lass."

"It's too early for dry humour, Bri."

"How about ironic sarcasm?"

"Hit me with some and I'll let you know."

Brian sighed.  "Brain hasn't cranked up yet, I have nothing."

"Then stop your jibber-jabber."

They stood outside their RVs, sipping steaming coffee from mugs and struggling with consciousness, until the open sided jeep arrived, pulling up in front of them.  The driver and tour guide, a Navajo man in a white cowboy hat, red chequered shirt and jeans, greeted them warmly but quietly.  They clambered on board and the driver set off immediately.

"I thought we'd have to wait for other people," Mark said.

"Other people have more sense," said Brian.  "Other people are, at this very moment, peacefully sleeping in their warm, comfortable beds."

"Oh don't," Mark wailed.

Faye put her head on Brian's shoulder.

"Don't go to sleep," he told her.

"Why not?"

"Because if your sleep makes me sleep, I'll topple and crush you."

He fidgeted in his tiny seat, then stood up as the jeep drove down the road and sat in the seat in front, opening his legs and resting his arms across the back.  "Space," he cried.

"Knees are pulverised but you can't have everything."

Mark moved to another seat so that Olivia could open up the sports bag.

"Who wants breakfast?" she asked.

"You have food?" Brian gasped.

"I do."

She pulled out plastic bags containing sandwiches of toast. "Peanut butter," she said, handing them out. "I was going to put jam on them, like the Americans do, but it just didn't seem right. I have snack bags, apples, and extra water if anybody needs it. No chocolate bars though, I thought they would melt, but," she added, pulling out a couple of plastic boxes, "There's chocolate chips in the home-made cookies, and I did some freshly baked cheese sticks."

"You, lass, are a bloody star."

Olivia blushed as everyone tucked in.

* * *

The tour was *magnificent*, better than they could ever have imagined, and the sunrise was breath-taking; the buttes and mittens looked like they were on fire. Their guide, Larry, was knowledgeable and friendly, telling them all about the history of the land and the Navajo people through a speaker in his cab. He even sang native songs to them.

They tightened the straps on their cowboy hats, Mark adjusting his cap, donned masks and sunglasses against the sand clouds raised by the jeep, and tried to take it all in. They soon ran out of adjectives, but the gasps continued.

When they stopped for photos on Forest Gump Hill, Brian stood talking to Larry. When Larry herded them back onto the jeep, Brian sauntered over to Sophie and said, "How much did this tour cost?"

"It's all taken care of, Bri."

"How is it taken care of, exactly?"

"We all pitched in," Tel said.

"We each put a couple of hundred pounds into the pot."

Brian looked at the others. "Didn't we?"

They all nodded.

He paused for a moment, seemingly deep in thought, before saying, "How can six hundred pounds cover all the extras? It doesn't seem enough."

"This tour is included in the camping fee," Sophie said, "My assistant is a whizz at finding the best deals on the internet."

Brian eyeballed her. She held his gaze, and her breath.

"Something's not right," he said, "And I intend to find out what it is."

He turned and walked off, clambering up into the back of the jeep. They followed, glancing nervously at each other.

Larry took them to different areas of Monument Valley. Every time Brian looked around at the scenery and mentioned a John Wayne film he thought might have been filmed there, Faye surreptitiously bent down and grabbed a good pinch of red sand, pouring it into the Absinthe bottle before pushing it back into her pocket. She did it several times, until the bottle was full.

Their final stop was the visitor centre, sitting high above the valley, where the women took dozens of pictures to add to the millions they'd taken at every stop along the tour. They dashed into the shop for souvenirs, whilst the men stood looking out over the vista. They wore their cowboy hats and sunglasses, their hands thrust into their jeans pockets.

"Wish I'd bought a cowboy hat now," Mark said.

"You can still be in our gang," said Tel, "As honorary member."

"I could have been a contender," he rasped, "If I'd just bought a hat."

Brian looked at them, standing in a row, and started whistling the theme tune to a spaghetti western.

Mark joined in with a "Wah wah wah."

Brian whistled, Mark wah'ed, and Tel added a melodic "Doo doo doo doo doo."

"Ooh, ah, ooh, ah."

They laughed at themselves.

"What's that film called, Bri?"

Brian hesitated, then said, "T'Good, t'Bad and t'Ugly."

They laughed again.

A small boy of about six or seven approached them, watched over from a distance by his parents. "Are you cowboys?" he asked, staring up at them.

Brian pushed up the rim of his hat and said, in his best John Wayne voice, "Y'know when you play cowboys and Indians with your buddies, Little Britches?"

The boy nodded.

"We're doing the grown-up version."

The kid stared at them for a few seconds more, then smiled and said, "You still get to play when you're a grown-up?"

"You sure do."

Happy, the boy ran off to his laughing parents. "Good advice," the dad shouted over.

"Always act your shoe size," Brian bellowed.

\* \* \*

"I can't feel my bum," Faye cried, wincing in pain.

"Me neither."

"I'm covered in bruises."

"I'll never be able to sit down again."

"Worth it, though."

"Oh yeah, absolutely."

"Wouldn't have missed that for the world."

They were back at the campsite, walking like cowboys who had spent too long in the saddle. Without a word, Brian climbed into his RV, with Faye hot on his heels shouting, "You okay, Bri? You haven't got sunstroke, have you? It's not like you to be *not* booming about something."

"I think he suspects," Mark said.

"I think you're right."

"He might just be tired," Olivia offered.

"No, it's more than that, he knows."

"Brace yourselves," Sophie said, "There might be a storm coming."

The others looked up at the bright, cloudless sky.

"Not from up there," she added, nodding towards Brian and Faye's RV, "From there."

\* \* \*

"So, what's the plan, man?" Mark asked, swinging his arms and clapping his hands in front of him.

"Exciting day ahead," Sophie beamed.

"What excitement is that, Sophie, baby?" Tel asked with a huge smile.

"Well, Teletubby, it's all on the itinerary in glorious, meticulously researched detail, if only you'd all bother to read it."

From the corner of their eyes they glanced at Brian, sitting outside his RV eating a Pot Noodle. Faye was inside, packing up.

"Maybe he's reached that point in the holiday when you just want to go home?" Tel whispered.

"More likely he's realised what sanctimonious, patronising gits we are."

"*Kind* gits," Olivia said.

"Cruel to be kind?"

"No good deed goes unpunished."

"We're so going to cop it later."

"I'm frightened, Mark."

"Me too, Livs."

Tel casually wandered over to Brian. "Hey, Bri."

"Hey, yourself."

"Faye nearly finished, is she?"

"Why don't you ask her?"

"You almost ready for the off, Faye?"

"Yep," she yelled, "Nearly done."

Tel sat down on Faye's camping chair next to Brian. The others hovered, pretending not to listen.

"You okay, Bri?"

"Yeah, why wouldn't I be?"

"You just seem a bit … off."

"Been doing a bit of thinking."

Tel laughed. "You want to watch that."

"Seems I haven't been doing enough."

Tel realised Brian hadn't looked at him yet, was staring straight ahead and blindly eating his Pot Noodle. He actually felt nervous. "We're a bit concerned."

"Oh aye? About what?"

"We're worried we may have inadvertently done something to … upset you." When Brian didn't say anything, he added, "Have we done something to upset you?"

"I don't know, have you?"

Tel leaned forward in the chair and rested his elbows on his knees, clasping his hands together. "We've been friends for a long time, Bri, we know when something's not right."

"Same here."

"Do you want to … talk about it?"

"About what?"

"About anything that might be … playing on your mind?"

"No." Brian suddenly stood up, making Tel flinch. "Not yet. Maybe later."

"Okay, Bri."

When Tel returned to the others, anxiously standing in a tight group, and Brian had climbed into his RV, Sophie said, "How is he?"

"He's … thinking."

"About?"

"He wouldn't say."

"He's onto us," said Mark.

"Look casual!" Olivia suddenly whispered, "He's coming over."

"Oh God, I feel sick."

Brian came to a stop in front of them, looked at the ground, looked at them, and tilted back his cowboy hat. He said, "I'm not going to dwell, not right now. Let's just enjoy the rest of our 'oliday." He smiled behind his beard. They weakly smiled back.

He turned and started walking back towards his RV. "But at some point," he boomed, "We're going to sit down and sort a few things out."

"Yes, Bri."

"Of course, Bri."

"Shit," Sophie breathed, "Really scared now."

Canopies rolled away and everything packed up, they got into their cabs and started up the engines, pulling off the camping area and onto the road running down from the lodges. Brian stopped to see if anything was coming.

A black Cherokee drove in front of him, the sun reflecting sharply off the windows.

Tel immediately came over the walkie talkie. "Was that the car?"

"Again?" Mark crackled.

Brian picked up the walkie talkie. "It does appear that we may have a stalker."

"*Christine!*" Faye suddenly gasped.

Brian stared at her. "You know who it is?"

"That film about an evil car that comes to life and kills people. Or *Duel*," she gasped even louder, "About a psychopathic killer in a truck chasing after Dennis Weaver in a car."

"Lay off the horror films, Faye."

"Won't, Bri."

The convoy pulled away. By the time they reached the main road the car was nowhere to be seen.

\* \* \*

Brian picked up the walkie talkie. "Sophie?"

"Yes, Bri?"

"I'm not entirely sure where we're going."

"What does your GPS say?"

"Not much, but the wife is saying 'idiot' a lot," he laughed, as Faye squinted her eyes at him. "I put the coordinates in but there's no destination, just directions."

They'd driven through Kayenta and were back on the 160, heading west.

"Follow the signs to Page until you see a sign on the right for 98."

"Copy." He put the walkie talkie down and sighed. "Hope there's a food stop planned along the way?"

"You and your food," Faye said.

"I'm a growing lad!"

"You can't possibly grow any more, Bri."

"I might."

"Upwards is done, the only way left is outwards."

"Bouncing around in that jeep burned off at least a million calories."

"You had loads of Liv's food on the tour."

"That was *five hours* ago!"

"I made you egg on toast when we got back."

"Three hours ago."

"And you had a coffee and half a packet of biscuits after that."

"Still not enough."

"Then you had a Pot Noodle before we set off!"

Brian grunted. He still felt hungry. Maybe it was the heat messing with his metabolism.

"You're not feeding me enough, wife!"

"Feed you any more and you'll pop, *husband*!"

"I'll never make it! I feel faint with malnutrition. I can't drive if I feel faint."

Tutting, Faye unclipped her seatbelt, said, "Don't crash," and went into the back of the RV to search through cupboards. She came back and threw a packet of crisps on his lap.

"That won't keep me going for long, it's like feeding

wafers to a whale."

"You'll look like a whale if you're not careful."

"Open them for me, would you?"

"I suppose you want me to feed them to you as well?"

"If you wouldn't mind.  Can't get salt all over the steering wheel, they might charge us for it."

Faye tutted again, but grinned as she popped them, one by one, into the hole in his beard.

In the second RV Sophie said, "Do you think Brian will be alright at the next place?"

"Why wouldn't he be?"

"Well, it's a bit narrow, and Brian's … "

"A big man," Tel laughed.  "He'll be fine."

"I hope your right, they might charge us for a helicopter rescue."

In the third RV Mark glanced at Olivia, curled up in the passenger seat with the sun shining on her, making her glow. "Do you know what?" he said.

"No, what?"

"I really, really love you."

She gave him a big smile.  "Do you know what?"

"No, what?"

"I can't believe this is my life."

"Believe it, it's real."

"When I think back to – "

"Don't look back," Mark said, reaching out to gently clutch her hand, "Look forward and enjoy."

"I am.  You make me very happy, Mark."

"Good, you deserve it."

Brian hauled on the steering wheel to turn right onto 98, secretly keeping an eye out for a shop or a café.  There wasn't one.

"I love that the roads are so straight here," he said, trying to take his mind off his grumbling hunger.  "No wonder the American rigs are so big, they don't have to fight with junctions or traffic islands.  Imagine one of those trying to navigate their way around the Cotswolds."

"They'd get stuck," Faye laughed.

"Hence the lack of American RVs on British roads."

"I love it here," she breathed, watching the scenery fly passed.

"We're not moving, Faye."

"We could look into it?"

"We couldn't. They probably wouldn't let us anyway."

"Why not?"

"Because we're old and we're poor."

Faye pouted, but dreamed about it anyway as they drove across the scrubby desert.

\* \* \*

Sophie crackled over the walkie talkie. "It's just here on the right, Bri, where all those cars are parked."

"Antelope Canyon?"

"That's the one."

"Is this a safari park?" Faye asked Brian, "Like a canyon filled with antelopes?"

"No idea."

They parked up, got out, and stretched.

"What is this place?" Mark asked.

"It's a slot canyon," Sophie said.

Mark shook his head. "Still none the wiser."

"It's a canyon that goes underground."

"Underground?" Olivia said. "It's not potholing, is it? I don't like tight spaces."

"Oh," said Sophie, frowning. "Are you claustrophobic?"

"I don't think so. I guess it depends on how small the space is."

Sophie thought, if they'd read their itineraries when she'd first sent them out they'd know ahead of time what was planned and wouldn't be springing phobias on her. "I'm a bit claustrophobic," she said with a forced smile. "But Etta said I should be fine.

"Hungry," Brian said irritably.

"Sandwich?" Olivia offered.

"Life-saver!"

Olivia hurried back to the RV.

Sophie headed off to one of the two Navajo ticket huts. She showed the woman behind the counter the booking number on her phone and handed over her driving licence as ID. As she turned round, she found Brian standing right behind her. He peered down at her, then at the tickets in her hand. Sophie stood still and silent, holding his gaze and her breath. Brian gave a grunt and walked off without a word. He and Olivia stood to one side as he scoffed her sandwich.

"He definitely knows," she whispered to the others.

"Do you think he'll hate us for long?" Sophie asked.

"No," Mark said, "He's a good bloke, he'll understand what we did and why we did it."

"Will he? Are you sure about that?"

"No."

As they waited with the gathering crowd, Faye read out the rules printed on a board. "No bags, backpacks, fanny packs – "

"Better leave your fanny packs behind, ladies," Mark snorted.

" – hydration bags or purses. No firearms or weapons – "

"That's a relief," said Tel, "Nothing worse than a ricocheting shoot out in a cave."

"Don't even joke," Mark said.

"No open toed shoes, sandals, or footwear with heels. Oh," she said, looking at the sandals on her feet, "I'd better put my trainers on."

"Me too," said Sophie and Olivia in unison.

The women dashed back to the RVs to change.

Mark continued to read out the rules. "Oh, says here they're not responsible if you trip and break your neck."

"Good to know," said Brian. "No jumping from ledges and definitely no neck breaking."

A young Navajo boy in his teens sauntered over to collect them.  Brian quickly pushed the remains of his sandwich into his mouth, just as the women hurried back.

Despite all the tour jeeps in the car park, the boy led them into the desert.  They assumed it would be a short walk.

It wasn't.

"Where is it?" Faye said, staring out over flat desert.

"Pretty sure the Navajo lad knows where he's going."

"Unless he's a psychopath leading us to our death."

"He'll have his hands full with all us lot."  There were four other people with them.

"He could have special Native American powers that call to the spirits of his ancestors, and *they* kill us."

While Faye was in the midst of a feverish nightmare scenario, Sophie had more realistic concerns on her mind. Staring at the ground, she called to the boy in front, "Are there any creepy crawlies around here?"

"Very occasionally rattlesnakes and spiders," the boy said, "Sometimes scorpions."

There was a couple of tiny screams, and when the front four turned around they saw Sophie in Tel's arms, still looking at the ground around her as she clung tightly to his neck. Behind them a woman had leapt up onto a man's back – presumably she knew him – piggy-back style.  The man hissed, "So it's okay if I die, is it?"

"Get a grip, Sophs," Tel gasped, prising her from his neck and lowering her to the ground.

"My hero!" she whined.

"I'm a lawyer, not a weightlifter."

"*Excuse* me?"

"I didn't mean it like that."

She turned to huff off, then gripped onto Tel's arm instead, walking close. "Keep your eyes peeled," she breathed.

They walked across soft sand, flat at first, then dipping down an incline.  The boy pointed out a dinosaur footprint, and they all stood around it, cocking their heads to the side, trying to make it out.

At the bottom of the hill, a covered walkway corralled them down, and down, and down.  The cliffs rising up around them were smooth waves of sandstone eroded by time and water, a kaleidoscope of natural colours.  At the end, several sets of steep metal stairs took them underground.  The voices of the people below echoed off the walls.

"You okay, Livs?" Mark asked.

"Yes, darling, I'm fine."

The canyon was beautiful; the light, the swirling sandstone, and the sense of unending time.  They squeezed through the undulating walls.  At one point Brian sucked in to manoeuvre himself through a particularly narrow gap, and pulled all the buttons off his chambray shirt.

"It's seventies man!" Tel's laughter bounced off the walls. "Shirt open to his waist, hairy chest on view to woo the women!"

"Anyone have a medallion?" Olivia giggled.

Mark started singing and dancing to *YMCA*.

"Shut up, the lot of you."  Brian's voice boomed through the cavern, making the people up ahead turn around.  Their eyes widened when they saw a giant of a man exposing himself.

Faye fussed over the shirt, pulling it out of his jeans and tying it around his significant waist.

"I look like a Kardashian!" Brian drawled miserably.

"You don't," Sophie laughed, "You really don't."

"No miniature sewing machine in your back pocket, Faye?"

"Left it in my bag in the RV," she winked.  To Brian she said, "Just hold it together."

Brian glared pointedly over her head at the others and said, "I am trying to hold it together."

They all gulped.

Brian spent the rest of the tour trying not to expose his nipples.  It was difficult on the steep ladders that kept going up, and up, but at least he wasn't as hot as everyone else due to the increased ventilation around his torso.

"Does the canyon flood often?" Olivia asked the boy.

"Not often, but they give us warning."

"How do they give you warning?"

"They call."

Olivia pulled out her phone and looked at it. "There's no signal down here."

The boy, still walking, said, "They *call*. They shout down to us."

"Does that give everyone enough time to get out?" Tel asked.

"Mostly."

They all mouthed 'Mostly?'

"Listen out for the sound of running water," Brian said, "Then run like hell."

"Wish I'd brought my arm bands," said Sophie.

Just over an hour later they climbed the final ladder up through a crack in the ground and emerged into the daylight, where they stood gasping for breath in a hee-haw kind of way until the eyespots faded.

Brian panted, "Ranulph Fiennes … would have baulked … at the steepness … of that last … set of … steps."

Mark looked back at the narrow crevice they'd just crawled out of and said, "I feel like I've been reborn." He threw up his arms and cried, "I AM REBORN!"

A man walking passed patted him on the shoulder and said, "Well done, man, Christ is our saviour."

"Christ," Tel laughed, "No more swearing around Mark then."

"'Tis the celibate life for you, lad."

Mark pulled Olivia close to him and cried, "Never!"

Olivia giggled.

They trudged across the sand back to the car park. It was hot and, despite their glasses, the sun blinded them.

But not completely.

Mark spotted it first and cried, "You have *got* to be kidding me."

They followed his gaze and saw the black Cherokee parked in the car park.

There was no one in it.

"Bri?" Faye said nervously, as they scoured the crowds for familiar faces. Their guide was already leading another party towards the canyon.

"It's okay, love."

"Is it?"

"It's just a coincidence."

"They're after me," Olivia breathed. "We should have just given them the money."

"I'm sure there's a perfectly reasonable explanation," said Tel. "They're probably visiting the sites, just like us."

"They didn't strike me as tourists," Sophie said, instantly regretting it when Olivia gave a little whimper and quickly adding, "But I'm sure Brian's right, it's probably a fluke."

"A glitch in the matrix," said Mark. "Nothing to worry about."

They walked up to the car and peered in. The back seat had a zipped-up bag and a crate of bottled water.

They shook their heads and walked on.

"Should we buy a gun at Walmart?" Olivia suddenly asked.

"Pretty sure it's illegal to shoot someone you think might be following you," Tel said. "As a lawyer, I wouldn't recommend it."

"As your fiancé," said Mark, "I have to say I wouldn't feel comfortable having a gun in the RV."

"I bet we never see it again and we're needlessly worrying," said Sophie.

"No point getting worked up over nothing," said Mark.

"Food," said Brian, "Let's concentrate on getting something to eat instead."

"Bri, the world doesn't revolve around your stomach!"

239

"My world does. I can't help having a healthy appetite."

"Massive, unabated, unrelenting appetite."

"Page is just down the road," Sophie said, "We can eat there."

"Herd 'em up, move 'em out!" Brian bellowed, climbing into his RV.

Faye climbed into the back and then handed him a shirt with buttons. "Cover yourself up, Bri, nobody needs to see your man boobs."

He slapped his flesh and said, "I'm a fine figure of a man!"

"If the figure is zero," Faye laughed.

"This isn't fat, this is *muscle!*"

"Looks like the result of a lot of overeating to me."

He changed in his seat and picked his hat off the dashboard, instantly feeling like John Wayne again.

John Wayne with a niggling, irritating problem – and it wasn't food or man boobs.

\* \* \*

They were on the road again.

Sophie came over the walkie talkie. "We have choices."

"Closest source of food?" Brian replied.

"There's loads, Bri, don't panic. Now, we can either find a restaurant – "

"Yes, nearest?"

" – or we can find a supermarket, get something for lunch and a bunch of meat for a barbecue when we stop for the night?"

Confused now, Brian looked at Faye, who said, "Be nice to have a barbecue."

"Supermarket," he reluctantly agreed.

Mark crackled, "Liv says she needs provisions."

"Okay," said Sophie, "Follow us."

The second RV peeled off from the back of the convoy and drove onto the left side of the road.

"Oh, this feels more normal," Tel sighed.

Grinning, and checking the long, straight road ahead was clear, Brian pushed down on his accelerator.

The RVs were neck and neck, racing down the highway. Brian turned his head and saw Sophie's expressionless face glaring at him through the passenger window, and let them pass.

They turned right towards Page and the empty desert became more populated. Walmart appeared on the left. They parked up and instantly looked around for a black Cherokee. There were two, neither of them *their* car, and inwardly they breathed a sigh of relief.

They burst through the supermarket doors and, led by Brian, who marched like a man on a mission, headed straight for the deli counter. His arms filled with food, he paid and marched out again.

They sat outside their RVs on their camp chairs, chomping.

"Never shop on an empty stomach," Brian declared, eating his foot-long with gusto.

"Funny how they call bread rolls 'sandwiches' here," Olivia said, delicately biting into hers.

"Cobs," said Faye.

"Teacakes," Brian insisted.

"Baps," Sophie laughed.

"Buns!"

"Did you know that you can park up for the night in a Walmart car park?" Sophie said.

"Why would you want to do that?"

"You just can if you want to, if you're travelling and need somewhere to stop, and it's free."

"We're not though, are we?" Faye asked, looking around. A supermarket car park wasn't her idea of a scenic place to pitch.

"No, Walmart might not be pleased if we lit up barbecues on their tarmac."

"Where *are* we stopping?" asked Mark.

"If you'd read your itinerary you'd know, but, since none of you have bothered, I guess it's going to be a surprise."

"Ooh, this trip is full of surprises, isn't it," Faye said.

"It certainly is," said Brian, eyeballing the others, who all looked away, pretending not to notice.

Packets of crisps were opened and consumed, along with bottles of water.

"Could do with a nap now," Tel said, stifling a yawn.

"Me too. Early mornings are a killer."

"Plenty of time for that later," Brian declared, standing up and walking back towards Walmart. "We have more important things to do first. Noticed they had a liquor store. Thank the Lord! I'm stocking up, and I swear," he boomed, thrusting a fist into the air, "I'll never go thirsty again!"

"I'll put the chairs away then, shall I?" Faye called after him.

In the meat section, Tel and Sophie rolled by with their trolley just as Faye was putting packs of burgers and sausages into theirs. "You don't need those," Sophie said, "We've got two packs of each, and spare ribs and flavoured chicken pieces, enough for everyone."

"Why?" Brian drawled, glaring at them.

"Because we're having a barbecue," Sophie grinned.

"Oh," Faye said, putting her packs back, "That'll save us a bit of money, won't it, Bri."

"Yes," Brian said, watching Tel and Sophie rolling away again, "I think that's the point."

They bumped into Mark and Olivia in the bread section. Their trolley was already full of bread rolls, or buns, or teacakes.

"We've got these," Olivia said.

Brian humphed and headed for the condiments section. He saw Tel and Sophie up ahead and quickened his pace.

"Is this a race?" Faye cried, struggling to keep up with him.

They reached the condiments at the same time. Tel and

Sophie furiously started putting bottles and jars into their trolley.

"I'LL GET THESE," Brian boomed. The whole supermarket fell silent, anticipating a fight somewhere – for most, it was the only reason they came to Walmart.

Sophie tutted dramatically and said, "They're in our trolley now. *So* much effort to lean down and take them out again."

"Faye."

"Yes, Bri?"

"Remove the condiments from their trolley."

Sophie physically threw herself across the top of their shopping, as if protecting it. Faye looked at Brian, who reached into his trolley and picked up four square, orange packs. "We got to the cheese first," he said, then threw back his head and indulged in an evil laugh. The supermarket fell silent again.

"I see you got the alcohol," Tel said, peering at the boxes of cans and the six bottles of Prosecco in his trolley – and, inexplicably, a giant container of Cheese Puffs. "You might want to change the beer though."

"No, no, they're mine now."

"Busch NA," Tel said, tilting his head to read the box. "Do you know what NA means, Bri?"

"Don't care."

"You might."

Brian looked at Tel. Tel looked at Brian.

Brian caved and said, "What does it mean?"

Tel grinned. "Non-alcoholic."

Brian grunted, spun the trolley round and hurried off, with Faye struggling to keep up with him. "This isn't Supermarket Dash, you know, Bri!"

"Non-alcoholic," Brian muttered furiously, "What's the point of non-bloody-alcoholic?"

* * *

Back at the now well stocked RVs, Sophie declared status

at the front of the convoy.

Tel looked shocked. "You're not ... you're not *driving*, are you?"

"I might be," she teased.

"But you're not."

"No, but I do know the way, so ... follow us."

"Is it far?" Olivia asked.

"About half an hour."

They headed towards Page, drove straight passed the bottom of it and across a bridge overlooking the Glen Canyon Dam. The panorama as they crested the hill on the other side and saw the lake down below was breath-taking. The buttes of Monument Valley were visible in the distance. It was all so ... American.

"Welcome to Utah!" Tel said into the walkie talkie as they drove passed the sign.

"Utaaaah!" Mark crackled.

"So, have we crashed through another time barrier into a different time zone?" Faye asked Brian.

"Who knows?" He shrugged his big shoulders. "Who cares?"

"I'll just throw my watch out the window then, shall I?"

"Might as well."

"Waaaahweap!" Mark crackled over the walkie talkie as they passed another road sign.

"Next right, Tel," said Sophie, checking the map in the folder, "And straight down to the water."

"Oh, I can see the lake again!" Faye cried.

"Mark, it's so beautiful."

"Nowhere near as beautiful as you."

Olivia looked over at him. "Do we have any sick bags in the van?"

"Use the washing up bowl."

"We are now approaching our destination," Sophie crackled like a tour guide, "Lone Rock Beach, where we shall be camping for the night on the shores of Lake Powell."

Multiple cheering came over the walkie talkies.

They pulled up at the entrance station booths. Tel was just winding down his window to pay when he heard quick, heavy footsteps coming up behind them. Suddenly, slightly out of breath, Brian stood between the RV and the man inside the booth, and slapped down his credit card.

"Three … RVs … one night … camping."

He struggled to turn around in the tight space between Tel's RV and the booth, and instead grinned and wobbled his head at them over his shoulder. He thought twice about sticking his tongue out, that seemed a step too far.

"And three passes for the National Park," Sophie shouted over, having consulted her notes.

Brian glanced at his receipt as he clambered back into his cab. It seemed pretty high for one night's camping, but he wasn't going to worry about it, he'd got one over on them and he felt pretty gloaty.

They drove onto the sandy beach. It was *massive*. And there, right in front, was Lake Powell, with a big rock sticking out the middle.

"Don't stop," Sophie instructed over the walkie talkie, "Keep going in low gear, otherwise you might get stuck in the sand."

"That's clever of you to know," Tel said.

"All courtesy of Etta, my fabulous PA, who said she's watched about a hundred YouTube videos and feels like she's already taken this road trip ahead of us."

Tel found a quiet spot between a dozen or so spread-out RVs, facing the water and the rock.

"Oh, this is lovely," Olivia said.

They got out to admire the scenery.

"Spectacular view."

"Good camp find, Sophs."

"It is, isn't it, and it's cheap."

"I beg to differ," Brian drawled, thinking of his receipt.

"You have to pay for a pass to the National Park as well.

Maybe should have thought of that before you rushed to booth, eh, Bri?"

"I thought it was about time I paid for something."

"U-shape configuration for the vans?" Tel deflected quickly.

They nodded and rearranged their parking, pulling out the canopies and creating a little space of their own.

Sophie jumped up and, hurrying into her RV, cried, "Last one in the water is a rotten egg!"

* * *

"It's cold!" Olivia squeaked, tiptoeing into the lake.

"Cold?" Mark laughed, swimming backwards, "My gonads are in my throat. Take that shirt off, Livs."

"No, no, I'll leave it on."

Faye stood behind her, nervously stepping into the water.

"Faye!" Brian yelled.

"What?"

"Take your dressing gown off."

"If I looked like Sophie or Livs I would, but I don't, so I'm not."

"Don't be daft, woman."

"You're amongst friends," Mark laughed, "We don't care."

"I care." She peered down at the water. "Is there anything in there?"

"More water," Tel shouted.

"Any fish with teeth, or alligators?"

"Alligators!" Brian howled, splashing her. "It's okay, Sophie has some brandy to kill any alligators; well, get them drunk enough to kill themselves."

Sophie tutted.

Brian suddenly stopped laughing and a look of terror washed over his face. He suddenly disappeared under the water with a lot of splashing and thrashing of arms.

"BRIAN!" Faye screamed.

His head bobbed up again, gasping for air, before he

started bellowing with laughter.

"*BRIAN!*"

"Come and get me. Come on, I dare you."

Faye shuffled in, staring down the whole time and trying to brush the surface of the water away so she could see underneath, despite its crystal clarity. She took a deep, calming breath, and took the dressing gown off, flinging it back onto the sand. She felt very imperfect with her middle-aged body that had birthed two children, but nobody seemed to take any notice; there were other imperfect people splashing in the water too.

Olivia stood on the edge, her shirt flapping in the breeze.

"You can swim, can't you, Livs?" Mark thought to ask.

"Yes."

"Then throw caution to the wind and launch yourself in like the brave woman you are."

Olivia quite liked the idea of that – Mark always seemed to know the right thing to say – and, like Faye, she tore off her shirt, threw it behind her, and shuffled in.

It was *freezing*.

"Sophie!" Tel shouted, "Considering it was your idea to camp here, you don't seem to be enjoying yourself very much."

Sophie had submerged herself up to her ankles and was standing with her hands bunched up under her chin. "Are you sure there's no snakes?"

"Get in!"

She quickly stepped in, squealing as the water rose up her body.

Suddenly, everyone was yelling and splashing like children.

* * *

Sophie ran to her RV and came running back with a plastic bottle.

"Let's get this sand and sweat off us," she said, squeezing gel into their hands. "It's hair and body wash. Don't know how good it will be, but it's environmentally friendly."

"Ah," said Brian, vigorously rubbing his armpits, "You can't beat a bit of outdoor washing."

"Do it all the time," said Mark. "Neighbours have complained about it."

"Such a view to do it in!" Olivia gasped.

As they sudded up, Sophie sensed eyeballs upon them and raised the bottle in the air, shouting, "IT'S OKAY, IT'S BIODEGRADABLE!"

People along the beach raised their thumbs. A man in a huge rig nearest to them laughed and shouted, "I WASN'T LOOKING AT THE BOTTLE!" The woman with him whacked him.

"Your head's steaming," Brian said to Faye.

"I've just washed it."

"You look like a blown-out candle."

"Flattery will get you nowhere, Mr Bennett."

He swam over to her and took her in his arms, gently spinning them round. "How about now, Mrs Bennett, will this get me anywhere?"

She tried to adopt a stern face but failed. "Possibly."

He lifted her hand out of the water to show her the ring, but … it wasn't there! He quickly lifted her other hand just as she started screaming, and dropped to his knees, pushing his head under the water to search around Faye's feet.

"MY RING!" she wailed, "MY RING!"

"What's up, Faye?"

"I'VE LOST MY RING!"

Four heads stared down at the crystal-clear water, just as Brian came up. He took a breath and dunked his head again, delicately running fingers over the fine pebbles and hoping the diamonds were good enough to sparkle underwater.

"You search where you are," Tel called out to Faye, who was spinning on the spot with her head down. "We'll line up and search from the shore. Try not to move your feet too much or you might bury it."

Long minutes passed. Faye started whimpering. Brian was too frantic to offer soothing words, he just wanted to find it.

Tel suddenly bent forward, his face going underwater. He straightened up again with his hand in the air and yelled, "GOT IT!"

"Oh, thank god!" Faye cried, as Brian threw his head to the sky and breathed a huge sigh of relief. She moved as quickly as she could over to him and took the ring from his fingers. She immediately ran back to the RV.

Brian hurried after her, as did Olivia and Sophie.

She was sitting at the table when they got to her, holding the ring tightly in her trembling hand.

"Is it too big?" Brian asked.

"I didn't like to mention it."

"You should have mentioned it."

"I know." She sniffed. "I'll put it back in the box for safekeeping."

"Wrap something round it," Sophie suggested, "Tape or something."

"I don't have any tape."

Sophie looked at Olivia, who shook her head, then said, "There'll be plasters in the first-aid box."

With a bit of plaster wrapped around it, Faye pushed it back on her finger. "It's a bit tight now."

"Better tight than loose," Sophie said.

"Said the bishop to the actress," Brian laughed.

The women glared at him.

Brian ambled out, muttering, "Tough audience."

\* \* \*

The men started up the two tripod barbecues, whilst the women gently baked on their towels; Faye back in her dressing gown to prevent sunburn and lifting her hand at regular intervals to check on her ring. Olivia got up at one point to make a marinade and salad, then resumed the sunbathing.

Along the beach, smoke rose from the other RVs.

"Ah, the smell of cooking," Olivia sighed.

"Not for me," Faye said.

"Oh, sorry, forgot you don't smell."

"She did before she washed," Sophie laughed.

"It's okay, it doesn't really bother me."

"Bothered us," Sophie laughed again.

"What's it like, not being able to smell?" Olivia asked.

"Like breathing fresh air all the time."

"Must be weird."

"Must be weird to smell something every time you breathe in."

Olivia lifted her head, "Can't you smell anything at all?"

"Vinegar, I can smell vinegar sometimes, but I think that's just the fumes."

"You're missing out on all the lovely scents."

"Missing out on all the bad ones, too, like cow manure and Brian's stink bombs in bed. When the kids were babies I used to change all the 'filled' nappies because I couldn't stand the sound of Brian heaving every three seconds, and when we had a dog I had to clear up the garden because Brian wretched every time he bent down. I do have to be careful I don't blow up the kitchen because the gas on the oven didn't light."

"You could get an electric cooker," Olivia suggested.

"I could," Faye grinned, "But where would be the fun in that?"

They tanned in silence, moving occasionally to rub in more suncream.

"Should we help the men?" Olivia asked, looking back at them laying meat on the grills.

"Nah," said Faye, "Let them get on with it, makes them feel like cavemen cooking dinosaur meat, and it's a good excuse for them to start drinking early."

"I agree," said Sophie, "I'm feeling very languid."

"Lazy."

"Lethargic."

"That's unanimous, then."

They resumed their sunbathing.

"Oh," Sophie suddenly exclaimed, "I know I keep talking about the wedding and the honeymoon – "

"The photos were lovely," Olivia said, thinking of the night at Sophie and Tel's flat before their flight.

"And the DVD was really good," said Faye, "Except for the bit where Brian's snoring sent us all to sleep."

They laughed.

"But I didn't tell you about Lizzie at the wedding." Sophie turned on her side and rested her head on her hand.

"Do tell," said Olivia.

"Tell us *everything*," said Faye.

"Well, Lizzie used to go out with a bloke who dumped her for another woman."

"The swine!"

"He was more Tel's friend than mine, hence the reason he was invited, but I got to know Lizzie quiet well. Nice woman, didn't deserve to be dumped like that, completely out the blue, *by text*!"

"The coward!"

"So, Tel's friend, Andrew, brought his new girlfriend to the wedding, the one he'd left Lizzie for. Then Lizzie arrived."

"No!"

"Wait, it gets better. Lizzie brought two men with her."

"Two?"

"Yes, her new boyfriend and, get this, the *ex-boyfriend* of Andrew's new girlfriend, the one she'd cheated on and left."

"Inspired," Olivia giggled.

"Lizzie walked into the wedding reception with a man on each arm, both incredibly handsome, by the way. She said the look on their faces when they saw her is burned into her memory for all time, said it was almost worth all the pain he'd caused her … almost. Andrew and his girlfriend left soon after."

"That's *awesome*," Faye laughed. "Good for her."

"Are they still together?" Olivia asked, "Andrew and his new girlfriend?"

"No." Sophie lay on her back again. "He wanted to get back together again, but Lizzie had already moved on with the new bloke. They're engaged now and very, very happy."

"Serves him right."

Faye checked the ring was on her finger for about the millionth time.

It was starting to hurt a bit now.

* * *

"Who wants what?" Brian shouted down to them.

"Bring me one of everything," Faye yelled back.

"Come and get it yourselves!"

"The service here is terrible," she said, stirring herself.

As they sauntered towards the laden tables, the men gawped at Faye.

"Wife?" Brian gasped.

The tone of his voice forced her to quickly look down at herself to check she still wore a swimming costume and wasn't – horror of horrors – walking around completely naked. She wasn't.

"What?"

"Your hair!"

"What about it?" She touched the top of her head: it was higher than she remembered. Her hair felt ... fuzzy, and quite widespread. She couldn't run her fingers through it, and it seemed very *bouffant*.

"Wild woman of Borneo," Mark laughed.

"Dragged through a hedge backwards," Tel sniggered.

"It's certainly a different look for you, lass. Have you tried brushing it?"

"Yes! Is it bad?" She raced into the RV to look in the mirror and they heard her scream, "It's terrible! I look like I've been electrocuted!" She came running out again, furiously brushing at it, but it refused to be tamed and kept bouncing up again.

Sophie came out of her RV with a plastic bottle. "Put some of this on."

"That's what you said with the biodegradable stuff and look at me now, pom-pom head!"

"This," Sophie breathed in a Marks and Spencer voice, holding the bottle to her face and pouting, "is the finest hair oil money can buy."

"No, leave it as it is," Brian urged, "It'll keep us amused all night."

"Shut up."

Faye took the bottle and squeeze the contents into the palm of her hand.

"Oh, not that much!" Sophie gasped.

"Oh?"

Sophie shrugged and sighed. "Try it and see."

Faye tried it, slicking her hair back with her fingers.

"Oh my life!" Mark cried, "You look like that woman in the *Addicted to Love* video!"

Faye smiled. She knew she didn't look like that woman in the video at all, more like some old bird with oily hair, but she appreciated the compliment. She looked at Brian.

"Gorgeous!" he said with feeling.

Her smile grew bigger. She felt quite trendy. Also, it was nice not to not have her hair constantly tickling her face.

Smiling, she jumped into the RV to look at herself in the mirror. Pleased, she took the sand filled bottle from her hoodie pocket and took it outside.

It was time.

"Brian," she said, sitting next to him at the table, "I have a special anniversary present for you."

"Oh?"

She handed him the bottle. He took it, looked at it, and said, "A tiny bottle of sand, just what I've always wanted."

"It's not just *any* sand," she breathed, copying Sophie's Marks and Spencer voice, "It's 'two Johns' stood here in

Monument Valley' sand."

Brian stared at the bottle with more interest.

"It's 'John Wayne was here' sand."

A big smile spread behind his beard.

"It's 'John Wayne filmed on *this sand*' sand."

"You mean – ?"

"Every time you mentioned a John Wayne film I put a little sand in the bottle. This bottle of sand," she said, tapping it, "is made up of layers of John Wayne and John Ford Monument Valley film sets."

Brian sucked in air. His eyes got bigger. He sat up straight in his chair and gasped, "Faye!"

"Yes, Bri?"

"This …" He stared at it. "This has got to be the *best* present I've ever had!"

"Better than a book?" she laughed.

"A thousand times better, although I love the book."

"Almost as good as a gold and diamond ring?"

He nodded and pulled her close for a hug. "Yes, Faye, we're even. Thank you, lass, I'm chuffed to bits. You've made me really happy."

"I'm glad, because you make me really happy."

"It's gone gooey!" Mark cried.

"I thought you like gooey," Olivia giggled, snuggling up to him.

"I like *our* gooey, other people's gooey, not so much."

They laughed, they ate, they drank and chatted. After a while Tel jumped up and said, "Oh, I almost forgot."

He came back out of his RV with a bottle in one hand and flute glasses in the other. He popped the cork on the champagne like an expert, and everyone cheered.

"What's this in aid of?" Brian asked.

"Your wedding anniversary, of course. Wanted to do it yesterday but – "

"It was a dry town," Brian gasped, clutching at his chest, "Worst night of my life!"

Tel handed out the bubbles, adding, "There's a couple more in the cool box."

"You shouldn't have," Faye said, taking hers, "You've already treated us so much already; the clothes, the hats, the beautiful bag."

"Yes," said Brian, clearing his throat and putting his glass and his special bottle of sand on the table, "I think it's about time we had a chat about that."

"Oh god," Mark muttered, swigging back his champagne and immediately refilling it, "It's happening. I feel sick."

"So, we're finally addressing the elephant in the room, are we?" Tel sighed.

"Elephant?" Faye asked, looking around. "What elephant?"

"I regret nothing," Olivia said firmly.

"It's okay," Sophie told them, "I've prepared the case for our defence."

# CHAPTER TWELVE

"What's going on?" Faye asked, "I'm sensing something's a bit off. What did I miss?"

"You missed our affluent friends sneakily subsidising the impoverished working-class folk."

"That's not fair," Tel said, "We were discrete about it, we weren't patronising you in any way."

"What's he mean, Bri? Why are you all so serious? I don't like it. What's going on?"

"They've been paying for all our stuff; camping fees, tours, restaurants, food, clothes." He turned to Sophie. "The RVs, were they *really* 'hire three, get one free'?"

She jutted out her chin. "No."

"Did our two hundred pounds in the kitty *really* cover everything?"

She hesitated. "No."

"In our defence," Tel said quickly, "We knew you were financially distressed after buying the new caravan and the ring for Faye. We were just trying to help."

"And lying about it."

"We didn't lie!" Olivia snapped, "We just … didn't tell you."

"Would you have come on this trip if we had?" Mark asked.

Brian paused, then said, "Probably not."

"That's why we did it."

"We wanted you to come," Olivia urged, "You were invited too, it wouldn't have been right to go without you."

Mark leaned forward in his chair. "You're a proud man, Bri, we get it. You were struggling and we wanted to help, but we didn't want to rub it in your face."

"Hence the subterfuge," Tel said.

"We did it purely for selfish reasons," said Sophie. "This road trip wouldn't have been the same without you both. You're our mainstays."

"The voices of reason."

"The wise ones."

"Our friends," Olivia breathed, "And we love you."

Brian jutted out his hairy chin and crossed his arms, eyeing them and thinking. "I'm not happy," he said at length.

"Which one are you then?" Tel quipped, hoping to relieve the tension.

"Grumpy, by the look on his face," Mark laughed.

Brian didn't laugh, he grunted, still thinking.

Faye said, "It's very kind of you, but … it's a bit embarrassing, having someone else pay for your holiday because you can't afford it yourself."

"We weren't doing this without you," Olivia declared.

"You're our friends," said Sophie, shrugging a shoulder. "You *had* to come."

"You're our biggest source of amusement," Mark grinned.

"Swallow your pride, Bri. Accept it in the way it was meant, with kindness and with love."

All four of them nodded their heads, and waited for the verdict.

Brian took a deep breath. He looked at Faye, who said, "They meant well."

"We did, we did!"

"And it has been brilliant, hasn't it, Bri?"

"Plus," Mark piped up, "It's done now and there's nothing you can do about it."

"Mark!" hissed Sophie.

"What?"

"Stop antagonising the plaintiff and leave the reasoning to me."

"How much do we owe you?" Brian asked.

"See?" Sophie snapped at Mark. She turned back to Brian. "I don't have the figures to hand."

"In the region of?"

"I've no idea."

"Perhaps you could ask your assistant for a balance."

"I could, but I won't."

"Just don't expect a Christmas present this year," Tel said. "When you're back on your financial feet again you can treat us all to a slap-up meal at the Woodsman or something."

"Oh yes!" Olivia cried excitedly, "That would be lovely."

"Come on, Bri," said Mark, giving Sophie a nervous glance, "If the shoe was on the other foot wouldn't you do the same for us? If one of us was in the middle of a financial crisis and you could afford it, wouldn't you want to help? Think of all those times you've helped *us*."

"The toilet cartridge in the Airstream!" Tel gasped, "Remember that? Blimey, the horror! And Faye coming to the rescue."

"Faye's caravan full of emergency supplies," Olivia giggled, "Never short of a cushion or a blanket or a cup of tea for waifs and strays."

"Brian standing up to Richard all those times," Mark said, holding Olivia's hand.

"Persuading me to marry Tel," Sophie said, staring at her handsome husband.

"Stop," Faye sniffed, "You'll make me cry."

"You see, Bri," said Sophie, "This is small payback for everything you've done for us."

Brian leaned back in his chair, his arms still folded, and they waited, sipping furiously at their champagne to steady their nerves.

"Okay," he finally said.

"To be clear," said Tel, "When you say 'okay'... ?"

"I mean it's okay, what you did, what you've done. We," he said, holding Faye's hand, "really appreciate it."

"We do," Faye sniffed.

There was a mass exhalation of relief, and then Sophie jumped up and into their RV. "First bottle is for your anniversary," she said, jumping down with two more bottles. "This," she said, struggling with the cork and then passing it to Tel, who said, "You have to take the cage off, Soph."

"I know! It was welded on."

The cork popped.

"This one," she said, refilling their glasses, "Is for good times, with good friends."

They clinked glasses.

"And the third one?" Olivia giggled.

"Oh, the third one is just to get smashed."

"I'll drink to that," Mark cried, raising his glass.

"I'd much prefer a beer, if you don't mind," Brian said. He lumbered into the RV to raid his cool box, returning with a four-pack.

"Cheers," Tel said, grabbing one, and then another when Mark nudged him.

The crisis was over.

* * *

They'd eaten their fill of the barbecue and there was loads left over, which Olivia diligently wrapped in foil and put in the fridge.

"Picnic tomorrow," she said, already thinking of dipping sauces and salad dressings – she missed her pub kitchen.

Faye, full and tipsy, said, "I still can't believe I've seen the Grand Canyon."

"Me neither," Olivia said, "Wasn't it *amazing*! And Monument Valley was just *epic*."

"I can't believe we've known each other for three years," Sophie said.

"Seem longer, does it?" Brian grinned.

"No. I think I can safely say it's been a life changing experience. I feel lucky to know you all."

"But that isn't what you thought when you first met us,"

Brian said with a wink.

She laughed. "No. I was a stuck-up cow then."

"Then?" Tel snorted.

"Shut up."

"So, what *did* you think of us?" Mark asked.

"Not much, to be honest, not at first. I was more concerned that my boyfriend had brought me *camping*." She looked at Tel and smiled. "I lived in Kensington, I didn't *do* shiny tin cans in the middle of a field, surrounded by strangers."

"And they don't come any stranger than Brian," Mark laughed.

"I just thought he was a big bloke who talked funny." Sophie reached across the table and put her hand on top of his. "Who knew he was a gentle giant with a big heart?"

"I did," said Faye, putting her head on his shoulder.

"His huge, hairy head filled with so much knowledge," Mark grinned.

"I'll have less of your cheek, lad."

"I thought you were lovely, but a bit sad," Faye said to Olivia.

"I thought you were a friendly chap," Brian nodded at Mark. "I was wrong."

"Don't make me get up and come over there, Bri."

"Come on, plant man, bring it on."

"I'm too full and too knackered. Take a rain check?"

"Yup."

"I thought Faye was, and is, the kindest, most generous woman I've ever met," Olivia said.

Faye modestly waved her comment away and, looking at Tel and Sophie, said, "I thought you two were *gorgeous*."

"Notice the past tense?" Tel laughed. "We've clearly lost our edge since then."

"You never had an edge," Sophie told him, "Mine is sharp enough to cut glass."

"Like your *enunciation*?" Tel laughed again.

"I'll deal with you later."

"Promises, promises."

"I'd never seen such beautiful people on a campsite before," Faye said dreamily, "You looked like film stars."

"Who'd wandered onto the wrong movie set," Brian snorted,

"Your babies are going to be stunning."

Sophie's hand shot up. "We'll have no talk about babies, thank you very much, far too early for that."

"Talking of babies," Olivia said, "What about Jim and Beth having *twins*?"

"Oh my god," Mark cried, "Two tiny Jims, it hardly bears thinking about, does it!"

"Don't be so mean! Besides, it could be two tiny Beths."

"Let's hope so."

"Or a boy that looks like Jim and a girl that looks like Beth. Mini-thems."

"She's going to be a brilliant mother."

"And I think he'll make a great dad," said Faye.

"Yeah," Mark said, "I have to admit, he does seem to have grown up quite a lot."

"Do you see much of Julie?" Brian thought to ask.

"I quite liked her," Olivia giggled, "She was so flaky and lascivious."

Brian took a deep breath and said, "She made a pass at me once."

"Only once?"

"She made a pass at everything with a pulse, Bri."

"Did she?"

"Yeah, if you were breathing you were a target."

"Oh, my ego just popped."

"Yes, we heard it," Sophie laughed, and Brian stirred uncomfortably in his chair, wafting the air around him with a giant hand.

"We see her every now and again," Mark said. "She works in MacDonalds in town now, got a boyfriend who looks scarily like Jim."

"She has a type then," Faye laughed.

"We mostly see Jim and Beth," Olivia said. "They pop into the pub most weekends. It's one of the reasons I didn't offer Julie a job as a barmaid."

"No, I can't imagine that would have gone down too well."

They sipped their drinks and stared up at the dark sky speckled with a million tiny stars.

"It's so peaceful," Faye sighed.

"Until you spoke," Brian said.

"Shut your face."

"I'm so glad we decided to stay longer and take this road trip," Olivia said, burping.

"Excellent idea of yours, Sophie."

"Not me, my amazing assistant, Etta. You met her at the wedding."

"Drunk lass?"

"That's the one. She did all the research and booking for us. Probably not the best use of company time but she won't say anything if I don't. She said she feels as if she's already taken this trip ahead of us. Which reminds me, she left a note for today in the itinerary." She jumped up into their RV and back out again with the plastic folder. *"Dear Road Trippers. Hope you're having a lovely time, bring me back gifts of gratitude for all my hard and very amazing work putting it together for you.* Oh, must get her something. *I've left the last full day fairly open to cater for anyone who might be flagging at this point."*

"That'll be the old folk," Mark laughed, and Brian threw a chewed spare rib at him, which missed.

*"At your next pitch tomorrow, don't forget to clean out the RVs, including the potty, before heading back to Las Vegas. I thank you in advance for the gratuities. Love, Etta."*

"Oh no, tomorrow's our last full day!" Olivia wailed.

"Last day!" cried Faye.

"Where is our last pitch?" Mark asked.

"Last pitch!" Faye wailed again.

Olivia cried, "Waaaah!"

"Waaaahweap!" Mark whooped.

"Hurricane," said Sophie.

"Hopefully a place name and not tomorrow's weather forecast?"

"It is."

"Shh," whispered Tel, "Brian's gone."

Brian was spreadeagled in the chair, beer can in one hand, hat tilted back on his head, snoring gently.

"The calm before the storm," Olivia giggled.

"Hope you've all still got your earplugs," said Faye.

"Been wearing them every night since we got here," Tel said. "Despite this, the crescendo last night was staggering in its intensity." They all nodded in agreement. "I don't know how you put up with it without going mad, Faye."

"Who says I'm not?" She rested her head on Brian's shoulder. "I'm used to it. It's like white noise to help me get to sleep; growling, hitching, air-sucking white noise."

"It's been good, hasn't it," Mark said quietly, "The trip of a lifetime."

"Certainly has."

"I'll be sad to go home."

"Me too."

Faye, with a smile on her face, now had her eyes closed.

"I knew the oldies would be the first to go," Mark breathed.

"It's been a long day." Tel stirred himself in his seat. "In fact, I could do with hitting the sack myself. Soph?"

She stretched and got up.

"Lightweights," Mark laughed softly. When he turned to Olivia, she was leaning sideways in her chair, her head on her shoulder, fast asleep. He glanced at his watch. "It's only eight-thirty!"

"Stay up if you want," Tel said, heading to his RV.

"On my own?"

"Suit yourself."

Mark stirred Olivia, who opened her eyes and immediately smiled at him. He loved that. "Bed, Livs?"

"Yes, please."

He stirred Brian, who snorted awake, assessed the situation with startled eyes, and roused Faye, who grumbled her way into the RV.

* * *

## DAY 6

Faye woke up in pain, which had invaded her dreams and disturbed her all night. Brian was already up, making coffee below with the lights on. When she lifted her hand in front of her face she flinched. The finger on her right hand was swollen, bulging from the ring like a balloon and throbbing like a bugger.

"Brian," she gasped.

"Yes, love?"

"My ring."

"So happy you like it, I wasn't sure if it was – "

"No," she said, holding it out for him to see. It looked like a sausage wearing a very tight belt.

"Bloody hell," he gasped, which instantly threw her into a panic – Brian was calm in any situation, but not now it seemed; it must be really bad.

He helped her clamber down from the bed and sat her at the table. He took a tray of ice cubes from the tiny freezer and wrapped them in a tea towel, gently placing it on her finger. He sat opposite her, holding her hand across the table.

"It really hurts, Bri."

"I'll bet. We'll take the swelling down and then hopefully slip it off." He lifted the ice pack and frowned. Faye was starting to feel slightly hysterical, which increased tenfold when Brian opened a drawer and took out a sharp knife.

"Don't cut my finger off!" she cried.

"Don't be daft, I'm going to cut off the plaster."

He angled the knife awkwardly, trying to avoid her

bulging red flesh, and carefully sawed at the layers they'd wrapped around the ring to stop it coming off.

"Don't slip," she laughed nervously.

"I'll try not to." He tutted. "Nothing worse than a blunt knife."

Brian, who had seen many injuries at the steelworks where he worked, didn't like the look of this. The ring was almost completely submerged in flesh. It must really hurt, and he didn't like to see Faye in pain. He sawed at the layers of plaster again and thought he might as well use a butter knife for all the cutting it was doing.

"Can you do it?" Faye asked.

He smiled at her to keep her calm, and then stood and moved towards the door.

Despite the early hour, Tel and Sophie were sitting outside at their table, sipping coffee in the dark. Mark and Olivia's RV was lit inside, so they were awake too.

"Sophie," he said quietly, and she looked up. "We have a problem."

They were on their feet in an instant.

"What is it, Bri?"

"It's Faye's finger, it's swollen around the ring. I think we need a hive mind to get it off. Do you have a sharp knife in your RV?"

"I'll check. If not, I'm sure Livs has one for her cooking."

* * *

Six of them were crowded into one RV, all looking at Faye, who had her hand in the air and was quietly crying in both pain and panic. Sophie and Olivia were on their knees next to her, and Brian sat opposite her at the table. Mark and Tel kind of lingered in the background offering moral support.

Liv's sharp paring knife had managed to cut through the layers of plaster, but they couldn't pull it out from beneath the ring, and the finger looked even more swollen by the minute as they tugged and pulled on it.

"We might have to take her to hospital and have it cut off," Mark suggested.

"My finger?"

"No, the ring."

"I don't want my lovely new ring cut!" she wailed.

"We need to get the plaster off," Olivia said, opening a cupboard and taking out some cooking oil, which she began slathering on Faye's finger to loosen up the sticky. "Anyone have any pliers to pull it out?"

Mark took Brian's RV keys to open up the outside compartment, which might contain a toolbox. It did, but no pliers.

Sophie left and came back with a makeup bag.

"Is that to make me look nice when they cut off my finger?" Faye asked with a dry, uneasy laugh.

Sophie took out a pair of tweezers. She managed to ease the oil further under the plaster with it, and then caught one end and pulled.

It came out with the third tug, and Faye gave a little sigh of relief as the pressure eased, just a little. With oiled fingers, Sophie gave the ring a gentle pull, but the swelling held it firmly in place. She wrapped the ice towel around it and lifted her arm in the air once more, and Brian stood and held it in place.

"Have I got time to make pancakes to boost morale?" Olivia asked. "This is quite nerve-wracking and cooking calms me down."

"Let's see if we can save Faye's finger first," Tel said, without thinking.

"*Try* and save it?" Faye cried.

"I meant, wait for the swelling to go down."

Sophie peeked under the ice towel.

They waited.

"What kind of pancakes?" Brian asked to fill the time.

"Thin ones, like crepes, with fresh fruit and cream, or the standard lemon juice and honey."

Five people went 'Mmmm'.

"How you feeling, Faye?"

"Okay."

"Is it throbbing less?"

"I … I think so."

Sophie took the ice towel off and delicately pulled on the ring.  It didn't budge.

"Sewing kit," she said.

"To sew my finger back on?" Faye cried.

"No, a little trick I just remembered from years ago."

Olivia hurried back with an emergency sewing kit, and Sophie took out a tiny spool of cotton thread, doubled it, and pressed down on the ring, making Faye wince.  Managing to create a tiny gap between the gold band and swollen flesh, she threaded the cotton through the gap, holding one end in place, and coiled the cotton tightly up her finger.

"Hold it at the top," she told Brian.

Olivia quickly drizzled on more oil.  With a determined look on her face, Sophie pulled on the cotton at the base of her finger, which started to pull the ring up.  When it got wedged on the knuckle, Brian took over and forced the ring up its spiral of cotton while Sophie gently pushed it.

And then it came off, and Faye, crying now with relief, rubbed at the finger.

"Here," said Brian, struggling to unclip the gold chain she always wore round her neck until Olivia took over with daintier fingers, "Put it on this, that'll keep it safe until we get it resized.  You okay, lass?"

"Yes," she sniffed, "Thanks, Sophie."

"No problem."

"Where did you learn how to do that?"

"Dad forced me to do a company course on *10 Things to Save Your Work Colleagues' Lives*.  I didn't think some of them were worth saving," she laughed, "But it came in handy today."

Relieved, and now hungry, they filed outside to partake of the fresh morning air …

… and Olivia's very delicious pancakes.

\* \* \*

A couple of hours later, they stood in a line on the shoreline, sighing and admiring the view as a glorious sunrise painted the sky red. Faye thought she was in the closing scene of a film where they lived happily ever after.

"Arizona sure knows how to do sunrises," Mark said, in his best American accent, which was terrible.

"I think we're in Utah," Sophie said, "Hence the 'Welcome to Utah' sign on the way in."

"Utaaaah," he cried, "sure knows how to do sunrises."

Tel looked up and down the beach. "Everyone else is still asleep."

"That's because," Brian said, widening his eyes to focus on his watch, "It's stupid o'clock in the morning."

"Amazing how much better you feel after almost ten hours sleep!" Sophie laughed.

Mark gazed at the rock jutting out in the middle of the lake. "Wonder how far away that is?"

"Dunno."

"Reckon we can reach it?"

Tel looked at Mark. "You want to try?"

"You want to race?"

"I could be persuaded. Brian?"

Brian gulped down the remains of his coffee and handed it to Tel. "Hold my mug," he said, standing and dramatically swishing off his dressing gown. He instantly felt fresh air where fresh air was not meant to be.

"Might want to put some swimming trunks on," Mark howled, as Brian frantically cupped himself.

"He's always showing off his dangly bits!" Tel cried.

"I thought I was wearing underpants!" he gasped.

"A likely story. Any excuse to flash the flesh."

"BRIAN!" screeched Faye, holding out her hands to cover Olivia and Sophie's eyes, "PUT SOMETHING ON!"

He bent down, which made Mark and Tel wince at the vision presented to them, and snatched up the dressing gown, wrapping it around his waist before making a bolt for the RV.

Suitable attired, the men raced into the water. Olivia and Faye didn't fancy it, and Sophie wasn't a strong swimmer, so they made a second breakfast instead – a mini fry up.

"You certainly know how to keep a well-stocked motorhome," Faye told Olivia, as they milled around the kitchen area.

"I'm a pub landlady, I know how to cater for people."

"Thank goodness for that," Sophie said, "Or we'd have all starved to death by now."

Tel won the race to the rock, thrusting his fist in the air with victory. Mark was a close second.

Brian gave up halfway across and backpaddled his way back to shore, mostly because he could smell bacon cooking.

\* \* \*

"Where to next, batman?" Mark asked Sophie.

"You know I'm not your tour guide, right?"

"Just asking."

"We have located our itinerary!" Brian boomed, waving a plastic folder in his hands as he stepped out of the RV. Standing by Mark, he flicked through a few pages and went, "Oooh."

"What?" said Mark.

"Very interesting. A straight bit, a wiggly bit, and," he said, deepening his voice, "a *dark* bit."

"What is?"

"The route to our next pitch."

Mark moved towards him, but Brian held the folder above his head.

"Give us a look."

"No."

Mark jumped up for it. Brian lifted it higher.

Huffing, Mark walked away, then turned, saw that Brian

was now standing reading the folder with his back to him, had an idea, and yelled, "RAIN CHECK!"

He launched himself at Brian, flew through the air towards him, and bounced off. Brian barely moved, hardly felt it at all. Mark threw himself against him again, and Brian casually turned his head and asked, "What are you trying to do?"

"I'm *trying* to knock you over for the comment you made last night."

"What comment?"

"I dunno, I can't remember now. I think I'm stunned, maybe concussed. I might have broken my shoulder," he said, rubbing it. "What are you made of, reinforced concrete?"

"Snips and snails and puppy dog tails."

"We saw the puppy dog tail earlier," Tel laughed.

"No fighting!" Faye yelled, coming out of the RV after washing up the breakfast things. Her hair was still slicked back, and she'd put on lipstick and drawn around her eyes with a dark pencil so they looked bigger than normal

"He started it," Brian said, pointing at Mark and thinking his wife looked really bloody nice.

"Did not!"

"Behave, or I'll send you both to bed," she grinned.

Tel raised an arm and cried, "Can I go to bed? And can I take Sophie with me?"

Grinning, Faye sat at the table. "So, what's the plan for today then?"

"I notice you're looking at me," Sophie drawled. "I'm never planning a trip again, it's too much responsibility."

"Here," said Brian, thrusting the folder at his wife. "It's all in here."

Faye flicked a few pages and went, "Oooh, interesting."

Mark huffed.

"A nice two-hour drive with stop-off for pees, lunch and sight-seeing."

"Peas for lunch?" Olivia asked, frowning.

"No, toilet breaks."

"Oh," she giggled.

Sophie looked back up the beach and said, "Look! Cars, they come."

"Not *the* car, is it?"

They all turned to look. Four cars, none of them a black Cherokee, had trailers hooked up, each carrying a jet ski. They backed up to the water not far from their pitch and unloaded the trailers. One raised a hand in greeting as he parked his car and trailer further up the beach, then jumped on the jet ski and was away. The others followed, the engines screaming.

"How lovely," Olivia said, watching them. "Mummy and I did a bit of jet skiing in Lanzarote, such fun."

"Never tried it," Faye and Sophie said together.

The jet skis zipped back and forth in front of them, the men yelling to one another. One of them came speeding over and cut the engine, letting his jet ski bob gently on the water.

"Want a lift?" a handsome young man said directly to Sophie.

"Erm."

"Take you round the rock?"

To everyone's surprise, Sophie suddenly splashed into the water and jumped on behind him. She waved as he pulled away, almost falling off and clasping tightly onto the driver.

"Bit unexpected," Brian said to Tel.

"Yes, very. Who knew my wife could be enticed away by a young stud on a jet ski. She doesn't even like water, can barely swim."

They watched the jet ski zooming towards the rock and could clearly hear Sophie's screams of delight. The other jet skis followed.

"Do you think she's coming back?" Tel asked Brian, when Sophie and the jet skis disappeared behind the rock.

"Let's hope so."

The high-pitched screaming slowly returned, and the jet ski, along with the others, pulled up in front of them.

Sophie got off, her t-shirt and shorts soaked, laughing so hard she could barely catch her breath. "Oh, you have to try it!" she gasped, "It's *so much fun!*"

"Jump on, mate," the driver shouted to Tel. Tel hesitated for a millisecond and then splashed into the water. As he struggled to clamber onboard, the other skiers shouted over to them, "Come on! Take you for a ride?"

Faye, Olivia and Mark dashed into the water and were helped onto the seats.

One of the drivers looked back at Brian, standing alone on the beach, and hollered, "Sorry, bud."

Brian raised a hand of acceptance. "I know, too big," he boomed, "Wouldn't want to be the cause of you going down with the ship."

Inside he was gutted, and also, like Tel, surprised that *his* wife could be lured away so easily. Faye evidently had a penchant for American men, cowboys or otherwise. It was probably the accents, she loved his Yorkshire one but it was clearly not exclusive. He worried that he was worried as he watched them, screaming and laughing and disappearing around the rock.

"Wife left you, has she?" Sophie laughed, coming to stand next to him in dry clothes.

"Temporarily, I hope."

Sophie stared up at his face. "You're not *jealous*, are you, Bri?"

"Bit."

"Don't be daft, she's just having fun."

"Without me."

She punched him playfully on the arm but hurt her knuckles. "You're like a man mountain," she grimaced, shaking her hand. "I bet you didn't even feel it, did you?"

"Feel what?" Brian grinned.

Thankfully, the four jet skis returned and deposited the drenched pillions on the beach. Still squealing with adrenalin and yelling out their thanks, they ran to their RVs to change.

"British?" one driver yelled over to Brian.

"You could tell from the hysterical screaming coming from behind you?"

"Mine kept saying 'Blimey!'," he laughed, "Kinda cute, so I guessed you were British."

"We are indeed."

"You come here often?" Sophie shouted over, hoping it wouldn't be construed as a pick-up line.

"We live in Wahweap – "

"WAAAHWEAP!" Mark yelled from inside his RV.

" – come here most weekends, and some evenings too."

"Nice lifestyle."

"It is. Enjoying yourselves?"

"Very much so."

"Here for long?"

"Leaving soon."

"Well, nice to meet y'all."

The skier raised a hand and they all zoomed off.

"Oh, have they gone?" Faye said, appearing in dry t-shirt and shorts and combing back her hair.

"Brian's jealous," Sophie told her.

"Snitch," said Brian.

"Jealous? Of me going on a water ski or of me being taken away by a handsome young man?"

"Oh, you acknowledge he was handsome then!"

"I'm married, Bri, I'm not dead from the neck up."

"Fair point, but if you could stop lusting after American men that would be much appreciated."

"I don't lust!"

"I think he needs some special attention," Sophie laughed.

"He's been needing special attention for years. Come here, you daft bugger."

Brian bent for a hug, wobbling his bottom lip, which made his beard quiver. "I didn't get to play on the water," he whimpered.

"There, there."

Satisfied, he stood up and bellowed, "Right, enough time wasted on frivolities, let's load 'em up and move 'em out!"

* * *

Back on the road again, with Brian leading, Sophie crackled over the walkie talkie. "Anyone want to stop and stare at any interesting rock formations along the way?"

"At this point," Mark crackled, "Unless the rocks are singing and dancing, I'm all rocked out."

"Does it involve walking?" Brian asked.

"Yes."

"Then no."

"So you don't want to stop at any interesting hiking trails either?"

"Definitely not."

"Fine!"

Mark crackled, "What's that noise in your background, Bri? You're not having engine trouble, are you?"

"You mean the high-pitched whining?"

"Yeah."

"Faye's got her headphones in and she's singing to her iPod."

"Blimey," Tel said to Sophie, "I thought you were bad."

"*What?*"

They passed sandstone buttes that looked like escapees from Monument Valley and small mountains streaked with colour. The long, straight road cut through red rocks that rose up around them like giants bending to have a good look at them. Pylons followed them for mile after mile. The sun shone from a clear blue sky. It was all so stunning.

"Ooh, we're at a summit," Brian said, passing a sign, "We're at 5690 feet. That's exciting, isn't it."

When Faye didn't reply he glanced over and saw that she was asleep.

"She sure looks pretty in the morning sun," he grinned,

and, in her sleep, she smiled.

They drove through the town of Kanab, which looked typically American and very pretty.

Tel crackled over the walkie talkie. "You need to stop at any of these fast-food restaurants, Bri?"

"No, I'm okay."

"You're not hungry?"

"Are you ill?" Mark crackled.

"Pancakes and fry-up are keeping me going."

"Go Livs!" Tel said, "You've actually managed to fill him up."

Olivia preened.

They turned right onto North 89, and Brian was glad Faye was sleeping as they drove passed shops he knew she wouldn't be able to resist. Then, up ahead, he saw a statue of a cowboy on a rearing white horse behind a sign that read Little Hollywood Land Museum & Trading Post, and knew he had to pull over, it was totally his thing.

The others followed.

"This isn't on the itinerary," Sophie said, hurrying over.

"Impromptu and impetuous stop."

"What's this place then?" Mark asked.

"Dunno," said Brian, clambering down from his cab and feeling a twinge of pain in his back, "I just got here."

Tel stared up at the horse and said, "Don't you ever get bored of cowboy stuff?"

"That's what I keep asking," Faye said, getting out and stretching.

"Never," Brian said, and headed towards the entrance doors.

They passed through a vast shop and Brian, not slowing his pace, said, "Step away from the merch, Faye." He paused only to put five dollars in the donation box, before going through the door marked MOVIE SET MUSEUM.

Brian spent a pleasant half an hour wandering around

the various wooden cabins, and a wagon attached to a life-size plastic horse. Brian, like a child in a sweet shop, read quotes from the description plaques, telling them the names of movies and actors like they were something wonderous. He handed his phone to Tel, who took an astonishing number of photographs with Brian standing in front of everything in his cowboy hat and sunglasses. The others trailed along behind. When Brian disappeared into a saloon cabin, still talking about actors and movies, four of them made a break for it, leaving Faye to fend for herself. They perused the gift shop instead, which was marginally less boring.

A short while later the door to the museum opened and Brian's voice boomed, "Stop pushing me, woman, I haven't finished looking yet!"

"One walk round was enough," she said, "I'm not doing it again. They're just wooden huts, Bri."

"They're not just wooden huts, Faye, they're – "

"M&S huts," Sophie breathed, and they all laughed.

"We're not buying anything," Brian pouted. "Faye, we're not … Faye?"

Faye bought a Good, Bad and Ugly t-shirt, primarily, Brian thought huffily, because it had Clint Eastwood's face on it.

Mark finally bought a cowboy hat. "On the last day!" he complained, paying and putting it on.

"Welcome to our gang at last!" Tel said.

"Wyatt Earp, at your service," said Brian, tipping his brim.

"Doc Holliday," Tel said, tipping his.

"Erm," said Mark.

In his best John Wayne voice, Brian said, "Y'strike me as Billy the Kid there, boy."

"I don't want to be a kid."

"Jesse James then."

Mark shrugged and said, "Jesse?"

"Buffalo Bill?" Tel suggested.

Mark crinkled up his nose.

"Wild Bill Hickok it is." Brian turned from a nodding Mark and, still in John Wayne mode, drawled, "And who might I be addressing here, li'l ladies?"

"Li'l?" Sophie scoffed, "I'm five foot ten!"

"Calamity Jane," Faye declared, pushing back her hat and, for some reason, doing a little dance on the spot.

"Erm," said Sophie and Olivia, looking at each other.

Brian pointed at Olivia. "Laura Ingalls," he said.

"Oh, from *Little House on the Prairie*?"

"The very same."

"I like that," she grinned.

"And you," Brian said, pointing at Sophie, "Can only be Miss Annie Oakley."

"Don't know who she is, but okay, cool."

They left, laughing; six Brits wearing cowboy hats, sunglasses and shorts, striding back to their RVs like the outlaws that they weren't.

Except Brian, who hobbled a bit.

* * *

"Dinosaur tracks?" Sophie asked over the walkie talkie.

"Seen one," Brian said. "Don't want to overdo it."

"I think I'm a bit over the whole rock scene," said Mark.

"Rock and roll is forever," Brian laughed.

"Caves?" Sophie crackled.

"That's a negative from me."

"That's a 'oh no, I can't be bothered' from me also," Mark said.

"I think we're suffering from geographical and historical overload."

"You're probably right, but I think," Brian said, stretching his back in the driver's seat, "We'll need to stop for a break soon."

"Pea break," Olivia giggled.

Brian, following his GPS, turned left at Mount Carmel Junction onto Route 9, and pulled straight into the petrol station.

They parked side by side and got out. The men gathered for a stretch, the women ran first to the loos and then, to Brian's dismay, into the gift shop.

"I'm off for a slash," Mark said, striding off.

"Delicately put!" Tel called after him. Then, after a moment of consideration, he followed, as did Brian.

\* \* \*

"Put it down," Brian hissed at Faye.

She held a pretty turquoise necklace and earrings in her hand. "But they're so purdy."

"Purdy expensive, Faye. Are diamonds not shiny enough for you?"

Lifting up her necklace with the ring, she smiled and put them back.

"Buffalo jerky to keep your strength up, Bri?" Mark shouted over. "Or would you prefer elk, venison or alligator?"

"Grab me an alligator," Tel yelled. "If it fights back we can hit it with some brandy."

"I'll just get a salad box for lunch," Brian said, moving towards the Subway counter. "I have a hankering for a salad."

Olivia opened her mouth to tell him she'd made a salad, but he was already gone.

"Did Bri just say 'hankering'?" Sophie asked Tel.

"He's been here too long, he's gone native."

Faye turned and gasped, "A salad?"

\* \* \*

Further down the road, Brian pulled into the left-hand booth of Zion National Park and took out his wallet, intending to pay for all three RVs, but Mark and Tel drove to the right-hand booth instead, laughing loudly and waving out of their windows. He tutted.

They drove on until they found a scenic parking space at the side of the road, at the foot of an overhanging rock which provided some shade. They got out their folding chairs and a table and sat eating their lunch stash; leftovers from last night's barbecue, with Olivia's dipping sauces and a dressed salad.

"I'm really enjoying this," Tel said.

"The food or the view?"

"Both."

"The landscape is just staggering, isn't it."

"They have so much empty space."

"I love the climate."

"I could live here," said Faye, for the umpteenth time.

"We're not moving," Brian said firmly, and she pouted at him.

"Our last full day," Olivia said softly. "Home tomorrow."

"Don't!" Faye wailed, "I might do a *Shirley Valentine*."

"A what?" Brian asked.

"You know, where a woman changes her mind at the airport and walks off to live a beautiful life in … I can't remember where, somewhere in Greece, I think."

"It was," Olivia said, "Mummy and I watched that film and immediately booked a flight to Mykonos."

"Are you planning to run off with a cowboy?" Brian asked, "Or some young stud with a jet ski?"

"How fickle do you think I am, Bri?"

"Fickle enough to fawn all over Dave, the cowboy, and the cee-gar smoking biker, *and* leap onto the back of a kid's jet ski at Lake Powell."

"He wasn't a *kid*, and I didn't leap onto his back!"

"You were running so fast you were practically skimming across the water, leaving me abandoned and alone on the beach."

"Get a grip, Bri."

"I can still see it in my head," he sniffed, brushing an imaginary tear off his hairy cheek, "My wife speeding off into the distance with barely a backward glance, arms clasped around his semi-naked body." He paused and looked at Mark and Tel. "She's giving me the evil eye, isn't she?"

"She is," Mark said. "I'd shut up now if I were you."

"Wise words. Tell her I still love her, despite her wanton ways."

"He said he still loves you."

"Big of him. He's a pain in the buttocks."

"She said you're a pain in the buttocks."

"But I love him anyway."

"But she loves you anyway."

"Most of the time."

"Most of the time."

"Is there an echo round here?" Sophie said, frowning.

"ECHO!" Mark yelled, "ECHO! ECHO! ECHO!"

A voice from the rocks above them shouted, "You folks okay down there?"

They looked up but couldn't see anything except the overhang.

"WE'RE FINE," Brian bellowed. "WE'RE BRITISH, BIT BONKERS, BIG SHOUTERS."

There was the sound of laughter and a voice yelling, "SAY NO MORE! YOU FOLKS HAVE YOURSELF A NICE TIME."

"THANKS, WE WILL, WE HAVE, WE ARE."

"Nothing like a peaceful picnic lunch in a national park, is there," Olivia smirked.

"At least it's not peas," said Sophie.

* * *

The road wiggled a bit as it rose up the side of a mountain, lined by numerous parking spaces to pull off the road to take in the view or catch your breath at the wonderment of it all.

"You're going to need to put your lights on," Sophie crackled over the walkie talkie.

Faye looked back inside the RV. "The lights?"

"Headlights," said Brian.

"Why do we need – ? Oooh!"

They were inside the Mount Carmel Tunnel, pitch black

except for the light and air windows carved into the rock which gave tantalising glimpses of spectacular views outside.

"This is just like the Birmingham tunnels, innit."

Brian threw her a quick, astonished look. "No, Faye, this is *nothing* like the Birmingham tunnels! Look through this gap ahead." She did, her face briefly illuminated by the light. "Do those mountains and valleys and perfect blue sky remind you *anything* of Birmingham?"

"No, Bri. I just felt a twinge of homesickness, but it's gone now. I definitely want to live here."

"We're not moving, Faye, and you're definitely not doing a *Shirley Valentine* at the airport. I'll put one of those child harnesses on you, and a tracker."

They emerged out the other side and faced possibly the most spectacular view any of them had ever seen. The road wriggled down from the mountain, every sharp turn displaying another impossibly stunning vista. Nobody spoke, except occasionally to gasp, "Oh my god," and Faye, who kept saying, "Don't drive off the edge, Bri," every time he turned the wheel.

"Well," came Mark's breathless voice over the walkie talkie when they reached a straight bit, "That was unexpectedly bloody awesome!"

"Most scenic road in the world, according to Etta's notes," said Sophie.

"I can believe it."

"Pull in here!" Tel cried, spotting a parking space up ahead, "We need to take photos."

They took dozens; some for other people, other people for them, in a crowd, bunched up together and smiling. That would be the photograph Olivia would print and frame and send to each of them after the trip; they all looked so incredibly happy.

# CHAPTER THIRTEEN

"National Park Visitor Centre?" Sophie asked over the walkie talkie. There was no reply from the jaded travellers, and she added, "Philistines."

Brian stretched his back in his seat and grimaced. "Need a break!" he bellowed into the walkie talkie and, at the same time, pulling onto the car park of a wood and glass building with 'Coffee' written on the side.

"Glad you pulled over," Tel said, "I was about to suggest it just so I could catch my breath after all that … amazement."

"No choice," Brian said, putting a hand on his lower back. "I'm not used to sitting for long periods and it's playing blue murder with my coccyx. Road trips are not like caravanning, are they, where you just pull up, pitch up and start drinking."

"You okay, Bri?" Faye asked, putting a gentle hand on his arm.

He winced and said, "I think I've pulled something in my back."

"I have drugs," Sophie said.

"I'd keep that quiet if I were you, lass."

"Ibuprofen, for muscle pain?"

"Aye."

Sophie reached into her bag and pulled out a blister pack, pushed two out and handed them to him. He swallowed them straight back and said, "You'd make an excellent drug dealer."

"Occurring?" Mark asked, coming over. "You okay, Bri?"

"I'm fine, just a spasming back pain, it'll pass."

"Poor you," said Olivia, moving to gently rub his back.

Faye, on his other side, started rubbing his back too. Brian widened his eyes at Tel and Mark, and said, "Double attention, I should spasm more often."

They went inside the coffee shop, Brian moving slowly and hobbling a bit.

Tel perused the huge menu board on the wall and said, "I'm going to seize the day and have a Carpe Diem."

There was no response from the cute barista behind the counter, she just prepared it.

Sophie ordered a 'South Kensington (London Fog) tea. "We live in Kensington," she gushed.

"Yeah?" said the girl, "Where's that then?"

Sophie pointed up at the menu board. "London. The clue is in the name."

"Oh, London, I know where that is. Canada, isn't it?"

Sophie tutted.

"What would you like, Faye?"

"I'll have a … Mona Lisa."

"One of those," Brian boomed at the young man behind the counter, "And do you serve bubble tea?"

"No, sir," said the barista, "We don't do bubble tea."

"Pity. What would you recommend from your vast array of hot beverages then?"

"Our most popular drink is the Vaughn Gogh Latte."

"Does it come with an ear?"

The barista looked blankly at Brian. "No, sir, it doesn't come with an 'eya', but we do have muffins."

Brian raised a hairy eyebrow. "Are they ear shaped?"

"No," he drawled. "I'm not sure I'm understanding you, sir."

"Forget it. I thought it was funny, but my humour obviously doesn't translate."

"Not even at home," Faye laughed.

Olivia had a FeelLove Latte and ordered a James Dean for Mark.

They sat outside on the rattan chairs, wanting to enjoy the heat and the fresh air and trying not to think of the weather they would face the next day. Brian stood grimacing, pushing a hand into his back.

"Is it hurting a lot?" Faye asked.

"On a scale of one to ten," Mark said, "How bad is it?"

Brian thought for a moment. "Eight," he said. "Eight and a half, edging towards a nine, which is when the screaming and sobbing will start."

"Sit down and take the weight off, Bri."

"I've had enough of sitting down."

"Jog?" Sophie suggested with a wink. "Cartwheels across the car park?"

"Pass. How much further to the next place?"

Sophie consulted her itinerary. "Probably another hour's drive, but pull over whenever you need to."

"Should you be driving after taking Ibuprofen?" Olivia asked. "It can make you drowsy."

"I'll be fine."

They finished their coffees and ambled across the car park. Brian struggled into his cab first and, as the others were opening their doors, they heard him cry out loud and raced back to his RV.

"My back!" Brian gasped, sitting stiffly and awkwardly in the driver's seat, "It's gone!"

"Oh Brian!" Faye cried.

"On a scale of one to – "

"*Fifty*!" Brian panted, "I felt something twinge and now I can't move."

Tel said, "Let's get him out, he won't be doing any more driving today. I'll push him out from the back."

Faye jumped out of the cab and Tel clambered into the passenger seat, bracing himself behind Brian. Mark held Brian's half-in, half-out legs, as heavy as tree trunks, and Brian pulled himself up by his arms however he could, gasping, "Ow! Ow! Ow!"

They gently lowered him to his feet, the women helping where they could. Brian was clutching onto the wing mirror for support. Olivia rushed to open the RV side door and Faye jumped in, pulling the cushions off the seats and laying them on the floor. The men helped Brian struggle up the steps.

By brute force they managed to get him inside and eased him down onto the cushions. Faye pulled the pillows off the bed above the cab and slipped them under his head.

"You okay, Bri?"

"No," he panted. "It hurts, a lot."

Tel and Mark looked at each other.

"What are we going to do?" said Tel, "He can't drive in this condition."

"I'll drive their RV," Mark said, "Liv can drive ours. That okay, Liv?"

"Yes, of course."

Faye cried, "Do you want anything, Bri? Can I do anything? Would you like a nice cup of tea?"

"Stop fussing, woman! We've just had coffee!"

"What can I do? Tell me what I can – ?"

"Leave me be! In fact," he said, struggling to move his head to look at her, "I'd much prefer it if you drive with Liv, keep her company."

"You want me to leave you?"

"Mark's here."

"But he'll be driving, what if you – ?"

"Faye," he gasped, "Please, just leave me to suffer in peace."

"That's what you always say."

"Because that's how I deal with excruciating pain."

Faye turned her sad, concerned face towards the gang standing outside the door. "That okay with you, Liv, if I ride with you?"

"Of course."

"We'll lead," Tel said. "Are you comfortable, Bri?"

"Not really."

"Hold tight," said Sophie, "Those tablets will kick in soon and take the edge off."

"Do you need a blanket?" Faye asked. "I could use a bath

towel, or get the sleeping bag down?"

"Why?" he grimaced. "It's as hot as Hades in here!"

"Should I open the skylight above the bed for ventilation?"

"Only if you want it popping off and smashing through someone's windscreen."

"It's good that you've still got your sense of humour, Bri."

"It's all I have left!" he wailed, then winced.

"Will you be alright on your own?"

"Get gone, woman, you're annoying me now."

She kissed his forehead. "Try and sleep."

"I won't be able to sleep. I'll just stare at the ceiling and moan a lot."

"Okay."

Outside there was a sense of tension and panic.

"Do you think he'll be alright?" Olivia asked.

"He probably just needs to rest up a bit."

"We could stop off somewhere and get him some stronger painkillers."

"Advil," said Mark, looking at his phone. "That's supposed to be good."

"Not sure we should be mixing his drugs," Sophie said, "He could overdose."

"Could he?" Faye gasped.

"We won't kill him, Faye."

"Good. I've grown quite fond of him."

"We all have."

"Okay," said Tel, "Enough faffing about, let's herd 'em up and move 'em out."

Brian shouted as best he could as they all started moving towards their RVs. "Could somebody shut the side door?"

* * *

They drove towards La Verkin, Tel and Sophie leading the way, followed by Olivia and Faye, with Mark and a now sleeping Brian bringing up the rear. Their sense of adventure was now tinged with some concern over Brian's wellbeing.

To lighten the mood, Mark pulled into the right lane of the dual carriageway, drawing level with Olivia and Faye in the left, waving at them and pulling faces. They were laughing at his antics when an unbroken white line on the road suddenly came between them, just as Sophie's voice crackled, "Left at the crossroads."

The lights ahead were green. Cars were lined up tight behind them. Mark had no room to manoeuvre back over to the left lane. A road sign read 'Right lane MUST turn right'. He had no choice but to turn right as the others turned left.

"What's he doing?" Faye asked Olivia, peering into the side mirror.

"He's going the wrong way!"

"Tel!" Faye said into the radio, "We've lost Mark!"

"Already? We've only been driving a few minutes!"

Tel pulled into a petrol station. They followed.

"Mark," Tel said into the walkie talkie, "Is there anywhere you can turn round?"

"Looking." Silence. "There's a car park but it doesn't look big enough for the RV." More silence. "You'd think, with all this bloody space, they'd have somewhere to turn around."

Tel said, quite urgently, "Follow the GPS."

"GPS doesn't work, it's never worked. When it does sporadically spark into life it brings up maps of Texas."

"What about the GPS on your phone?"

"I … I don't have my phone."

"It's here in the cab," Olivia crackled.

"Okay, turn three lefts and you should be back on 9 again."

"Will do."

They all waited in their cabs, holding the walkie talkies in their hands, waiting for Mark to speak again.

"I've turned left. Looks like a housing estate."

"Next left."

"Turning."

"Where are you now?"

"In a cul de sac."

Tel huffed.

"Ask Brian what to do," Faye said, "Brian always knows what to do."

"I can't."

"Why not?" Faye gasped.

"He's asleep. Listen."

They all heard the sonorous sound of Brian snoring.

"At least he's still breathing," Olivia said comfortingly to Faye, who wasn't comforted at all.

"Turn around, Mark."

"I am." Silence. "I've lost my bearings now, do I turn left or right?"

"Left, left, left." Silence. "Where are you now, Mark?"

"It's a dead end. I'm turning round. I'm just going to keep turning left. Oh, this looks promising. No, I'm in the desert. I'll turn round and go back."

Tel put the walkie talkie down and sighed heavily.

"Do you think we'll ever see them again?" Sophie asked, half-joking.

"We're already a man down, now we have one missing in action."

"You're the only man left amongst three women."

"Normally that would excite me," he grinned. "Now, not so much. Mark, where are you?"

"No bloody idea."

"Mark!" Olivia cried, "Come back to me, darling."

"I'm trying, Liv, I'm really, really trying." Silence. "Okay, I'm on a long, straight road. I'm going for it, it's got to bring me out somewhere. Wish me luck."

"Good luck, darling."

"Love you, Livs."

"Love you too."

Silence.

"Looks like I'm on the outskirts of town," Mark finally

crackled. "I can see mountains in the distance."

"I'm not sure that's a good sign," Sophie said to Tel.

"Wait! I'm at a crossroads! Do I turn left or right?"

"Are there any road signs?"

"None that make any sense, they're just numbers."

"Aim for 9, the number nine."

"I can see a sign for 9, but it looks weird."

"What do you mean, it looks weird?"

"It's pointing both left and right, but my gut instinct – "

"Is rubbish," Tel cut in. "Turn right, right, *right*."

Silence.

"Where are you, Mark?"

"God knows."

"Pull over somewhere, we'll come and find you."

Tel started up the engine. Behind him, Olivia did the same.

"Where have you pulled into, Mark?"

"A place called El Rancho, it's a Mexican restaurant."

"No kidding," Sophie laughed. She pulled out her mobile phone and searched for the restaurant. She laughed.

"What?" Tel asked.

"He's just across the road."

\* \* \*

Mark and Olivia ran to each other across the car park like they'd been separated by war or famine for years, hugging tightly. Faye rushed to their RV and flung open the side door.

"*Brian*!"

"Uh?"

She threw herself down on him and he humphed loudly, losing all the air from his lungs. Something in his back clicked and shifted under the weight of his semi-hysterical wife. There was a sharp moment of absolute agony, and then … nothing.

"Oh Brian, I thought I'd lost you!"

"What's up? Where are we? What's happened?" He felt

no pain. "I'm either paralysed," he said nervously, "Or your brutal pummelling has fixed my back."

"Brian?"

He gingerly sat up, stared off into space for a moment, moved his enormous shoulders, and said, "You've unbroken me!"

"Oh Brian!" Faye cried again, carefully wrapping her arms around his neck, "I was so worried."

"Calm down, lass."

"Can you stand?"

Brian used the edge of the table and the top of the fridge unit to lift himself up. He felt stiff, but pain free. Mark and Tel came running over to help steady him down the steps.

"How are you feeling?" Mark asked.

"Not too bad, surprisingly."

"It could be the painkillers," Sophie said. "It might be a temporary thing."

"So get things done while you can," Tel laughed.

Brian turned his head and spotted the restaurant. "Mexican," he said with feeling. "I could eat."

"Food?" Faye said, "You're thinking of food at a time like this? You've already had pancakes, a fry-up – "

"Mini fry-up," he corrected.

" – and the leftovers from last night's barbecue *with salad*!"

"Salad doesn't count." He looked over at the restaurant. "We are in their car park, it would be rude not to partake of a taco or two."

"My treat!" Olivia cried, suddenly running for the door.

"No, mine!" Sophie yelled, running after her.

The rest ambled slowly across the car park on either side of Brian, who walked slowly but at least he wasn't doubled up in agony.

Olivia reached the counter first and ordered a selection of Mexican food in perfect Spanish.

\* \* \*

It was decided, over tasty tacos, that due to Brian's medication he shouldn't drive. Without much argument, he allowed himself to be helped into the passenger seat of his RV, while Mark once again jumped in behind the steering wheel.

Back on the road again, Mark insisted on bringing up the rear to make sure Olivia and Faye were okay in the middle.

"Try to stay with us this time," Tel told him over the walkie talkie.

"Do my best."

"If you get lost again, we're leaving you."

"Bit harsh," said Sophie. "I thought we left no man behind."

"What about my husband?" Faye crackled, "He doesn't deserve to be left behind."

"But I do?" Mark said curtly, "You're quite happy to abandon me, never to be seen again, lost and alone in America?"

"I didn't mean it like that," Faye said, and then Olivia's voice saying, "I won't leave you, darling."

"Thank you, Livs."

"Just stick with us, Mark."

It took twenty minutes to drive from La Verkin to Hurricane. Tel was on the walkie talkie for most of those minutes.

"Still with us, Mark?"

"Yep."

Silence. The desert flew passed. Country music played from the speakers.

"Still with us?"

"Right up against Liv's rear end."

"Does she mind?"

"Get away from my rear end!" Olivia laughed.

Silence. Desert. Music.

"Do you still have us in sight, Mark?"

"Affirmative, Teletubby."

"Stop calling me that!"

Silence. More desert. More music.

"You haven't wandered off on your own again, have you, Mark?"

"No, still here."

"Pity," Tel laughed.

"Shut your face."

The convoy drove into town and down the main street. Tel suddenly slammed on the brakes, causing Olivia and Mark to slam on theirs. Tel pulled into the car park of a tyre shop. The others followed.

"What's up?" Sophie asked him.

"I thought I saw something."

He drove into the adjoining car park of an AutoZone. They followed.

"Where's he going?" Liv asked Faye.

"Could be a toilet break. Those tacos were a bit spicy."

He drove into the front car park of the Wingate Hotel.

"Maybe he's had enough of camping?" Mark suggested.

"He could have picked somewhere cheaper," Brian said, "This place looks expensive."

Tel parked up and turned off the engine. He turned his head. Sophie followed his gaze and said, "Is that ...? No, it can't be!"

There was the black car, the Cherokee.

"Same reg number," Tel said. "Saw it as we drove passed."

They got out and went up to the car, peering in through the windows. There was the same zip-up bag and box of bottled water on the back seats.

"It can't be a coincidence," Sophie said.

"They could be doing the same trip as us."

"What, two young Americans lads driving the exact same route?"

"It's a possibility."

"What do they want with us?" Faye gasped, running

over with the others, while Brian winced and inched his way towards them. "They must be in the hotel," she cried, "They must be following us!"

"Can't be following us," Brian said, "They were here first."

"They're anticipating our movements, hoping to catch us unaware."

"Let's not jump to any conclusions, lass."

"We should have just given them some money," Olivia said nervously. "They must be chasing us for the money."

"Don't worry, Liv, there's only two of them and six of us. Well, five now that Brian's injured."

"Two," said Tel, "I don't expect the women to do any fighting."

"I've brought many a man down with my moves," Olivia said, striking a karate pose. "Mostly Richard, but I'm willing to expand my repertoire."

"I pack a mighty punch," Sophie winked.

"You could probably paralyse them with your death stare," snorted Tel. "I've seen you glance at opposing prosecutors and turn their innards to jelly."

"Shall we look inside the hotel?" Mark asked.

"Are they likely to be loitering in the lobby, do you think?"

"Won't know till we look."

"We'll go," Tel said, "It might look suspicious if we all pour through the doors at once."

Tel and Sophie strode towards the doors. They walked across the modern, crisp lobby casually checking the faces of the people sitting on grey sofas next to the reception desk. Nobody seemed familiar. The woman behind the desk looked up and smiled. "Can I help you?"

"No, we're just looking for someone," Tel smiled back.

In the room off the lobby a few people sat at white tables, eating and drinking. They didn't recognise any of them.

"They're probably up in their room," Sophie said. "Maybe staring out of their window at everyone standing around their car. They could come rushing down at any minute and – "

"Hello!" came a man's voice from behind them.

They turned and saw Evan and Brynn, the couple from Cardiff they'd met at the Grand Canyon.

"Hello!" Sophie gushed. "How lovely to see you again!"

"We've been all over the place," Brynn said excitedly. "We've had a wonderful time. How's your trip been?"

"Excellent," Tel said. "We're really enjoying it."

"Marvellous country, isn't it," Evan said. "We're already planning to come back again, not to the same place, mind, we're thinking more Florida way next time."

"Maybe do what you're doing and hire a motorhome," Brynn added.

"We'd highly recommend it," said Sophie.

"Anyway, we won't keep you, we're just off for a late lunch."

"Or an early dinner," Brynn giggled. "We were very naughty and had an afternoon nap, I highly recommend it. Anyway, lovelies, enjoy yourselves."

"Bon appetite," Tel said, "And enjoy the rest of your holiday."

"We will. You too."

The couple turned and headed for the main doors.

"They're so sweet," Sophie said, watching them go. "I want to be like them when I grow up."

"Come on, let's go, they're not here."

They followed Evan and Brynn out of the doors. The couple walked towards the parked-up RVs. They thought they were going to have a look in preparation for their next holiday, or maybe indulge in a quick conversation with the group standing around them.

They didn't.

They nodded at everyone as they passed.

And then they unlocked the black Grand Cherokee.

The group turned as one to stare, wide-eyed. Evan and Brynn, sensing several sets of eyeballs upon them, nervously turned around. Tel and Sophie hurried over.

"Is this your car?" Tel asked.

"Yes.  Well, not *ours*, exactly, it's a hire car."

"You've had it the whole time?" Brian asked.

"Yes."

Brynn said, "Remember Williams, Evan."

"Oh yes!"  He shook his head.  "Couple of young buggers stole it while we were staying in Williams, went on a brief joy ride in it."

"Brief?"

"We informed the police and the hire company immediately, as per the instructions on our hire lease.  The police managed to stop them a few miles away using their registration recognition thingy and called us, said we if we cleared it with the hire company we could collect it from Williams Police Department, which happened to be right across the street from where we were staying."

"Yes," Brynn giggled, "How lucky was that?"

"No damage or anything," Evan continued.  "Lucky really, it could have disrupted our entire holiday waiting for another hire car."

"We thought you were following us," Sophie explained. "The young men who stole your car nearly ran into the back of one of our RVs and demanded money from us."

"Oh dear," said Brynn, "How awful for you."

"It all makes sense now," said Brian.

Evan looked up at him.  "You're a big chap, aren't you."

"So I've been told," he winked.

"It's his eat-everything-in-sight diet," Faye laughed.

Brynn said, "We're going to a nice little restaurant up the road, if you'd like to join us?"

"Very kind," said Tel, "But we're on our way to our last pitch."

"Last pitch!" Faye wailed.

"Well, have a good journey and a good trip back to Blighty."

"You too."

Evan got into the car, and they reversed out of the parking space, waved, and drove off.

"Can you believe that?" Faye cried. "And all this time we were worried we were being followed."

"*You* were worried," Brian said. "The rationale menfolk were just curious."

"I'm glad we got that cleared up," said Mark. "We can relax and enjoy our last day now."

"Last day!" Faye wailed.

* * *

Five minutes outside of Hurricane, they turned left onto Southern Parkway and then right down a smaller road. A lake appeared in the distance.

"Good afternoon, ladies and gentlemen," Sophie crackled over the walkie talkie. "Welcome to Sand Hollow State Park. That's actually a reservoir you can see on your right. Naked man to the left."

"Funny!" Olivia crackled back.

"Did you look?"

"Of course. I'm very disappointed."

"Oh wow!" Faye gasped, as they pulled onto the huge campsite. "I can't choose a favourite, but I think this has got to be the best pitch so far."

"So, this is your favourite?"

"Yes, but don't tell the other pitches."

"My lips are sealed."

A winding track took them through the vast, opulently-spaced campground. Each pitch was a different-sized offshoot from the track, with their own picnic table beneath a pavilion.

"Etta booked us the best spot," Sophie said over the walkie talkie, as Tel pulled into a curved pitch big enough to accommodate all three RVs. It was right beside the vast blue lake, surrounded by orange sand beaches. The nearest pitch to them was some way off.

They parked up and got out. Faye went to wake Brian in

the passenger seat and they helped him hobble to the picnic table.

"Etta said this place is a bit out of our way but definitely worth it," Sophie said, looking out over the lake, mere metres away.

"She's not wrong," Mark sighed.

"Paradise," said Brian.

"It's gorgeous, Sophs. I hope you're paying your secretary enough."

"She keeps telling me I'm not, and I keep my fingers crossed she's not whisked away by another company." Sophie glanced at her now familiar folder. "My excellent secretary-stroke-PA also reminds us, once again, to get our RVs cleaned out before we take them back to Las Vegas tomorrow."

"Let's not talk about tomorrow," Tel said, throwing the back of his hand against his forehead, "Tomorrow is another day."

"And the best acting Oscar goes to … "

"How's your back, Bri?"

Brian nodded. "Not too bad, actually. My wife flinging her full weight on top of me must have clicked something back into place."

"Happy to leap on you any time, Bri."

"It just aches a bit now."

"A gentle swim might do it the world of good," Olivia said, jumping into the back of their RV, "Who's coming?"

"Skinny dipping?" Mark said, hopefully.

"In your dreams, darling."

"It is, quite frequently."

"Brian?"

"I'll sit this one out, but maybe later."

The women hurried to change into their swimming costumes.

"And while the women enjoy themselves," Tel said, "Us men can stoke up the barbecue."

"And drink," Brian grinned.

* * *

"This," Sophie breathed, floating on her back with her arms stretched out in the water, "is Paradise."

Faye, floating next to her, said, "I don't want to leave."

"I can't hear you," Olivia said, "I have water in my ears, you'll have to speak up a bit."

"I SAID!" Sophie laughed.

Olivia stood up. The water was up to her waist. Sophie didn't want to go out any further as she wasn't a good swimmer, didn't normally like water, so they were gently bobbing on the periphery of the lake. Olivia cocked her head to each side and relaxed back into the water again.

"Hasn't this been the best trip ever," said Faye.

"It has."

"Well, apart from the sinister black car following us."

"And Brian doing his back in."

"And me nearly losing a finger with my new ring."

"And Mark getting horribly lost," Olivia said.

"All good things must come to an end," Sophie sighed.

"Not always." Faye grinned, thinking of Brian. "Sometimes a happy ending lasts a long, long time."

"Road trips don't have happy endings," said Olivia, "They just have endings."

Faye pretended to cry. Sophie and Olivia joined her; three women, floating on the edge of the water, wailing up at the sky like a trio of Lucille Balls.

* * *

Faye came back from the showers with super-shiny, super-smooth hair.

"Faye!" Brian cried, "You look bloody gorgeous! Not that you don't normally, but you look gorgeous-er than usual."

Next to him, Tel and Mark made invisible notes in their imaginary Little Books of Mens answers and nodded sagely to each other.

"It's the oil Sophie gave me," she said with a huge smile,

"It's made my hair all soft and shiny."

"Looks lovely, lass."

The men had laid out the camping tables next to the picnic bench and now sat comfortably in their chairs, resting their feet on their cool boxes with a cold can in their hands.

"Isn't it a bit early, Bri?"

"Early, Faye?"

"You know, for partaking of the booze juice."

"I don't know, love of my life, I've lost all sense of time."

"It's only three in the afternoon at home."

"So, by your reckoning, I should have started drinking at – " He did a quick calculation in his head, couldn't figure it, and guessed instead. " – nine o'clock this morning, local time, to reach the 5pm UK criteria?" He leaned towards Tel and said, "That's right, isn't it?"

Tel shrugged. "Time is irrelevant."

"There, see?" Brian said, turning back to Faye and clicking open another can, "Time is irrelevant."

She huffed and flicked back her shiny hair.

"We can't take them home with us," Mark said, "We'll have to drink them all tonight."

"All?" Sophie said. "How many are left?"

"Not telling," said Tel.

"Where's our drinks?" Faye asked.

Brian lifted up a giant arm and looked at his watch. "But it's only – "

"Shut up, Bri, and break out the bubbles."

The men reached into their cool boxes and took out a bottle of Prosecco and a flute glass each. "Chilled for madams' enjoyment," said Mark.

They sat, staring out over the lake, each with a drink in their hands. It was a peaceful, memory-making moment. Jet skis bounced across the lake, buggies bounced over the sand; pleasant sounds of engines and people enjoying themselves. What looked like an eagle flew overhead, although none of them could decide if it was or not so chose to believe that it was and felt chuffed to see one. Talking and laughing, gentle music coming from all directions, each of them knowing that this was a special moment, a memory to look back on.

Tel lifted his head off the back of the chair to stare at the buggies bouncing over the sand dunes behind them. "That looks fun. Fancy it, Sophs? I saw a hire place as we came in."

She nodded and got up.

"Anyone else wanna eat my dust?" Tel laughed.

"I'd prefer to cool down in the water," Mark said, getting up, "I might hire a jet ski. Want to join me, Livs?"

"Yes, please!"

"Brian?"

Brian, half asleep in his chair with his feet up on the cool box, said, "There's a big difference between a young person's holiday and an old person's holiday."

"You speak for yourself, Bri!"

"I speak for both my wife and I when I say we'd much prefer to stay here and relax due to lack of stamina."

"Yeah," said Faye, closing her eyes again, "What he said."

"Suit yourselves."

"Have fun!"

The youngsters ran off.

The old folk dozed, holding hands.

Even the screaming coming from the sand dunes and the hysterical laughter bouncing across the water didn't wake them.

Hunger did.

\* \* \*

"Famished!" Brian boomed.

"Again?" Faye gasped. "Have you got hollow legs?"

"No, just a big appetite, I'm a big man."

Tel leaned over and patted the mound underneath Brian's chambray shirt.

"Are you insinuating that I'm *fat*?" Brian asked in faux horror.

"You're not fat, Bri, you're just wide in all directions."

Indignant, Brian stood up, slowly and carefully, and lifted his hairy chin. "I have to work hard to maintain this Adonis-like physique, y'know."

"Eat hard, more like," said Faye.

"Adonis?" Tel snorted.

"Abominable snowman," Sophie giggled.

"I must admit," said Mark, taking out his phone and tapping on the screen, "I'm a bit hungry myself after all that young person exertion. There's a curry takeaway over in Saint George."

"Oooh," Faye frowned, "Should we risk a curry on our last night? Remember when we had curries in the Cotswolds that time?"

"How could we possibly forget?"

"Took a week for the odour to dissipate," Olivia said, "I was there, it permeated the entire site for *days*."

"Chinese?" Mark suggested. "They deliver."

As Mark was placing the order, Sophie's phoned beeped with a text message. She ran her eyes over it and then laughed. "It's from Iain Flemmingway," she said. "He hopes we had a good time in Vegas, courtesy of his publishing company and MGN."

Laughter filled the air, but before anyone could say anything she jabbed at the screen. "I'll tell him about the good time we've had, shall I?"

She put it on speakerphone and lay the phone on the table.

"Hello, Mr Flemmingway's office."

"Hi, could I speak to Iain please?"

"I'm afraid he's not in at the moment, would you like to leave a message?"

Sophie glanced at them all, grinning. "Yes, do you have a paper and a pen handy? It's a long message."

"Okay, go ahead."

"We would like to thank Mr Flemmingway for our very

*unusual* trip to Las Vegas, where we completely bypassed the Caesar's Palace Hotel we were expecting and ended up in a trailer park with the film crew. We slept in derelict motorhomes – "

"Held together with rust and gaffer tape," Brian loudly added.

" – showered in tents with cold water, fed entirely on junk food, and were roped in to play extras, for free."

"I quite enjoyed that part," Faye said.

"Even the heat stroke you got pushing an RV up a sand bank?" Mark asked.

"Well, not that bit, obviously."

Sophie continued, "I would very much like to discuss these events with Mr Flemmingway. If he could call me back at Avery & Forbes Solicitors next week to explain the circumstances of our trip, I'd be grateful."

"Anything else?" the secretary asked.

"The beds were lumpy and smelly," Tel shouted at the phone. "I think something died in ours."

"And there was no air-conditioning," Faye cried out, shuddering at the memory of being hot, hot, hot, "We nearly boiled to death in the RVs."

"Overall," Sophie concluded, "It was a dreadful, awful, traumatic experience. I think that's it?" She looked at the others, who nodded. "Thank you," she said, and hung up.

"Enjoyed it though," Faye said.

"Yeah, it was good," said Brian.

"We've driven thousands of miles across three states," Mark said.

"Three states?" Faye gasped.

Brian leaned into her and said, "You remember those road signs that said 'Welcome to Nevada,' 'Welcome to Utah,' and 'Welcome to Arizona'?"

"Ah," said Faye, "That's quite impressive."

"It is, lass."

"In hindsight," Tel said, "it was quite an adventure."

"It was."

"Yeah, but we won't tell Iain Flemmingway that," Sophie said. "Let him sweat for a bit."

"He won't be interested," said Olivia.

"Oh, he will," Sophie said. "Don't forget, we're lawyers, people have been sued for less."

"Really?"

"We won't sue him, so don't get your hopes up," Sophie laughed, "But we'll let him stew for a while thinking we might, just for retribution purposes."

They all nodded, grinning.

"Revenge is a dish best served cold," said Faye.

"Talking of dishes," Mark said, standing up and watching a car driving across the beach towards them, "Here's our takeaway."

That night they ate straight from the takeaway tins to cut down on washing up and sipped at their drinks, too full to over-indulge. The women, gossiping and giggling, went from one RV kitchen to the next, cleaning, tidying and packing. The men sat outside, looking up at the stars and reminiscing.

It was the perfect last night.

Almost.

* * *

"Alone at last," Tel said, drunkenly snuggling up to Sophie in the bed above the cabin. "Fancy a little light gymnastics before sleep?"

Sophie grinned, and was just about to kiss him when, from close by, almost like he was there with them, Mark said, "We can hear you, you know."

"We'll have to be quiet, Tel whispered.

"We can still hear you."

Sophie giggled softly.

"Giggling in bed only leads to one thing," said Mark, "And we certainly don't want to hear *that*."

"I think the RVs are parked too close together," came

Brian's voice.

"You think?" said Tel.

"What about our last amazing night in America?" Sophie breathed.

"It's cancelled," said Mark.

"Bugger!"

There was some thumping noise and the squeaking of a canopy being hastily rolled up, followed by the sound of an engine starting and a vehicle pulling away.

"What's that?" Faye whispered.

"Newlyweds on the move," Brian grinned. "Now, where were we?"

Mark coughed. Brian flopped onto his back with a heavy sigh.

"If we can't," Mark said, "You can't!"

"Bugger!"

# CHAPTER FOURTEEN

**Day 7**

"BRIAN! BRIAN!"

Heavy pounding permeated Brian's brain. "Hmm?"

"BRI-AN! GET UP! IT'S LATE! WE'RE GONNA BE LATE!"

Faye lifted her head off the pillow. "Late?" she gasped.

Brian would have quickly sat up, except he'd vowed he wouldn't concuss himself on the roof getting up in the morning again. Instead, after Faye had jumped down and opened the RV door to Mark, who was bouncing in agitation from one foot to the other, he rolled over and eased himself down like a very large, very hairy Spiderman.

"BRIAN!" Mark cried frantically, "BRIAN! WE OVERSLEPT!"

Behind him, Tel and Sophie roared up the beach in their RV, with Tel leaning out of the window yelling, "DO YOU KNOW WHAT TIME IT IS?"

"WE DO!" Mark yelled back. "WE NEED TO GET A WOBBLE ON, AND FAST!"

It was then that Brian looked at his watch. His eyes widened, his mouth dropped. He bawled, "LET'S GET MOVING!"

"How late are we, Bri?" Faye asked, as she quickly pulled on clothes whilst, at the same time, shoving the last of their belongings into the sports bags, hand luggage, handbag and several carrier bags.

"It's gone nine!"

"And when is our flight?"

"Three o'clock!"

"Oh, that's plenty of time."

"It would be if we didn't have a two-hour drive into Vegas first, and we have to be at the airport three hours ahead of time. If we hit any traffic we're stuffed."

Faye hissed a swearword he didn't hear her say very often and knew she understood the seriousness of the situation.

"TEL!"

"BRI!"

"HOW FAST CAN YOU BE READY?"

"MINUTES!" Sophie screamed, to the sound of objects being thrown around.

"WE DIDN'T SWEEP OUT THE RVS!" Olivia cried.

"NEVER MIND THAT!" Mark yelled, as he wound up his and Brian's canopies like a dervish on speed, "LET THEM CHARGE US, WE CAN'T MISS THAT FLIGHT!"

Banging, thumping, yelling. Their amassed belongings wouldn't fit into the sports bags they'd brought, having shopped their way around the American West. They were still packing as the men drove to the dump station for the last time.

There were some brooms outside the shower block and the women picked them up as the men emptied the loos, frantically brushing as much sand off the floor and surfaces as possible. Red clouds poured out of open doors. Afterwards, Faye, looking decidedly crimson, said, "Have I got time for a – ?"

"No!"

"But my hair!"

"Looks beautiful," Brian told her, not looking up from the sluice.

Faye quickly brushed herself off as best she could and made copious use of a packet of baby wipes in lieu of a shower. She emptied the kitchen cupboards into carrier bags and bagged up the rubbish. When she took them to the waste area nearby she found a gaggle of women apparently waiting for her.

"Heard you were leaving," one said.

"If we can help in any way," said another, eagerly eyeing

Faye's bags.

"What's going on?" Sophie asked, hurrying over with two plastic bags of food.

"Happy to relieve you of any excess tins or fresh produce," a blonde woman said.

"They'll only go to waste otherwise," said another.

They happily handed over the food bags and the women happily took them. As they walked away, picking out and comparing the contents of each, they heard one say, "What the hell are baked beans?"

Men casually sauntered over to the RVs at the dump station and hung around expectantly.

"Can we help you?" Brian asked.

"You off to the airport?" one said.

"We are."

"Relieve you of any excess alcohol?"

"I didn't think there was such a thing as *excess alcohol*," Brian grinned, pulling out his cool box and handing the whole thing over. Tel and Mark did the same, and the men excitedly wandered off again.

"Mind doesn't feel very heavy," one said, shaking the box.

"Mine neither."

"Right," said Sophie, joining them, "Check your passports and tickets."

"Why?" Olivia asked.

"To make sure you have them."

They rushed off for their handbags.

"Got ours," Faye yelled out.

"Ours too," Olivia shrieked.

"Tel!" Sophie cried, "Where's your passport?"

"With yours."

"It's not!"

"Where is it then?"

"I don't know."

"You had it last."

"I gave it to you."

"I DON'T HAVE IT!"

"I'll come back and visit you often, Tel."

"Sophie!"

"I'm looking!"

Tel jumped into the RV. Seconds later they heard him say, "What's this then?"

"Your passport."

"And where was it?"

"In my bag."

"Get a smaller bag, Sophs."

"But then where will I put all my things?"

"Time check?" Mark asked, once they'd finished their tasks.

Brian looked at his watch and made a strange, strangled noise.

"LET'S GO!" he boomed. "WAGONS ROLL!"

They fairly skidded out of the campsite and were too frantic to take a final glance at the big blue lake as they roared onto Route 7, eventually flying passed the outskirts of Saint George and its tiny airport.

The women continued repacking the bags, trying to get everything to fit in, folding and rolling and pummelling as they sped down the road towards Las Vegas.

Faye, giving up on the bags, took the last two slices of bread off the counter, having disposed of the wrapper, and tried to fold one. It cracked. She pushed it into Brian's mouth anyway before sitting in the passenger seat with two bottles of water and a packet of plain biscuits.

"This is stale," he said, taking the bread out and staring at its dryness. "Any butter? Margarine? Dripping?"

"All given away or chucked," Faye said.

"Nothing to put on it at all?"

"No, it's all gone. Pretend it's a biscuit."

"A dry, tasteless biscuit." He threw it out of the open window. "I can't eat that, Faye, feed me something else before my sugar levels drop to dangerous levels."

She opened the packet of plain biscuits and began slotting them into Brian's mouth at regular intervals.

"Not much of an improvement," he said.

Olivia, who hated waste, made Mark a sandwich using what was left in the fridge. When she placed it in his lap, on a plate with a folded paper napkin and a side order of olives, he took one look at its several-layered thickness and said, "How am I supposed to eat it?"

"Do you want me to feed it to you?" she grinned.

He grinned back and wiggled his eyebrows.

In the last RV, Tel was saying, "There's no food at all?"

"I gave it all away."

"Before breakfast?"

"I didn't think about breakfast, I just thought about emptying the RV before we returned it."

Tel pressed the button on the walkie talkie and said, "Mayday, mayday, driver without sustenance! I repeat, driver without sustenance!"

"Would you like a sandwich?" Olivia crackled back, just as he'd hoped.

"Yes, please."

The RVs pulled onto the side of the dusty road and ticked over for a minute or two, before Olivia's door sprung open and she ran back to Tel and Sophie with two plates holding sandwiches, paper napkins, olives and a packet of crisps each, which she passed through Sophie's window.

"Star, as always," Tel winked, grabbing one and pushing it into his mouth.

Olivia ran back to her RV. Brian poked his head out of his open window and hollered, "WHERE'S MINE?"

"WE'RE GOING TO BE LATE!" Mark hollered back.

"THAT'S OKAY FOR YOU TO SAY, YOU'VE PROBABLY JUST EATEN SOME FABULOUS GOURMET SNACK. I'VE *LITERALLY* HAD DRY BREAD AND WATER!"

"It won't take a minute," Olivia told Mark, quickly spreading and layering another two sandwiches.

"We don't have time for this, Livs!"

"Chill your boots, darling, you can't march an army on an empty stomach."

"*Liv!*"

"If you don't stop doing your white rabbit impersonation your head is going to explode, and they'll *definitely* charge us for the blood stains."

Olivia jumped out the door and raced up to the leading RV, passing two plates through the window. Brian grabbed one and started chomping on it, instantly making happy noises.

"What would we do without you?" Faye said.

"Starve," she giggled, and ran back towards the irate man furiously mouthing to himself behind the wheel of their RV.

They roared off down the road again. Faye tried playing some country music to calm Brian down, but the songs were about dogs dying, wives leaving and trucks breaking down, which did nothing to soothe his increasing panic as they sped towards Vegas.

"Truck stop!" Mark cried over the walkie talkie.

"I concur," came Tel's voice.

They pulled onto the side of the road again and jumped out of the drivers' seats, standing in a line on the edge of the desert with their backs to the RVs. The women peered and jeered at them.

"Don't watch us!" Tel hissed.

"Ain't nothing we ain't seen before," Sophie laughed.

"Shy bladders?" Faye teased.

Brian started first. There was a tinkle, a sigh of relief, and a hissing noise.

"Brian," Tel said, "Have you sprung a leak somewhere?"

"Not that I'm aware."

"It sounds like you're deflating."

"Brian!" Mark whispered harshly.

"What?"

"Don't move."

"I normally give a little Irish dance of victory at the end."

"No," Mark whispered with more urgency, *"Do not move."*

The tinkling stopped. The relieved sighing stopped. The hissing continued.

Brian looked down at his feet. A small area of dusty ground seemed to be moving in a gentle, circular motion.

He slowly took off his sunglasses and focused.

A wet or very shiny snake was curled up against the toe of his trainer. It looked like a rattlesnake, but his knowledge had been gained from watching cowboy films and this one wasn't rattling, it was hissing. Brian sucked in air and held it.

"Step back, slowly," Tel whispered.

"You're the group snake whisperer, are you?"

"Maybe he should stand still," Mark breathed.

"And wait for one of us to die?" Brian squeaked. "My bet's on the snake, it's familiar with the climate, whereas I can feel my brain boiling in my skull, despite the very fetching cowboy –"

The snake stopped slithering. Brian wondered if that was a good sign or a bad one. Should he run or stay? He realised he'd stopped breathing and felt a bit faint. Would a dead faint onto a hissing snake be a good thing or a bad thing? He wasn't sure. He exhaled slowly and sucked in air. The snake raised its head and seemed to look up at him.

His survival instinct kicked in then and he leapt up and backwards, grabbing onto the wing mirror of his RV and hanging off it with his feet pulled up.

Faye, who was busy putting on lipstick, peered at him. "You alright, Bri?"

He nodded, glancing down at the ground. The snake was still there, undulating gently. Tel and Mark were frozen to the spot, holding but no longer peeing.

"Snake," he told her.

"What?"

"Snake." He nodded to the ground where he'd recently been standing.

Faye looked down.

She saw.

She screamed so high and so loud that Celine Dion would have been impressed.

Sophie poked her head out of her window and yelled, "WHAT'S UP, FAYE?"

Faye jumped like a scalded cat into the back of the RV, the single note following her and reverberating around the interior.

Olivia half opened her door, thought better of it when she saw Mark and Tel standing stock still and Brian curled around the RV wing mirror, and slammed it shut again.

"WHAT'S GOING ON?" Sophie yelled.

"SNAAAAAKE!" Faye screamed.

"WHAT?"

Sophie, terrified of snakes, added her own falsetto note to Faye's as she scrambled straight up onto the over-cab bed area, beating the sleeping bag and walls with a pillow.

"Why is everyone screaming?" Olivia called over to Mark.

"Snake."

"Snake?"

"Yeah, those long, slithery, hissy things."

"Oh."

Mark slowly turned his head to glance at her. "No screaming?"

"It's just a snake."

"Could be poisonous."

"Don't annoy it then."

The snake, obviously not a fan of skull-splitting shrieking, slowly uncurled itself and slithered off into the desert.

Brian uncurled himself from the wing mirror and set himself down, putting a hand on his twinging back. To stop the shrill notes drilling into his head he bawled, "IT'S GONE!"

"IT'S GONE?" Sophie screamed.

"BRIAN?" cried Faye.

"THE SNAKE IS NO MORE, LASS."

"DID YOU KILL IT?"

"NO, IT JUST SORT OF WANDERED OFF ON ITS OWN, DRIVEN AWAY BY ALL THE CATAWALLING."

Brian looked at Mark, standing next to him. "You appear to have missed your aim there, lad. In fact, you don't seem to have had any aim at all."

"Lucky it's just the front," he said, puffing out his cheeks.

Tel looked down at himself. "I think I've burned the end of my todger."

"Use some of Sophie's lip cream," Brian laughed, mostly in relief, "Prince Harry swears by it."

"I thought that was for frostbite," Mark said, as they turned back to the RVs.

"Works with sunburn too, apparently."

"Good to know."

Tel slamming the driver's door was quickly followed by a short, sharp cry of pain and Sophie saying, "Don't be such a baby!"

And then they were roaring down the road again, glancing at watches and hoping the route ahead stayed straight and clear.

* * *

They were on Interstate 15, shooting across the desert and roaring through rock canyons like heat-seeking missiles; target, Las Vegas. Brian read out the remaining miles and glanced at his watch, muttering, "We'll never make it."

"We have to," Faye urged. "Go a little faster."

Brian put his foot down. The telegraph poles pulsated rhythmically alongside them as they headed towards Mesquite at a vast rate of knots. Brian spotted blue lights flashing behind them, followed by a wailing siren. Thinking the cruiser would roar straight passed, he slowed down and pulled over to give it more room. The others followed.

The cruiser pulled up in front of them and a big, burly police officer got out. As he sauntered back towards them,

Faye said, "He looks like he got out of bed the wrong side this morning."

"Could just be his resting face," Brian said, pulling his documents out of the glove compartment.

"His resting face looks like a bag of wasps."

"Don't tell him that," Brian warned. "Say nothing, let me handle this."

The officer stood next to the driver's door and squeaked, in a remarkably high pitch, "Licence and registration please, sir."

Brian stopped shuffling through his papers and looked at the tall, wide officer with the voice of Micky Mouse. Faye leaned forward in her seat to get a better look. Brian willed her not to laugh.

"Do you know the speed limit on this stretch of road, sir?" the officer asked, as he flicked through the documentation.

Now Brian was struggling not to laugh, and the more he thought about not laughing the more he wanted to.

"Eighty," he spluttered, "But I doubt these RVs could get anywhere near that unless they had a couple of jets fitted at the _"

"Briddish?" the officer asked.

"Yes, officer, right there on the driving licence."

"You all together?" He nodded at the two RVs parked behind, and Brian resisted the urge to gasp out loud and say 'Never seen them before in my life.'

"Yeah," he said instead. Being pulled up by the police in a foreign country was probably not the best time to make jokes, he thought, unless you particularly enjoyed the feel of metal bracelets.

"You were doing eighty-five, sir."

"Aye?" Brian said, patting the steering wheel with some pride, "Must have had the wind behind us."

The officer stared at him. "There's no wind, sir."

"It's a figure of speech."

"Any particular reason you were doing eighty-five in an

eighty limit?"

"We're in a bit of a rush."

"Dangerous to drive at those speeds."

Brian looked at the empty road ahead, then glanced over his shoulder to look at the empty road behind. "Dangerous for who?"

"Brian!" Faye hissed, "Don't antagonise the officer."

The police officer peered across at her. "Are there any drugs in the vehicle, ma'am?"

"I have a prescription for lansoprazole, for my acid reflux, and Brian, my husband, takes warfarin, which is a rat poison." She laughed nervously while Brian willed her to stop talking. "Makes him run around the edges of the room a lot."

The officer was silent for a moment, then asked, "Anything else? Coke?"

"No, I much prefer lemonade."

The officer tilted his head. Brian thought he detected a flicker of a smile twitching at the corners of his mouth. "Any other drugs?" he squeaked.

"Paracetamol and some diarrhoea medication in case we reacted badly to the American diet, which we didn't. There's also some throat lozenges, do they count?"

"Marijuana?" the officer asked, covering his mouth with a hand.

Faye shook her head. "Wacky baccy? Not since the nineties." She looked at Brian. "Can he still arrest us for that?"

"No, Faye."

"Oh, good."

The officer took a step away from the door, stared at the ground until he'd regained his composure, and said, "Would you mind getting out of the vehicle, sir?"

Brian was desperate to ask why, but thought it prudent and quicker to do as he was told. Once standing on the tarmac he was a good head and a half above the officer, who peered up at him and slowly slid off his sunglasses.

"Walk with me, sir."

Brian had to physically restrain himself from singing *Walk This Way* as the officer strode towards Mark and Olivia's RV. Instead, he said, "Could we go a little faster, only we're a bit short on – ?"

"It'll take as long as it takes, sir."

At the back of the convoy Tel was just opening his driver's door.

"STAY IN THE VEHICLE PLEASE, SIR," the officer yelled in his high-pitched voice, and Tel closed the door again, their anxious faces peered through the windscreen.

"Licence and registration," the officer squeaked up at Mark.

Mark had sweat rolling down his face and the top of his t-shirt was drenched. His breathing was erratic, and his eyes were wide and terrified and focused entirely on the gun hanging off the officer's hip.

"Licence and registration, sir," the officer squeaked again.

"D-don't s-shoot me," Mark gasped.

"Pardon me? Are you okay? You're perspiring a lot, is that nerves? You look nervous. Could you step out of the vehicle?"

"I haven't done anything! Don't shoot me!"

"Step out of the vehicle, sir." The officer backed away from the driver's door, and Mark frantically fumbled with it and fell out, staggering forwards to maintain his balance. He had an empty plastic bottle in one hand.

"Is that an open container you have with you in the cab, sir?"

"It's water," Olivia shouted across. "He was drinking it when you put your siren on and it went everywhere."

"Please don't shoot me!"

"Darling, can you stop saying that?"

"Why? Will it make him shoot me?"

"I'll shoot you in a minute," Brian growled. "Just give him your documentation."

Olivia leaned over with the papers. The officer glanced at them and said to Brian, "Is there something wrong with your friend here?"

"I've often thought so," he said, half laughing, "But no, he's just afraid of guns."

"Afraid of guns?"

"Alien concept for you, I guess, but we're British, we don't have guns back home.  Also, being British, we're slightly nuts, its hereditary, like our bad teeth."  Brian wriggled his finger at the side of his head for emphasis and exposed his tombstone teeth behind the beard, making him look a touch psychotic.

The officer let out a high-pitched squeal of laughter. "Yes, of course, eccentric Brits."

"We're more crazy than eccentric," Brian said.

"What's the difference?"

"Eccentrics have money."  He pointed at Mark and back at Tel and Sophie.  "Crazy," he said, pointing at himself and Faye, "is poor."

"Interesting."

Brian frowned, glancing at his watch and gasping. "Officer, is there anything else we can help you with?"

The officer handed a drenched Mark his papers, who took them with shaky fingers and promptly dropped them on the floor.  As he was scrabbling to pick them up the officer said, "I'm going to let you off with a warning."

"Thank you, officer," Brian said, "Much appreciated."

"Just keep your speed down."

"Of course."

He started to walk back to his cruiser, saying, "Enjoy the rest of your vacation."

"We're just on our way back."

"Enjoy your flight."

"If we catch it, otherwise we might be forced to stay over awhile."

"Well, if you do," the officer said, opening his door and glancing back, "You be sure to give to give Immigration a call."

Brian laughed. "Will do."

The officer curled into his car and drove off.

"Mark?" Olivia called out. "Mark, are you alright?"

Mark was staring after the cruiser with his mouth open and his eyes wide. Panting, he patted his body for any holes and looked weak with relief when he didn't find any.

"You okay, lad?"

Mark nodded, but his eyes were still glazed.

Olivia shuffled over to the driver's seat. "Get in," she said, "I'll drive, you recover from your close encounter of the law enforcement kind."

"LET'S GO!" Tel shouted over, tapping on his watch.

Brian marched back to his RV and they skidded back onto the tarmac.

* * *

They kept a steady pace, slowing only to drive through Mesquite and shooting passed off-freeway towns. The scenery was still stunning, arid and beautiful, but their attention was solely on time; which seemed to be passing at a faster rate than normal.

"A watched kettle never boils," Faye said, when Brian glanced at his watch for the millionth time.

"That's for slow passing of time. What we're experiencing here is literally time travel; we go fast, but the road goes on forever."

"Like in a dream, where you're running and going nowhere."

"Nightmare, Faye, this is a nightmare."

The high-rises of Vegas came into view in the distance and slowly got bigger. Desert and rocks gave way to buildings. The roads, after days of empty highways and fresh air and freedom, suddenly seemed very crowded. Their eyes were assaulted by billboards and signs, and people, so many people. It all seemed very overwhelming.

They stayed on the main road until they hit The Strip, where they came to a virtual standstill.

"Traffic!" Brian cried, hitting the steering wheel. "Why is

there so much traffic at – ?" He glanced at his watch and gave a strangled cry. "We're never going to make it!"

"Calm down, Bri, we'll make it."

"Will we? Will we, Faye?"

"Well I don't know, do I! I'm just hoping for the best."

"Hoping won't do us much good, *praying* is what we need now. Pray for a miracle, Faye, pray hard!" Brian pipped his car horn and hollered, "COME ON!"

"Pretty sure having a hissy fit behind the wheel isn't going to help."

"Maybe not, but it makes me feel better."

"Out with the rage, in with peace and tranquillity."

"If we miss our plane we'll have to pay for another flight that might not even be *today*!" he growled, pounding the steering wheel again. "What are we going to do if – ?"

"BRIAN!" Her sharp voice reverberated through the cab, so loud it was almost a physical thing. "WILL YOU CALM DOWN!"

Brian gripped the steering wheel, his lips tightly pursed, thinking only of panic and rage and abandonment in a foreign country and feeling Faye's stern eyes upon him. What was he afraid of most, he wondered; panic and rage and abandonment, or Faye's wrath?

Faye's wrath, he decided. She had a slow-fuse temper, rarely seen, that could beat his to a pulp.

Brian took his cowboy hat off the dashboard and put it on, asking himself, 'What would the Duke do in a situation like this?' He imagined the big man riding down the strip on his horse, shooting guns from each hand and yelling, 'AIN'T NO MAN STANDING IN MA WAY!'

Except, in reality, *everyone* was in his way and stopping him from getting where he wanted to go, and he didn't have any guns. Or a horse. And John Wayne would probably be run out of town by a slow but ceaseless wave of traffic, racing off into the desert and vowing never to return.

Brian took a deep, calming breath. The traffic moved

forward inch by agonising inch. He forced a smile and glanced at Faye, saying, "Peace and tranquillity, my love."

She smiled back. Wrath averted, he felt a tiny speck of relief in the maelstrom of volcanic anxiety.

Tel crackled over the walkie talkie. "We could dump the RVs and make a run for it with our luggage?" he suggested.

"They'll just charge us," Mark said, "And we'll get fined, and they might get stolen or damaged and then – "

"Okay, okay, it was just a suggestion!"

Sophie looked at him. "You okay, Tel?"

"Not really. Kind of a disastrous end to a rather brilliant holiday."

"Better than a brilliant end to a disastrous holiday."

He laughed and nodded.

"How you doing, Liv?" Mark asked.

"I'm okay." She threw him a smile. "I actually prefer the slow traffic to belting down empty roads, I always imagine what would happen if a tyre blew out."

"Want me to take over?"

"No, we're nearly there."

"Let's hope so." He stared out of the window at the traffic, willing it to open up like the parting of the Red Sea.

It didn't.

They crawled on down the road.

* * *

They followed the signs to the payless return area at the RV hire place. They jumped out, hauling their luggage behind them, hats on their heads, sunglasses on their faces, the women clutching handbags and a multitude of carrier bags. Men with the hire company logo on their fleeces jumped in and drove their RVs away.

Brian boomed after them. "OI! HOW DO WE GET TO THE AIRPORT?" The last RV slammed on its brakes and a surprised face leaned out of the window. "Shuttle buses over there, every five minutes."

They headed towards the shuttle queues at a jog, dragging the bulging sports bags behind them, bags over each shoulder and hanging from their hands and the crook of their arms. They had twice as much 'stuff' than when they'd arrived and felt every extra ounce.

The queue was small and they joined in an agitated, watch-glancing group.

The shuttle promptly arrived. They got on, feeling the extra ounces turn into pounds, and sat surrounded by their bags, hats and sunglasses askew in the overheated bus.

It took seven minutes to reach the Harry Reid Airport.

It seemed like forever.

They ran down corridors and concourses, asking almost everyone they passed, "Terminal Three?"

Mark, throbbing with panic, didn't even notice the policemen or their guns as ran.

They reached the check-in desk hot, sweaty and breathless.

"Are we on time for the flight to London?" Mark gasped, letting the luggage drop from his body and slamming down their tickets and passports.

The pretty counter clerk glanced at her computer screen. They all waited, holding their breath. Tel crossed his fingers. Brian whispered to Faye, "A watched kettle never boils."

"Look somewhere else, then."

He stared up at the ceiling. It was very high.

"Plenty of time," the counter clerk finally said. "You're an hour early."

"What?" Brian glanced at his watch, confused. "An hour early?"

"Yes, sir, you only need to book in three hours before an international flight."

Sophie pointed at the clock on the wall behind the counter clerk. "Time difference," she grinned. "Our watches say midday, but the clock says eleven."

They all exhaled, slumping on their feet.

"Are you ready to check in your luggage?" the counter clerk asked, and Faye suddenly went into ultra-faff mode. "No!" she cried, waving her hands by her head as she stared at all the bags around her feet. "I haven't sorted out our hand luggage."

"Well, you have four hours to do it so don't get too excited, lass."

"We have *too much stuff!*"

"And who's fault is that?"

Faye huffed.

"Hand luggage!" Olivia cried. "I'd forgotten about carry-on."

"You've had hours to get it sorted before we got here," Mark sighed irritably.

"*Me?*" Olivia pushed her face into his and said, "I was *driving* for most of those hours because *someone* had a *panic attack* over a *gun*, and I didn't notice *you* packing anything, *you* are responsible for *your own stuff!*"

Mark, taken aback, lowered his head, duly reprimanded, and made a mental note in his Little Book of Men's Answers never to bring up the subject of packing ever again.

"If you'd like to step to the side while you sort yourselves out," the counter clerk said, "And I can get other passengers booked onto the flight."

They shifted over, adrenaline still running high after their race across the desert.

"Why are you making this look difficult?" Tel snapped at Sophie, who was kneeling on the floor, peering into various bags and tutting a lot.

"Accumulation," she snapped back. "Same sized bag, more belongings."

"Just hurry up so we can get rid of it."

"Unreasonable behaviour," she muttered, pulling out clothes from one bag and pushing them into another, "That's what I'll put on the divorce papers, *unreasonable behaviour*! Or maybe I'll just suffocate him in his sleep."

"I can't find my Kindle!" Faye shrieked. "I can't do a twelve-hour flight without my Kindle!"

"I can't get everything into the sports bags!" Olivia wailed, sitting on them and trying to zip them up.

Brian tutted and wandered off.

"You could at least *try* to help!" Faye shouted after him.

"I am," he boomed.

"By walking off?"

He disappeared into the crowds.

"Are you going to help at all?" Sophie snarled up at Tel.

"What do you want me to do?"

"I don't know, just get all of this – " She indicated the bulging bags and the spillage of contents. " – into this," and she indicated the sports bag.

"I'm not a miracle worker! Do you really need all those clothes?"

"Yes! Do you really need all of yours?"

"We didn't think this part through enough," Mark muttered.

"We didn't think this part through *at all*!" Tel huffed.

"We'll need water," Olivia said, taking out two bottles. "Will they let us carry water on board or will they be serving drinks? Mark!"

"What?"

"Stop standing there like a stuffed cabbage and *help me*!"

The women were on their knees on the floor, surrounded by their accumulated possessions. The men stood over them, looking down but not sure what to do without getting their heads bitten off.

Sophie was just fighting with Tel about shoe abandonment, mostly his, and Olivia was just asking Mark if he'd consider sacrificing everything he'd brought with him, when a giant suitcase landed in the middle of their scattered debris.

"Extra stuff in here!" Brian boomed.

They stared at the suitcase, then up at Brian.

"Bloody brilliant!" said Mark.

"Why didn't we think of that?" Tel asked Sophie.

"Because we were too busy indulging in a domestic dispute, that's why."

"You clever sausage," Olivia said, pulling off the price tag and opening it up.

Everyone took off their hats, except for Brian, who refused to hand it over, and packed them neatly in the suitcase. With everything sorted, they hauled six sports bags and the suitcase onto the check-in weighing machine. Six faces dropped their smiles and their jaws when the counter clerk told them how much the excess baggage was going to cost them.

Tel said, "I'll get this."

"No, let me," said Mark, reaching for his wallet.

Brian slapped his credit card down on the counter and grinned at them. "Take a third of this off my bill," he said to Sophie.

"What bill?"

"The bill for the holiday expenses."

"I don't know what you're talking about, Bri."

Olivia giggled and said, "I'll get lunch then."

\* \* \*

They ate at the Village Pub, washing the food down with beer and mimosas. They were delightfully squiffy as they walked past slot machines and settled into a line of chairs in front of the slanting windows overlooking the runway. A sharp voice suddenly came over the tannoy system: "Passengers to Frankfurt, you vill board ze plane now!"

"You vill not dilly-dally," Mark mimicked, "You vill board ze plane *immediately!*"

They laughed.

Tel wandered off, returning with an ice bucket containing a bottle of champagne in an ice bucket and six glasses dangling from his other hand.

"I don't know if we're allowed to bring this out here," he whispered, glancing around as he popped the cork and started pouring, "But we'll be leaving soon – "

"Leaving, on a jet plane," Mark warbled.

"Wah!" cried Fay

" – and we're going to have a toast."

"To the fabulous United States of America," Sophie said, raising her glass. "Thank you for your splendour and your hospitality."

"To the road trip of a lifetime," said Tel.

"Viva Las Vegas," Mark cheered.

"To the best time ever."

"To friends."

"To us," said Brian, "A bigger bunch of scallywags you'll never meet."

"Speak for yourself," Sophie winked.

"If you're in my gang you're a scallywag."

"I want to be in his gang," Mark whined.

"Me too."

"Apprentices," Sophie said, raising her glass to Brian. "I see us all as being Brian and Faye's apprentices, training our way up to becoming unique and caring human beans, just like them."

"Stop," Brian said, throwing out a giant hand.

"God help you all," Faye laughed.

"How many mimosas did you have?" Tel asked Sophie.

"Enough to celebrate our trip, not enough to kill the pain of leaving."

"Hear, hear," said Olivia. "I feel awfully sad. I wished we could have stayed longer."

"Me too," Faye sighed. "It's gone so fast."

"Holidays always do," Mark sighed, "Time only slows down at work."

"Or on The Strip when you're in a rush," said Brian, shuddering at the memory.

They stared out of the floor-to-ceiling window at the

plane waiting to take them all home, and sighed, and smiled, and resigned themselves to going back to the real world.

\* \* \*

The first three hours of the flight were unremarkable; boring and quiet, with only the constant distribution of food to stupefy the masses to break up the tedium.

And then one of the passengers a few seats in front of them started getting a bit loud.

"What do you mean, I can't have another drink?" a man yelled at a young flight attendant.

"I'm sorry, sir, but I think you've had enough."

"*I'll* decide when I've had enough, now bring me another beer!"

"I'm sorry, sir, but – "

"*Bring me another beer!*"

The flight attendant looked a bit flustered. Another, older attendant came to settle the man down, but he got more belligerent and demanding.

"I can have what I bloody well like, now get me a beer!"

"Quieten down up there," a man from the back shouted.

It was like igniting a bomb. All hell broke loose.

The drunken man stood up, turned around and searched the sea of faces for the one who had dared to shout out.

"Who said that?" he growled. "Come on, who was it?"

The woman seated next to him reached up and tried to grab hold of his arm, but he furiously pulled it away, his fists clenched and his jaw set firm, ready for fighting.

"Show yourself! Who said that? Stand up!"

Nobody moved. Brian, sensing animosity oozing from the bald, wiry man, straightened up in his seat.

"Come on, *coward*, stand up and show yourself!"

"Sit down, Ben," the woman next to him hissed, "You're making a spectacle of yourself!"

"I want to know who told me to be quiet! Who do they think they are? What business is it of theirs?"

"*Ben!*"

The man again pulled his arm away from the woman's appeasing hands and stepped into the left aisle. "I WANT A DRINK!" he yelled into the young attendant's face. She looked ready to burst into tears. The older attendant was uttering soothing words, which did nothing to curb the man's ire.

"I think you've had enough, lad," Brian said. "Sit down and sleep it off."

"WHAT?" The man stomped towards him. Brian held his gaze. The man loomed over him, his face red with intoxicated fury. Brian was instantly assaulted by beer fumes. "WHO ARE YOU THEN, EH? THINK YOU CAN TELL ME WHAT TO DO? WHAT BUSINESS IS IT OF YOURS?"

"You're spoiling my peaceful flight with your drunken rant, that makes it my business. Just sit back down and – "

The man lunged forward and thrust his face into Brian's, hissing, "Ain't none of your business, *mate*."

Next to him, Faye gasped in horror. Tel and Mark sat alert in their seats, ready for action if action was required. Olivia wondered if she could take him down with some self-defence moves in the aisle and decided she probably could.

"Sir," said the older attendant, "Can you return to your seat, please?"

"Bring me a beer and I will. Do it *now!*"

Brian clutched the seat in front of him with both hands and slowly pulled himself up, stepping into the aisle to fully uncurl himself. The man's head followed his ascent. His fists uncurled when he saw how tall and wide Brian was, and he took a step back.

Mark and Tel stood up, as did five or six other men. The drunken man's eyes widened as he surveyed his opposition.

"Sit down," Brian breathed menacingly.

"Get back to your seat and shut up," said another man.

"I'd do as he says if I were you," Mark said.

The man looked from one to the other. He still seemed angry, but now he was alarmed too and clearly unsure what to do next.

And then the fighting started.

The man pushed Brian, trying to make him sit down. Brian didn't budge. The older attendant touched the man's arm to urge him back to his seat, and the man spun round with his arm raised, as if about to hit her. Brian pounded the arm down with his own and gripped him in a tight body lock, lifting him up off his feet and squeezing the air from his lungs, silencing his obscene tirade.

The man kicked out, hitting the young attendant, who cried out in alarm and pain. People immediately leapt from their seats, two grabbing at the man's legs. He kicked out again and again, rolling his head from side to side in an effort to try and escape the vice-like grip around his body.

A big man in a kilt thundered down the left aisle, squeezed passed the men holding the legs and rugby tackled the man, pulling him from Brian's arms and pinning him to the floor. Several women whooped as the kilt flapped up the man's back, exposing his plump buttocks. A woman in the seat next to the action casually reached out and flipped it back again. Several women glared at her.

"LET ME GO!" the man hollered, struggling to push the kilted man off him and kicking out at the ones holding his legs.

Brian rested a foot on the man's chest to hold his bouncing head in place. When the man continued screaming obscenities he gave a gentle push down, forcing the air from his lungs like he was pumping up an airbed, and the obscenities all ended with an *uhhh*; Faye shouldn't have to listen to language like that, he thought, nobody should.

Another man came running down the left aisle. "STAND BACK!" he cried, pulling a set of handcuffs from his belt, "I'M THE AIR MASHALL, LET ME THROUGH."

Brian glanced at his watch. "Good of you to come," he drawled. "Had something more important to do, did you?"

People around them laughed and the Air Marshall glared at him. The kilted man struggled to his feet in the tight space.

The drunken man's legs were released, and Brian removed his foot. The man instantly started thrashing about, struggling to get up and screaming abuse. Brian gently pressed him down onto his back and pumped his chest with his foot again; *uhh, uhh, uhh.*

"Need a hand?" Brian asked, as the Marshall failed to turn the man over and put on the cuffs.

"It might help if you took your foot off him!"

Brian did and the man, his face now so red it looked like an overripe tomato, thrashed and screamed and spat. Brian indicated to the men by his feet, twirling his finger and nodding, before lowering himself and gripping the man's shoulders. On the count of three, they flipped him over onto his stomach. Brian stood up and resumed the pumping on his back; *uhh, uhh, uhh.*

The Marshall finally managed to get the cuffs on his wrists and they hauled the man to his feet. His language was foul. The older attendant came running up with a roll of gaffer tape. Brian, who considered himself to be the King of Gaffer, took it from her, pulled off a strip, and pressed it against the man's mouth. Finally, there was silence. The Marshall led his thrashing body to the back of the plane and sat him on the floor, where he continued his muted screaming, interspersed with some furious head banging against the wall.

Everyone returned to their seats. The atmosphere was filled with triumph and excited chatter, drowning out the sound of the gagged man on the floor at the back.

Brian wriggled back into his teeny-tiny seat, careful not to kick the cowboy hat he'd stored underneath.

"My hero," Faye said, snuggling up to him as best she could in the tight space and adding, "Don't do it again."

Mark and Tel reached over and patted a giant shoulder.

"Team work," said Mark.

"You didn't do anything!" Tel said.

"No, but I was ready to leap in at a moment's notice."

"You were all marvellous," said Olivia.

Just as everyone was settling down again, a voice came over the tannoy system.

"Ladies and gentlemen, this is your captain speaking. Unfortunately, due to technical issues, I have to inform you that the flight is now being redirected to Keflavik International Airport."

Faye turned to Brian with wide eyes and gasped, "Russia?"

\* \* \*

When they landed in Iceland they expected to be deboarded whilst the drunken man was taken care of, but he'd fallen into a deep sleep and was quietly carried from the plane by the police. One collected his hand luggage from an overhead locker.

"You two together?" the officer asked the woman next to the now vacant seat.

"No, not any more," she said, and there was a gentle cheer, which spurred her on to say, "First holiday together and he spends the whole week drunk, and then he does this! So no," she said, looking earnestly at the police officer, "We're not together."

Landing in London, only a couple of hours later than scheduled, the same woman took down her bag, rummaged through it, then burst out laughing. "His passport is in my bag!" she declared to all the people around her. "He'll have a job getting home then, won't he, and serves him right."

There was a brief burst of applause.

The group collected their luggage, trying not to fall asleep on their feet, and trudged to the taxi rank outside, where Faye screamed, "Oh my God, it's cold!" They felt as if they'd been awake for days.

Back at Tel and Sophie's flat, they dropped their luggage to the floor and shuffled to any available sleeping space; Mark and Olivia on the shag-pile rug in the living room, Brian splayed like a starfish on the leather sofa, and Faye curled up on the leather armchair.

Tel and Sophie fell face first onto their bed and were asleep in an instant.

* * *

## Zoom Meeting – three weeks later

"I'll be quick," Sophie told the boxed faces on her computer screen, "I have a client waiting to see me. First off, Etta thanks you for her gratuities, she was most grateful. In particular I want to thank the person who thought it a good idea to get my alcoholic PA a large bottle of bourbon. She thought it best to share it out amongst her colleagues and the entire workforce on our floor spent the whole afternoon drunk, two of whom were found fornicating in the stationery cupboard and another two found sitting on the photocopier while it spat out multiple copies of their privates."

Brian howled with laughter.

Mark said, "Do we get to see those?"

"They were shredded," said Tel.

"A likely story. Bring them with you next time we're at the Woodsman."

He noticed on screen that Olivia, sat next to him at the dining table with her laptop, snapped her head towards him. "For what reason?" she asked.

"I have a penchant for grainy, black and white erotica?" he mumbled.

"They're in colour," Tel said.

"Present tense?" Sophie questioned.

"They *were* in colour."

"Oh," said Mark, "Not interested then."

Olivia nudged him. "You'll buy *proper* porn magazines from the newsagents like everyone else."

"Anyway," Sophie continued, "Just to let you know that I've been negotiating with Iain Flemmingway about our American trip."

"Negotiating?" Brian asked.

"Compensation for our poor accommodation, stress levels, and a few other things I threw in for good measure."

"I quite liked roughing it in those old trailers," Mark sighed.

"In retrospect," said Brian.

"What?"

"In *retrospect* you liked it. How would you feel about doing it again?"

"Well … "

"Anyway," Sophie said, glancing at her watch, "He didn't want anything to affect his pet project, the camping-slash-alien film, so he's made a generous offer to cover our expenses and distress, and I've accepted it. So, it gives me great pleasure to inform you that our road trip across America has been fully paid for courtesy of Flemmingway's agents, pending your signature on an NDA."

"NDA?" said Faye.

"Non-Disclosure Agreement. It means you won't say anything to anyone about our experience or anything derogatory about the film, the movie company, or Hemmingway himself."

"Excellent!" Brian said.

"How much?" said Mark.

With a grin, Sophie scribbled on a piece of paper and held it up to the camera; four numbers.

Mark whistled.

Brian's beard split with a huge grin.

Faye's mouth fell open.

Olivia giggled and clapped her hands.

Mark started counting on his fingers. "Split six ways, that makes – "

"Not split," said Sophie, "*Each.*"

"Each?" they all gasped, with Brian adding, "Minus mine and Faye's American expenses."

"You know," Sophie said, "I asked Etta about that and she can't find a single receipt, so we all get the same. I can see you taking a breath to argue, Bri, but the case is closed.  I thought we could use it for our next trip."

"Excellent," Olivia said, "Where to next?"

If you enjoyed this book, or any of my books, please do leave a rating or a review (for extra brownie points) on Amazon.

I thank you.
I'd also be thrilled to hear from you about anything!
Email: deborahaubrey01@gmail.com
Facebook: AuthorDebbieAubrey
Amazon Author Page: Deborah Aubrey

Until next time, ta ta.  Dx

# BOOKS BY THIS AUTHOR

## Book 1: Pitching Up!

The adventures begin! You'll be so emotionally exhausted after reading this you'll need a holiday to recover.

## Book 2: Pitching Up Again!

The Woodsman pub and campsite is under new management, with new staff and improved facilities. The old gang, plus some new ones, return by invitation to 'check it out', and the adventures begin. Perfect holiday reading.

## Book 3: Pitching Up In Style!

The camping gang are back together and someone's getting married, in a big house, with lots of guests and lots of chaos. Funny, emotional, and a whirlwind of delightful celebration.

## Book 4: Pitching Up In America!

Ian Flemmingway, the 'creepy guy' from Pitching Up!, has written a book about their Cotswolds escapades and its being turned into a film! The campers are invited to Las Vegas, to the film set, all expenses paid ... but not all is as it seems. This is armchair travelling at its finest, with plenty of laughs, lots of camping chaos, and a few surprises.

## Tipping Point

It'll make you laugh (a lot). It'll make you cry (a bit). It'll make you go "Ooh" and "Ahh" and "Oh my God!" Emotional drama blitzed with huge dollops of humour, you'll love it.

## How Not To Kill Your Teenager

Welcome to the wonderful world of teenagers. Trust me, nothing will have prepared you for this moment, nothing. Living with teenagers is akin to kicking jelly up a ladder; it's horrible, they're horrible, and your life will collapse from the weight of their physical and emotional angst. Read this for a bit of light relief.

## Oobe Doobie Doo

A SHORT STORY. Life is bleak for Malcolm. He has a domineering wife and a miserable life. At a dreary dinner party, sitting next to the woman he's secretly in love with, he suffers a suspected heart attack and finds himself at the midpoint area between heaven and earth - except the fuse has blown and everything's in darkness, and heaven is a bit full.

Printed in Great Britain
by Amazon

24450617R00188